MUCH ADO ABOUT MURDER

Much Ado About Murder

EDITED BY

Anne Perry

BERKLEY PRIME CRIME, NEW YORK

MUCH ADO ABOUT MURDER

A Berkley Prime Crime Book
Published by The Berkley Publishing Group,
a division of Penguin Putnam Inc.,
375 Hudson Street, New York, New York 10014.

Visit our website at
www.penguinputnam.com

First edition: December 2002

Library of Congress Cataloging-in-Publication Data

Much ado about murder / edited by Anne Perry.— 1st ed.
p.   cm.
ISBN 0-425-18650-4
1. Shakespeare, William, 1564–1616—Adaptations.   2. Detective and
mystery stories, English.   I. Perry, Anne.

PR2877 .M83 2002
823'.087208—dc21
2002074766

PRINTED IN THE UNITED STATES OF AMERICA

10   9   8   7   6   5   4   3   2   1

CONTENTS

Introduction to
Much Ado About Murder

Part of the genius of Shakespeare is that he is universal and can be infinitely adapted. He speaks to the human condition; therefore, with a twist here and a tweak there, he can become just about all things to all men—and most women.

There is no need to be a scholar to enjoy this collection of stories with a Shakespeare twist, only a lover of mystery, adventure, travel in time and place, and to have a thoroughly good imagination. And it will definitely help if you have a sense of humor and curiosity as well.

Have you a fancy to visit Elizabethan or Jacobean London, to attend a performance at the Globe Theatre—but from the comfort of your armchair—and to meet Shakespeare himself? Would you like a flavor of the teeming streets, the taverns, but in safety, and without the smells and the noise—which were horrendous? Human living with farmyard immediacy—but it seems too vivid and too well described not to be accurate. It is another world, and yet the people who inhabit it, who love and hate, burn with jealousy, kill, and solve crimes, are moved exactly as we are, and we identify with them.

There are subtle and devious plots of actions and murder in the alleys and by the river as in Jeffery Deaver's, "All the World's a Stage." There is a glimpse of Shakespeare in the doldrums of self-doubt, and then on fire with ideas, high detection, and wit in Simon Brett's "Exit, Pursued"—by a bear—of course!

Vivid feel for scenery, a touch of Cornish history and language, and a great compassion in "Let the Game Begin!" by Peter Tremayne.

Hamlet is so rich a store of passion, thought, experience, and drama, so filled with quotes we can scarcely put unfamiliar passages between them. Perhaps that is why it has come to us in a thousand different garbs, and yet remains unspoiled in its original. It is unalloyed tragedy to leave you—or me anyway— in tears at the end. I've certainly used it myself. But in "The Fall of the House of Oldenborg," by Robert Barnard, you can smile all the way through. This will be one version of the story you had not thought of! But you will now.

Sharan Newman's "Jack Hath Not His Jill" is a long letter from Princess Anne of France, after her visit to the court of the King of Navarre. It is all perfect period, and yet the passions, the tricks, and the issues are timeless. Not much is as it seems, and yet such an honest voice.

"Gracious Silence," by Gillian Linscott, takes us to the Rome of Coriolanus, and makes me feel immediately in *I, Claudius* country, all violent emotions hidden by soft words, and even softer lack of them. And yet I felt with her all the way, and am profoundly grateful for my modern freedoms.

Edward Marston's story "Squinting at Death" takes us to Plantagenet England, with the feuds, the heroism, and the slaughter of battle, and as always a mystery, a wrongful death in among all the others, and detection, but as should be with Shakespeare, loyalty and tragedy as well. The loss matters.

"Richard's Children," by Brendan DuBois, is as immediate as today, or even tomorrow. Could it be true? What a twist! I think that possibility might keep me awake.

Shakespeare deals much with ambition, with the crown and its perils, its love and poison as power corrupts, envies, corrodes, and changes everything we thought we knew. How appropriate that we should also deal with those who aspire, by fair means or foul, to seize that prize for themselves. The lust is real—the tragedy is real.

Then a little farther back in the world's history: Who does not know what was done by "Cleo's Asp" as postulated by Edward D. Hoch? But did you know the private murder that went hand in hand with that most famous suicide? Well, read this story—and you will!

P. C. Doherty's "The Serpent's Tooth" is of a different sort, a spiritual tooth with poison in the sac. Exactly how did William Shakespeare die? What was his own family like? How about a good detective story that will unravel to give you a possible answer? And would you like a thoroughly sinister detective to do it for you?

Kathy Lynn Emerson brings us "Much Ado About Murder," and love and faith, persecution, loyalties, women you will have to like, issues to care about, and some very charming domestic scenes. I can hear the laughter as well as feel the fear and the pain. And in the best tradition of what is known as a "comedy," a thoroughly satisfying conclusion.

"The Duke's Wife," by Peter Robinson, also left me with a feeling of total completeness. I had always wondered about what happened afterward, feeling Shakespeare had stopped a trifle too soon in that tale. This is all very much as it should be. Enjoy it!

I did a short story on Macbeth once, from Lady Macbeth's point of view. I never thought of making the three witches the heroines! This is hilarious and so believable. Marcia Talley's "Too Many Cooks" is a cautionary tale with a vengeance. A smile and a shiver all the way through. It could have been that way!

"Ere I Killed Thee" is my own contribution, featuring late Victorian traveling actors. It is totally unfair, but that woman has always irritated me! This was my chance to tell the Othello story from another angle altogether. Isn't it fun being a writer? As long as the story works, you can do any damn thing you like! Or at any rate, you can try to.

With thanks and our apologies to Shakespeare—we had a ball!

I hope you will equally enjoy reading them!

All the World's a Stage

BY JEFFERY DEAVER

Master Deaver's novels have appeared on many best-seller lists around the world, including those in such pamphlets as the *New York Times*, the *London Times* and the *Los Angeles Times*. The instigator of fifteen novels, he hath been nominated for five Edgar awards from the Mystery Writers of America and an Anthony Award and he be a two-time recipient of the Ellery Queen Reader's Award for Best Short Story of the Year. His novel *The Bone Collector* hath been magically converted into a feature film from Universal Pictures, starring the able players Denzel Washington and Angelina Jolie. Producer Joel Silver and Warner Brothers do, at the present time, labor mightily to create a film of the scribe's novel *The Blue Nowhere*. That tale, together with his *The Stone Monkey*, *The Empty Chair* and *Speaking in Tongues,* do constitute his most recent work. He doth make his home in the territory of Virginia, though he mitigates his rash decision to reside in the barbarous Colonies by traveling to London with some frequency to hawk his wares. Readers are humbly encouraged to visit his website at *www.jefferydeaver.com* (whatsoever a website may be).

The couple was returning from the theater to the Thames ferry, winding their way through a deserted, unsavory area of South London.

It was four hours past candle-lighting, and Charles and Margaret Cooper ought, by rights, to have been home now with their small children and Margaret's mother, a plague widow, who lived with them in a small abode in Charing Cross. But they had dallied at the Globe to visit with Will Shakespeare, whom Charles Cooper counted among his friends. Shakespeare's family and Charles's had long ago owned adjoining acreage on the Avon River and their fathers would on occasion hunt together with falcons and enjoy pints at one of the Stratford taverns. The playwright was busy this time of year—unlike many London theaters, which closed when the Court was summering out of the city, the Globe gave performances year 'round—but he had been able to join the Coopers for a time to sip Jerez sherry and claret and to talk about recent plays.

The husband and wife now made their way quickly through the dark streets—the suburbs south of the river had few dependable candle-lighters—and they concentrated carefully on where they put their feet.

The May air was cool and Margaret wore a heavy linen gown, loose on the back and with a tight bodice. Being married, she cut her dress high enough to cover her breasts but she eschewed the felt or beaver cap customary among older married women and wore only silk ribbons and a few glass jewels in her hair. Charles wore simple breeches, blouse, and leather vest.

" 'Twas a delightful night," Margaret said, holding tighter to his arm as they negotiated a crook in the narrow road. "I thank thee, my husband."

The couple greatly enjoyed attending plays, but Charles's wine-importing company had only recently begun to show profit and the Coopers had had little money to spend on their own amusements. Until this year, indeed, they had been able to afford only the penny admission to be understanders—those crowded in the central gallery of the theater. But of late, Charles's industry was showing some rewards, and tonight he had surprised his wife with threepence seats in the gallery, where they had sat upon cushions and shared nuts and an early-season pear.

A shout from behind startled them, and Charles turned to see, perhaps fifteen yards away, a man in a black velvet hat and baggy, tattered doublet, dodging a rider. It seemed that the man had been so intent on crossing the street quickly that he had not noticed the horse. Perhaps it was Charles's imagination, or a trick of the light, but it appeared to him that the pedestrian looked up, noted Charles's gaze, and turned with undue haste into an alleyway.

Not wishing to alarm his wife, though, Charles made no mention of the fellow and continued his conversation, "Perhaps next year we shall attend Black Friars."

Margaret laughed. Even some peers shunned paying the sixpence admission at the theater, though the venue was small and luxurious and boasted actors of the highest skill. "Perhaps," she said dubiously.

Charles glanced behind them once more but saw no sign of the hatted man.

As they turned the corner onto the road that would take them to the ferry, however, the very man appeared from an adjacent alleyway. He had flanked their route at a run, it seemed, and now stepped forward, breathing hard.

"I pray you, sir, madam, a minute of thy time."

A beggar only, Charles assumed. But they often turned dangerous if you did not come forth with coin. Charles drew a long dagger from his belt and stood between his wife and this man.

"Ah, no need for pigsticking," the man said, nodding at the dagger. "This pig is not himself armed." He held up empty hands. "Not armed with a bodkin, that is to say. Only the truth."

He was a strange sack of a creature. Eyes sunken in his skull, jaundiced skin hanging upon his body. It was clear that some years ago a whore or loose woman had bestowed upon him the bone-ache and the disease was about to work its final misery upon him; the doublet, which Charles had assumed to be stolen from a fatter man, undoubtedly was his own and hung loose because of recent emaciation.

"Who art thou?" Charles demanded.

The man replied, "I am one of those to whom you owe this evening's play-going, to whom you owe thy profession as a bestower of grape's nectar, to whom you owe your life in this fine city." The man inhaled air that was as sulfurous and foul as always in these industrious suburbs, then spat upon the cobblestones.

"Explain thyself and why thou hast been dogging me, or faith, sir, I shall levy a hue and cry for the sheriff."

"No need for that, young Cooper."

"Thou know me?"

"Indeed, sir. I do know you too well." The man's yellow eyes grew troubled. "Let me be forthright and speak no more in riddles. My name is Marr. I have lived a life of a rogue and I would have been content to die a rogue's death. But a fortnight ago the Lord our God did appear to me in a dream and admonish me to make amends for my sins in life, lest I be denied entrance to the glorious court of Heaven. In truth, sir, I warrant that I should need *two* lifetimes to make such amends when I have merely a fraction of one left, so I have but chosen the most worrisome deed I have committed and have sought out he whom I have wronged the worst."

Charles looked over the puny man and put the dagger away. "And how have thou wronged me?"

"As I said before, it is I—and several of my comrades, now all gone to the plague and infesting hell, I warrant—who be responsible for ending your idyllic life in the countryside near Stratford and coming to this mischievous city so many years ago."

"Howbeit that this is so?"

"I pray you, sir, tell me what great tragedy befell your life?"

Charles did not need a moment to reflect. "My loving father taken from us and our lands forfeit."

Fifteen years ago, it was claimed by the sheriff near Stratford that Richard Cooper was caught poaching deer on the property of Lord Westcott, Baron of Habershire. When the sheriff's bailiffs tried to arrest him, he launched an arrow their way. The bailiffs gave chase and, after a struggle, stabbed and killed him. Richard Cooper was a landed gentleman with no need to poach deer and it was widely believed that the incident was a tragic misunderstanding. Still, a local court—sympathetic to the noble class—decreed that the family's land be forfeited to Westcott, who sold it for considerable profit. The rogue would not give so much as a tuppence to Charles's mother, who died soon after from grief. Eighteen-year-old Charles, the only child, had no choice but to walk to

London to seek his fortune. He worked labor for some years, then apprenticed to the vintner's trade, became a member of the guild, and over the years turned his thoughts away from the tragedy.

Marr wiped his unpleasant mouth, revealing as few teeth as a puking babe, and said, "I knew well that this would be your answer." He looked about and whispered, "Faith, sir, I have intelligence about what truly happened that sad day."

"Continue," Charles commanded.

"Westcott was as many nobles then and now," Marr said. "His life was lived far beyond his means and he found himself increasingly in debt."

This was well known to anyone who read the Fleet Street pamphlets or listened to gossip in the taverns. Many of the nobles were selling off their goods and portions of their estates to meet the costs of their extravagant lifestyles.

"There came to Westcott an ignoble scoundrel named Robert Murtaugh."

"I know the name," Margaret said, "though for reasons I recall not, there be an unsavory association accompanying it."

"Faith, good lady, I warrant that is so. Murtaugh is a peer of the realm, but a lowly knight, an office he himself did purchase. He hath made an enterprise of seeking out nobles deeply in debt. He then arranges various schemes whereby they come into lands or property through illicit means. He himself then takes a generous percentage of their gain."

Charles whispered in horror, "And my father was a victim of such a scheme?"

"Faith, sir, he was. It was I and those other scoundrels I made mention of who waylaid him on his own land and conveyed him, bound, to Lord Westcott's fields. There, by prior arrangement, the sheriff's bailiffs did arrive and kill him. A dead hart and a bow and quiver were set next to his cold body to testify, by appearance, that he had been poaching."

"Thy father, murdered," Margaret whispered.

"O merciful Lord in heaven," Charles said, his eyes burning with hatred. He drew his bodkin once more and pressed the blade against Marr's neck. The rogue moved not an inch.

"No, husband, thou cannot. Please." Margaret took his arm.

The man said, "Verily, sir, I did not know the bailiffs had murder in mind. I thought they were merely going to extract a bribe from thy father for his release, as such rustic lawmen are wont to do. No one was more shocked than I by the deadly turn the events that day took. But I am nonetheless as guilty of this heinous crime as they, and I will not beg for mercy. If God moves thy hand to slit my throat in retribution for what I have done, so be it."

The memory of that terrible night flooded through Charles—the sheriff ignominiously carting the body to the house, his mother's wailing in grief, then the long days after: his mother's decline, the poverty, the struggle to start a new life in the unforgiving city of London. And yet Charles found his hand unable to harm this pitiful creature. Slowly he lowered the dagger and replaced it in the scabbard on his girdle. He studied Marr closely. He saw such penitence in the man's face that it seemed he had spoken truly. Still, he asked, "If Murtaugh be as thou say, then many would have cause to despise him. How know I that thou art not merely one of those aggrieved by him and have spun this tale to—as thy very name suggests—mar his reputation?"

"By God's body, sir, I speak the truth. Of bitterness against Sir Murtaugh I have none, for it was my choice to corrupt my soul with the foul deed I have revealed to you. Yet your jaundiced view of my motives I do comprehend, and can offer unto you a token of proof."

Marr took from his pocket a golden ring and placed it in Charles's hand.

The vintner gasped. "It is my father's signet ring. See, Margaret, see his initials? I remember I would sit with him some evenings and watch him press this ring into hot wax red as a rose to seal his correspondence."

"I took this as part recompense for our efforts; my comrades partook of the coinage in your father's purse. I oft thought: Had I taken and spent his money, as did they, thus disposing of the mementos of our deed, perhaps then the guilt would not have burned me like smelter's coals all these years, as hath this tiny piece of gold. But now I am glad I kept it, for I can at least return it to its rightful owner, before I cast away my mortal sheath."

"My father, not I, be the rightful owner," Charles muttered darkly. He closed his hand tightly around the ring. He leaned against the stone wall beside him and shook with rage and sorrow. A moment later he felt his wife's hand upon his. The fierce pressure with which he gripped the ring subsided.

Margaret said to him. "We must to the courts. Westcott and Murtaugh will feel the lash of justice upon them."

"Faith, madam, that cannot be. Lord Westcott is dead these five years. And his brigand son after him spent every pence of the inheritance. The land is gone to the Crown for taxes."

"What of Murtaugh?" Charles asked. "He lives still?"

"Oh, yes, sir. But though he is well and keeps quarters in London, he is further from the reach of justice than Lord Westcott in heaven. For Sir Murtaugh is much in favor with the Duke and others highly placed at Court. Many have availed themselves of the villain's services to diminish their debt. The judges at Queen's Bench will not even hear your claim, and in truth, you will put your freedom, indeed your life, in jeopardy to bring these charges into the open. My desire this night was not to set your course on a reckless journey of revenge, sir. I intend merely to make amends to one I have wronged."

Charles gazed at Marr for a moment and then said, "Thou art an evil man, and though I am a good Christian, I cannot find it in my heart to forgive thee. Still, I will pray for thy soul. Perhaps God will be more lenient than I. Now, get thee gone and I swear that, should ever thou cross my path again, my bodkin hand will not be stayed from its visit to thy throat and thou shall find thyself pleading thy case in the holy court of heaven far sooner than thou did intend."

"Yes, good sir. So shall it be."

Charles's attention turned momentarily to the ring so that he might place it on his finger. When he looked up once more, the alleyway was empty; the ruffian had vanished silently into the night.

Near candle-lighting the next day Charles Cooper closed his wares-house and repaired to the home of his friend, Hal Pepper, a man near to Charles's age but of better means, having inherited several apartments in a pleasant area of the City, which he let out for good profit.

Joining them was a large man of deliberate movement and speech. His true name was lost in the annals of his own history and everyone knew him only as Stout, the words not referring to his girth—significant though that be—but to his affection for black ale. He and Charles had met some years ago because the vintner bought Stout's wares; the man made and sold barrels and he often joked that he was a cooper by trade while Charles was a Cooper by birth.

The three had become close comrades, held together by common interests—cards and taverns and, particularly, the love of theater; they often ferried south of the Thames to see plays at the Swan, the Rose, or the Globe. Pepper also had occasional business dealings with James Burbage, who had built many of the theaters in London. For his part, Charles harbored not-so-secret desires to be a player. Stout had no connection with the theater other than a childlike fascination with plays, which he seemed to believe were his portal to the world outside of working-class London. As he would plane the staves of his barrels and pound the red-hot hoops with a smithy's hammer, he would recite lines from the latest works of Shakespeare or Jonson or from the classics of the late Kyd and Marlowe, much in vogue of late. These words he had memorized from the performances, not the printed page; he was a very poor reader.

Charles now told them the story that Marr had related to him. The friends reeled at the news of the death of Robert Cooper. They began to question Charles but he brought all conversing to a halt by saying, "He who committed this terrible deed shall die by my hand, I am determined."

"But," Stout said, "if thou kill Murtaugh, suspicion will doubtless fall immediately upon thee, as one aggrieved by his foul deeds against thy father."

"I think not," Charles replied. "It was Lord Westcott who stole my father's land. Murtaugh was merely a facilitator. No, I warrant that this brigand hath connived so much from so many that surely to examine all those with reason to kill him would keep the constable busy for a year. I believe I can have my revenge and escape with my life."

Hal Pepper, who being of means and thus knowledgeable in the ways of the Court, said, "Thou know not what thou say. Murtaugh hath highly placed friends who will not enjoy his loss. Corruption is a hydra, a many-headed creature. Thou may cut off one head, but another will poison thee before the first grow back—as it surely will."

"I care not."

Stout said, "But doth thy wife care? I warrant thee, friend, she doth very truly. Would thy children care if their father be drawn and quartered?"

Charles nodded at a fencing foil above Hal's fireplace. "I could meet Murtaugh in a duel."

Hal replied, "He is an expert swordsman."

"I may still win. I am younger, perchance stronger."

"Even if thou best him, what then? A hobnob with the jury at the Queen's Bench and, after, a visit to the executioner." Hal waved his arm in disgust. "Pox. . . . at best thou would end up like Jonson."

Ben Jonson, the actor and playwright, had killed a man in a duel several years ago and barely escaped execution. He saved himself only by reciting the neck verse—Psalm 50, verse 1—and pleading the benefit of clergy. But his punishment was to be branded with a hot iron.

"I will find some way to kill Murtaugh."

Hal persisted in his dissuasion. "But what advantage can his death gain thee?"

"It can gain me justice."

Hal's face curled into an ironic smile. "Justice in London town? That be like the fabled unicorn, of which everyone speaks but no one can find."

Stout took a clay pipe, very small in his massive wood-worker's hands, and packed it with aromatic weed from the Americas, which was currently very much in style. He touched a burning straw to the bowl and inhaled deep. Soon smoke wafted to the ceiling. He slowly said to Hal, "Thy mockery is not entirely misplaced, my friend, but my simple mind tells me that justice is not altogether alien to us, even among the denizens of London. What of the plays we see? Oft-times they abound with justice. The tragedy of Faustus. . . . And that which we saw at the Globe a fortnight ago, inked by our friend Will Shakespeare: The story of Richard III. The characters therein are awash with evil—but justice doth out."

"Exactly," Charles whispered.

"But they be make-believe, my friend," Hal countered. "They are of no more substance than the ink with which Kit Marlowe and Will penned those entertainments."

Charles would not, however, be diverted from his goal. "What know thou of this Murtaugh? Hath he any interests?"

Hal answered, "Other men's wives and other men's money."

"What else knowest thou?"

"As I said, he is a swordsman, or so he fancies himself. And he rides with the hounds whenever he quits London for the country. His is intoxicated with pride. One cannot flatter him too much. He strives constantly to impress members of the court."

"Where lives he?"

Stout and Hal remained silent, clearly troubled by their friend's deadly plans.

"Where?" Charles persisted.

Hal sighed and waved his hand to usher away a cloud of smoke from Stout's pipe. "That weed is most foul."

"Faith, sir, I find it calming."

Finally Hal turned to Charles. "Murtaugh hath but an apartment fit for a man of no station higher than journeyman and far smaller than he boasts. But it is near the Strand and the locale puts him in the regular company of men more powerful and richer than he. Thou will find it in Whitefriars, near the embankment."

"And where doth he spend his days?"

"I know not for certain but I would speculate that, being a dog beneath the table of Court, he goes daily to the palace at Whitehall to pick through whatever sundry scraps of gossip and schemes he might find and doth so, even now, when the Queen is in Greenwich."

"And therefore what route would he take on the way from his apartment to the palace?" Charles asked Stout, who through his trade knew most of the labyrinthine streets of London.

"Charles," Stout began. "I like not what thou suggest."

"What route?"

Reluctantly the man answered, "On horse he would follow the embankment west then south, when the river turn, to Whitehall."

"Of the piers along that route know thou the most deserted? Charles inquired.

Stout said, "The one in most disuse would be Temple wharf. As the Inns of Court have grown in number and size, the area hath fewer wares-houses than once it did." He added pointedly, "It also be near to the place where prisoners are chained at water level and made to endure the tides. Perchance thou ought shackle thyself there following thy felony, Charles, and in doing, save the Crown's prosecutor a day's work."

"Dear friend," Hal began, "I pray thee, put whatever foul plans are in thy heart aside. Thou cannot—"

But his words were stopped by the staunch gaze of their friend, who looked from one of his comrades to the other and said, "As when fire in one small house doth leap to the thatch of its neighbors and continue its rampaging journey 'til all the row be destroyed, so it did happen that many lives were burned to ash with the single death of my father." Charles held his hand up, displaying the signet ring that Marr had given him yesterday. The gold caught the light from Hal's lantern and seemed to burn with all the fury in Charles's heart. "I cannot live without avenging the vile alchemy that converted a fine man into nothing more than this paltry piece of still metal."

A look passed between Hal and Stout, and the larger of the two said to Charles, "Thy mind is set, that much is clear. Faith, dear friend, whatever thy decision be, we shall stand by thee."

Hal added, "And for my part, I shall look out for Margaret and thy children—if the matter come to that. They shall want for nothing if it be in my means to so provide."

Charles embraced them then said mirthfully, "Now, gentlemen, we have the night ahead of us."

"Wherefor shall we go?" asked Stout uneasily. "Thou art not bent on murder this evening, I warrant?"

"Nay, good friend—it shall be a week or two before I am prepared to meet the villain." Charles fished in his purse and found coins in sufficient number for that evening's plans. He said, "I am in the mood to take in a play and visit our friend Will Shakespeare after."

"I am all for that, Charles," Hal said as they stepped into the street. Then he added in a whisper, "Though if I were as dearly set on saying heigh-ho to

God in person as thou seem to be, then I myself would forgo amusement and scurry to a church that I might find a priest's rump to humbly kiss with my exceedingly penitent lips."

The constable, whose post was along the riverbank near the Inns of Court, was much pleased with his life here. Yes, one could find apple-squires offering gaudy women to men upon the street and cutthroats and pick-purses and cheats and ruffians. But unlike bustling Cheapside with its stores of shoddy merchandise or the mad suburbs south of the river, his jurisdiction was populated largely with upstanding gentlemen and ladies, and he would often go a day or two without hearing an alarum raised.

This morning, at nine of the clock, the squat man was sitting at a table in his office, arguing with his huge bailiff, Red James, regarding the number of heads currently resting on pikes upon London Bridge.

"It be thirty-two if it be one," Red James muttered.

"Then 'tis one, for thou art wrong, you goose. The number be no more than twenty-five."

"I did count them at dawn, I did, and the tally was thirty-two." Red James lit a candle and produced a deck of cards.

"Leave the tallow be," the constable snapped. "It cost money and must needs come out of our allowance. We shall play by the light of day."

"Faith, sir," Red James grumbled, "if I be a goose, as you claim, then I cannot be a cat and hence have not the skill to see in the dark." He lit another wick.

"What good art thou, sir?" The constable bit his thumb at the bailiff and was about to rise and blow the candles out when a young man dressed in workman's clothing ran to the window.

"Sirs, I seek the constable at once!" he gasped.

"And thou have found him."

"Sir, I am Peter Rawls and I am come to raise a hue and cry! A most grievous attack is under way."

"What be thy complaint?" the constable looked over the man and found him to be apparently intact. "Thou seem untouched by bodkin or cudgel."

"Nay, it is not I who am hurt but another who is *about* to be. And most grievously, I fear. I was walking to a wares-house on the embankment not far from here. And—"

"Get on, man, important business awaits."

"—and a gentlemen pulled me aside and pointed below to Temple wharf, where we did see two men circling. Then I did hear the younger of the two state his intent to kill the other, who cried out for help. Then the dueling did commence."

"An apple-squire fighting with a customer over the price of a woman," Red James said in a tired voice. "Of no interest to us." He began to shuffle the cards.

"Nay, sir, that is not so. One of them—the older, and the man most disadvantaged—was a peer of the realm. Robert Murtaugh."

"Sir Murtaugh, friend to the Lord Mayor and in the Duke's favor!" Alarmed, the constable rose to his feet.

"The very same, sir," the lackey said breathlessly. "I come to you in haste to raise hue and cry."

"Bailiffs!" the constable cried and girded himself with his sword and dagger. "Bailiffs, come forth at once!"

Two men stumbled into the room from quarters next to the den, their sensibilities muddled by the difficult marriage of this morning's sleep and last night's wine.

"Violence is afoot upon Temple wharf. We go forthwith."

Red James picked up a pike in the corner, his weapon of choice.

The men hurried out into the cool morning and turned south toward the Thames, over which smoke and mist hung thick as fleece on a lamb. In five minutes they were at the porch overlooking Temple wharf, where, as the lackey had assured, a dreadful contest was under way.

A young man was fighting vigorously with Sir Murtaugh. The peer fought well but he was dressed in the pompous and cumbersome clothing then fashionable at Court—a Turkish theme, replete with gilt robe and feathered turban—and because of the restrictive garments, was losing ground to the young cutthroat. Just as the ruffian drew back to strike a blow at the knight, the constable shouted, "Cease all combat at once! Put down thy weapons!"

But what might have ended in peace turned to unexpected sorrow as Sir Murtaugh, startled by the constable's shout, lowered his parrying arm and looked up toward the voice.

The attacker continued his lunge and the blade struck the poor knight in the chest. The blow did not pierce his doublet but Sir Murtaugh was knocked back against the rail. The wood gave way and the man fell to the rocks forty feet below. A multitude of swans fled from the disturbance as his body rolled down the embankment and into the water, where it sank beneath the grim surface.

"Arrest him!" cried the constable, and the three bailiffs proceeded to the startled ruffian, whom Red James struck with a cudgel before he could flee. The murderer fell senseless at their feet.

The bailiffs then climbed down a ladder and proceeded to the water's edge. But of Sir Murtaugh, no trace was visible.

"Murder committed this day! And in my jurisdiction," said the constable with a grim face, though in truth he was already reveling in the promise of the reward and celebrity that his expeditious capture of this villain would bring.

The Crown's head prosecutor, Jonathan Bolt, an arthritic, bald man of forty, was given the duty of bringing Charles Cooper to justice for the murder of Robert Murtaugh.

Sitting in his drafty office near Whitehall palace, ten of the clock the day after Murtaugh's body was fished from the Thames, Bolt reflected that the crime of murdering an ass like Murtaugh was hardly worth the trouble to pursue. But the nobility desperately needed villains like Murtaugh to save them from their own foolishness and profligacy so Bolt had been advised to make an example of the villain Charles Cooper.

However, the prosecutor had also been warned to make certain that he proceed with the case in such a way that Murtaugh's incriminating business affairs not be aired in public. So it was decided that Cooper be tried not in Sessions Court but in the Star Chamber, the private court of justice dating back to his highness Henry VIII.

The Star Chamber did not have the authority to sentence a man to die. Still, Bolt reflected, an appropriate punishment would be meted out. Upon rendering a verdict of guilt against the cutthroat, the members of the Star Chamber bench would surely order that Cooper's ears be hacked off, that he be branded with a hot iron, and then be transported—banished—probably to the Americas, where he would live as a ruined beggar all his life. His family would forfeit whatever estate he had and be turned out into the street.

The unstated lesson would be clear: Do not trouble those who are the de facto protectors of the nobility.

Having interviewed the constable and the witness in the cases—a lackey named Peter Rawls—Bolt now left his office and proceeded to Westminster, the halls of government.

In an anteroom hidden away in the gizzard of the building, a half-dozen lawyers and their clients awaited their turn to go before the bench, but Cooper's case had been placed top on the docket and Jonathan Bolt walked past the others without delay and entered into the Star Chamber itself.

The dim room, near the Privy Council, was much smaller and less decorous than its notorious reputation imported. Quite plain, it boasted only candles for light, a likeness of her majesty, and upon the ceiling, the painted stars that bestowed upon the room its unjudicial name.

Inside, Bolt observed the prisoner in the dock. Charles Cooper was pale and a bandage covered his temple. Two large sergeants at arms stood behind the prisoner. The public was not allowed into Star Chamber proceedings but the lords, in their leniency, had allowed Margaret Cooper, the prisoner's wife, to be in attendance. A handsome woman otherwise, Bolt observed, her face was as white as her husband's and her eyes red from tears.

At the table for the defense was a man Bolt recognized as a clever lawyer from the Inns of Court and another man in his late thirties, about whom there was a slight familiarity. He was lean, with a balding pate and lengthy brown hair, and dressed in shirt and breaches and short buskin boots. A character witness, perhaps. Bolt knew that, based on the facts of this case, Cooper could not avoid guilt altogether; rather, the defense would concentrate on mitigating the sentence. Bolt's chief challenge would be to make sure such a tactic was not successful.

Bolt took his place beside his own witnesses—the constable and the lackey, who sat nervously, hands clasped before them.

A door opened and five men, robed and wigged, entered, the members of the Star Chamber bench, which consisted of several members of the Queen's Privy Council—today, they numbered three—and two judges from the Queen's Bench, a court of law. The men sat and ordered papers in front of them.

Bolt was pleased. He knew each of these men and, judging from the look in their eyes, believed that they had in all likelihood already found in the Crown's favor. He wondered how many of them had benefitted from Murtaugh's skills in vanquishing debts. All, perhaps.

The high chancellor, a member of the Privy Council, read from a piece of paper. "This special court of equity, being convened under authority of her royal highness Elizabeth Regina, is now in session. All ye with business before this court come forward and state thy cause. God save the Queen." He then fixed his eyes on the prisoner in the dock and continued in a grave voice. "The Crown charges thee, Charles Cooper, with murder in the death of Sir Robert Murtaugh, a knight and peer of the realm, whom thou did without provocation or excuse most grievously assault and cause to die on fifteen June in the forty-second year of the reign of our sovereign, her majesty the Queen. The Crown's inquisitor will set forth the case to the chancellors of equity and judges of law here assembled."

"May it please this noble assemblage," offered Bolt, "we have here a case of most clear delineation, which shall take but little of thy time. The vintner named Charles Cooper did, before witnesses, assault and murder Sir Robert Murtaugh on Temple wharf for reasons of undiscerned enmity. We have witnesses to this violent and unprovoked event."

"Call them forth."

Bolt nodded to the lackey Peter Rawls, who rose and, his oath being sworn, gave his deposition, "I, sir, was making my way to the Temple wharf when a man did bid me come running. He said, 'Behold, there is mischief before us, for that is Sir Robert Murtaugh.' Faith, sirs, before our eyes the prisoner there in the dock was challenging Sir Murtaugh with a sword. Then he did leap toward the unfortunate peer and utter words most threatening against him."

"And what, pray, were those words?"

"They were somewhat to this order, sirs: 'Villain, thou diest!' Whereupon the dueling commenced. And Sir Murtaugh cried, 'Help! Help! Murder, Murder!'

"I did run to seek the aid of the constable. We did return, with the advantage of bailiffs, and arrived to see the prisoner strike poor Sir Murtaugh. He fell through the railing to his death. It was a most awful and unpleasant sight."

The court then allowed the defense lawyer to cross-examine the lackey Rawls, but the attorney for Cooper chose not to ask any questions of him.

Bolt then had the constable rise and take the witness's dock and tell much the same story. When he was finished, Cooper's lawyer declined to examine this man either.

Bolt said, "I have no more to present by way of the Crown's case, my lords." He sat down.

The lawyer for the defense rose and said, "If it please this noble body, I shall let the prisoner report on the incident, and thy most excellent chancellors and most noble judges will behold, beyond doubt, that this is but a most egregious misunderstanding."

The men on the bench regarded each other with some irony and the high chancellor administered the oath to Charles Cooper.

One of the judges from the Queen's Bench asked, "What say thou to these charges?"

"That they, my good lord, be erroneous. Sir Murtaugh's death was but a tragic accident."

"Accident?" a Privy Council member said with a laugh. "How say thou 'accident' when thou attacked a man with thy sword and he fell to his death. Perchance the instrument of his death was the rocks upon the embankment but the instigating force was thy thrust, which sent him headlong to them."

"Aye," offered another, "I warrant to say, had the unfortunate Mr. Murtaugh not fallen, thou would have skewered him like a boar."

"I respectfully submit, Lord, that, nay, I would not have harmed him in any way. For we were not fighting; we were practicing."

"Practicing?"

"Yes, my lord, I have aspirations to be a player in the theater. My profession, though, as thou have heard, is that of vintner. I was at Temple wharf to arrange for delivery of some claret from France and, having surplus time, thought I would practice a portion of the role, which chanced to involve some swordplay. I was so engaged when Sir Murtaugh happened by, on his way to Whitehall Palace. He is—sadly, *was*, I should say—quite an accomplished swordsman and he observed me for a moment then reported to me what, alas, is true— that my talent with a blade be quite lacking. We fell into conversation, and I said that if he might deign to show me some authentic gestures, I would inquire about getting him a small part on the stage. This intrigued him and he offered me the benefit of his considerable expertise at dueling." The prisoner cast his eyes toward the Constable. "All would have gone well had not that man disturbed us and caused Sir Murtaugh to lose his stride. I merely tapped him on the doublet with my sword, Most High Chancellor, and he stepped back against the rail, which tragically was loose. Before I could run to his aid, I was struck by a huge bailiff and fell to the wharf. . . . For my part, I am heart-sick at the good man's demise."

There was some logic to this, Prosecutor Bolt thought grimly. He had learned something of Cooper in the hours before the trial and it was true that he frequented the theaters south of the Thames. Nor could he find a true motive for the murder. Cooper was a guildsman, with no need or inclination toward robbery. Certainly much of London would regale at the death of a lout like Murtaugh. But as the nobles wished the case prosecuted swiftly, Bolt had not had time to make a proper inquiry into any prior relationship between Cooper and Murtaugh.

The knight, for his part, as everyone knew, was vain as a peacock and the thought of getting up on a stage and preening before members of the Court would surely appeal to him.

Yet even if Cooper were telling the truth, the nobles would want Murtaugh's killer punished, whether his death was an accident or not, and indeed the five men on the bench seemed little swayed by the prisoner's words.

Cooper continued, "Those words of anger and threat reported by the lackey there? Sirs, they were not mine."

"And whose be they, then?"

Cooper glanced at his lawyer, who rose and said, "Prithee, sirs, we have a witness whose deposition shall bear on the events. If it please the bench, may we have William Shakespeare step forward."

Ah, yes, Bolt thought, *that* is who the witness is: the famed playwright and director of the Chamberlain's Men troupe. Bolt himself had seen several of the man's plays at the Rose and the Globe. What was transpiring here?

"Master Shakespeare, thou will swear oath to our holy Lord that thy deposition here shall be honest and true?"

"I so confirm, my lord."

"What have thou to say that bears on this case?"

"I pray you, Lord Chancellor, I am here to add to the deposition thou have previous heard. Some weeks ago, Charles Cooper did come to me and say that he had always been a lover of the player's craft and had hoped to try his hand upon the stage. I bid him attempt some recitation for me and observed that he performed several passages, of my own creation, with exceeding grace."

Shakespeare continued. "I told him I had no place for him just then but I gave him portions of a draft of the play I am presently writing and told him to practice it. When Court returns in the fall, I told him I might find a part for him."

"How exactly doth this bear on the case, Master Shakespeare?"

The playwright withdrew from a leather pouch a large sheaf of parchment with writing upon it. He read, " 'Enter CASSIO. RODERIGO: I know his gait, 'tis he. Villain, thou diest! Makes a pass with his blade at CASSIO. . . . CASSIO draws his own weapon and wounds RODERIGO. RODERIGO: O, I am slain! IAGO from behind wounds CASSIO in the leg, and exit. CASSIO: I am maim'd for ever. Help, ho! murder! murder!' "

" 'Villain, thou diest . . . Help, ho, murder. . . .' But those," the high chancellor said, "with some alterations, are the very words that the witness heard the prisoner and Sir Murtaugh exchange. They are from thy play?"

"Yes, my lord, they are. It is as yet unperformed and I am in the midst of reworking it." Shakespeare paused for a moment, then added, "I did promise her highness, the Queen, a new play for her enjoyment when she and the Court return this fall."

A Privy Council member frowned and then asked, "Thou art, if I am not mistaken, much in the Queen's favor."

"Humbly, sir, I am but a journeyman playwright. But I can say with little exaggeration that Her Highness hath from time to time offered expressions of pleasure at my work."

Hell's bells, thought the prosecutor. Shakespeare is *indeed* much in the Queen's favor. This fact was well known. It was rumored that Her Highness would name his the sole royal acting company within the next year or two. The course of the case was now clear: To find Cooper guilty would require the judges to disavow Shakespeare's testimony. The Queen would hear and there would be consequences. Bolt recalled an expression he had heard years ago: A hundred dukes versus a single queen leaves a hundred coffins on the green.

The high chancellor turned to the rest of the Privy Council and they conferred again among themselves. A moment later he pronounced, "In light of the evidence presented, this court of equity rules that the death of Sir Robert Murtaugh was caused by no man's intent and Charles Cooper is herewith free to go forth unfettered, and untainted by any further accusation in this matter." He cast a stern gaze toward the prosecutor. "And . . . Sir Jonathan, if it be not too taxing in the future, the court would be honored if thou might at least *peruse* the evidence and consult with the prisoner *before* thou deign to waste the time of this court."

"I shall do, my noble lord."

One of the judges leaned forward, nodded at the sheaf that the playwright was replacing in his sack, and asked, "May I ask, Mr. Shakespeare, what will this play be called?"

"I know not for certain, my lord, what the final title shall be. I presently call it, *Othello, the Moor of Venice.*"

"And might I be assured from the testimony we have heard today that the audience may look forward to some good swordwork in this play?"

"Oh, yes, your honor."

"Good. I far prefer such plays to thy comedies."

"If I may be so bold, sir, I believe you will then enjoy this piece."

Cooper and his wife left with Shakespeare. The hawk-billed shyster followed, though not before casting a gaze toward Bolt. It was a look that seemed to contain some import but the prosecutor had no idea what the meaning might be.

Near candle-lighting that night, three men sat in the Unicorn and Bear tavern in Charing Cross, tankards of ale before them: Charles Cooper, Stout, and William Shakespeare.

A shadow filled the doorway as a man walked into the tavern.

"Behold, 'tis the mysterious gentlemen on the wharf," Charles said.

Hal Pepper joined them and was served up an ale of his own.

Charles lifted his tankard. "Thou did well, my friend."

Hal drank long and nodded proudly to acknowledge the compliment. His role in the daring play, as writ by William Shakespeare and Charles Cooper in collaboration, was critical. After Charles had stopped Murtaugh on the wharf and, as he'd told the court, piqued the knight's interest with the promise of an appearance on stage, it had been Hal's task to snare a passer-by at just the right moment so that he witness the exchange between Charles and Murtaugh at the start of their mock duel. Hal had then given Rawls a half-sovereign to raise the hue and cry with the constable, whom Shakespeare, as master plotter, had decided should perforce be a witness to the duel as well.

Shakespeare examined Charles gravely and said, "Regarding thy performance in court, friend, thou need some study as a player, yet on the whole"— the man from Stratford could not here resist a smile—"I would venture to say that thou *acquitted* thyself admirably."

Will Shakespeare often deflected the course of the conversation to allow for the inclusion of puns, which he loved to contrive. But neither was Charles Cooper a stranger to word games. He riposted, "Ah, 'tis sadly true, friend, that my talent for bearing witness in court is no match for thy overbearing witness in taverns."

"Touché," cried Shakespeare and the men laughed hard.

"And here is to thee too, my friend," Charles tapped his tankard against Stout's.

It had been the big man's task to wield his barrel-maker's tools with sufficient skill to loosen the railing at Temple wharf just the right degree so that it would not give way under casual hands, but would fall apart when Murtaugh stumbled against it.

Stout was not as quick as either Shakespeare or Charles and attempted no cleverness in reply. He merely blushed fiercely with pleasure at the recognition.

Charles then embraced Shakespeare. "But thou, Will, were the lynchpin."

Shakespeare said, "Thy father was a good man to me and my family. I will always remember him with pleasure. I am glad to have played a small part in the avenging of his death."

"What might I do to repay thee for the risks thou took and thy efforts on my behalf?" Charles asked.

The playwright said, "Indeed thou have already. Thou have bestowed upon me the most useful gift possible for a dabbler in the writer's craft."

"What might that be, Will?"

"Inspiration. Our plot was the midwife for a sonnet which I completed just an hour ago. He drew a piece of paper from his jacket. He looked over the assembled men and said solemnly, "It seemed a pity that Murtaugh knew not the reason for his death. In my plays, you see, the truth must ultimately out—it needs be revealed, at the least, to the audience, if not the characters. That Murtaugh died in ignorance of our revenge set my pen in motion."

The playwright then read slowly:

> When I do see a falcon in the wild
> I think of he, the man who gave me life,
> Who loved without restraint his youthful child
> And bestow'd affection on his wife.
> When I do see a vulture in its flight
> I can think of naught but thee, who stole
> Our family's joy away that evil night
> Thou cut my father's body from his soul.
> The golden scissors of a clever Fate
> Decide how long a man on earth shall dwell.

But as my father's son I could not wait
To see thy wicked soul entombed in hell.
This justice I have wrought is no less fine,
Being known but in God's heart and in mine.

"Well done, Will," Hal Pepper called out.

Charles clapped the playwright on the back.

"It be about Charles?" Stout asked, staring down at the paper. His lips moved slowly as he attempted to form the words.

"In spirit, yes," Shakespeare said, turning the poem around so that the big man could examine the lines right ways up. He added quietly, "But not, methinks, enough so that the Court of Sessions might find it evidentiary."

"I do think it best, though, that thou not publish it just yet," Charles said cautiously.

Shakespeare laughed. "Nay, friend, not for a time. This verse would find no market now, in any case. Romance, romance, romance . . . that be the only form of poesy that doth sell these days. Which, by the by, is most infuriating. No, I shall secrete it safe away and retrieve it years hence when the world hath forgot about Robert Murtaugh. Now, it is near to candle-lighting, is it not?"

"Very close to," Stout replied.

"Faith, then. . . . Now that our real-life tale hath come to its final curtain, let us to a fictional one. My play *Hamlet* hath a showing tonight and I must needs be in attendance. Collect thy charming wife, Charles, then we shall to the ferry and onward to the Globe. Drink up, gentlemen, and let's away!"

Those Are Pearls That Were His Eyes
BY CAROLE NELSON DOUGLAS

 Ex-journalist Carole Nelson Douglas is the award-winning author of forty novels and two mystery series. *Good Night, Mr. Holmes* introduced the only woman to outwit Sherlock Holmes, American diva Irene Adler, as a detective, and was a *New York Times* Notable Book. The series recently resumed with *Chapel Noir* and *Castle Rouge*. Douglas also created contemporary hard-boiled P.I. Midnight Louie, whose first-furperson feline narrations appear in short fiction and novels (*Cat in a Leopard Spot*, etc.).

As a college theater major, Douglas played the title role in *The Taming of the Shrew*. She collects vintage clothing and stray cats, and lives in Fort Worth, Texas.

Prologue

Humility is only doubt,
And does the sun and moon blot out,
Rooting over with thorns and stems
The buried soul and all its gems.
This life's dim windows of the soul

Distorts the heavens from pole to pole,

And leads you to believe a lie

When you see with, not through, the eye.

—WILLIAM BLAKE

"What's past is prologue."
—ANTONIO

Dramatis Personae

Prospero, right Duke of Milan	*Antonio, usurping Duke of Milan, brother to Prospero*
Miranda, daughter to Prospero	*Ferdinand, son to the King of Naples*
Ariel, an airy spirit	*Gonzalo, an honest old counselor*
Caliban, a savage and deformed slave	*Balthasar, a doctor of law from Rome*

ACT I

"The wills above be done, but I would fain die a dry death."
—GONZALO

Scene I. *On an island. Enter a* MONSTER.

The sea's soft fists beat upon the beach, its salty lips kiss the cool sand senseless. He hears murmur after murmur, a tide of whispers from the mermaids in Poseidon's deepest, watery dungeons.

You are alone, the mermaid voices hiss like sea snakes. *You are alone.*

He huddles in his cave, knowing naught else to do. *The island is my own again,* he answers the mocking voices. Perhaps it is not he they mock. Perhaps they do not mock, but he has never known anything but mockery and in some wise the taunting chorus brings sweet familiarity.

The island is his own again. His alone.

He tallies his solitary kingdom. Every blade of grass and upright sword of reed, each drop of dew, each thorn upon each briar and bramble. Each blast of wind and knife-flung dirk of rain. All that is called human has left. He had crouched among the lacerating froth of mermaid tongues to watch the ships's white-sailed masts joust with the clouds of heaven. The fleet had rocked upon the frothy breast of mother ocean until it vanished into her lapping, salt-laced sleeves.

He heard them speak before they left, those strangers, though they little marked him. Once shipwrecked, they now sail on fresh ships, bound to climes called Algiers, Milan, and Naples, fair-sounding names for unseen places.

He is bound to this unnamed island, cursing a god of whom he knows only his name, Setebos, remembering a long-dead mother he knows only from the old man's curses. She had named him Caliban and then died. The old man who came after had called her as many foul names as he called the son she left behind. The blue-eyed hag Sycorax, the old man had named her.

Caliban cannot say how old or hag-ridden his mother was, what color her eyes. Her memory was soon supplanted by the old man, Prospero . . . and by one other creature, the only fair thing he ever saw upon this island, the maiden Miranda. She the old man will wed to a prince, the son of his once-mortal enemy, the King of Naples.

They are all gone, enemies to each other no longer. And no longer will he, the one left behind, be called Caliban the slave, the monster. No more shall he be pinched blacker than pitch and given groaning cramps by the vexed and invisible spirits Prospero called to berate him. Nor shall he carry bruising burdens of wood and huddle apart in his foul cave, nor be called villain and misshapen knave and poisonous filth.

The island is his own again.

When the rain comes, drowning out the mermaid taunts, he ventures into its stinging curtains. He trudges the island's length and width as if to measure with his naked feet the rich cloths worn by the men of Milan and Naples. The old man saw that even when these, his bitter mortal enemies, were shipwrecked on this shore, not so much as their garments were salt-wracked and ruined.

No harm to those who harmed him, but to Caliban who has harmed no one, all incivility.

Still, he howled when they left. So in the rain he runs to the island's every selvage edge. This lone rugged rock is his kingdom, as it was his mother's, and he howls at wind and water, who howl back like brothers.

He is not quite alone. The mischievous spirits his mother imprisoned in twisted pine trees around this island home scream their solitary agony in chorus as he passes their binding places. They do not sing as sweet as mermaids, but like wild pigs. Sometimes he joins them, as if they were all dogs of the same unlucky litter. At other times he laughs and curses them as Prospero cursed Caliban. Sometimes he is silent. And at other times he thinks that the ceaseless howls of trapped spirits will drive him mad.

The island is his own again. Yet the powers his hated mother had in full measure remain to him only as weak memories. When the storm has passed, he will huddle in his cave, whipped by wind and wave into a shivering cur, hiding from the unholy wails of helpless spirits.

Sun and moon are his only visitors.

He taught Caliban them, the old man. He had a long beard and hair that flowed like the white froth at the waves' rabid mouths. His eyes were the cold churning green of a wall of water tall enough to oversweep the isle entire. He told Caliban of the bigger light and the smaller light that come and go in dark and brightness above. At first he taught Caliban kind words. Sun. Moon. And at length he taught Caliban that he was a monster.

Caliban will still build the fire, which the old man taught him, though he eats only roots and sere fruits. There is nothing living on this island save him. Save Caliban.

And the whispering mermaids and the howling spirits trapped for eternity. Like Caliban.

Scene II. *Outside* CALIBAN'S *cave.*
Enter ARIEL, *invisible, singing.*

Ah, brothers, sisters, on this strand
Take heed, take heart and then take hand,

This free and ever dancing sprite
will deliver thee from spite.
So touch the earth and spring to air
I banish foul and make all fair.

ARIEL *darts into the cave.*

Caliban flees his only shelter, wincing beneath invisible blows. What madness is this? What dream, what nightmare? He is at last alone, yet the same pestilence that had beset him under the reign of Prospero bedevils him still.

"Away! I have done with invisible things, save the wind."

A spiteful funnel of dust shimmers in the salt air until a narrow, wild face surmounts it.

"You are not done with me, foul fiend!"

"Ariel, blasted spirit! You were freed. I saw the old man unleash you. You were free to serve the wind alone, and your own will."

"I have become the wind, and grew used to buffeting such foolish beasts as you hither and yon. Get thee to a woodpile, slave, or I shall pinch thee blacker than thy villainous heart!"

"Strike me not! You need obey no one now."

"None but my own willful nature. If you wish me gone, you will tell me how to free my brethren in the trees."

"Did not the old man tell you that I had no powers? Why else would I suffer his insults and blows, and yours?"

"You know the ways of your foul dam, the witch Sycorax, driven from Algiers to exile on this island, with sprites all her unwilling servants, until she treed us in fury at our disobedience. You told Prospero enough spells that he released me for his body servant."

"Softly, ungentle Ariel, who pinches and spits and tricks at another's command. You would not serve my mother, but you served the ill-usage of that old man. Even Prospero spoke to me softly at first and taught me words and warmth of the fire, all the better to charm the secrets of my dead mother's spells from me. Have you learned nothing from your former master but his cruelty?"

"Have you learned even less, to think that you dare disobey a higher spirit? Away! To the trees that weep bitter sap. I will have my kin unleashed."

Scene III. CALIBAN *alone.*

He sits by the trees who wail with only the wind for company now. He has come to a sore state. He misses his old enemy and all his kind and even Prospero's cruel disembodied servants, even the eternal howls of the imprisoned sprites. But he was not completely cowed by the airy tormenter. This pine conceals one last bound sprite. He swallows, then croaks out a song that mimics Ariel's spell.

> *"Come to my bidding as I sing*
> *You shall fly to ev'ry unkempt thing,*
> *You shall do a task at my command*
> *When I call you forth with clutching hand."*

His gesture is crude, a fist not a flourish, but the tree splits as if peeled by lightning. From its raw, pale fissure swirls another disorder of air. A wicked face appears in the sulphurous mist.

"Sprite, you must obey my command 'ere you fly free."

"Woe that I must heed a witch's hellish spawn!"

"Before you take to air and cloud, you will follow foul Ariel's example. Blow me a tempest, Sprite, that will drive near shore a ship to take me far from here. No tricks. No shipwreck, no dead school of sailors stranded on my island's frothy petticoats. I will have an argosy to waft me to such shores as Naples."

Whirling into a blur like a water spout, the sprite vanishes into the kettle of thunder and lightning cooking above.

Caliban looks to the darkling sky. He can see no large light and no little light, no sun and no moon. The coming storm smells of human fear. This island soon will be as dead to him as is his mother and even now-distant Prospero. He offers a vow to the lightless heavens:

"I have been a monster and a slave." His knotted fist shakes as if it brandishes a weapon, but it is empty and any weapon is invisible. "Now I will try my hand at aping a man."

ACT II

"Let me live here ever; So rare a wondered father and a wife Makes this place Paradise."
—FERDINAND

Scene I. *A market in Milan.*
Enter MIRANDA *and* FERDINAND.

Among the bustling citizens of Milan flourishing jeweled lengths of burnished silk and bright vessels of Venetian glass, the young couple strolls as if lost in a garden by themselves.

He wears velvet tunic and silken shirt. Her gown of sky-blue silk is full and plain, as if borrowed. Simplicity frames her features, both serene and struck with wonder, as richly as gold-leafed haloes embellish some Tuscan friar's latest fresco.

"What sights and sounds of joyous souls are these, Ferdinand?" she asks in fine Italian, but with an accent strangely innocent of the intonations of the region. "I blink in wonder to see a land thronged with people instead of my father's spirits and my fraught imagination. My island home now seems no larger than a wedding band."

He takes her hand, bare of any decoration. "An apt comparison, my sea-borne bride-to-be, for soon such a loving ring shall circle thy finger. But look about. Thy father bade you on the island to be sure I was the fairest man you did ever look upon, yet you had never seen none but his own venerable brow." He frowns with an unwelcome memory. "And, I trow, the shaggy, lowering head of that brute slave of his. Here you see the young noblemen that populate a dukedom. How stands Ferdinand now?"

"Oh, my love. First sight is best."

She has stopped to gaze into his eyes. Jugglers, pedlars, and the good wives of Milan flow around the island these twain have made of themselves.

He may be the son of the King of Naples, but since he has been shipwrecked on Prospero's island he marvels at seeing only one, while she stands shocked by multitudes.

"What kind of bold seafarer are you," he asks fondly, "to sail across half the salt ocean, and swear you need only Ferdinand for captain and crew?" The question is meant to have but one answer.

" 'Tis true. My sire did well by both of us when he his magic caused your father's fleet to stumble to its knees upon our island shore."

"O, happy accident! I have won a wife, but Prospero has won his dukedom back from his treacherous brother, Antonio. Now they are bosom brothers, or at least act so. It astonishes me that Prospero should forgive where he was so sinned against."

"I can only think he does it for the welfare of his child. His every thought was always of me."

"Prospero is truly a noble man. I almost bless the unjust exile that has brought you safe and unsullied to me. Blush indeed. You are not a bride yet."

"I had no cause to blush upon the island, save in one instance." She glances away to avoid a troublesome memory, then her smooth face lightens with delight. "Look, Ferdinand! What is the hue and cry over there? Is it a dancing bear?"

"We shall see at once. If so, we must engage him. Even the bears will dance at our wedding."

Moving nearer brings the maiden to a halt. "Ah, the poor beast is in a cage."

"I have never sensed a heart tenderer than yours."

"And it is dressed in satin foppery, poor brute, as if to mock its hairy soul."

"If the entertainment distress you, we shall leave."

"Distress me? Only in that I have come to think that another's misery is not entertainment. I have seen such civility in Naples and now in Milan as would shame the island."

"Naples is my father's seat, and he is a king. Civility is first courtier there, but the larger world is seldom such. Fine clothes may disguise the foulest intention."

"I begin to think back upon the island with dismay. Only now do I see my father's sorceries as strange and frightening. Were you not dismayed by them?"

"Your father spoke harshly on our meeting. I was dazed from swallowing half the salt sea. With my kin and party lost in the waves, I did fear his gruffness. Yet I had only to drown in your sweet eyes to grow brave again."

"And I yours. His harshness tested our swift enamorment, I think."

"A man of consummate wisdom."

"Look! Listen. Does the beast sing? What a harsh, rough tongue."

> *"Full fathom five thy father lies,*
> *Of his bones are coral made;*
> *Those are pearls that were his eyes,*
> *Nothing of him doth fade."*

"O, Ferdinand! So pale you grow. What has the beast done?"

"I heard those very syllables when first wandering on your island. I took them for a kind of death knell for my own father. I had feared our entire party drowned but I. Then I heard those dread words. I had forgotten that cruel song."

"And so you shall forget again, that mere ditty sung by that most mischievous spirit, Ariel. My father permitted him too much taunting. He was ever tormenting my father's slave and even myself on occasion. But he is free to mock the winds of the wide world now, and shall not bother us here."

"Then why has his cruel song followed us half a world away?"

"Can Ariel, freed from an island tree, have found another fettered lodging in the body of a beast? I must see for myself. But what fiend is this! Caliban!"

CALIBAN, *singing.*

> *"Full fathom five thy father lies,*
> *Of his bones are coral made;*

Those are pearls that were his eyes,
Nothing of him doth fade.
But doth suffer a sea-change
Into something rich and strange."

"This is not possible," Ferdinand says. "This is the unearthly burden I heard upon the isle, thinking it played the death knell for my drowned father. It was no mortal business then, and is not so now. I feel a chill. Will my father die soon, in Naples?"

"That city is far away, my love. Come with me. I feel the beast's stare. I will not have so fair a day darkened by a brutish scowl and a lying song."

Scene II. PROSPERO's *garden in Milan.*
Enter MIRANDA.

She moves through the garden like Eve through Eden, knowing herself alone, speaking to her only friend, herself.

"How it amazes me, that my father has ended as he begun, ruling a dukedom in this fruitful land amid a garden trained to flower in neat rows and trellises, where the only spirits on the wind are fragrance and unanchored petals like a fairy ship's sails.

"When all I knew was island, I was satisfied with every sight and sound. Now I see our safe anchorage as a harsh and unhappy land. Even my father's temper there was stern as some distant storm. I knew him not then for a deeply wronged man, nor knew his care of me, a toddling child. Yet his magic brought his enemies to his exile place. And some spirit other than Ariel stirred in him when he forgave the brother who had set us loose upon the sea without provision. So now we are returned to solid land and solid souls and cultivated gardens, to rank of place and myself to a bridal bed. I feel a fool among these city-bred folk and wonder if my eyes are opened yet."

Enter CALIBAN.

Miranda's eyes widen more to see the gaily caparisoned form of the misshapen slave from her father's island.

"What is this? Say it is that sprite of all appearances, Ariel, playing some new trick on me. This cannot be the shape of nightmare we left behind on the island."

"Say nothing louder than a whisper," Caliban orders, edging nearer. "I have no love for your father, though he accused me of overmuch love for you."

"You have escaped your cage in the marketplace!"

"I could not escape my cursed birth and the woe life brought me, so I have escaped all else at every opportunity. First I fled the island upon which my unfortunate mother was stranded and on which your unkindly father left me stranded again. Even the sprite who found me a ship to leave the island waxed fat with deceit and trickery. The sailors who rescued me decided I could save their purses from a lack of coins. I went from lonely cave to a cage within a gibbering circle of men I was told were not monsters."

"Perhaps you had better stayed alone upon the island."

"What, and never strut before my masters in the threads and tatters of their dress? See what I have to wear! Jacket and pantaloons, like the veriest puppet. I pass as a man, and they much remark that I can speak and stand amid gawking circles while they wait panting to hear what pearls will fall from my stuttering tongue. Are not men more splendid than monsters?"

"Why have you come to this garden?"

"Fear not. I have already paid the price a thousand times over for gazing upon the daughter of Prospero."

"You mean to violate me before my marriage! Get away, or I shall cry down all of my father's spirits upon you."

"He has released them all, maid. Only I remain of that time and place, and I am no spirit. This place is ripe with bud and bloom. Perhaps Prospero's ill words spoke from his loss of such a paradise. You do not remember when he spoke me fair, and stroked my head as a favored pet and taught me all my words, when you were but a blithering babe?"

"I do not remember."

"Or when we sat together on the cave floor, you and I as children, thinking it a kingdom, and I brought you stones to pile into walls. I was the elder. I spoke first. I ranged far to show your father the secrets of the island and my mother's hidden spells. You do not remember."

"I do not remember."

"I do not remember this, but I am told I was born of an exiled witch. Your father cursed her as a blue-eyed hag, and said that age and envy had hooped her over like a barrel stave. No wonder I was born misshapen and ugly. Yet my infant brain remembers eyes like the sky before it o'erclouds to weep rain. I remember that she stroked my head before your father showed like kindness, and she crooned to me like wind through rocks, spoke soft and was in no ways a witch to me."

"Even a witch may be a mother."

"And even a monster may be a child! No. Do not flee. I never harmed you."

"Foul, lying fiend! My father found you. He said you would have violated my innocence had he not come upon us at that very moment. To that vile intent you owe your sad estate, not to your mother's magical history, but to your own evil nature."

"Is that what you remember?"

"I remember my father coming upon the two of us in the cavern, and waxing wilder than a tempest. He beat you away from me, from the cave, almost off the island into the sea, with his staff and mighty powers and a hail-storm of furious words. I cowered myself, there on the stony floor, as if I, too, had sinned. But I was too innocent for that."

"Mayhap I was too."

"What mean you, beast, who has never spoken true?"

"Hark. Someone comes, and I must go. Beast I am, and hunted. Was it not ever so?"

Exit CALIBAN, *enter* FERDINAND.

"You grow pale as an April lily, Miranda," Ferdinand says, hastening to her side, an arm around her shoulders. "What ill thoughts turn your temper so cool in this warm and nurturing clime?"

"Memories."

"Memories are what the future will make. I remember nothing before I gazed into your eyes. I wonder if it was an enchantment of thy father's making."

"He harnessed many enchantments to make much happen on the island. Perhaps I am but another captive spirit of his powers."

"I did but jest, fairest maid! You require no enchantments but the level gaze of your honest eyes. I have never seen a truer pair. So smile, and let your cheeks warm to the regard of your lover."

"I will, most excellent Ferdinand. As my father forgave his brother Antonio his treachery, so I must forgive the past its mysteries. Perhaps I must even forgive . . ."

Tumult without. GONZALO *enters, distraught.*

"Woe! Oh, woe. What perfidy is this? Death in the dukedom. Murder has struck. We must clothe ourselves in ashes and midnight stuffs. Dead. Drowned, as he had not drowned upon the island. What wreck of a man is this?"

Miranda seizes Ferdinand's hand, but her eyes cannot leave Gonzalo's woe-racked face.

"My father!" she cries. "He said that he came home only to die. But say not so soon!"

"No, no! Take her hand, good Ferdinand. She has naught so close to home to mourn. Prospero lives. It is Antonio who has been struck and felled, until the blood ran from his head into a ribbon of scarlet fishes in the pond not two minutes walk from here."

Shaking his white-locked head, Gonzalo leaves the pair. Miranda paces away from Ferdinand's loving custody, as if suddenly lost in this most civil garden.

"My heart rejoices and breaks in the space of one beat," she breathes. "How can grief and joy ride tandem in such a narrow alley of emotion?"

"When evil expectation becomes unexpected deliverance of one dear to us, yet at the cost of another, grief becomes guilt. Mourn not," Ferdinand counsels her. "Antonio died a shriven soul. He had confessed his crimes against your father and yourself and had been forgiven. Show me a finer surety of paradise upon this earth! Wait here, and I shall see to the sad event."

Kissing her hand, Ferdinand follows in Gonzalo's footsteps.

Miranda remains unmoving in the tranquil garden, unsoothed by the curried comfort of nature. Her thoughts form soft phrases that fall like strings of broken beads upon the heedless flowers.

"My heart still beats in twain." She approaches a small orange tree and almost seems to address it. As a child she had heard the moaning spirits pent in the island's trees and had regarded them as friendly winds and almost-playmates. This tree solaces her now. "Surely the beast Caliban has done more evil here." She paces away to a soldiering stand of sentry pines. "Yet doubt has entered into my house of memory, and I teeter upon the threshold of my own abode, afraid."

Shaking her head, Miranda strides to the carved marble bench at the center of the bower, and declaims loud words as if making a speech makes her words toll true. " 'Tis clear Caliban will stand for this crime and that I must bear witness to his recent presence in this garden, not many steps away from where Antonio fell dying. It is only fitting that the beast must pay."

Again she walks away from her own brave words, muttering, "Yet if I have learned anything since leaving my father's island, it is that all is not what it seems. Oh, woe indeed! What shall I do?

Scene III. *A house in* VENICE.
Enter BASSANIO.

" 'A Daniel come to judgment' I seek! 'A Daniel come to judgment.' "

Laughing, the Venetian pauses to watch his wife set aside her fancy work.

Her eyes widen as they move from stitches smaller than eyelashes to a well-clad canvas as large as a man, and they warm with new-made marriage.

"Good Bassanio, has my husband become the town crier? What paper bear you?"

"This? A trifle. A summons fresh brought from the dukedom of Milan for the learned Doctor Balthasar. It seems a murderous monster requires an advocate."

"I have done with masquerades and the sickening compromises of the law. When your good friend Antonio stood to lose a pound of flesh and thus his very life to the Jew, Shylock, I did not hesitate to don a doctor's robe and play at manhood for thy friend's sake. But we are wed now, and Venice is in good temper. Why should I venture to Milan to seek more travail? Besides, Nerissa has sworn never to visit court more."

"Still, my Portia, this old Bassanio beseeches aid for a new Antonio, my role this time played by the daughter of the long-lost Prospero, Duke of Milan, one Miranda. It seems the murdered man was her uncle, Antonio, and the monster thus accused, one Caliban, is a servant from an island she and her father were marooned upon for many years."

"The niece of this dead Antonio seeks counsel for the monster that slew him? What kind of monster is it? Or is she?"

"This creature, I understand, is a low beast cast up like Duke Prospero and Miranda upon the deserted isle, rough of skin and feature and speech, the very likeness of a monster within and without, Caliban by name, and by fact Prospero's servant upon the island. I have heard of Milan's lost duke, this Prospero, that he was a learned man."

"A Daniel come to judgment, doubt it not."

"Not so learned as thee, noble Balthasar."

"Flatter me no more, husband. 'Tis you should hie to Milan. And I must go in my doctor of law disguise, to do what, I ask you?"

"Evoke the right and wrong of it and preserve some ignorant savage from death if he is innocent."

"I will go, noble Bassanio, but not because I believe the golden shower of praise that slips from thy lips. So ducats escaped Shylock's grasp when his daughter took his treasure and hied off to wed a Christian and the Jew argued himself into losing even more. Willful, stubborn man! I tried every persuasion to urge mercy for his claim upon Antonio. He had been ill used in his own turn, and argued well himself: 'Hath not a Jew eyes, If you do cut us, do we not bleed?' and so on. And if you bleed then, Jew, answer this: should you bleed another?

"Yet my own arguments for mercy, my every plea, pelted ears of stone. In the end the court stripped him of all his wealth. I can still hear his plaint for his lost treasures, one soft posterity, one hard currency. 'My daughter and my ducats.' Now we have another daughter and the dark deed of murder. Will ducats weigh in the balance here as well?"

"Ducats, no doubt, always weigh in a court of law."

"But gold has no way with you. You stand here with me, husband, because your eyes were blind to the glitter of the chest of gold and the chest of silver. Where nobler suitors chased false gleams, you chose the casket of lead, wherein the real treasure lay, and thus gained my hand. My wealthier suitors chose the surface glister and went home poorer. The truth most often lies inside the leaden casket, Bassanio, and is always the heaviest of any burden. I think that truth is crueler than ever mercy was kind."

"Then if you venture into bearing such burdens again, fair Portia, I will accompany you as the learned Doctor Balthasar's humble clerk, and hope that Nerissa will pardon my usurping her role."

"No woman of sense would settle for a maid when she may have a man to wait upon her pleasure. 'Tis done. We are off to Milan, which is not so long a journey. I am most eager to meet this monster from a world of water far away."

ACT III

"And thence retire me to my Milan, where Every third thought shall be my grave."
—PROSPERO

Scene I. *Milan: a court of justice.*
Enter PROSPERO, GONZALO, MIRANDA, *and* FERDINAND.

Prospero moves slowly under the weight of brocaded velvet robes, restored in raiment to the nobility of his office and his heritage.

"I would I were not here, my friends and daughter. Murder is foul enough a deed in its own person. To meet the beast that did it and know him for the monster that he always was only further affronts my breast."

Gonzalo, accompanying the Duke, attempts to reconcile him to the coming judgment. "Cruel it is to lose a land and a brother, then reclaim both, only to lose the one again so soon."

Miranda gazes upon the ornate chair that her father will soon occupy as judge. It is a thing of gilded elegance unseen upon the island.

"It is not certain that Caliban did the deed," she says.

Prospero assumes his seat. "O, my daughter, too long have you lived on seaweed and bright air, on Ariel's songs and caperings. You saw every day the scabrous underbelly of our island home, that stinking clod of animal earth that threatened to cloud o'er all our joy. Can you doubt his guilt, who was born thus?"

"I cannot doubt that he was born, and born upon the island we came to as castaways. He was not wrong in claiming the island first. No matter how we berate him then or now, Caliban was our Eden's only Adam."

"And you are not his Eve! Nothing Christian or fair ever dwelt within that cankered hide. I have taught thee too well the finer things of life and breath. You overflow with the honey of mercy, like hive in apple orchard. Yet you have no sting to defend yourself."

Ferdinand joins hands with Miranda as she stands uncertain before her father, like one seeking judgment.

"I would not change a jot of her, sir," he says, "and mercy is the crown jewel of an unsullied mind."

"Mind, King's son, that you are wed to your jewel soon. She shows a sinew of stubbornness that would power a long-bow. Such does not make for a meek wife."

"As long as she makes for my wife, I will not ask for meekness in the maid."

Gonzalo comes to clap Ferdinand upon the back and restore peace. His role has always been thus. "Well spoken, Prince. She much reminds me of her mother, so soon taken from hence."

"You knew her, sir?" Miranda asks with eagerness. "I have heard so little of the one who bore me. Am I like her?"

"Enough." Prospero speaks gruffly, with the finality of a judge decreeing. "There is naught to say of her. In birthing, Miranda, she gave twin life to you and to her own death, and a ghost of my life perished with her."

"Forgive me, Father. I forget the losses that wreathe your brow: a wife, a land, and now a brother. I cannot allow a daughter to leave you also. Much as my soul leans toward my Ferdinand as the shadow of the sun-dial creeps 'round to tell each hour, following time like a faithful hound, I cannot leave you thus."

"All will be well once this fiend has been laid low for his crime. It is good that I have renounced the practice of my powers, or I would have the winds tear him gristle from sinew without the gentle intervention of a court."

Enter CALIBAN, *in chains, with two guards.*

"O, be thou damned, inexorable dog!" cries the Duke. "Ingrate spawn of an unhappy, unhallowed dam. I gave thee the sweet suckle of human knowledge, but thou art a beast from fangs to cloven feet and have moved from lust to slaughter like the wolf from lamb to shepherd in the winking of an evil eye."

"If I am wolf, then you be bear, old man, who stole sorceries I gave you as freely as air itself gives loft to the pinions of the eagle. And for your thanks you filled my island's ether with the screeching burdens of malicious spirits you called servants; though I was always but your slave."

"Did you not stand accused long ere this? Is not the roster of your savage wrongs longer than a fjord of forgotten Hyperborea? And does it not point as cold an accusing finger? You deny that you did lust after my girl-child?"

"I do!"

"Liar! I saw with my own eyes. And at the very moment of our delivery from the isle, whilst I was newborn in forgiveness of those who worked against me here in Milan, did you not conspire to murder me?"

"Not so! I was innocent of the ills that may hide in a bottle, and made drunk by those noble shipwrecked savages of Milan, the lords of your former land, yet not too high to mislead one naked of all knowledge of the world from whence you had been driven by your own brother."

"This will not do," Gonzalo objects. "The beast is to be tried for Antonio's death, not his misdeeds in another place. The past is not meat for today's repast."

"What's past is prologue." Prospero pauses to pronounce his unofficial judgment. "And so shall Caliban pay the debt of past and present evil today."

Scene II. *Enter* PORTIA *and* BASSANIO, *clothed as doctor and clerk.*

"Who are these strangers?" Prospero asks.

"My master is a young doctor of Rome," answers Bassanio, "most esteemed by the learned Bellario, who oft assists in thorny matters of justice. In Venice this young solon overcame the bloodthirsty claim of the Jew Shylock for a pound of flesh from the merchant Antonio."

"I have heard of this case," Gonzalo says, nodding.

"He is young and bare of beard for such powers of judgment," Prospero notes doubtfully, settling into the cushions of his high seat.

"Youth is a disadvantage," Portia concedes, her voice low in tone and modest, "except in cases where it is an advantage."

"You speak like a well-tried doctor of law, at least, in paradoxes, Balthasar.

Are you acquainted with the case before this court, the murder of my brother Antonio, previously Duke of Milan?"

"The dead I know, but not much of the living. Since you are judge, m'lord, and this creature Caliban is criminal, and you both are two of three persons to come from the distant island that was your home, your daughter, sir, is the only one left to play the witness. From her I will elicit the founding facts as to the history of this matter."

"There is no history!" Prospero says. "My brother lies but three days dead, struck down in his garden . . . my garden now and previously. That is the only history worth investigating."

"Ah," says Portia, bowing in agreement. "That is true. You and your dead brother have traded roles like actors in a play. First you were Duke of Milan, and then you were not, but were the exiled master of an unnamed island while Antonio duked it here in Milan. Then he became as you, shipwrecked and thrown up upon a foreign shore, a tiny strand where you were master. Master of more than earthly things, I gather. There two brothers came to see each other again as friends, and Antonio freely gave the dukedom back to you, so here he was again your subject. This is a very model of justice, save for Antonio's death."

"That is so."

"And is it not so, noble Prospero, that you used the strange powers you found upon the island to drive your brother's ship to your very feet? That you conjured the wind that united the brothers once riven?"

"Not I. A certain sprite I found upon the island."

"Enough. A judge should not play witness. I will ask the maiden Miranda to stand forward. Ah. I should have said the fair maiden Miranda. My apologies."

"You need not bow to me, learned doctor. I have no knowledge but the things my father taught me during our durance on the island."

"How long this servitude?"

"I was but three years old when we were cast upon the ocean's bosom in a boat with little water, and I mark but seventeen years now."

"Fourteen years upon a deserted island: the blood chills to think a well-born maid must grow in such an untamed place. Yet your father provided every comfort that he could."

"He did indeed, though little comfort was on the island save the presence of each other."

"Then you were alone except for servants?"

"I would not say we had such soft attendants as servants."

"Was not Caliban a servant?"

Miranda glances uneasily from the young doctor of law with his many questions to the figure of Caliban, still clad in gay raiment, but now decorated with chains.

"Perhaps that is a question," says Portia with the smooth command she has now employed in two courts of law, "that the creature Caliban may best answer. Let Caliban come forward."

He shuffles toward Portia, a huge and heavily burdened beast. As he moves forward, Miranda edges away.

"You speak?" Portia asks.

"Speak indeed, and walk upright when I am not laden with ropes of iron or pallets of firewood."

"There is no firewood here."

"There was wood aplenty on the island, and I carried it from one end to the other."

"Then you were a servant."

"I was a slave, for such old Prospero called me often enough that I forgot my given name."

"Hellhound!" the duke roars from his judgment seat. "The names I called thee were too fine by half and half again, though I called thee dog and cur and fiend and slave 'til the sea itself should dry and all its shells lie revealed from here to Gibraltar, like Neptune's treasury of pearls abandoned in the desert."

"So Caliban was your slave," Portia says, turning to Duke Prospero.

"Yes, and be damned to him! Slave was too good a word."

"And was this air spirit you commanded also a slave?"

"Ariel?" The Duke frowns. "My words and their usage are not on trial here. Ariel was a creature of that foul witch Sycorax, this monster's monstrous mother."

"This Sycorax had been in like straits to yourself, sir, and so came to the island under similar force, though sooner than yourself."

"Like to myself, young Balthasar? Thou art mad to draw parallel where there is only deep loathing. There was nothing like between Sycorax and myself, and besides, the witch was dead 'ere I came upon the island."

Portia strolls with deliberation toward the Duke's ornate throne, as though to consult a superior more closely, despite the listening ears all around.

"My lord, perhaps I am not informed as well as I should be. You must forgive my newness to the circumstances, even this cast, so to speak, of cast-aways."

" 'Tis true, for one small island, the place drew shipwrecked souls to it as if it were a last outlook of lost Atlantis."

"Indeed, my lord. So is it not a strange parallel, then, that the outcast witch Sycorax should be spared death in Algiers because her womb bore an unborn soul? That she was then left upon the island by sailors, long before you and your infant daughter were likewise spared assassination in Milan and given leave to take a boat to where the winds would send you?"

"You tell a tale rather than pose a question, young doctor of law. You will learn better soon. I suppose a stranger like yourself could draw some common line between our fates, that of this cursed Sycorax and her thrice-cursed son Caliban, and that of myself and my innocent daughter. But the circumstances are as opposite as the likeness of my angelic Miranda to this devilish whelp of a fiendish dam, this slave Caliban."

"And so too Ariel served, more slave than servant?"

"Ariel also was a malicious spirit, too headstrong to serve even Sycorax and thus punished with the cell of a tree trunk for eternity. With such harsh creatures only hardness will be heeded."

Portia nods as if well satisfied by this explanation, and returns to face Caliban.

"You claim, sir," she says with ironic dignity, as if the crouching, hairy beast is like unto a man, "that you are the heir and owner of the island, having been born there?"

"I was the only living thing upon that strand once my mother died."

"And did she die soon after your arrival, and hers?"

"I cannot say how long. I grew enough to walk, but she had always seemed weak. That is why she pent the spirits in the trees. She had not the will to control them and they would have played mischief until some unending tempest would have sunk our island."

"So your mother was ill, perhaps from the time of your birth?"

"I cannot say, but it would seem so."

Portia turns to Prospero. "Another strange coincidence, Duke. This creature's mother sickened and died of his birth."

"Not so strange. Look at the monster! If you were a woman, would you not have died of sheer fright from distaste at mothering that?"

Portia does not answer, but looks upon Caliban as Prospero had bade young Balthasar do. "Miranda's mother also died upon her birth, am I not right?" she says mildly. "Two motherless babes marooned upon the same lone island."

"Caliban was the elder, and never a fit object of pity!" Prospero cries, half-rising from his seat. "I tried to tutor the creature, as I did my daughter, using the library of books Gonzalo put as ballast in the leaky boat where our enemies had stored scant food and water. But we reached the island, and the books became our food. I taught that ingrate rascal to speak and then he turned upon the most precious pearl in my possession and sought to dirty it with his ragged claws."

"Is this true, Caliban?" Portia asks.

"I speak because he taught me, yes, but he only taught me so I could take him to the places where my mother penned the sprites and tell him the spells she used to seal and unseal them. Once he had Ariel free to obey his every whim, it was Caliban the slave, the dog."

"Then he was master of the island, and master of you and Ariel?"

"Oh, aye. And when Ariel tired of being his creature, the damned sprite put hedgehogs into my path to spear my feet, and adders to bite me into madness in my bed, and unseen demons to pinch me to a bruise as big as the moon."

"And no creature was kind to you upon the island?"

Caliban frowns and does not answer.

"No matter," Portia says, returning to a table to consult papers as high and thick as a plum pudding. "Kindness is not the issue here."

"At last," Prospero cries, "you come to the charge of murder."

"And so I must question . . . Ferdinand."

The young man starts, and almost drops Miranda's hand from the fond custody of his own. He had expected to be witness, not testifier.

But young Balthasar calls him forward. "You will answer true, all that I ask of you?"

"As true as man may talk."

"You are the son of the King of Naples, once Duke Prospero's bitter enemy, who conspired with the Duke's brother Antonio to exile Prospero and take his home and title?"

"Yes, and yes to all. The sad tale is admitted by all, and all is forgiven and restored."

"More than restored, for not only does Prospero resume the Dukedom, but the shock of shipwreck brought Antonio to remorse. And did not Prospero oversee your island courtship of his own fair daughter, Miranda?"

Ferdinand smiles to find his testimony is on a subject so simple and dear to his heart. "He was quite canny in the way he first decried us to one another, yet forcing us closer, until it was clear our hearts had met and were meant to stay together."

"In short, Duke Prospero, then an exiled lord of only empty acres, acted as matchmaker between his daughter and his royal enemy's beloved only son and heir."

"Our love was our own idea."

"So love always claims, but I have reason to know that there is more wit and sense in it than one would believe." Portia takes a slow turn around the court, eyeing every witness.

"Thus comes a happy ending to all but Caliban. The Duke sails home, restored in every respect; the king's son sails home, with a lovely, unspoiled maiden for a bride, whose father has recently been named a duke. The island orphan shall wed a prince. Even Antonio merely retreats to his previous position of second to his brother.

"Only Caliban is left upon the island, with nothing, not even the company of his ancient enemy Ariel."

"O clever lad," cries Prospero. "You show how Caliban lay writhing on the beach, mad from lack of everything. How he conspired to fetch a ship to take him in the wake of those he'd known, there to wreak the ruin upon their lives that he had failed to do upon the island. Cruel envy, jealous wrath, and anger unmatched stirred his monstrous soul. And so he came to Milan and in the garden struck down the first of us to cross his crooked path: my brother, Antonio."

The onlookers stir, and make angry mutterings, but Portia does not heed them. She again comes before the chained monster.

"You speak wisely, Duke. There is no bitterness on earth or island as bleak as losing all."

"Then the judgment is plain."

"Judgment is never plain. It is a gemstone of many facets, each of which may blink as bright as the sun, then shrink to a dark cinder of doubt. Soon another facet catches the fickle light of reason. This, we say, must be the fact, the truth that shines like the sun upon us. But a cloud comes and our judgment darts behind it as beyond a curtain. What role shall Judgment play when next the curtain draws back to reveal . . . Dame Fortune, plump and shiny as a miser's purse? Or is it Sir Self-Deception, wearing ribboned tights upon his skinny shank and making courtier's bow to Lady Prevarication, whose starched collars quite obscure the expression on her face? I believe she would be smirking to see Judgment tricked up in so many costumes as we do view in court each day."

"Then forget this pointless questioning and declare what all must know to be true: Caliban has killed Antonio in revenge, and in revenge must pay the price with his own debased life."

"No life is debased, my lord, unless we let it be so. Caliban." Portia turns sternly to the prisoner. "You are an unwholesome thing to look upon and I do not doubt that the soul within is as deformed.

"You stand accused 'ere this of conspiring on the island to kill its departing lord, your admitted master, Prospero."

The creature's head bows as if under the weight of unseen chains.

"You do not deny it?"

"Two shipwrecked lords made me drunk, and I became their monster-servant, as they called me. They promised me fair treatment and we conspired together. I meant it not."

"Still, you cannot deny it and there were witnesses. So, Caliban. Even before you came here as a caged beast to amuse the people at market, you had been caged into servitude upon the island and held no love for Prospero."

"No," he mutters.

"Nor had you reason," Portia observes.

Prospero protests. "What excuse is this?"

"No excuse, mere fact, my lord. So, Caliban. You broke free of your cage and came straight to the ducal gardens, is that not truth?"

"Truth," the beast mutters.

"You came to kill Prospero."

The beast is silent.

"You came upon his brother Antonio in the garden, from behind, mistaking him for Prospero, and struck him down."

The beast is silent.

"Or you recognized him for Antonio, and still you struck him down, because he was brother to your enemy. Did not the King of Naples conspire to put Antonio in Prospero's place because he was brother to his enemy? So you unseated Antonio from the role of brother as he had been unseated from the role of Duke."

The beast is silent.

"Why else would you have come here, Caliban, but to kill your betters?"

The beast is silent.

"I call the royal bride," Portia says. "Miranda."

Ferdinand's hand tightens upon hers, as if to keep her by his side.

She does not move.

"I have spoken earlier," she whispers.

"I would have you speak more," Portia says, unswayed.

Miranda approaches, keeping well away from Caliban, looking neither up nor down, to one side or the other.

"This," says Portia, gesturing to the girl whose hair is golden wires, whose lips are coral, whose throat is alabaster, and whose skin is pearl, "is another of Caliban's would-be crimes called to testify against him. Murder is nothing to a creature who would violate his master's daughter, and she but a child upon the brink of girlhood then. Is that not true?"

"What? What is true?" Miranda cries.

Upon his judgment seat, Prospero writhes with swallowed action, but Portia has taken command of the courtroom and all eyes are upon the young doctor of law from Rome, Balthasar.

The gathered people hush in the presence of such vile intention, and Gossip slips among them and whispers until Miranda's skin is rose quartz.

"Is it true," Portia demands, "that this debased beast, this ugly, useless, spiteful monster, did try to force himself upon you in the cavern on the island? That he did attempt this crime in those days when your father taught him to speak and took him around the island as a favorite child to learn from the pines with their moaning spirits?"

"I do not remember! I cannot remember. I cannot say!"

Gossip swells into a murmur like a spirit wind among the trees, and Miranda must answer the whispers.

"I remember my father descending up on us like Ariel from a storm-cloud, screeching, flailing in a tempest I had never seen before. Caliban was there, Caliban was—"

The beast is silent.

Miranda's cool palms chill her flagrant cheeks. She stares ahead, distracted. Ferdinand paces in his place as if on a leash. The merchant Bassanio from Venice has ceased to breath and move. The crowd sways against itself, whispering, conferring, leering at the maiden and the monster.

Prospero dares not speak.

Nothing stops Portia from speaking, from suggesting to Miranda . . . "Caliban was about to lay foul hands upon you, whisper lewd words in your ear, claw at your garments—"

"No!" Miranda's hands drop. Her head rises. "He had brought me stones to build a palace with. We used to play together. I had no other playmate and Ariel even then tormented him, and myself as well. Caliban taunted Ariel, so

Ariel would forget me. Caliban was my playmate then." Miranda is thinking as a child, remembering as a child. "He was my only brother. I did not know he was ugly, who saw no other thing than Ariel, who was lithe and spiteful, and my father, who was wild of beard and hair as any wizard. Caliban . . . Caliban—"

"What did Caliban do?"

"He leaned toward me."

The crowd gasps.

"To kiss my cheek."

The beast is silent.

"And then?" Portia asks, so quietly it seems that Miranda is the only one who hears her, although the two words strike like small hissing serpents at every ear.

"My father coming. The noise. The blows. A tempest of fury I have never seen before. He is like an angry God. There is no answering him, no escaping him. I feel such fear. I have not recalled that day clearly until now."

Miranda looks at Caliban at last. "He did not attack me. He loved me."

"What does this nonsense matter?" a voice roars from on high. Prospero has stood before his throne. "She was a child. Her memories are worthless, deceptive. This has naught to do with the death of my brother Antonio."

Portia paces toward him, tilting her stern profile under its tasseled doctor's hat up toward the Duke. He is the figure of an Old Testament prophet, despite his rich robes, and now every eye in the courtroom sees the tempest that is within him.

"You studied many strange and magical matters when you were first a Duke," Portia says. "Had you not been lost in your studies, you might have noticed that the brother you allowed to rule the Dukedom in your stead wished to supplant you."

"I was bound to scholarship, yes. But a man should not lose his birthright from mere inattention, not if his kin are true."

"Even on your desert isle, kind Gonzalo had seen that your precious books followed you, along with some clothes and other stuffs. The books were all, except for your daughter."

"This is no crime, no matter to investigate."

"What's past is prologue." Portia tolls the words like a bell. "We have heard testimony that the first crime attributed to Caliban the monster is false. Why should the last crime attributed to him not be false as well?"

"Look upon him! He is a monster! He has always been a monster!"

"Sin seldom wears an obvious face, my lord. Methinks Caliban is too convenient a monster. I do not doubt that you saw what you saw. You saw this rough, unhandsome creature leaning toward your daughter in tenderness. And who should not lean toward the likes of Miranda in tenderness? You have made her for the world to love. But love is not lust, Duke Prospero, and you could not see the sibling kiss for the concealed guilt that sank its teeth into your soul."

"My guilt! I have always been the one sinned against!"

Portia's voice raises to match Prospero's. "There was no one on that island but Master and Slave. Two slaves, Caliban and Ariel. And your daughter Miranda. She you reared to be the best and gentlest of humankind. Him"—Portia gestures to Caliban as if accusing him, but her voice is directed at Prospero— "you reared to be beset, bullied, reviled, abused. And then you blame the beast. I am looking at the beast, my lord, and it sits upon the throne of judgment. Judgment is a bawd, my lord, and will paint on many faces, even yours."

Even Gossip purses her lips and is still. The courtroom is silent.

Finally Prospero finds his voice again. It is low, hollow. "What has this to do with the murder of my brother Antonio?"

"What's past is prologue. Does not the phrase echo with familiarity in thy ear? Gonzalo tells me that Antonio was fond of saying it. Poor Antonio, he gave me the clue to all in all, and never lived to know it."

"I do not understand," says a small voice behind Portia.

The false doctor of law turns with a smile. Miranda and Caliban stand side by side, not looking at each other, but unafraid of each other as well.

"I understand all too well," Portia tells Miranda with a warm but weary glance at Bassanio. "If my lord Duke will answer but a few more questions—?"

Prospero sinks back upon his seat, looking truly shipwrecked now, an old man with no more props for his seniority, not even the false truth he embraced like a lover.

"You knew of Sycorax of old," Portia declares as fact. "Your magical readings acquainted you with her powers."

"Yes," says the Duke.

"You sought her out to learn her charms."

"Yes," says the Duke.

"You brought her here to Milan in secret, or went in secret to Algiers."

The Duke is silent.

"She was the 'blue-eyed hag' from the North. Not such a hag, not until she had been ill served by you. When you were marooned upon the same island, you recognized her magic, you knew she had been with child and driven from Algiers with nothing but her empty life and swollen womb. You knew exactly who and what she was, though all that remained of her by then was her sole, barely surviving child. She was the mother of Caliban."

The Duke is silent.

"You are the father of Caliban."

Screams. Gasps. Shouts. Curses.

Portia stands against the storm like the Rock of Gibraltar. Sometimes Judgment wears the face of the mob. Sometimes Judgment kills.

Miranda swoons, but Ferdinand is there to catch her before a lock of her golden hair touches tile.

Caliban looks into Portia's eyes for the first time during his trial.

She strides toward him, takes the clumsy face into her hands, and tilts it to the Duke upon his high seat. She brushes the brutish eyebrows back from the rough brow, until the eyes that glint through the brambles of his face shine bright as sun and moon together.

"The eyes are the window of the soul, my lord. Sycorax had the sky-blue eyes of the North, but Caliban has the sea-green eyes of the South, as do you."

"I could not have spawned this, not even on an ancient witch who could assume any shape to suit her purpose."

"She was old, Sycorax, yes, but we only have your testimony that she was a hag, and perhaps she was after you were done with her and had leeched all the

secrets you wanted from her bones. Was she hideous, or only so after you had
made the memory of the woman you had used and abandoned into that of an
ugly old hag? And no, you could not have spawned a son like Caliban, so you
spelled him into the likeness of a repellent monster. Show us now Caliban's
true likeness. You can conjure tempests and command sprites. You have bent
the sea and kings and delinquent brothers to your will. You have married your
daughter well and resumed your seat. Cast off your last, unworthy spell. Free
this spirit from the husk you entrapped it within. Show us the son who is the
fruit of your quest for power at all cost, whose very existence belies you, whom
you had to turn into a monster to hold the ugliness of your own soul.

"Show us Caliban as he is, not as you needed him to be."

Prospero has shrunken into an old man, whom age and envy have bent into
a hoop. He clings to his ducal seat. His snowy beard and hair hang like hoar
frost around his sunken features.

"Ariel." His voice is a croak that could barely command a pond frog. "Ariel!"

The air bestirs itself in the gilded rafters of the chamber. It becomes a cloud,
then a mist, then a disembodied face ever-youthful, ever-old.

"Free him from the last enchantment," Prospero asks, not commands.

Ariel's malicious features hesitate. He glances at his shrunken master and
spite shines forth like a full moon. For once it pays him more to benefit Caliban
than to harm him.

A sudden whirr of air, a shimmer of cloud.

Caliban rises, straightens, a brown-haired young man, straight and fair-
skinned, with islands of sea-green eyes in the calm expanse of his face.

He lifts hairless hands, as if the iron manacles had fallen away, although
they have not. Miranda gazes on him with amazement, and Ferdinand comes
to join her.

"O brave new beast," she murmurs.

"It maddened you," Portia tells Prospero, "to see your son and daughter in
fond embrace despite the lies you had erected like a wall between them. Knowing that they were half-brother and sister, you feared the worst, and thus saw
the worst. The wrong was all yours."

"But he admitted it."

"Stung by pride and despair, he did not bow to give the lie to yours. You had left him nothing to be but your monster."

"And so all my spells and schemes have brought me only grief. Yet someone has killed my brother Antonio."

"And sometime Judgment dresses as a ghost, a teasing spirit that calls forth truth. Would it be justice, my lord Duke, if your maltreatment of your bastard son had made him into the monster you disguised him as?"

"No. No, not that. I never wished him ill. I simply thought that he was born to be evil in punishment for my sins. If he has done this murderous deed, I will serve the sentence for it."

Caliban steps forward, his face still slack and unaccustomed to its new geography. Yet there is something that might be called pity on it.

"Father!" Miranda cries, half protesting, half accusing still.

Portia spies Bassanio's knowing eyes among the crowd. It is now her turn to choose the right box, the chest of lead among the deceptive glitter of more apparent choices.

"Can we sentence the wind?" asks the wise young doctor Balthasar. "We have heard testimony how on the island Caliban was led astray time and again to his pain and suffering by an invisible enemy. Antonio indeed was mistaken for your self, Duke Prospero, and led down the garden path to a fatal misstep on the brink of a stone-edged pool."

"Ariel? My Ariel has killed him?"

"The sprite grew used to mischief and missed having a butt for his ill will. Shall he deliver himself now to our judgment? I ask you, spirit, will you come answer to us?" She looks around the courtroom and to the air above it. Not so much as a dust mote twinkles. "I think not. As with every ending, we answer only to ourselves. Beasts and sprites have fled this company and only mortal men and women remain to make what peace with past and present that they can.

"And now I must repair to Rome. Clerk, come take me hence. I grow tired of Judgment."

Epilogue

SPOKEN BY CALIBAN

Now my past becomes the present,
Turns my life from bleak to pleasant.
Prospero and his spells o'erthrown
Make any deceptions now mine alone.
I stand here like a new-made man
To sin or save as best I can.
To ev'ry spirit foul or fair
I offer this most savage prayer:
Handle souls within your power
As you would a precious flower.

Judge not lest ye be someday deemed
As one who is not what he seemed.
Give fellow creatures all you may
Of nature's sweetness and full sway
To some unspoken sense of justice
That gives the lie to what must us
Believe about each and ev'ry other,
As we bow to any unnamed brother.
I take my leave, no more a beast,
But what you will, I am at least.

The Fall of the House of Oldenborg
BY ROBERT BARNARD

Robert Barnard's most recent novel is *The Bones in the Attic*. His other books include *Unholy Dying, A Murder in Mayfair, The Corpse at the Hayworth Tandoori, No Place of Safety, The Bad Samaritan, The Masters of the House, A Scandal in Belgravia,* and *Out of the Blackout.* Winner of the prestigious Nero Wolfe Award as well as the Anthony, Agatha, and Macavity Awards, the eight-time Edgar nominee is a member of Britain's distinguished Detection Club and lives with his wife, Louise, in Leeds, England.

When he emerged from the Grand Audience Chamber, the Prince was in a right pet.

"It makes me absolutely sick!" he muttered. "Sick to the pit of my stomach. Did you hear that, Pat? The odious endearments to his new wife. My mother! The King my father not two months dead, and my mother is now my aunt and he is now my stepfather! Did you hear him calling me 'son'?"

"I did, and I heard your reply, Hammy."

A smile of satisfaction lightened his petulant face.

"Did you? Pretty neat, I thought it."

And totally unwise, like everything he did. After a great deal of "son" talk had made him more and more tetchy, his mother had commented on the cloudiness of his brow.

"On the contrary, I've had too much 'son,' " he said. Quick, I suppose, but not the way to behave in the new King's court. Claudius is a soldier, and not to be played with.

Hammy was peeved. Naturally he was peeved. The moment his father, the old King, died, his uncle called a snap election, won it, and was crowned before Hammy could get back to the Danish capital. He was studying, as I was, at the University of Wittenburg, where he was a very ineffectual President of the Student Union. I was his deputy, and I did all the work and took all the decisions, with typical Irish efficiency. He spent most of his time in amateur dramatics—the traditional resort of the totally unserious student—which was how he had acquired the diminutive of his name. I read whatever books were available in English or Latin, and financed my studies as Diplomatic and Foreign Affairs Correspondent of the *London Sunne*.

"The man is a *brute!*" exclaimed Hammy. "If only I'd been here to stand against him. As it was, the Danish aristocracy was bound to elect a man of that type. They're still Vikings at heart."

I wasn't inclined to deny, after a mere week or two of observations, that King Claudius was a thug, albeit a thug with an expensive education. Still, Hammy was deluding himself if he thought that, even if he had been on the spot, there had been any hope of his winning a disputed election. He made no decision as President of the Students' Union that he did not reverse or rescind on the morning after. Of such stuff are kings *not* made.

My column in the *London Sunne* was much less diplomatic and discreet than it had been under my predecessor. I was turning it into a high-class gossip column, with a strong line in royal scandals. My proprietor (an excentric thousandaire whose place of origin is as yet undiscovered) had written to praise what he called my "looning down" of the feature, and said he had made this a model for the work of all his other scribblers. It was for this reason, scenting scandal and blood, that I had followed Hammy to Denmark. Denmark was obviously a place where news was being made. But more than that: if Hammy had a future there, I had no objection to being his right-hand man. Nor, for that matter, if Hammy was out of the picture, to being the right hand of his uncle Claudius, though the fact that he had been heard to refer to me as an "economic migrant" did not bode well for any future cooperation.

I had not been pleased, on my arrival, to find another Irishman already in place. His title was Deputy Armourer to the Royal Guard, but I suspected he supplemented this by spying for the English Queen's Council or by scribbling for one of the *London Sunne*'s miserable competitors. I was even less pleased to see this fellow approach as Hammy spoke.

"Hello, O'Ratio," I said glumly. He gave me the most imperceptible of nods and turned at once to my companion.

"Strange news, Your Royal Highness."

"Call me Hamlet," said the Prince. "What news?"

"In confidence"—he drew the Prince aside and continued in sibilant whispers that my newshound ears had no difficulty picking up—"the palace guards are in turmoil. They say they have seen your father."

"My father? Impossible. They kept him on ice till I came home so I could be sure he was dead. Considerate, wasn't it?"

"His ghost. It's been seen patrolling the battlements. It was definitely seen by Barnard and Marcel."

"Barnard!" I said scornfully. "A credulous, dull-witted fellow, and Marcel is hardly better."

"You weren't supposed to be listening!" O'Ratio said bitterly, turning and glaring at me.

"Well, if you will talk like a camp hairdresser who's been had by all the NCOs," I replied . . .

That was a bit unfair. It was true O'Ratio was never to be seen in the red lantern district down by the Elsinore docks, but I had no evidence he was a pansy by nature. His friendship for Hamlet, however, was compounded of starry-eyed royalty-worship and the sort of sentimental gush that the companions of reasonably attractive young men seem to go in for. O'Ratio was a typical penniless Irish soldier of fortune, attaching himself to anyone who offered. Not surprising if he found buggery more enticing than beggary. Hammy's bedroom tastes I had had several indications of in Wittenburg.

"The ghost," continued O'Ratio, "has indicated a desire to talk to Your Royal Highness."

"And by what feat of drumb crambo did the ghost convey this to a pair of dimwits like Barnard and Marcel?" I asked.

"A being from the Other Side has ways and means," said O'Ratio.

"Quite," said Hammy, serious. "There are more things in Heaven and earth, Pat, than a cynical worldling like you could imagine."

And he wandered off with O'Ratio, talking low and serious. "I'm gonna put that white sheet on again," I carolled, though only mentally. When I thought about it, the last person I'd seen in a white sheet was Hamlet himself, playing the ghost of Julius Caesar at Wittenburg in a translation of the play by William Shaksberd (rumoured to be a pseudonym of the essayist Francis Bacon). He'd got the part because his ambitions for a crown were well-known.

I was pretty sure what was going to happen next. Hammy was going to go up on to the battlements and the ghost would appear (in the white-sheeted person of O'Ratio or one of his soldierly mates), and take Hamlet aside and tell him he'd been murdered.

How did I know this? Because O'Ratio was one of those hangers-on of royalty who find out what the royal personage most wants to hear, then tell him it.

I was confirmed in this view two days later when Hammy came to me all ineffectually excited and told me he'd had an encounter with the ghost of his father.

"He took me apart from the others," he said solemnly, his language becoming suitably elevated, "and imparted a matter of great moment."

"Oh?" I said. "The color of the fourth horse of the Apocalypse?"

"My sire was murdered by his brother," said Hammy, ignoring me. "Claudius poured poison in his ear while he slept."

"How does he know if he was asleep?"

"He has passed through to that state where knowledge is not limited as it is limited by our worldly state, Pat."

"Ah," I said. I wished he wouldn't call me Pat. Royalty should not be matey. And he should give me my title: Earl of Duntoomey, in the County of Killarney.

I had no seat, no money, no post at court but I was descended from the second last King of Ireland, on both sides of the blanket, and I wished he would use my title, to distinguish me from that direct descendent of an itinerant Irish mathematician, O'Ratio.

I was meditating how to take this matter of the supposed ghost further when we were fortunately interrupted by Ophelia, the daughter of the new King's First Minister. She had been making a great nuisance of herself since Hammy's return to court. And so had her poisonous rat-pack jerk of a brother on her behalf.

"Hamlet, what ails you? What does this change towards me mean?"

"Nothing, Madam, except that I have seen a wider world."

"Before you went, we had something together—"

"Nothing, Madam. Nothing whatever. If you had something, it was entirely in your imagination. A Royal does not marry into the political class. It would destroy all our credibility."

"But you said—"

"I said nothing. Go and find some religious order, preferably a closed one, and shut your disappointments away with others of your self-deluded kind."

Ophelia dashed off weeping. I had little sympathy. I had every reason to doubt that Hammy had ever given cause to hope to any member of her sex. But she had given me time to think.

"Did you know there's a travelling theatre company in town?" I asked.

"Really?" said Hammy, perking up. "Do they have any parts unfilled?"

"Nothing suitable for your rank and talents," I said hurriedly. "They are performing *The Mousetrap*."

"That old thing. Everyone's seen it."

"I doubt whether your Uncle Claudius is a great playgoer," I said. Hammy raised his eyebrows enquiringly. "Do you remember that bit towards the end acted in dumb-show?" I asked him.

That was a cliché of that branch of the Revenge Tragedy commonly called the Whodiddit. The audience was shown the truth of what had happened by having the murder silently reenacted.

"The murderer comes in while—right!" said Hammy. "While the victim is asleep."

"Exactly. And poisons the glass of aquavit that the victim always keeps at his bedside."

"Ah—pity . . ."

"What if you, Hammy, commanded a royal performance here at Elsinore. They're only crap actors. They'll be happy with a few ducats and a square meal. In return for all the publicity they'll get, you could persuade the manager—"

"Yes?"

"—that instead of the dumb-show murder suggested by Mr. A.C., the play's perpetrator, the poison will not be put into an aquavit glass—"

"But in his ear!" Light was breaking, but slow as sun on an Irish winter morning. "But—what then?"

"Then your eyes will be on the King. If that's how he murdered your father, his guilt will be clear to you and to the whole court."

And if he didn't, it won't, I thought. I had no doubt that this was a story fed to Hamlet by O'Ratio and his mates, to spur Hamlet on to action, and to get themselves cushy places at court once he had gained Claudius's crown. Nice work if you can get it. Only I was determined that if anyone got it, it was going to be me.

Hamlet was in his element. He loved having actors around him, particularly bad ones. He lectured them, told them how scenes should be played, how the verse was to be spoken. They listened respectfully, and tittered behind his back, though in truth he was no worse an actor than they were. The afternoon of the Command Performance came. The court assembled in the palace ballroom, where an improvised stage had been erected. The King and Queen arrived last, she with all the dignity that could be mustered by one who had married her husband's brother a month after her husband's death, he with a pretense of being a regular attender at cultural events of every kind. His steward, though, had put a bottle of aquavit (double-strength Royal Danish Breweries brand, "for added effectiveness against the grippe and the clappe") by his throne, and a large glass. He knew his man.

King Claudius just about kept awake during the play, taking copious draughts of his tipple, and even offering it jokingly to his wife, who equally jokingly slapped his hand, then sipped. At last the dumb-show began. Hamlet was watching. I was watching. What I was expecting to see was nothing—business as usual. I was surprised then to observe the King shifting uneasily on his throne at the sight of the King in the play sleeping alone on a bed. Then the figure of the murderer came in. He approached the bed. He bent over the sleeping man. He took from his pocket a phial, and he brought it down towards the sleeping man's ear—

"Bloody awful play!" bellowed the King, throwing his glass at the stage. "Ordure, pigs manure, horse droppings! I hate all poets and playwrights. Stop the rubbish. Come on, Gertrude. I'm not watching any more of this."

Well, of course that was the end of the cultural entertainment. The court streamed out after the royal pair, Hammy came over and shook my hand in gratitude, and I noticed Ophelia in the melée slipping over and appropriating the royal bottle of state monopoly gut-rot. Me, I went off to my room in the West Tower and began to pen my weekly article for the *London Sunne*. DANISH COURT IN DISARRAY, I headed it. It began: "Last night tensions threatened to erupt in the royal House of Oldenborg. The new Danish King attended a performance of that old chestnut *The Mousetrap,* organized by his nephew, the son of the late King who died only two months ago. When the King angrily disrupted the performance during the dumb-show, rumors began to fly around the court concerning the manner of the late King's death, which occurred while his son was studying at the prestigious University of Wittenburg. With the state machine in chaos and rumors of a possible Norwegian invasion proliferating, the international order seems threatened by a sordid family row with criminal overtones. A central figure is luscious Queen Gertrude, wife and mother of the two rival princes. . . ." And so on. I signed it, The Danish Bacon.

But while I was penning the sort of rubbish that my undereducated British reading public loved, my mind was active. So the King *was* murdered—and murdered in his sleep by having poison poured into his ear. Hammy was right. But he was right not by reason of any supposed revelation by a ghost (I am a man of the Renaissance, not some medieval superstition-monger) but because somehow O'Ratio or one of the guards had become cognizant of the secret—perhaps suspecting Prince Claudius, as he then was, and following him at night. So far I had done rather well in capitalizing on O'Ratio's inept plotting. That's what I had to keep on doing. If there was going to be a new King Hamlet, the man who did the real work, as in the affairs of the Student Union of Wittenburg, was going to be me.

I went off to find him. Somewhat surprisingly I found him at the door of the royal chapel. Coming up beside him and looking through the door, I saw, before the altar, King Claudius on his knees and at prayer. What did he and God have to say to one another, I wondered?

"Now might I do it, Pat," said Hamlet.

"Well, go on and do it," I urged. "You'll have the support of the whole court, after his exhibition of guilt today."

But of course Hammy was not displaying a resolution for action, merely putting the point of view that he would immediately contradict.

"What, and send his soul straight to heaven?" he demanded. "As the souls of those killed in prayer immediately do go?"

"Your theology is positively Dark Ages," I said. "Nobody in their senses believes that sort of stuff now."

"I couldn't take the risk," said Hammy.

"Then what are you going to do? Raise an army and start a civil war? With you two at each other's throats in the country, and Fortinbras coming from the North with a force of fresh Norwegian troops, you'd be handing him the country on a plate."

"Hmmm," said Hammy. "This needs thinking about."

"Quickly," I urged.

But by now things were moving at double time at Elsinore. We had no sooner got back to the main body of the Castle, where the Queen was distractedly looking for a bottle of something to calm her frazzled nerves, than the court was electrified by the appearance of the Lord Chamberlain at the Great Door in obvious perturbation.

"Your Majesty, Ophelia is dead."

"Dead? But how!"

"Drowned, my lady."

"Drowned?" She threw a look of reproach at her son. "Disappointed in love, poor girl. Betrayed by one she believed she could trust. No doubt she walked

into the river, letting her court dress hold her up until the weight of the water
pulled her down to the reeds below."

"Not quite, Your Majesty. She slipped on a muddy patch on the river bank
and died with her head in the water clutching a bottle of aquavit."

"I knew it was somewh—" began the Queen, but there came a second
interruption. I think I've mentioned Laertes—a loud-mouthed and poisonous
nerd whose idea it had been to hitch his sister up with Hammy. If this alliance
(of whatever sort) had come about, his low-born family's grip on the levers of
power would have been unbreakable. Now that ambition was shattered, and
he burst into the Great Chamber making an almighty fuss and noise. He was
followed by his father, Polonius, looking as if his politician's instinct to be all
things to all men was affecting his mental grasp. Laertes, as usual, had to hold
the floor.

"Where is he? Where is that trifler with a young girl's affections? Where is
that so-called *Prince*? Where is he?"

"Here," said Hammy, coming forward with chin raised, with an expression
of disdain perfected for Julius Caesar being petitioned at the Capitol.

"What have you to say to my poor sister's death—you who drove her to
it?"

"I no more drove her to it than I drove her to drink. It was your preposterous
ambitions drove her to get ideas above her place. A Prince marries a Princess."

"As, I suppose, a King marries a Queen," sneered Laertes, looking towards
Gertrude. "If there is one *available*."

Hamlet started towards him (Hammy let no one insult his mother but
himself), but to keep the initiative, Laertes removed his glove and whipped it
across Hammy's face.

"I challenge you to a duel," said Hammy.

"I've already done that," said Laertes. "That's what the glove means."

"Enough!" shouted the King, entering from his prayers. "A duel there shall
be."

You can say what you like about the old King, courtiers were muttering as
they discussed this development behind their hands in nooks and corridors
(and what they mostly said about him was that he was much too fond of

aquavit, and he turned, if not a blind, then a bleary eye to his wife's serial infidelities), but he would never have allowed an upstart politician's brat to challenge a royal Prince. Laertes would have been shipped off down to the Danish equivalent of the Tower of London with a price on his head (fifty kroner for a nice clean cut). The fact that this did not happen said something about Claudius's indebtedness to the Amundsen family, father and son.

Before the day was out, many had made their way to the back door of the health food shop near the vegetable market, the standard source for effective and out-of-the-way poisons in Elsinore. The whole thing seemed to be getting out of my hands, and I was reduced to trying to ensure that Hammy remained alive.

"How can you be sure that Laertes won't be fighting with a poisoned sword?" I asked him.

"I shall reject the swords supplied by the King and insist that he choose a sword from one of the Royal Guards," he said. "There are ten guards on duty, and he can choose at random."

"He will insist that you choose yours from one of the Guards as well."

"Very well, it will be a fair fight."

"Laertes was champion fencer at the Copenhagen University Fencing Club," I said meaningfully.

"A provincial establishment, our university," he said airily, "fit only for the boors and bumpkins who attend it."

"Academically laughable," I agreed. "The university is notable only for its jousting, its beer-drinking, and its swordsmanship. Laertes was the best from among the best in the world."

Hammy thought.

"Then I shall make sure all the Guards' swords are smeared with poison. Then a mere scratch will kill him."

"His sword will also be poisoned. A mere scratch will kill you too."

"Hmmm. . . . Advise me, for God's sake, Pat! That's what you're here for!" The note of panic in his voice boded ill.

I told him I had a plan, and when darkness came, I slipped off to Mensana, the health food shop. I went to the back door, but there stood a hard-faced lad handing out queue tickets with times scrawled on them. I filled in the hour and a half between with a visit to the red lantern district and a girl from Belfast who was earning her ticket home and reduced her prices to anyone with an accent that made her nostalgic.

When I returned to Mensana, I was shown into a dark back room in which sat a figure of indeterminate sex with whom I was forced to communicate in dog Latin.

"This concerns a duel, I would guess," said its hoarse voice.

"Yes. We fear poisoned sword-tips," I said.

"Client confidentiality forbids—" it began.

"Of course, of course. But I wondered if there was something that could be administered *before*—"

"To kill?"

"No. Preferably something to disable for combat—something that will prevent the victim from performing at the top of his bent."

There was a few seconds' silence.

"Balance . . . Successful swordsmanship depends on balance. Administer this and the . . . the patient will have the gait of a newborn calf for twenty-four hours thereafter."

"And how is it administered?"

"For maximum effect, in the ear while sleeping."

I laughed out loud at that. Perfect! There were problems, of course, but I thought that with O'Ratio one of the big cheeses in the Royal Guard, I could surely get one of the men who guarded Laertes while he slept—and someone would, Claudius would see to that—to do the necessary for a bag of kroner. Hammy was, in fact, my main problem.

"From now on," I told him, "we are inseparable. I send out for food to town. You drink nothing but wine from my own store."

"But I don't like your wine. You have rotten, English taste. I prefer my own wines."

"They could be already poisoned. In Claudius's court you are worth killing, while I am not. When it comes to the fight, I shall hold goblets of both wine and water, and you will drink nothing else. There will be bottles of wine and jugs of water set out for the contestants. Don't touch them."

"You'll have to remind me."

"Oh, for heaven's sake!" I said disgustedly. "Whose life is this I'm protecting?"

Anyway that showed me there could not be a moment's relaxation in my vigilance. We had a disgusting pork chop meal sent up from the Kongelig Dansk Hotel in town, and then I locked the bedroom door and we settled down to get what sleep we could. Heaven knows what rumors started going round the court. My only concern was whether O'Ratio would manage to get the destabilizer administered into Laertes's ear. One thing was in our favor: it would be just like Laertes to sleep soundly, so hideously confident as he always was.

The Great Hall next day was stripped for action. All furniture had been moved to the walls, and the great central area was bare. Claudius was no doubt used to masterminding such affairs of honor from his army days. At the far end of the hall were two thrones, and on the table in front of them bottles, a carafe, and goblets. The King and Queen were already seated when Hamlet and I arrived. When the King saw I was carrying a bottle and a glass, a shadow passed over his face. Hammy cast a glance at the two épées laid out at either end of the long table.

"Your Majesty, I demand fresh swords."

"Fresh swords?" All injured innocence.

"Swords I can trust. I demand that we choose swords from those borne by the Royal Guards."

He gestured in the direction of the assembled picked troop. The King hummed and hahed. Then he gave way. He knew the abilities as swordsmen of his stepson and his First Minister's son, and he trusted to the latter's superiority.

"Very well. When Laertes arrives—ah, here he is."

But the words almost died in his throat. Weaving his way like a drunken porter, Laertes came into the Hall, lurching from left to right, stumbling, and finally weaving his way erratically up to the thrones.

"Your Majesty, I demand a postponement! I have been poisoned! You see the result. Please God it does not prove fatal."

"Hah!" said Hamlet, with an expression of stage disgust. "The man's feigning. He's an arrant coward. The Court yesterday saw whose the offense was—a rank insult to the blood royal. I demand satisfaction now, at the place and time Your Majesty appointed."

Now the King really was in a quandary. He knew that his behavior at the play the day before had sent waves of suspicion rippling through the Court. To be seen to favor his First Minister's son—the upstart grandson of Jens Amundsen, a backstreet fishmonger—over his stepson would set tongues wagging furiously. At this point O'Ratio made a rare positive contribution.

"Your Majesty, I pray this unhappy matter be settled with all speed. The Norwegian threat is imminent. There are rumors of a landing—"

"Very well. The contest will take place," the King said, with palpable reluctance. An expression of arrant terror suffused Laertes's face. Everyone in the room must have suspected that he had been set on to challenge Hamlet by the very man who now signed his death warrant.

The swords were chosen, directions given. Laertes made desperate attempts to gain some kind of control of his movements.

"Swords at the ready!" said the King, his voice quivering. "Let battle commence."

Laertes lurched forward, his sword flailing. Hamlet parried it a couple of times, then he stood back, sword raised. His adversary saw his next move, and a look of pleading came into his eyes. Hamlet plunged his sword through his heart.

Advantage Hamlet.

He pulled out the sword, dripping blood on to the flagstoned floor, then he turned and bowed to the two thrones. He went forward.

"Oh, the poor young man," said Queen Gertrude. "And his poor father. To have lost both his children! Hamlet, are you all right?" Her priorities seemed less than motherly. Confused, she bent forward and picked up a goblet full of red wine from the table.

"Gertrude!" said the King.

"I am faint. Hamlet, you are sweaty and scant of breath. Drink too."

"Hamlet!" I shouted, running from the far end of the Hall. As I reached the table, he was quaffing deep. As he set down the goblet, he caught sight of his mother: her face was blue and she was struggling for breath. His eye went from her to the King, guilt deeply etched on his sensual, cunning face.

"Murderer. Twice, thrice murderer! Die thyself!"

And he plunged his sword into the guilty King. At last the blood of the Kloakkgate fishmongers was mingled with that of the Oldenborgs. Hamlet sank to the floor. I knelt down beside him and began to press his stomach, trying to make him vomit up the deadly draught. He, too, was going blue, he too breathing with difficulty. All my efforts were in vain, but as I pressed and struggled, I heard a commotion at the Great Hall door. I turned and looked. Coming under the great arch, flanked by a fearsome troop of men, was a superb armored figure, six feet or more in height, proportionately broad, fair of beard and hair, steely of eye. He advanced at the head of his army. Fortinbras!

He came towards us, his cold eye observing the scene. His demeanor seemed to say that he'd seen worse sights on the field of battle, but not many. He stopped beside Hamlet, looking down on him from his great height. The Prince half-opened his eyes and spoke his dying word.

"Dishy!"

The breath left his body. The face of the invading Prince was twisted with disgust.

"How absolutely vile! I had heard the Danish court was a sink of iniquity, but this is beyond anything. The realm needs cleansing—needs a purging of the rottenness and foulness which has infected it to the heart. I shall use the gallows and the stake should they be necessary, but I shall bring back decency and godliness to this unhappy land. It will be my first priority as King."

My heart sank. I knew those tones, those absolutes. I'd heard them in my native land. Thus spoke the upright Ulsterman with a mission, and a sword to enforce it. Thus speak men who know that God is on their side, and all decent men too. It was the authentic voice of the Moral Majority.

Flee it, I thought.

Gone were all hopes of serving this or that Danish king. I had thought to bring international sophistication to the Danes' conduct of foreign affairs, but serving in an administration formed by King Fortinbras would be a nightmare.

As soon as it was safe to do so, I stuffed my belongings into a backpack and scuttled down to the docks. As luck would have it, I found a fishing vessel ready to depart for Aberdeen. I breathed a sigh of relief as we crossed the bar and headed for the North Sea.

Thinking it over, the idea of Scotland appealed to me. The cussed old English Queen had, as near as dammit, named the King as her preferred successor. A fine, learned man, James VI, or so I'd heard. He had his drawbacks: a Danish Queen and an antismoking obsession. But on the plus side, he had two fine sons, a ready wit, and strong views on the divine rights of Kings. He would need advice from some worldly-wise figure, someone with connections to the courts of Europe. Yes, there was no doubt about it: the Stuarts were the coming men. With my help, they could become the foremost dynasty in Europe. I made a firm resolve to hitch my waggon to the rising star of the Stuarts!

NOTE: I first heard the theory of the Silent Irishman in *Hamlet* at parties at the University of New England, New South Wales, told by my colleague in the English Department there, Bill Hoddinott. This was of course the Irishman addressed in the line "Now might I do it, Pat." Later in the evening he might expatiate on other Irish characters in the play, including O'Ratio and O'Phelia. Bill was the funniest, most generous, and most open of colleagues. He died young, after gashing himself while swimming in the Great Barrier Reef. This story resulting from his revolutionary theory is dedicated to his memory.

Jack Hath Not His Jill

BY SHARAN NEWMAN

Sharan Newman has been both a writer and a medieval historian for many years and doesn't seem to be able to stop doing either. She is the author of the Guinevere fantasy series set in Late-Roman Britain, the Catherine LeVendeur mystery series, set in twelfth-century France, and has coedited three anthologies of historical mystery short stories, the *Crime Through Time* series. Her most recent mystery is *Heresy*.

EDITOR'S NOTE: The following letter was recently discovered in the Vatican Library between two pages of a thirteenth-century edition of Trotula. If there was a response, it has been lost, although the Vatican Library being what it is, it may yet appear. The translator would like to mention that there has been no attempt to render this into Shakespearean English since it was written in Rabelasian French.

To his Eminence, the most Holy Cardinal Antoine Capet from his sister, Anne, Princess of France:

My dearest Antoine:

I hope this finds you enjoying good health, both in Body and in Spirit. It is widely understood in Paris that you are passing your days in Rome making life so miserable for the Pope that he will soon send you back to us. How I hope this is true! Until that happy time, I must content myself with sending this missive by my most trusted courier, trusting that the course to you will be true and that your response will soon reach my eager hands.

You will have heard that our Noble Parent is very ill and not expected to live. I pray it is not so and, *voire*, he seemed in good spirits when I saw him last. Some may say that this is the only reason he was persuaded to send me on a diplomatic mission of such delicacy. While it is true that I pleaded to be of use since our Brother, the Dauphin, should not be far from home at this dangerous time, with Heretics abroad and at home and the Wicked English always ready to attack; nevertheless, it was logical that I should be the one to go. I am not insensible to the gossip that a Union with the Kingdom of Navarre would be good for France and, looking about, I saw no other royal princess available to be cast onto the Pyre of Duty. Therefore, rather than wait in Paris while my Fate was decided, I decided to attempt the negotiations myself.

Antoine, I must tell you in strictest secrecy that the situation I found upon my arrival was most Dire. I have no idea how Navarre has remained free of invasion with such a King! Forgive me for unburdening myself to you. In this you must be both my dearest Brother and a Priest and advise or at least absolve me concerning what has passed.

Wishing to impress my Lord Navarre with my economy, especially since I did not wish him to become too eager for my Dowry, rather than my Self, I traveled with only three ladies-in-waiting, all good friends. You may remember them: Katherine, Rosaline, and Maria—especially Maria, who sends her respects to you and asks often after your health. The only other persons of the court were Lord Boyet and his attendant, Mercade. Above that we had no more than twenty servants, barely enough to tend to our daily needs. Hardly enough to cause difficulty in housing, you will admit, since we naturally brought our own beds, linen, and kitchens.

You can but imagine my Surprise and Chagrin when, upon our arrival, I was told that the King could not receive us in his palace, instead proposing to situate us all in a tent in a nearby field! This Insult did not sit well with any of us. But there was worse to come. When I inquired if there were Plague at the palace that we might contract should we enter, or some other domestic Disaster, I was told that there was no illness at all but that the King had enclosed himself within with a few friends in order to spend three years in Study and had forbidden by decree any Woman to come near him.

What can one make of that?

Katherine surmised that His Majesty did not count maids and laundresses as women for she thought it unaccountable that the lowly, but necessary, tasks they performed would be done by the men of the country. Even monks find laundresses indispensable, as you know well. Maria opined that any man who found that the sight of a woman distracted him from his book was too light-minded to learn from in it any case. I fear that my countenance made clear my agreement with their assessments.

The final Affront was to realize that in his Eagerness for Learning, the King had quite forgotten Our imminent Visit.

We were, of course, tempted to return Home at once. Woe to the country that has a madman for a King! Who would wish to be Queen of such a Land? I confess that it was only my own Feminine Curiosity that persuaded me to remain. That, and the knowledge that part of my objective in this Journey was to keep the Aquitaine from leaving the French Domain, as Navarre had brashly proposed. I would not admit myself thwarted by the Folly of my Host.

First I commanded Boyet to attend upon the King and discover what had brought on his Uncivil Condition.

Boyet soon returned, shaking his head as if to clear the cobwebs from it.

"What have you found?" I demanded without ceremony.

"All I can say, Madam," he answered. "Is that it were better that Navarre turn monk and leave the business of the land to his brother. I have spoken to one Holoferenes, a scholar or schoolmaster of sorts. He must be most learned for I can barely find the sense in his sentences."

"Is he the one proposed to educate the King?" I asked.

"If so, there will soon be a great wind from Navarre that will make the

Mistral seem tame," he replied. "He cannot answer 'Yea' or 'Nay' without amending it with puerile Latin phrases and paraphrases. But no, I believe he has only been the instigator of this change. My understanding is that the King and his men are resolved to educate themselves through reading and conversation."

"Then I pray they begin with Apuleius," I commented, cruelly, I own. "They will find fellowship in reading of another Ass."

I must admit that at this point I was most befuddled. There seemed no Reason for the King's vow and no manner in which I could undo it. I decided that there was nothing to do but wait and hope that Good Sense and Manners would prevail.

His Most Gracious Majesty did finally deign to attend upon us in our rude accommodation. At once he showed he was not without a certain Awareness of the World when he repeated his Outrageous Demand for Aquitaine as repayment for the amount expended by his late Father to our Father for his assistance in our mutual War against the English. As if the cursèd Heretical Beer Swillers were not his enemies as much as ours! Yet I was not overly concerned by these dictates as papers had been sent after us from Paris proving that the old King had been paid his mercenary fee in full. I countered Navarre's haughty words with this fact and vowed to give them the lie as soon as they arrived.

The King agreed at once, proving to me that his petition had been so much Smoke, and changed the Subject to one more Banal. In further conversation, I began to sense that his was not the Hand guiding the kingdom nor had the terms of the negotiations sprung from his Mind. No, a much more Subtle and Devious intelligence was at work here and I was determined to discover whose.

The King was accompanied by three of his Lords, all of whom were known to my Ladies from various stays at Courts of their relatives. Only one of them, a man named Berowne, seemed to have the Sense required for Subtlety. But there was something of the Honest Man about him and my dear Rosaline vouched for him. Therefore, I hesitated to name him our Machiavelli.

Still we did not see the inside of the Palace. His Majesty did offer to forswear his Oath and rescind his recent Law commanding that any woman coming within a mile of the place should have her tongue cut out! I informed him that I refused to be a party to the breaking of a Sacred Vow, however Stupid and Mean Spirited. I also own to you, Antoine, that I felt safer out in the Open surrounded by my own People and guarded by my loyal Attendants.

The next day a Hunt was organized for us. Now, I enjoy hawking as much as anyone but I find a-hunting the deer far too exerting. I had already passed far too many days on the back of a horse just in getting to Navarre, but I acquiesced. We were provided with bows by the forester and shown the spot to begin. When I asked how far we were to ride that day, he seemed astonished and told me that we would remain upon the hill and the deer would come to us! To my Amazement, no sooner had we seated ourselves when deer began trotting across the clearing. What Sport is this, to shoot at tame animals? I should just as lief aim at my lap dog, a much harder target. I can hear your Unkind Comment now, Antoine, but she wouldn't have bitten you if you hadn't teased her.

With no delight I let loose an arrow anywhichway and, to my Chagrin, brought down a pricket. This occasioned much Bawdy Merriment among the men, who assumed I didn't know their Purport.

While all were recovering from the Entertainment, such as it was, Costard, the king's clown, approached with a letter for my Lady Rosaline. With her approval, it was opened by my good advisor, Boyet.

"This letter is mistook," he exclaimed. "It importeth none here. It is writ for one Jaquenetta."

I commanded that he read it aloud. If it did not bear upon our Mission, it might at least provide more Amusement than a hunt that was naught but Theatrics.

There is no need to bore you with the contents, my dear Brother. Suffice to say that it was a most Arrogant profession of love from one Armado, a Spaniard of the Court, to a country maid, Jaquenetta. While my Ladies and Boyet made merry over this, I took the clown aside and queried him regarding the error.

"Thou hast mistaken his letter," I said. "I think not without intent."

He gave me a look that told All. I have never met a Clown who was not the wisest man of the Court. Had I found the hand that moved the puppet King?

"Jaquenetta is my Love," Costard told me. "Armado wants her only as a Lord does a Possession, less valued than a fine horse or favorite bitch."

"His words would proclaim otherwise," I said. "He offers Marriage, if I be not mistook."

"She loves me!" he insisted. "She is but bedazzled by his wealth and position."

I refrained from remarking that both were logical reasons for a poor maid to wed.

"I would speak with this Jaquenetta," I said instead. "Send her to me. If she truly finds the suit of Don Armado repugnant, I shall aid you as best I can to win her."

When the clown had gone to fetch his low-born love, I called my Lady Rosaline to me.

"What makest thou of this Matter, sweet Flower?" I asked her.

I motioned her to sit whilst she pondered all that had occurred since our arrival in this Fantastical Kingdom. Ros is one who never speaks but to the point. I value her wisdom above all others, including yourself, save in the Care of my Immortal Soul.

Finally, she gave forth with the fruit of her thoughts.

"My Lady, I do believe that we are caught in a net of deceit," she said. "What form of king makes a vow to renounce the World and then, instead of retreating into a wild and desolate spot, forbids the World to enter his castle, where all the business of the kingdom must be transacted?"

"Also, if it be truth that our clown Costard was meant to give a missive to you from one of the King's lords then Navarre has oath breakers among his nearest friends." I added, nodding agreement. "It speaks not well of the loyalty he engenders."

"I know Berowne of old," she told me, hardly blushing. "I believe that if he entered into this agreement, it was under protest and only through loyalty to the King so that argument will not sail."

"So, where think you the letter went that should have been given to you?" I asked, accepting her judgment for the present.

"I cannot say," she answered. "This Costard does know 'A' from 'B' and, I am sure, misdirected the missives knowingly. So, would he have given my love note to his own demoiselle?"

I considered this. "Perhaps so. For unless the craving for learning in Navarre has become Epidemick, milkmaids are not taught to read. Therefore, she would take it to someone learned to con it for her."

And this, Dear Brother, is what I later learned happened. The letter was brought to Master Holofernes, the school master, who at once delivered it to the King, thereby proving Berowne forsworn of his Oath. However, the young lord was not at once Banished, as you might expect, but welcomed into a New Circle, that of self-perjured Lovers.

The Inconstancy of Men is beyond belief! Can you credit it? No sooner had these celibate scholars laid eyes upon us than they all conceived a great affection, each for a different woman. The convenience of that is Remarkable. Even the King professed himself hopelessly attached to my Poor Person. They then endeavored to trick us by dressing themselves as Russians and pressing their suits incognito. Of course, we instantly saw through their feeble disguises, although, oddly, they were totally cozened when we women masked and traded tokens.

I am half resolved to marry the King simply to keep Navarre from disaster. The man is not Fit to rule a Hen Coop. The event made me even more determined to find the Mind directing Recent Events and destroy its evil Influence.

But who could it be? So far I had met no one who appeared to have the Intelligence and the requisite Intimacy with the king. Costard, the Fool, was perhaps wise enough, but could his japes turn the King on such a drastic Course? My Lady Rosaline was much taken with Berowne, but that did not mean that he had no Plan to Undermine his Ruler having nothing to do with his feelings for her. And what of these Billets Doux gone astray? I could not but feel that they were somehow connected to the matter.

Shortly after these counterfeit Cossacks departed, the clown returned with the milkmaid, Jaquenetta. I saw at once that she was most comely and had nothing of the jael about her. I'm well aware that Our Royal Father has often said that any peasant wench will put her heels over her head in exchange for the price of a new petticoat, but I reserve Judgment to myself in this matter, since I have also heard such things said of the Ladies of my entourage, save that the price is more dear.

I motioned for her to sit and for Costard to depart.

She sat nervously on a tuffet balanced on the carpet in our tent. I believe if I had allowed her to stand, she would have fled at once.

I took out the letter that had been addressed to her and read it aloud. She seemed pleased at the start, where she was called fair, nay, beauteous. But as I read further, her brow puckered in puzzlement.

"What does he mean, '*veni, vidi, vici, videlicet*'? she asked timidly. "And why should he 'profane his lips on my foot'?

"I cannot be certain," I replied. "But I believe he is offering marriage to you, along with his title and wealth."

She recoiled from this statement as if struck, overbalanced, and went in a circle off the tuffet, like a child doing a somersault. I waited until she had righted herself and regained her dignity.

"Does this offer please you?" I asked. "Is the man Armado disfigured or diseased?"

"He is a fine figure of a man," she answered. "Although the outline is fading a bit. I would be a wealthy widow."

"And yet, I hear doubt in your voice," I commented. "Is your heart set elsewhere?"

She looked at me directly and I could tell I was about to be the recipient of a Confidence. I braced myself.

"My Lady." She stopped, then recovered herself. "The moon has waxed and waned twice now without me. I must marry soon or lose my Name."

I presume she expected me to be Shocked, although I don't know why.

"And is the Don Armado the cause of your contrariety with the moon?"

She shook her head. "But if I married him, my child would have wealth and power. Costard is a dear, but when all is said and done, a Clown."

"So, you would give your husband horns even before the wedding." I said this as Fact not Censure. The woman showed great Sense in her deliberations. However, "Have you family or friends who would advance your cause should Armado die?"

"I don't understand," she said.

I thought her Understanding of the world was not Complete.

"Without friends, once you are a widow, his family would converge at once to deprive you of all you own. Your child would be declared a bastard, even if he were not, and you would be fortunate to be tossed back onto the dungheap from which you came."

She overlooked the insult and appeared to be thinking.

"Master Holofernes would speak for me," she said. "He would ask the King to protect me. It was Master Holofernes who told me to take Lord Berowne's letter to the King and ask his advice. And Lord Berowne would help, as well. He has encouraged my meetings with Costard and speaks Kindly to me always."

"Has he now?" I said, more to myself than her. I was beginning to fear that my dear Rosaline would have to find herself another suitor.

I sent the woman away with a warning to guard the secret of her burgeoning womb until I gave her leave to reveal it, or until she was safely wed to Lord Armado. Then I called my Lord Boyet to me and bid him discover what he could of the men whom I suspected of being False to the Welfare of the King.

As a finale to the Farce of our visit to Navarre, the King had been persuaded to present us with a pageant put forward by Master Holofernes, Costard, Lord Armado's page, and some other simple countrymen. I was most Astonished to discover that Lord Armado had joined them. To impress his milkmaid? What lengths the man would go to for a simple peasant wench. Perhaps he had earned her, after all.

The motley group announced that they would represent themselves as the Nine Worthies of Old. We settled ourselves to be amused by the absurdity of this, but Boyet, who had returned just as the performance commenced, seemed determined to jumble the already misspoken speeches of the poor actors.

"I am Pompey!" Costard declaimed.

"You lie, you are not he!" Boyet leapt up as if poor Costard had attempted to extort taxes from us under a false name.

We endured this through Pompey, and Alisander the Great as well as Hercules, in infancy no less. Boyet mocked them all and my lord Berowne soon joined in the merriment.

Poor Master Holofernes came off the worst. Lord Armado had told us earlier that "The schoolmaster is fantastical, too too vain, too, too vain." It was clear that his pomposity could not abide mockery. And most unfortunate that he had chosen to be Judas Maccabeus.

"Judas I am . . ." he intoned, his chin pointed skyward.

"A Judas!" someone shouted.

"A kissing traitor! How art thou proved Judas?" Lord Berowne laughed.

The rest of the men joined in the banter, most mercilessly, and I must confess that Master Holofernes remained on his Dignity throughout although, at the end, he owned himself put out of countenance. I felt rather Sorry for him. His bladder of Self-Importance had been so thoroughly pricked. He never did finish his Speech.

As he turned to go, he fixed them all with a melancholy glance.

"This is not generous, not gentle, not humble," he told his tormentors.

I did agree and was about to put an end to it, when the schoolmaster departed.

"Alas, Poor Maccabeus," I said. "How he hath been baited."

I would have thought on this more but the next worthy, Lord Armado, was challenged by Costard for the hand of Jaquenetta. They were about to duel in some fashion, as is usual, without asking the Woman her mind in the matter, when Mercade, our servant, appeared with the grave news of Our Father's demise.

Would you credit it, Antoine? Even as I prepared to return home to Paris, my eyes aflood with tears and grief cracking my heart, the King and his men did still press their suit!

The King declared that I had a moment before leaving, to decide.

"A time, methinks, too short to make a world-without-end bargain in," I answered sharply.

I was no longer bemused by the lack of courtliness in the Court of Navarre!

My ladies and I put them off with preposterous demands of penance which they insisted they would perform. Even Lord Armado vowed to wed the unfortunate Jaquenetta, and I wish her well, a short marriage and a long and happy widowhood.

It was not until we were once again across the mountains and into Our Aquitaine again that I was able to piece together my Impressions of this incredible sojourn. It appeared that all whom we had encountered were Fools. But one must have been working with a Purpose beneath his Folly. Which one?

The matter went back, I believed, to the letters. Who would be helped and who harmed when they were mistransported?

Lord Armado certainly was embarrassed by the public knowledge of his love for the milkmaid. And Costard might have benefited from this, so he may well have done it a-purpose. But since Armado had not signed the oath to forswear the companionship of women, there was no shame other than his low tastes.

I came to the conclusion that Armado's letter coming to us was a Ruse, meant to divert us from the other letter that should have gone to Lady Rosaline. Berowne, a great friend of the King, would be forsworn and banished if it were known that he had written a love note. While this is not what occurred, since all the other men were likewise besotted oath breakers, the one who misdirected the letter could not know this.

And that person, the kindly man who read the letter for Jaquenetta and counseled her to take it to the King, was the schoolmaster, Holofernes.

I had encountered the man but once, in the guise of Judas Maccabeus. He had seemed the very portrait of the pompous scholar, using a dozen words when none would suffice. And yet isn't that a fine way to hide one's true self, in a forest of pedantic persiflage?

I pondered this some time before taking my conclusion to Lord Boyet.

"What do you make of it?" I asked him.

Boyet bowed his appreciation.

"My lady," he said. "I had resolved, in the light of your recent Sorrow, not to burden you with the results of my Investigation. However, I discovered that this Holofernes is but half of Navarre. His mother was English and he hath spent much time in Study there."

"I see," I said and thanked him.

So, Antoine, as I hurry to Paris and this letter to Rome, I lay the Problem before you. I have given myself a year and a day to Resolve the Matter.

Perhaps by then a better match will be found for me. If not, I do believe that my Duty lies in keeping the English from turning our Southern Neighbor into an Appendage of their Kingdom, one that they might use as a home for Madmen.

Advise me, dear Antoine.

In Sadness and perplexity, I remain, your dear Sister,

Anne, Princess of France.

TRANSLATOR'S NOTE: Since Shakespeare's grasp of history was roughly equal to that of Cecil B. DeMille's, it has proved impossible to situate this incident in time. Therefore we do not know if the King of Navarre ever won his Princess. It is to be hoped that future scholars will apply themselves to this mystery.

Gracious Silence

BY GILLIAN LINSCOTT

 Gillian Linscott is the author of ten historical mystery novels featuring her suffragette sleuth, Nell Bray. One of them, *Absent Friends,* won (in the United States) the Historical Mystery Appreciation Society Herodotus Award for the best international historical mystery of 1999 and (in the United Kingdom) the Crime Writers' Association Ellis Peters Historical Dagger. She lives in a three-hundred-year-old cottage in a village in Herefordshire, England, with her husband, who's also a writer.

"My gracious silence, hail!
Wouldst thou have laugh'd had I come coffin'd home,
That weep'st to see me triumph?
—*Coriolanus,* Act II, Scene 1

Gracious silence. That's what he called me in front of the whole rejoicing city. I've always been silent by nature. The gracious part took longer, but by that day when he came home in triumph with a crown of laurel on his head and the crowd drunk on cheering and cheap wine, I'd had ten years of working on graciousness under the best tutor in the history of Rome. Dear Volumnia, noblest of mothers-in-law. I was a shy seventeen-year-old when my education started. Caius Marcius—not Coriolanus yet—arrived one summer evening with his friends at my father's house to carry me off in the traditional way. By arrangement, of course, and all very properly done. I know now that she must have chosen me as her son's bride after careful consideration of my pedigree, constitution, temperament, soundness of teeth, father's military service, and dam's record of fertility. Not quite good enough for Caius Marcius, of course, but then only Juno freshly down from Mount Olympus might just about have matched up to that high privilege provided she'd minded her manners and been suitably grateful. As for me, I suppose I was grateful. Over-awed, certainly. For one thing, he was thirteen years older than I was and already Rome's most famous soldier. His face was burned brown by the sun, except for two shiny scar slashes, one across his forehead and right cheek just missing the eye, one down the left side of his chin and neck. By no means bad looking, though. Broad shouldered and muscular, thatch of black hair newly trimmed for the wedding rites, surprisingly well-shaped lips almost as full as a woman's. Eyes bright and very watchful. Like his mother's. As soon as he brought me over the threshold, she was there to welcome me formally to their home. My home now. I'd been well coached by my parents in the little speech I must make in return but somehow when I needed it, it wasn't there. She seemed pleased rather than otherwise by my silence and downcast eyes. "Can't find your voice, Virgilia? Well, better that than a chatterer." How could she know that there was a voice inside my head, speaking just to me? It was the first time even I'd heard it and in the beginning it was so quiet, so nervous and hesitant, that I could pretend it wasn't there at all.

Why isn't there any laughing? When my friends' husbands came to take them, there was laughter, people getting the words all muddled in the wedding songs, rose petals in the bridegroom's hair and down the neck of his toga. This time nobody got the words wrong, as if they'd been practicing all day, and if petals landed in his hair he must have brushed them off before anybody could see them, so there was nothing to laugh at. I'm never going

to sleep in my own bed again, and perhaps I've already had all the laughing
I'll ever be allowed to do. Help me, somebody. Help me.

Our son was born three years after the wedding. She didn't blame me for
the delay—at least not entirely. After all, Caius Marcius was away campaigning
for at least half the year and naturally he'd come back tired. There'd been a lot
of work for the army over those three years because our old enemies the Volsci
were in one of their more active phases. They'd always been there, roving
around outside our walls from way back when the city was founded. Sometimes
they simply went in for a little cattle stealing and ambushing bands of travellers.
But now and again a more than usually ambitious leader would emerge among
them and Rome itself would be under threat. This was one of their surging
times and the more nervous citizens scared each other with nightmares of the
Volsci breaking down our gates, burning our homes, and carrying off the
women over their saddle bows. So it was a good time to be a soldier and Caius
Marcius had all the fighting he wanted.

Naturally he'd be tired when he came home and it was hard for him to
adjust from a world of men and action, from sleeping on the muddy ground
under a tent of stitched skins that let in the wind and rain (he was a good
leader, you see, and shared his men's hardships) to this softer world of women
and soft voices and baths with sweet smelling oils. Harder to get through the
long evenings of political talk with the greyheads over the wine cups. "Another
few years, Caius Marcius. Another year or two and a really decisive victory
over Tullus Aufidius, and it's in the bag. You'll have our voices, the people's
voices, the fund raising will be no problem. You'll be unstoppable." Volumnia
would sit drinking her wine and putting in her opinions like a man. I'd spin
and listen and say nothing. He had no great taste for wine, no head for it, but
he had to drink to be companionable because a man trying for high public
office has to tread a careful line between being pleasure-loving or prudish, so
naturally by the time we got to our room, he'd be drowsy. To be honest I think
I liked him most, came nearest to loving him, those nights. Away from the
greyheads, his soldiers, and his mother there was a lost quality about him, like
a puzzled child left on his own. One night he ruffled my hair, yawned, and

said to me, "Why do we put ourselves through all this? Do I want the consulship so much?" Well, I knew the answer. *No, but your mother wants it for you.* But I couldn't say it, of course, so I just kissed him, then we both turned over and went to sleep. So there was a delay, but when I duly produced a healthy boy, she quite forgave me. No question, of course, that it would be a boy. If it had started out otherwise, I think her determination would have reached into my womb and swapped its sex as it grew.

Life changes once you're a mother. For one thing, you're allowed to laugh again. I laughed at little Marcius cooing in his basket and he laughed back, waving pink fists no bigger than poppy buds. ("Looking for a fight already, bless him," his grandmother said. "He's the image of his father." As if I'd had nothing to do with it.) We laughed, he and I, as I taught him to take his first steps along the stone paths between the borders of herbs. She was always watching, there before me when he fell over, but not to sympathize. "Roman soldiers don't cry, Marcius. Your father's been wounded nineteen times and he never cried." I suppose I should have known then, but I was happy for a few years, playing with him in the sun. It didn't dawn on me until the day of the butterfly, when he was five. He loved chasing butterflies, of course, as all children do and hardly ever caught them. There was one day in late summer when a particular butterfly moved too slowly. Maybe the night had chilled it or its wings were wearing out. Anyway, he made a grab for it and for once got it in his hand. He came running to show it to me, tripped, opened his hand, and off it flew, unsteadily with one wing torn. His childish roar of rage brought her in a second. "Don't let it get away, Marcius. Get up and go after it." With her yelling him on, he chased that limping butterfly up and down the paths, over the vegetable beds, up the steps and down until he'd got it again, firmly crushed in his fist. "Now kill it, Caius. Pay it back for escaping." His eyes were locked on hers, hers on him, while he tore the creature into pieces until his fingers were clotted with the yellow ichor from inside it and the rainbow dust of its wings. When it was over she smiled her approval at him and he smiled back at her, not looking at me, leaving me out of it. I knew then, as I should have known from the start, that he wouldn't be left as mine for much longer. A few years—a few very short years—and he'd be campaigning with his father, learning to be a hero. I think I saw then what was going to happen—not the details of how we'd get there of course—but where we'd be at the end. Sharp eyed as ever, she noticed something in my face. "Virgilia, have you been crying?" Only from laughing, I said.

Another thing about becoming a mother is that your women friends feel they can talk to you about sex. Unmarried girls and young brides must blush and pretend not to understand the coded remarks over the spinning wheels or the bowls of watered wine, but a child in the cradle is your entrance fee to the school of double meanings. "You're looking a little tired, Flavia. Restless night?" Or, "A little tetchy today are we, Marcia dear? How long has Marcus been away?" It took me a long time to realize that they envied me. Because Caius Marcius was such a famous warrior, they assumed that he must be more than usually rampant in bed. When I realized at last what they meant by the remarks about building up my stamina for when he got home and the warrior's return and so on, I didn't reply in kind. I'd blush and concentrate on my spinning or sewing and say nothing. Volumnia was always there, of course. I could see that she was pleased with the compliments to his virility, but she approved of my modest silence, implying that the pleasures of our marriage bed were too sacred for gossip.

In fact, my spinning friends, you've no cause to feel jealous, really no cause at all. It isn't all you imagine in that department, being married to a famous soldier. The wounds, for one thing. Two or three more in every campaign and—he being a hero—all on the front, of course. If you think about it, you can see that hardly makes for joyful abandon. Then there's her, on the other side of the wall. Every creak of the bed joints, every whisper, and you imagine her lying awake and wondering if this is going to be the night that produces another little hero. And if not, what's the silly girl doing wrong? So please

spare me the remarks about Venus and Mars. I wish you would, because
you see they make me wonder what you and your husbands do in bed. Is it
really fire and rushing waters, rose scents and beating wings like the poets
say? I wish somebody would tell me.

It must have been around this time that I happened to catch the eye of a
young man of about my own age when I was walking with Volumnia to a
friend's house. He was tall, with dark curling hair, and when he saw me looking
at him, he smiled such a frank open smile that I couldn't help smiling back.
Back at home, she told me that it wouldn't do. I must understand that as wife
to Caius Marcius, consul-in-waiting, I could not risk the slightest hint of gossip.
My spotless reputation must be as important to me as his courage was to him.
Then, with her eyes on my face and in a tone of voice as ordinary as if we were
discussing household accounts, she said, "If I ever found you'd been unfaithful
to Caius Marcius, I'd kill you. I'd kill you with my own hands. You understand
that?" I nodded, bowed my head, and said nothing.

Or is it something different altogether? Not fires or perfumes or roses but
simply something that two people can laugh about together, like a secret that
can't be told to anybody else. Am I going to have to live my life without
knowing?

The rats were particularly bad that summer. What made it worse was that every
grain of wheat and drop of oil mattered because we expected any day to find
Tullus Aufidius and his barbarian horde besieging us. Caius Marcius hardly
came home at all, and when he did, he could hardly talk about anything except
Tullus Aufidius. He was becoming obsessed by the man. Aufidius said this.
Aufidius might do that. Aufidius has an almost-Roman grasp of military tactics.
One night, when the greyheads were round for earnest conference, he said,
"My only fear in the world is that somebody else will kill him." Then, when
they asked why, "Because his head belongs to me." He said it in almost a loving

way. Later, when we were alone, I asked him what Tullus Aufidius was like. "A fine soldier," he said. "I mean what does he look like?" That surprised him and he had to think about it. "Red hair, red beard. Quite tall for a barbarian." Then, trying hard. "Very white teeth when he smiles." "Young?" "Quite young, younger than I am, but a lot of military experience." Then he patted me on the shoulder and said I wasn't to worry. He would protect us all from Tullus Aufidius. Then he went back to his army and the bed was all mine again.

Come and rescue me, Tullus Aufidius. Come galloping through the city gates with your red hair flying in the wind and your white teeth smiling through your beard, sweep me up out of my white bed and ride away with me. She won't be able to stop us. We'll laugh at the look on her face and our laughter will trail behind us like a red comet's tail as we gallop over the flat fields with the full moon in the sky until Rome is just a misty wall in the distance and we'll lie down under an olive tree and make love all night until I beg you to stop then laugh and say I didn't mean it and you laugh too and press down on me with all your weight and make me forget him and her and Rome and everything. I'm your city, waiting here for storming. My gates are open to you. Come and take me.

Only he didn't, of course. What happened that summer was exactly what should have happened. Caius Marcius stormed their citadel, Corioli, and although Tullus Aufidius lived to fight another day, his defeat was so thorough that we thought Rome would be in no danger from his Volsci for years to come. We could all sleep safely in our beds again without fear of the barbarians coming to carry us off. And my husband—Coriolanus now—came home to a triumph the like of which the city had never seen. That was when he kissed me and called me his gracious silence. And that's when, with my gracious silence, I started killing him. It wasn't clear in my mind then. It isn't clear even now, but I suppose I must have had some warning again of what was going to happen because I started crying. He thought it was because I was so relieved to see him home safe and made a joke of it. If I was crying to see him come home in triumph, would I have laughed if he came home in a coffin? That went down well with the part of the crowd that could hear him. Under her tuition, he was cultivating the art of seeming natural and easy in public. Of course, I said nothing, as if my feelings were too deep for the world to know. Which they were.

Well, my noble husband, since you've raised the subject, I have to admit that I have been wondering what I'd do if you came home dead. I wouldn't have laughed. Not exactly. Certainly not outwardly and in full view of the whole of Rome. Not laughed, no. I'd have been quite sorry—the way you feel if a pet bird dies, or an aunt who was quite kind to you sometimes or a dog you didn't know but saw crushed under somebody's chariot wheels. But then I'd have gone away into my own room and thought to myself, "Well, that's over then, so what next?" And I might have laughed then— shakily perhaps and without making a noise—but yes, I might have laughed. Well, you did ask.

So with the fighting over for a while the political campaign began, before the effect of that welcome home could go cold on us. The greyheads agreed that there'd never be an opportunity better than this one. The aristocrats, the common people, the money men were all in the camp of our genuine hero, still only forty with a lot of scars and a few grey hairs gained in the city's service, and a background and home life that were models of all that Rome expected. That was where I came in again. I'd thought at least I'd be left to myself while he and Volumnia got on with the politics, but not a hope of it. "We must visit as much as possible, Virgilia. The women's voice is essential." Surprised into argument, for once, I said, "But they haven't got a voice. We don't vote." She smiled. She was pleased when I showed my naivety. "We don't need to. In our homes we have a voice." So for weeks it was an endless round of visits, seven or eight of them a day, all over the city. Sitting there, sipping herb teas or spiced wine with the women, talking about nothing in particular with her eyes and ears on me all the time to make sure I didn't say a thing out of place. So of course, I said as little as possible. Usually, Marcius Junior had to come with us to complete the picture. He was at the fidgety age by then and didn't like it, but though he argued with me, he couldn't stand out against his grand-mother. My one consolation was that as soon as Coriolanus was safely elected—and it seemed a certainty—I could go back to my old life, dreaming and thinking my own thoughts in my rooms or along the herb walks in the garden. Then she put me right on that too. All this was good training for the duties I'd have once I was the consul's wife. I didn't even belong to myself anymore, I belonged to Rome. There was no way out.

Only there was a way out and I found it. I swear by all the gods that I didn't mean it. If I prayed to them to save me—and yes, I suppose that other voice inside my head did pray to them—I didn't mean it to be that way. I didn't intend to kill my husband. I didn't intend to kill Coriolanus. It was my silence that did it. How could I help my silence? It was the thing I was good at, after all.

You know the story, I suppose. It's our custom in Rome that before a man can be elected consul he has to put on a ragged working man's tunic and cap and go into the market place to beg the commoners for their votes. It's really no more than a carnival, a break from the serious campaigning and a chance for the candidate to show his so-essential sense of humor and common touch. He buys a lot of wine, makes a comic speech written by a friend who's good at that kind of thing, making sure to put in a reference to the latest wrestling results. They cheer him to the echo and that's that, everybody happy. Now, I know the way she's managed to rewrite what happened to make him look good, even in all this wreckage. Her version—Coriolanus was too proud, too noble to go along with this humiliating farce. So he loses his temper with the mob and is forced into exile. No, I'm sorry, Volumnia, but it wasn't quite like that. I come from a military family so even I know that you can't lead men unless you can share a joke with them, look at things through their eyes. He could have come through the ragged tunic business quite well, if he'd wanted to. Only, I think he was tired. It had been a long campaign after all and we were near the end of it. I know I was tired. The heat in the city was like a bludgeon, I had a sick headache and a list of eight visits to make that day and

Marcius Junior was irritable, probably a touch feverish. I'd heard Volumnia's laughter from her room next door and him laughing too, an unusual sound. Then he came into our room in his stained and torn tunic (borrowed from one of the slaves but well-washed, naturally) holding an old squashy cap in his hand. "Well, Virgilia, how do I look?" He struck an attitude in the doorway and squashed the hat on his head, still laughing. Now, I know I should have laughed too, entered into the joke, told him he looked good or looked awful or anything. Just anything. Instead, I looked away and said nothing. "Oh," he said. Just that, but I could feel the confidence going out of him like air from a puffball when you tread on it. Why it should have mattered to him so much that day I've wondered and wondered. Why, when nobody cared much what I thought, should a few words not said have such consequences? Perhaps, all along, he'd cared for me more than I thought but if so why didn't he tell me? Didn't she let him tell me in case tenderness made him less of a warrior? Whatever the reason, he should have said.

Anyway, the result was that he started the whole thing off balance, forgot his jokes, lost his temper, and got forced into exile. And killed, of course. Killed by Tullus Aufidius. Or by my silence.

He died among the barbarians so he had no grave in Rome. Volumnia decided to devote the rest of her life to putting up a statue to him. My life too. This statue wouldn't be made out of stone or metal but of our lives, our visible and noble grief. In all we did from then onwards, we were to be a reminder to Rome of the city's ungratefulness to its most deserving son, a souvenir of all the virtue that had gone out of the city the day they drove him away. We walked together through the forum, she and I and young Marcius, dressed in mourning clothes, eyes cast down on our daily journey to the temple of Mars. We did it for weeks, for months. At the end of a year I asked her how long we should go on with it. She looked at me with eyes as hard and dark as jet. "Forever," she said. At the end of two years a message came from my father asking if I had thought of marrying again. As a respectable widow, I was entirely free to marry if I wanted. My father had in mind a distant cousin I remembered and quite liked. When I raised the subject with her, very diffidently, I thought she was going to hit me. "What did I tell you? If you're ever unfaithful to Caius

Marcius, I'll kill you with my own hands." "But he's—" "That makes no difference." Her face looked as if it had already willed itself halfway to stone. Her
hair had greyed to the color of flint and her back was as straight as Minerva's
on a temple frieze. She must have been in her sixties but age meant nothing.
I knew she wouldn't let herself die, not for decades, because she was too busy
making us his monument. I said nothing.

*But I'm not ready to turn to stone like her. It would be a waste. My hair is
still thick and dark and heavy. When I let it down, in my own room, it
swirls round my body like the river round a willow tree. My toenails are
pink like shells, my knees soft and rounded as those of Venus herself in the
mosaic on her temple floor. But I'll be thirty next year. Soon it will be too
late. Last night, I heard two of the slaves whispering and giggling under the
window. I recognized the girl's voice, a little scrap of a thing, younger than
I am but not pretty. I heard their whispers dying away and lay awake all
night, imagining where they'd gone and what they were doing, and cried
with envy.*

All this morning I kept out of her way and made myself busy in the storerooms. Even living statues have to eat and drink. I checked the level of grain
in the bins and the olive oil in the big jars. We were running short of oil so I
sent the steward out with some slaves to buy more, warning them to be careful
with it on the steep dark steps down to the storerooms. It was evening when
I decided to go to her, with the low sun throwing a wash of copper-colored
light over the courtyard and the corners of the rooms dusky. It wasn't quite
dark enough to light the lamps yet. We've turned economical now that we
don't have many guests. She was sitting there at her spinning wheel in the dusk
of the living room on a low stool, upright as ever. The only sound was the
whirr of her wheel. I found another stool so that our eyes would be on the
same level and positioned it carefully between her and the door. I said, "There's
something I should tell you."

For the first time since I'd known her, the regular sound of the wheel fal-
tered. She couldn't have guessed what was coming but she knew the sound of

my voice was different. It was different in my ears too, the secret voice of a silent woman but now speaking so that somebody else could hear it.

"It's about Caius Marcius."

I had to time it carefully, not let it out all at once.

"What about Coriolanus?"

She insisted on the title in spite of everything. She'd stopped spinning altogether. Outside I could hear the low tones of the steward giving orders to a slave. I was glad there were other people not far away.

I said, "You know he was away such a lot. That was why it happened."

"Why what happened?"

The judge beyond the River Styx probably sounds like that, a voice telling you there will be no mercy but you've got to confess in any case.

"My lover."

And I poured it all out, like a bird that knows it's only going to sing its song once. I looked her in the eye and told her about how my lover crept past the guards on hot summer nights and I let him in at my window. I told her about those other times when it was my turn to creep past the guards and meet him waiting for me on the other side of the walls with his horse so that we could gallop away and find a place to make love by a river under the trees. He was a wonderful lover, I said. I'd no idea of what love was until we found each other. All the time she stared at me without moving. If it hadn't been for her eyes, I'd have thought she really had finally turned to stone from hearing it. But the eyes were like rats' eyes, two glossy berries in what was left of the light, only black not red. And there wasn't much light left. I stood up, took two steps towards the door.

"What was his name?"

I looked at her over my shoulder.

"Your lover's name?"

"Tullus Aufidius," I said.

Then I threw myself at the door, opened it, and ran for my life. The screech that came after me as I ran into the corridor and along the side of the courtyard was like nothing I'd ever heard before. Some winged monster might have made it, diving on its prey, but nothing human. It came behind me, louder and louder, as she chased after me. I'd never guessed that she could run so fast, let alone scream at the same time. I didn't know then and I don't know now whether she believed me. If she'd thought about it for a moment, she'd have seen that I'd never had a chance to go galloping over the plains with a lover, not with her eyes and ears on me every minute of the day. But saying it was enough. I heard from behind me things crashing over, slaves and servants shouting to each other. They must have known that she'd kill me when she caught up with me. Perhaps some of them tried to stop her, but I don't know. I think probably not. Her word had been law for a long time, and if she chose to kill her daughter-in-law, that was her affair. I'd counted on having a good start, on being a lot younger than she was, but her vengeance was a force of nature and I thought, beginning to panic, that I hadn't given myself long enough. I lost a sandal, kicked off the other one, and heard that screech coming closer and closer until she was only a few strides away. Ahead of me, at the far side of the courtyard, was the door to our storerooms. I grabbed the latch, wrenched it open, then threw myself through and slammed it behind me. It was quite dark with the door shut. My heart was thumping but I made myself go down the steps slowly and carefully, keeping well to the side, with one hand against the wall. By the time I got down to the floor among the jars and bins, the screeching had stopped. The next sound was the door at the top of the steps grinding open. She stood there above me, a darker shape against the dark blue sky.

I said to her, quietly, "Even if you kill me, he was worth it."

The dark shape came down the steps at me. She came quite slowly at first, taking her time because she knew she had me cornered. Then suddenly the shape changed and she was flying at me, head first as if she really had changed herself into an avenging Fury and was hurtling at my throat, beak and claw. That was how it looked to me and I screamed, even though I knew that everything was happening just as I'd planned it, that she'd slipped on the olive oil I'd poured so carefully all down the middle of the steps and was falling headlong. She didn't scream. She landed at my feet and, apart from the snap of her neck breaking, died quite silently. Which was strange, because silence was my speciality, not hers.

In a while, I shall go upstairs. I have a funeral to arrange, a household to run. I shall make it very clear that the slaves must not be punished for the oil spilt on the steps. After all, accidents can happen in the best households. Young Caius and I will mourn properly for the appointed time, and I shall write to my father and tell him that the distant cousin might be worth thinking about. Unless, that is, anybody more interesting comes along. After all, I am a rich young widow and free as a bird. As for that other voice, the one that spoke in my head, I don't think I shall be needing it anymore. The rest is silence.

A Dish of Poison

BY LILLIAN STEWART CARL

 Lillian Stewart Carl writes what she calls "gonzo mythology" fantasy novels, as well as mystery and romantic suspense novels. She began writing as a child growing up in Missouri and Ohio, and has continued all her life, even while traveling to Europe, Great Britain, the Middle East, and India, among other places. He novels include *Garden of Thorns, Memory and Desire,* and *Wings of Power.* Her short fiction has appeared in *Alternate Generals, Past Lives, Present Tense,* and *Murder Most Medieval.* She lives in Carrollton, Texas, with her husband.

When Viola caught a glimpse of herself in the tall mirrors lining the drawing room, she had to look twice. That slender youth in the blue and gold uniform of the Duke's household was truly her.

She squared her shoulders and lengthened her stride toward the far end of the room. Duke Orsino stood there, the focus of his retainers as a planet was the focus of its moons.

Unlike some of the tasks that had already fallen her way in the Duke's employ, those involving tobacco, guns, or dice, waiting upon Orsino was effortless. Viola could've stood all day at his elbow, feasting her eyes on his profile, clean as that on a Roman coin, or listening to his firm but melodious voice.

The gold braid on his collar set off his tanned complexion. His crisp black hair was cut short in the new fashion that rejected the elaborate powdered wigs of an earlier generation. When his guest Captain Bassanio bowed deeply, Orsino inclined his head in a nod so gracious, so polite, it was hard for Viola to envision him leading his ships into the fire and storm of battle. Warriors of old, though, were known for their courtesy as well as for their prowess on the battlefield.

"My thanks, Captain," said Orsino, "for allowing your nephew Cesario to join my household."

Bassanio's eyes twinkled in his weathered face, but his gesture toward Viola was carefully neutral. "So young a lad needs a protector, my lord. My thanks are due to you."

"I'm sure," said Orsino, "we'll get on famously."

She almost ducked, sure that intelligent gaze would see through her disguise. But his blue eyes touched hers, light as a feather, and returned to Bassanio's guileless smile without changing their expression.

Viola didn't dare present herself in this strange land in her true female form. Her respectable name, her blameless ancestry, would count for nothing without the income to shore them up. Making her way as a man, no matter how young, was infinitely preferable to the life she'd have as a woman lacking friends, family, and dowry.

She and her brother Sebastian had planned to make a new life after their father's death in Messaline. Even though many of their father's former patients conveniently forgot how he'd treated their ailments for promises rather than payment, still they'd managed to put together a meager purse. But that purse, and much more importantly, Sebastian himself, had been lost in the shipwreck which cast Viola, Bassanio, and a handful of crew members onto the shores of Illyria.

She tightened her lips. No, she wouldn't cry for her brother, not here, not now. He was gone. She had to make her own way in the world, without a father, without a brother, without a husband. . . . Not that she had any objection to taking a husband when the world held men like Orsino.

Bassanio was leaving. He patted Viola roughly on the shoulder. She knotted her fist and punched his arm. "Thank you, Captain."

"You take care, young man," he returned with another twinkle, and was gone.

Orsino turned in the opposite direction. "Gentlemen, attend me." Viola fell in with the others at his back. It was time for the afternoon ride.

What a good thing it was that she and Sebastian had been born in the same hour, that sad hour which had seen their mother's death. They'd grown to be friends as well as siblings. Viola had scandalized the neighbors by climbing trees and riding astride just as her brother did. And she'd unsexed herself even further by helping her father at his surgery. No wonder she'd chosen to shed the garments of womanhood, when in many ways they clung so indifferently to her.

Orsino led his retainers into the stable yard. It was as redolent of horses and hay and sunshine this afternoon as it had been the day before. A groom was waiting with the Duke's horse, a tall, muscular bay. Viola turned toward the small horse, little more than a pony, which had been assigned to her. A genuine youth might've complained, asking for a larger and more assertive beast. But while she might be devious, she wasn't stupid.

A ragtag figure skulked in the shadows of the tack room. On this warm day he wore an old army greatcoat, its bits of braid tarnished, its pockets sagging. His coat was gray, his hair was gray, his face was gray. His eyes were bits of flint. A lute hung like a sword across his back.

"Who is that?" Viola asked her colleagues Curio and Valentine.

Curio shrugged. "His name is Feste, a poor madman. The Countess Olivia provides him with a hut beside her wall and food in her kitchen. She finds his songs and pranks amusing, I suppose. So does Orsino, asking him to sing and play when the melancholy falls upon him."

"Or perhaps the songs Orsino hopes to hear from Feste are those of Olivia herself." Valentine reached for the reins of his own horse.

Orsino stepped into the tack room and bent his head close to Feste's wizened form. Feste spoke. Orsino nodded, his eyes straying more than once to the road leading south.

"Olivia?" Viola asked. This wasn't the first time she'd heard that name.

"Countess Olivia's estate is to the south of the city," answered Valentine. "Orsino courts her but she'll have none of him, says she'll consider no man's suit while she mourns her brother's death some six weeks past."

Orsino's heart was pledged? Viola pretended her own heart didn't sink a bit at the news. "Her brother was killed in the war?"

"Not exactly," Curio replied. "Count Leonardo returned wounded, yes, but was well on his way to regaining his health when he sickened suddenly and died. Some lingering contagion of his wound, no doubt."

"No doubt," repeated Valentine, a slight edge to his voice. "His death left his sister an heiress with a large household and a title in her own right. I daresay Orsino presses his suit because he wishes to recoup the expense of equipping a company for war."

No, surely he loved her for herself, and pitied her brother's death. . . . Viola looked down at her boots, a bit too big for her feet, mottled with dust and dung. So Olivia was a solitary woman, too, without father, without brother, but with a very tidy dowry indeed. Some are born fortunate, some achieve fortune, and some have fortune thrust upon them.

Orsino plucked a coin from his pocket and pressed it into Feste's hand. The madman turned to go, but not without shooting a shrewd glance around the stable yard. Something glinted in his eye, a subtle sardonic understanding. But if Curio or Valentine or Orsino himself couldn't penetrate her disguise, Viola told herself, why should this poor fool be able to?

Orsino leaped onto his horse and, without looking around to see if anyone was behind him, rode off to the south. Their horses jostling in the gateway, the others followed. None of them sat their saddles as elegantly as Orsino, Viola thought. His lithe body swayed so perfectly to the rhythm of the hoofbeats he and the horse might have been a centaur.

Gaining the crest of a hill, Orsino turned aside from the road and led his small troop along a cliff overlooking the sea. Viola lagged behind, her pony ambling through tall grass that bent double in a cool breeze with a premonitory taste of winter to it. Below her the sea heaved and shuddered and spilled in a white froth onto the rocky beach.

Sebastian had been carried away by waves much fiercer, beaten into foam by a shrieking wind. At least his soul hadn't entered Elysium alone—with him disappeared the French officer, Antonio, who'd enlivened their table with stories of Austerlitz and Waterloo, and who'd worried about sailing so close to the coast of his enemy Illyria. Death, thought Viola, was capricious indeed. Look at Count Leonardo, surviving battle only to fall ill and die in his own household. Or so Curio had said, although Valentine's tone seemed to imply something else.

Orsino's voice broke into her reverie. "Cesario!"

After a long silent moment, Viola thought suddenly, *That's me.*

"Cesario, attend me."

Viola tightened her knees and her horse strolled forward. She looked up at Orsino. He didn't seem annoyed with her—if anything, the slightest of smiles played at the corners of his mouth. But then, he wasn't looking down at her but inland. She followed the direction of his gaze.

Below them a church nestled into a fold of green land. The spreading fronds of an ancient yew tree sheltered several ancient tombstones and one fresh new one. The grave before it was still mounded, covered in new-grown grass and flowers. Three people stood there, two of them deferring to a woman clothed head to toe in black. Only the handkerchief she pressed to her eyes was white, little brighter than her pale skin.

"The Countess Olivia?" Viola asked, remembering in the nick of time to speak in her deepest voice.

"The very same." Orsino shifted in his saddle. "I'm sure Curio and Valentine, as given to gossip as any woman, told you of my thwarted love for her."

"Well—yes, they have."

"Ah, an honest lad. Good. And did they tell you of her brother's death?"

"Only that he died."

"He died. He died indeed."

The group in the churchyard walked slowly toward the gate. The brim of Olivia's bonnet caught the wind and tugged her face upward, so that she saw the group of horsemen on the ridge above her. Shaking her head, she turned away and rested her hand on the arm of the fastidiously frock-coated man beside her. Another, more plainly dressed, woman acknowledged Orsino's presence with a subtle wave and then followed Olivia and the man into a waiting carriage.

As far as Viola could tell from this distance, Olivia was beautiful enough to warrant Orsino's attentions. And worldly enough to enjoy them—no, that was unkind. The woman had probably commanded that stylish straight skirt, the short jacket with its puffed sleeves, and the feathered bonnet in anticipation of her brother's homecoming, only to find herself dying them black soon after. "He died," Viola prompted Orsino.

"The manner of his death, there's the rub. The Countess announced that he died honorably from his wound. And yet the madman tells me he died from a gastric fever."

"Ah," Viola returned noncommittally, but she told herself, a suppurating wound wouldn't cause violent distress to the digestive tract, not at all.

The carriage disappeared around a bend in the road. With an extravagant sigh, Orsino turned to Viola. For just a moment his eyes held the image of the black-clad woman. Then they cleared and brightened, and Viola knew he saw—a stripling youth, not her. "I find myself in a difficult position, Cesario. If I ask for your discretion, you'll not deny it me, will you?"

"Of course not, my lord."

"Today I heard an evil rumor concerning Count Leonardo's death."

"From the madman?"

"From him, yes, although I doubt he's the only rumormonger about. Feste told me Leonardo may have died by his own hand. That would explain much. If Olivia thought such a terrible secret needed concealing, she could well withdraw herself from the world and from me."

A thrill of horror gathered Viola's shoulder blades like cloth. "To lose a brother in such a way would explain much."

"But Feste asks, as much as the fool asks anything in his roundabout way, why a soldier like Leonardo would take his life by poison when his weapons, sword, dirk, and gun, are ready to hand."

"Perhaps to make his death appear an accident," Viola suggested, "so as not to lay the burden of the truth upon his sister."

"Honest, and clever as well." Again that hint of a smile curved Orsino's lips. "His death might genuinely have been an accident, don't you think?"

Viola did think that. And her mind reached further, to another, more sinister possibility. Should she voice that sudden suspicion? No, not just yet. Not unless Orsino himself spoke it first.

One of the waiting gentlemen laughed. A horse whickered softly. Black birds circled the tower of the church. Orsino leaned forward over his saddlebow, his look so intent Viola had to keep herself not from shrinking away but from bending closer. "If I could find the truth of the matter, the means and manner of Leonardo's death, I could ease the Countess's mind. Then she might be pleased to hear my suit."

"Or might reject it utterly, if the truth is the harshest of all possible truths."

"I'll make that gamble," Orsino said. "I knew Leonardo, he was under my command. If he took his own life, then I'll—I'll assume Feste's rags and wander the roads of my own dukedom, unheralded and unknown."

Those keen blue eyes, that noble stance, unrecognized? But Viola allowed him his rhetoric, for his heart followed close behind. "You yourself couldn't find such a truth. Better to place someone in the Countess's household, there to make discreet inquiries.... Oh." Her face grew hot. She hoped Orsino thought it was the wind that colored her cheeks so prettily.

"Yes, I should place some trustworthy retainer in the Countess's household. You, Cesario? You could play a gardener or a footman."

"Or," Viola responded somewhat giddily, "like the boys of old who played the female parts upon the stage, I could profit by my as-yet smooth cheeks and present myself as a maid. Then I could gain access to the innermost recesses of house and so uncover its secrets."

"Brilliant!" Orsino's smile at last broke free of constraint and illuminated his face, like the sun dispelling a storm's murk.

Viola basked in the glow. Answering the mystery of Leonardo's death seemed little enough, if she could earn another such smile.

"If you would stoop to such a ruse for me," Orsino murmured, "if you could acquit such an important task for me, why, I would be so deeply in your debt it would take my greatest galley to hold your reward. Will you do it?"

Yes, Viola wanted to cry, but instead she bowed stiffly and said in her gruffest voice, "As you wish, my lord. What you will."

Fire leaped upon the vast hearth, its orange gleam playing across the polished copper and pewter of the kitchen implements. The scents of smoke and baking bread teased Viola's nostrils. She settled her cap over the cropped ends of her hair, smoothed her apron, and sat down at the table. Knees together, she reminded herself. Eyes downcast demurely.

Armed with a letter of reference from the Duke's palace, she'd quickly secured a position as scullery maid in the Countess's mansion—her role within a role, she thought with a smile. Within a day she'd grasped Olivia's cast of characters, from the servants downstairs to the Countess and her guests upstairs. Now she had to learn the lines of Leonardo's death.

Viola reached into her basket of peas. She stripped one pod, and the next, and the next, pouring the green pellets into an iron pot. Across the table Bianca, Olivia's maid, sewed tiny stitches into a shimmering fall of silk—a nightdress, probably. Viola said, "What a lovely gown. But then, the Countess owns many lovely gowns, I expect."

"Oh yes, that she does. Has her dresses made up in Vienna."

"If I owned such fine clothes, I'd hate to dye them all black."

Bianca's long nose and lashless eyes twitched nervously as a rabbit's. "No help for it, a death in the family's a death in the family, isn't it?"

"And decorum must be observed," said a stern male voice behind Viola's back, "in life as well as in death."

She looked up. As the Countess's steward, Malvolio had interviewed her, hired her, and then lectured her on behaving herself and keeping her place in the household. He was the model of frock-coated propriety, his manner as starched as his white neckcloth and the pointed wings of his collar.

He walked on by, not expecting Viola to answer his pronouncement. Bianca's narrow cheeks flushed crimson. At the other end of the table Helen thumped a cleaver down on a joint of meat. She was as hearty as Bianca was frail—but then, Viola never trusted a thin, pale cook.

"Did you send for a cat?" Malvolio asked her.

"Yes, I did."

He waited.

"Sir."

"There will be no more poisons in this house, will there?"

"No, sir." Helen's cleaver rose and fell emphatically, as though she was imagining the bloody joint beneath her hands to be one of his.

Malvolio tasted the soup steaming over the fire. "Too much coriander deranges the mind. Next time use parsley." He marched out of the room.

Viola asked quickly but quietly, "Poisons?"

"Arsenicum. To kill the rats and mice. It was Maria who bid me purchase a packet of it and sprinkle it about the cellars. It was no doing of mine that the Count . . ." Biting off her sentence, Helen piled the bits of meat in a pan.

Bianca leaned toward Viola, whispering, "Count Leonardo drank the arsenicum with his posset one Sunday afternoon after dinner and was dead before Monday's dawn."

Yes, Viola thought, a fatal dose of arsenicum would produce a great upheaval in the stomach and bowels, and kill within hours.

"We don't know that he took the arsenicum," Helen insisted. "The Count wasn't at all despondent, was he? No, he'd been out riding that very day, and told Ferdinand before dinner he was tired and achy, but still recovering well from his wound."

"Could he have taken the arsenicum by accident?" asked Viola.

"I used only half the packet, not wanting to be overgenerous with a poison. The rest I hid away. I noticed the morning the Count died that it had gone." Her knife flashing, Helen sliced a carrot over the meat.

"And you never found it?"

"No. Vanished like the snow in spring, it did."

The back door opened and Ferdinand himself stepped inside, carrying a pair of large, freshly polished shoes. Like Curio and Valentine, his face was fresh if callow. He walked with the loose-limbed gait of a colt.

Bianca turned to him. "Ferdinand found traces of the arsenicum, though— in the Count's chamber."

"That I did," said Ferdinand. "A fine powder on the tray beside the empty posset cup."

"You're sure that was arsenicum?" Viola asked.

"Who'd be bold enough to taste it?" retorted Ferdinand. "Not I."

"The Count drank the arsenicum of a purpose," Bianca concluded. "There's no other explanation."

Yes, there was, Viola told herself. Murder. Leonardo showed no signs of despair. He might have destroyed the paper packet that had held the arsenicum, meaning to spare his sister the certainty of his suicide. And yet why should he have known there was arsenicum in the house, let alone where it was kept?

Olivia, Viola thought. She could've dosed Leonardo with the poison. But why? She was already wealthy. She was already titled. Perhaps instead of taking her dowry to a husband's household, she wished to draw a husband to hers. . . . No. Olivia was rejecting Orsino, the most suitable, the most desirable of husbands. And there was no reason to think she knew about the arsenicum any more than Leonardo did.

Orsino would laugh Viola out of his presence if she cast a crime upon Olivia. The Countess had been sinned against, she was no sinner herself. Orsino's love for her was not misplaced.

For a moment Viola envisioned returning to Orsino with her verdict, that Leonardo had indeed taken his own life, that Olivia's shame would keep her forever from his embrace and he should look elsewhere for a wife. But no. While she, like Olivia, would have compromised her honor to protect her brother's, in this there could be no compromise.

Helen clanged the pan of meat down on the hearth. "After the Count lay dead, Malvolio called us together and told us the Countess's will, that it be known her brother died of his wound. And may God forgive her her lie, he said, and for burying her brother in consecrated ground, but she was our mistress and we owed her our obedience. And we owe Malvolio, too, I'm thinking."

"If he tried to smile, he would break his face," said Ferdinand.

"Who are you to criticize him?" Bianca demanded. "Who is the steward here, and who the footman, eh?"

Ferdinand opened his mouth to retort. Maria, the housekeeper, walked into the kitchen carrying an armful of autumn flowers. "Fetch me a vase, Ferdinand, if you can tear yourself away from idle talk."

Ferdinand disappeared out the door into the front of the house. Bianca turned her attention to her mending. Viola split the last pod and let the peas fall into the pot. Helen whisked it away and hung it jangling from a hook above the flames.

She reached for a basket. "Viola . . ."

That's me.

". . . go into the garden and collect rosemary for the lamb, savory for the peas, sorrel to make a sauce for the fish. Leeks and lettuces, too. The Countess may be in mourning, but still Sir Toby and Sir Andrew will have their cakes and ale. Came for the funeral, they did, and stayed like a plague of locusts upon Egypt."

Bianca gasped. "How can you speak that way of quality folk?"

"Peace, Helen. Such talk helps nothing." Maria's buxom body, clad in a plain dark dress, reminded Viola of a pigeon. As did her eyes, black beads of perception. "While my lady's uncle and his friend worry her with their antics, at the same time those antics distract her from her melancholy."

Viola took the basket and a small knife and turned toward the door. "Savory. Sorrel. Leeks, lettuce. Rosemary."

"Rosemary flourishes where there's been a death." Bianca bit off the thread and shook out the gown.

"No," Helen corrected, "it flourishes when the house is ruled by a woman."

"Rosemary makes a fine hair and scalp lotion," added Maria, "although my lady prefers the scent of rose petals in her cosmetics."

Unlike Malvolio, Maria probably approved of Olivia's decision to give her brother a proper burial. Viola herself would've allowed Sebastian the benefit of the doubt, that he'd not intended the sin of suicide. But Sebastian's death wasn't at all mysterious.

With a sigh, she stepped out into the bright if cool afternoon. The trees beyond the garden wall were touched very lightly with gold and russet. Still the roses bloomed. Marigolds and Michaelmas daisies lined the path where the

Countess and her guests were walking. Fabian, the gardener, waved a pair of shears over a hedge and leaned forward. Viola could almost see his ears quivering.

No, a bit of eavesdropping wouldn't go amiss. She took the long way round to the kitchen garden, curtseying to the Countess, Sir Toby, and Sir Andrew as she passed. Olivia nodded, but didn't really see her.

The Countess was hardly older than Viola herself. Her face was fair as pearl, set against her black clothing like a jewel in a velvet box. She was so beautiful even Viola would've run a marathon to fan the bloom only hinted at in those pallid cheeks. She could imagine how Orsino felt.

Olivia's uncle, Sir Toby Belch, had the red face, big belly, and booming voice of the habitual drinker. His companion, Sir Andrew Aguecheek, strutted like a bantam rooster. Producing a small enameled box from his pocket, he said, "My thanks, dear lady, for doing me the honor of presenting me with your late brother's snuffbox."

"A fine appetite he had, for all the pleasures of the senses. Never to excess, of course—like some I could name." Olivia looked reprovingly at the two men. Their smiles ranged between sheepish and belligerent. "Even so, it could well be divine justice that he died purged and purified and so entered heaven without delay."

Sir Andrew sneezed so mightily the daisies waved in the breeze. Viola thought, Count Leonardo took snuff? What if the powder on the tray beside the fatal glass was snuff and not arsenicum at all?

So where, then, was the arsenicum? Accidentally misplaced? Or deliberately destroyed by someone who wished to profit from the ambiguous circumstances of Leonardo's death?

Behind her she heard Malvolio's voice, his tone no longer peremptory but unctuous. "My lady, it's a bit chilly today, perhaps you'd prefer taking tea in the Chinese gallery rather than the summerhouse."

The clang of the garden gate covered Olivia's reply. Viola set about her task, taking care to cut only the tender ends of the rosemary and choosing a variety of green lettuces. She pinched a bit from the magnificent clary sage bush with its pinky-purple blooms, even though Helen hadn't asked for it, just to inhale its tangy scent. A shame the kitchen garden with its vegetables and herbs was hidden away behind the stable yard as present fashion dictated.

The household refuse pile filled the far corner of the yard. Viola walked by it, then doubled back. The noisome mound glinted with myriad bits of glass, some small, some large enough to show the curve of their original shape. A couple of champagne bottles lay unbroken amid the trash. Were Sir Toby and Sir Andrew responsible for emptying all those bottles? What about Count Leonardo? Viola went on her way wondering if he'd indeed drunk himself to death, on alcohol, not arsenicum. But no. His symptoms were of a much faster-acting poison.

She found the madman, Feste, lounging beside the fire in the kitchen, holding a bowl of soup to his lips. Beside him sat a sleek calico cat, looking round the room with a professional air and all but polishing its claws. *Mice, rats, what you will. . . .* Its ears flicking forward, it disappeared beneath the sideboard.

Over the rim of the bowl, Feste's flint gray eyes took in Maria's flowers, Helen's kettle, Bianca's needle, Viola's basket. "A cat's a cat for all that," he murmured.

Viola had the uneasy feeling not that he recognized her from Orsino's palace, but that he recognized her true nature. No help for that. She sat down and started peeling the potatoes Helen handed her. "I met the Countess and her guests in the garden. Sir Toby and Sir Andrew must be famous drinkers, judging by the vast number of broken bottles on the refuse pile."

"She sees well," crooned Feste, "who looks well."

Helen arranged the tea dishes on a tray and lifted the kettle from the fire. "Yes, Sir Andrew and Sir Toby enjoy their cups. And it was Sir Andrew who sent many of those bottles to the Countess. But they contained not liquor but food."

"Food? Oh." Viola answered her own question. "I've heard of M. Appert's new method of preserving food. He became a wealthy man, didn't he, provisioning the French Emperor's armies?"

"Very much so," said Maria, jamming a larkspur into the midst of the other stalks. "A fact that has not escaped Sir Andrew. He's built a manufactory here in Illyria, and began sending along samples of his product some months ago, wishing first the Count and now the Countess to join him in his enterprise."

"By marriage," Bianca commented, "if by no other way."

"Her knightly guests wait upon her night and day," sang Feste, "and seek to set the date of nuptials long denied."

So Sir Andrew was also a suitor? If Olivia rejected Orsino, Viola told herself, she wouldn't give Andrew Aguecheek the back of her hand.

"There," Helen said, and set the tea tray so emphatically on the end of the table the porcelain dishes clattered. She turned to the sideboard and threw open its doors. "Look—meat stew, milk, beans, cherries, raspberries, apricots, asparagus, peas, artichokes. I wasn't sure about these foods at first, to tell you the truth, but the Countess ordered me to serve them. And with herbs and spices to correct the seasonings, they're not too bad, although I wouldn't give the milk to that cat, let alone the Countess."

Viola considered the ranks of champagne bottles, their corks held on as carefully by twisted metal hoods as though they contained the finest vintage. But the lumpy shapes of fruits, meats, and vegetables showed through the tinted glass. Each bottle bore a neatly written label.

The damp potato peels wrapped her fingers. The peas she'd shelled boiled merrily away. When either peas or potatoes came to the Countess's table, they'd be nestled in porcelain, lapped with butter and fresh herbs. The bottled foods, too, were decanted, heated, and flavored.

Dinner. Leonardo had been taken ill after dinner. Could she make a case for him dying of food poisoning? Was it Sir Andrew who'd hidden the arsenicum, not wanting it to be known that his food was tainted? And yet Sir Andrew had come here only for the funeral.

Feste shrank back into his corner. Malvolio walked in the door like Alexander entering Persepolis, followed closely by Ferdinand in the guise of a pack animal. The steward looked over the tea tray, repositioned an item or two, and then gestured to Ferdinand to pick it up and carry it away.

Malvolio's beaked nose turned toward the sideboard. "Bottled, preserved, food. What's the world coming to? No good comes from interfering with nature. We've all suffered from this novelty, haven't we? But the Countess—well, she's young and unmarried, without guidance now."

"Sir Andrew," Maria commented, "would hardly have invested his fortune if he didn't think preserved food was the way of the future."

"And his fortune is squandered, I daresay. I overheard him telling Sir Toby he's desperately in need of funds to support this mad enterprise of his. Gluttony and greed are two of the seven deadly sins, but sinners seldom recognize the error of their ways." Malvolio stalked out the door.

Bianca looked after him. "He's right. That food isn't fit to eat."

"Why not?" asked Viola. "Has it made anyone sick?"

"Hard to say," Helen answered. "We all have upsets from time to time."

Feste put aside his bowl and picked up his lute. "The spirit is willing, but the flesh is weak, both the flesh you eat and the flesh that is eaten."

Viola perservered. "Were any of these bottled foods served the night Count Leonardo died?"

"Oh yes," said Maria. "I know what you're thinking. It was the first thought on my mind, too, and on Malvolio's—he was adamant, at first—but only the Count was taken ill that night."

"If the food were tainted, we would all have suffered," Bianca added. "No, it was poison that did for him, I'm sure of it."

"Tainted food is a poison," Viola told her. "Almost anything can make a poison, whether intended or not. The leaves and stems of these potatoes. The seeds and leaves of that larkspur. Gastric fever is always a symptom of food poisoning, but there are other signs . . ."

She caught herself, but it was too late. Every eye in the room was on her now. Flower stem, ladle, needle, lute—every implement was held aloft in its owner's hand. "Out with it, girl," Maria commanded.

Viola laid down the knife. "I have some experience as a nurse. And I can tell you this: arsenicum strikes within the hour. Food poisoning takes several to manifest itself."

"Well then," Bianca said. "It was arsenicum."

"Was it? In his extremity, did the Count suffer from cold, clammy skin?"

"No." Ferdinand walked into the room and shut the door behind him. "I helped the Countess as she labored over him, I was there when he took his last breath in her arms. He moaned that his limbs were numb, but his skin was flushed as though with a fever."

"Did he have vertigo or double vision?"

"Not so's I could tell, no."

"He fell unconscious before he died?"

"No, he suffered a seizure and then was gone."

"What are you thinking?" Helen asked.

Viola frowned. "That he died neither of arsenicum nor of tainted food, but of some other poison. Ferdinand, did you notice anything else?"

"He could take no food or drink," the youth offered.

Maria scoffed, "Of course not, with his bowels in revolt."

"Well yes, that, but also his mouth and tongue were horribly blistered, as though his posset cup had been boiling hot."

"It was lukewarm," said Helen. "And cooled further before you bestirred yourself to take it to him."

"A cup, a stirrup cup, let the cup pass from me," Feste muttered.

Blisters. Viola smelled the aroma of the clary sage on her fingertips, faint beneath the pasty scent of the potatoes. The sage bush filled an entire garden plot, and yet there'd been something else. . . . "I'll return in a moment," she said, and hurried out the door.

Fabian stood in the kitchen garden maneuvering his hoe between the lush tiers of plants. Several fragrances mingled into one, overcoming the stink of the refuse pile. Viola walked briskly to the clary sage and thrust her arms into it, pushing its limber branches aside. Yes, there, its sparse, shiny leaves thrusting up into the lower shoots of the bush, was a black hellebore.

"Fabian," Viola called. "Did you know this was here?"

He looked over her shoulder. "There were several plants in the woods, bloomed prettily at Christmas, they did. I warned the Countess off picking them, though. I don't know how this one got here."

Covering her hand with her apron, Viola reached out and with one good tug pulled the hellebore up by its roots. Yes, its stem was scarred where several shoots had been recently stripped away. "And who would know, Fabian? Who comes here, to this enclosed spot behind the stableyard?"

"Helen gathers herbs for her cooking, Maria to make lotions. Bianca, too. Malvolio misses nothing, not one tarnished horse-brass, not one beetle-ridden rose. And the madman, well, the madman is everywhere."

"Thank you." Leaving him scratching his head, Viola carried the plant back into the kitchen. Every eye followed her as she walked across the room and cast the limp stem onto the hearth. "This may be odorless," she announced, "but it stinks of death and deception even so."

"Black hellebore!" exclaimed Helen. "How did that get into the garden?"

Maria shook her head. "Not by Fabian's hand, he knows better."

"Someone's hand put hellebore in the Count's dinner," Viola stated.

The room fell so silent the bubbling of the cooking food sounded like rain. When the cat popped out from beneath the sideboard, each person jumped and shot a wary glance at someone else.

Triumphantly, the cat laid a dead mouse at Feste's feet. "Hell bore his soul, and bore it well indeed," the madman said.

"Poisoned with hellebore?" Maria demanded. "How can that be? Thanks to the Countess's generosity, everyone in the house eats of the same dishes. No one else suffered the least twinge that night."

"What was served?" asked Viola.

Helen thought for a moment. "The usual soup, fish, meat. I made a sauce from the bottled raspberries, and a small dish of the apricots for the Count—he was very fond of my apricots dusted with cinnamon, although the Countess doesn't care for them at all."

"He ate that entire dish himself, with good appetite," offered Ferdinand, "as he'd been out all day."

"But he killed hims . . . Ow!" Bianca stabbed her own finger. She dropped needle and silk and watched as a ruby drop of blood welled from her skin.

Maria, Helen, and Ferdinand looked around at her, but no more closely than Viola did. She was Olivia's maid. Of all the people Fabian had seen in the garden, Bianca had the least excuse. Unless. . . . "You are interested in herb lore, Bianca?"

"Asks enough questions," said Helen, "though she gets half of it wrong."

"No harm in that," Bianca replied hastily. "If I learn to cook or make cosmetics I could better myself, couldn't I? Malvolio tells me I have many skills and can in time rise above my station."

Maria set her hands on her hips. "I've seen you loitering in the pantry, where you have no business, simply to drop Malvolio a courtesy. I thought him too haughty to take notice, and yet you tell me now he's had private conversation with you?"

"And why not?" retorted Bianca, her voice shrill.

"You were hanging about the pantry before dinner, beside the serving dishes, the night of the Count's death," Ferdinand said. "And later, when the Count rang for me and bid me alarm the Countess, I found you here in the kitchen shaking and weeping, and Helen going on about the missing arsenicum."

"It was you pointed out the arsenicum was missing, now that I think about it." Helen waved her ladle. "It was you rinsed off the serving tray, saying the powder on it was arsenicum."

"It was, it had to have been . . ." Bianca thrust her injured finger into her mouth.

Viola looked down at her apron, at the faint yellowish-green stain left by the hellebore plant. She knew what would happen next, and for just a moment she rued her place in it. But if Orsino had been willing to gamble on the truth, she could do no less.

Maria asked, very quietly, "What have you done, Bianca?"

Bianca's colorless eyes seemed too large for her face. Her complexion wasn't the appealing pallor of Olivia's but the flat white of a fish's belly. She slumped down in the chair and spoke around her finger, thickly and reluctantly. "Malvolio praised me for learning herb lore. He told me the plant behind the sage was a restorative. When Count Leonardo complained of being tired and achy after his ride, Malvolio said a restorative would be just the thing. So I stripped off a bit of the plant and brewed a tisane."

"But since it wasn't your place to carry food and drink to the Count," Ferdinand said, "you poured the tisane in his favored dish, the apricots."

"Thinking," Maria said with a scowl, "to go to Malvolio later on, when Count Leonardo recovered, and earn even more praise. Foolish girl."

Bianca looked desperately from face to face but saw nothing to help her.

"She meant for the masquerade with the arsenicum to cover her horrible mistake." Viola picked up the sewing basket and poured it out. Colorful loops of thread spilled across the tabletop. Among them was a square of brown paper studded with pins and needles. Creases showed where it had once been folded into an envelope. "Is this the packet that held the poison?"

"It was made of such paper," said Helen. "What did you do with the arsenicum itself, Bianca, pour it down the necessary?"

With the short wail of a trapped animal, Bianca began to cry.

"She is indeed guilty of foolishness," Viola said sadly. "The question is whether she's guilty of murder. She didn't mean to kill Count Leonardo. His death was as much an accident as if he'd died of tainted food."

"A court of law would find her culpable." Maria's look crossed Viola's. "Helen, Ferdinand, take Bianca to the shed and lock her in."

Feste strummed his lute. "The Count is counted among the dead, died a glorious death for his country and for the Duke's honor, for honor cannot be tainted even if apricots can." He, too, looked at Viola.

She offered him a thin smile, sure now he knew of her mission here. "No court would find Malvolio culpable. And yet, if only he had a motive to dispose of the Count, I would think he directed the entire plot."

"I can guess at his motive. Come with me." Gathering her skirts, Maria led the way into the back hall. Around a corner, at the corridor's far end, she threw open a door. "This is Malvolio's chamber."

The room was comfortably but plainly appointed. One window looked out over the front drive and another into the gardens, as though the room were a sentry post. Just inside the door stood a writing desk, papers and books arranged in their individual slots. Viola inspected the spines of several books and picked up one. "An herbal."

"Is one of the pages marked, by any chance?"

Viola leafed quickly through the book. "No. Not a one. But here's an etching of the black hellebore, with its fatal properties clearly set out. And yet he told Bianca it was a healing plant." She glanced at a couple of chapbooks containing popular romances, not the sort of thing she'd expect Malvolio to be reading. "Here's the story of the Lady of Strachey, who married a yeoman of the wardrobe. And here's another, similar tale. Surely he can't dream of . . ."

"He can, yes." Maria pulled a piece of paper from a stack of inventories and receipts. On it was written several times, with flourishes, "Count Malvolio."

"Infamous!" Suddenly Viola saw the entire play, act and scene. Her stomach turned.

Maria slapped the paper back into its pile. "Malvolio has the Countess's favor, having been appointed by her late father. If I tell her of our suspicions, she'll have none of them. . . ."

A step in the door. Viola and Maria spun around. There was Malvolio himself, his eyes slitted with rage, his chin so stiff above the wings of his starched collar Viola could imagine pulling his head off like a cork from a bottle. "How dare you trespass in my chamber! Leave this house at once, you impertinent wench, and in the future remember your station! As for you, Maria. . . ."

Maria drew herself up. "The Countess might hear nothing against you, Malvolio, but she'll hear nothing against me either."

Malvolio snorted indignantly.

"Bianca told us of your attentions to her."

"Bianca? That ignorant baggage? She claims I've paid her attentions? Who would take her word over mine?"

Gritting her teeth, Viola answered silently, *No one.* Even if a court did believe Bianca's testimony, there was no real case against Malvolio. With an abrupt curtsey, she walked out of the room.

Behind her she heard Maria say, "The girl Bianca poured a tisane of hellebore into the Count's dish of apricots, thinking it was a restorative. The same dish of apricots you commanded Helen make for him."

"As was my duty, to please my employer by serving a favorite dish. A shame Bianca's stupidity and Leonardo's taste for contrived food led to his death."

"Oh yes," said Maria, stamping out of the room, "it is indeed a shame."

In the distance Sir Toby and Sir Andrew exchanged bray for bray, with Olivia's quiet but steady voice as counterpoint. Viola waited until she and Maria were around the corner, away from Malvolio's baleful glare, before she asked, "What will you tell the Countess?"

"I'll tell her the truth, that her brother died accidentally of apricots tainted by mistake."

"Bianca must face a court of law even so."

"I'll plead her case with the Countess and with Sir Toby, who has a good heart beneath his bluster, and suggest they do the same with Duke Orsino."

"As I've been ordered to leave this house," Viola said dryly, "I'll take a letter to the Duke and resume my place in his household."

Maria stopped outside the kitchen door and turned her most penetrating look on Viola. "Did Duke Orsino send you here to spy upon the Countess?"

"Not at all. He sent me here to learn the truth of her brother's death and so ease her mind."

"You've done that," said Maria, even more dryly. "While the Countess will be grateful, gratitude won't necessarily further the Duke's suit."

"He knows that." *As do I,* Viola admitted to herself, and went on, "The Countess won't be grateful to Sir Andrew, who introduced the bottled food into the house. I daresay that was Malvolio's plot to begin with, to leave the Countess a wealthy spinster and rid himself of a rival suitor with one blow. He intended for at least one other person to eat of the apricots and sicken as well, to support his argument against the food. When that didn't happen and Bianca told the tale of the arsenicum, then sly Malvolio played along."

"If others of us had sickened then we—you—would never have discovered the truth."

"If the Count hadn't eaten the entire dish, he might not have taken enough of the poison to kill him. . . ." Viola shook her head. "If, if, if."

"Death is certain," said Maria. "Life is ambiguous."

So is love. "Surely the Countess wouldn't hear Malvolio's suit, even if he dared press it."

"I don't know what manner of man would tickle her fancy. Neither does Malvolio, I warrant." Maria grimaced. "Perhaps I can use his ambitions against him, and dress him a dish of poison appropriate to his nature, thereby toppling him from his high horse. Bianca was most notoriously abused. Malvolio deserves no less."

Viola followed Maria into the kitchen. Malvolio had said that sinners seldom recognize the errors of their ways. True enough. He was himself corrupt, his righteousness bearing poisoned fruit.

Feste sat beside the fireplace, the cat curled next to him, strumming his lute. The fool, thought Viola, had the most reason of them all.

He winked at her, and his cracked voice sang softly, "Journeys end in lovers meeting."

Do they? Viola asked herself. *Do they?*

Orsino gazed thoughtfully at the parchment marked with Olivia's seal. His brows were drawn down, his mouth a straight line. "So that was the way of Leonardo's death. And the Countess and Sir Toby have already been acquainted with the particulars, leaving me little role to play."

"Oh no, my lord. As magistrate, your role is the greatest of all, the disposition of the criminal." Viola refilled his wineglass and set the bottle down. *Legs apart,* she reminded herself. *Shoulders back. Voice rough.* "Mercy is as a gentle rain from heaven upon the parched earth beneath."

"Mercy, yes." Orsino's lips softened. "I'll set out a decree of banishment and send the poor foolish girl beyond Illyria's borders."

Viola thought of Bianca far from her native land, lacking friends, family, and dowry. She would live, but she would suffer for her crime even so. As for Malvolio—well, vengeance might more properly belong to God, but just now Viola was rooting for Maria.

"Surely this tragedy," Orsino went on, "will lead Olivia to reject that coxcomb Andrew Aguecheek's suit."

"It may well do so, my lord."

"Isn't it nobler to love the woman herself rather than her wealth, as he does?"

"Oh yes," Viola said. "That it is."

Orsino lay back in the corner of the settee and stretched out his legs. He smiled. "Well then, Cesario. You have done my will admirably. What reward would you have of me?"

"The honor of attending upon you." She couldn't keep the irony from her voice.

For a long moment Orsino considered Viola—Cesario—standing before him. His bright blue eyes reflected something between puzzlement and recognition, as though he heard a distant strain of music but couldn't identify the instrument. Then, with a slight shrug, he threw his confusion away.

Indicating the harpsichord in the corner, he said, "Then play for me. Something by Herr Mozart. Your touch is much more delicate than Curio or Valentine's blunderings about the keyboard."

Her smile repeating his, Viola sat down and stroked a light arpeggio.

Orsino lifted his glass to his lips. "I'll try my suit with Olivia once again, sending a new ambassador this time. After Leonardo's tragedy, perhaps she'll now share my taste for romance."

Romance, Viola thought, which can just as well become comedy. She began to play.

Orsino closed his eyes. "If music be the food of love, play on."

As you wish, my lord. What you will.

Too Many Cooks

BY MARCIA TALLEY

 Marcia Talley's first Hannah Ives novel, *Sing It to Her Bones*, won the Malice Domestic Grant in 1998 and was nominated for an Agatha Award as Best First Novel of 1999. *Unbreathed Memories*, the second in the series, won the *Romantic Times* Reviewers Choice Award for Best Contemporary Mystery of 2000. Both were Featured Alternates of the Mystery Guild. Hannah's third adventure, *Occasion of Revenge*, was released in 2001. Marcia is also the editor of a collaborative serial novel, *Naked Came the Phoenix*, where she joins twelve best-selling women authors to pen a tongue-in-cheek mystery about murder in an exclusive health spa. Her short stories have appeared in magazines and collections including "With Love, Marjorie Ann," which received an Agatha Award nomination for Best Short Story of 1999. She lives in Annapolis, Maryland, with her husband, Barry, a professor at the U.S. Naval Academy. When she isn't writing, she spends her time traveling or sailing, and recently returned from the Bahamas, where they lived for six months aboard *Troubadour*, their 37-foot sailboat.

History is not what you thought. It's what you can remember.
—W. C. SELLER AND R. J. YEATMAN, *1066 AND ALL THAT*

Merab wrapped her fingers tightly around the neck of the burlap sack and, with her free hand, gathered up the skirts of her gown and scrambled over the stile. Once over the wall, she relaxed against the smooth stones, grateful for their warmth as it penetrated the light fabric of her cloak. She closed her eyes, turned her face toward the sky, and inhaled deeply, delighting in the sweet smell of new-mown hay baking in the afternoon sun. A blissful moment later, she glanced back the way she had come, the hint of a smile on her lips. It had been only a small incantation, after all, but powerful enough to topple that ruffian, to send him sprawling with a satisfying *splat,* facedown into a puddle of mud that hadn't been there only seconds before.

A pity she hadn't been able to remember the spell before that other rogue had hurled an egg at her. She picked at the yolk spots on her plain, gray gown. She shrugged—a small matter. They would hardly be noticed among the other stains—brown and tan and iridescent green—that speckled the panels of her skirt.

Dragging the sack and stepping high, Merab crossed the field. A soft breeze lifted her hair, sending the dark, tightly coiled strands dancing about her shoulders and drifting lazily across her cheeks. Overhead, a sparrow circled leisurely. "Later," she sang to the bird with a friendly wave of her hand. "Zipporah's expecting me and it doesn't do to keep Zipporah waiting."

The field ended at a dirt track deeply rutted by the wheels of the King's wagons. Merab followed the track for half a mile, then veered left at the three-trunked birch tree that marked the path through the wood to the cottage she shared with her sisters. "Cottage" was perhaps too grand a word for the elaborate lean-to of lashed timbers that made a shallow vestibule just outside the entrance to their true living quarters: a deep natural stone cave. In a sunny clearing to the left lay the garden, stoutly fenced to discourage the deer, and just beyond it, the hives.

As she emerged from the trees, Merab noticed white smoke drifting lazily from the roof hole and she feared she would be late for dinner. She slipped through the door and leaned, slightly breathless, against the jamb.

"There you are!" Zipporah set aside the mortar and pestle with which she had been grinding herbs for the stew, now cheerfully bubbling in an iron pot hanging from a spit over the grate. She wiped her hands on her apron. "I was beginning to think I'd have to send Little Miss Feckless out to find you." She nodded toward the hearth where Merab's younger sister, Dymphna, sat on a stool busily shelling peas into her skirt. "As much good as that would have done."

Merab flinched as Zipporah snatched the sack from her hand and snapped, "Let's see what you've brought us today, sister." Holding the sack by the bottom corners, she upended it, sending a cascade of small parcels, wrapped in brown cloth and tied with rough string, spilling over the tabletop. Zipporah felt along the edges of the sack, then shook it vigorously until the last packet, a small leather pouch, dropped out. She began sorting through them. "Dried whelk, laver, lizard's toe, shark's tongue, wolf teeth . . ." She looked up. "Where's the pepper?"

Merab picked up a twist of cloth, sniffed it, then placed it next to a small loaf of sugar. It wasn't always easy to separate the items they used for cooking from those they would need for spells. She sneezed.

"Bless you!" Zipporah muttered, barely pausing in her inventory. "Tiger gut, eye of newt . . ."

Merab froze as Zipporah untied the packet and fingered the small, dried pellets it contained. Newt eyes had grown so expensive that Merab had substituted toads' eyes for their slightly smaller and scarcer cousins. The bat wool she'd scraped from the inside of her own cloak, and although she couldn't say for sure, the Turk's nose the old leech had sold her that morning bore a remarkable resemblance to the nether end of a chicken. The pennies Merab had been able to save weighed heavily in her pocket, but oh! how she wanted a new gown. And how else to afford the fine wool, soft as eiderdown and blue as the Highland skies, she'd been admiring each week at the market?

While Zipporah refolded the packet of toads' eyes and continued sorting, Merab inched toward Dymphna, whose head was bowed, her face nearly invisible in the smoky room. She'd been oddly silent.

"Dymphna?"

Dymphna shuddered, and when she looked up, it was with red and swollen eyes. To Merab's utter astonishment, the girl's cheeks and chin were covered with a straggly beard the same cinnamon color as her hair.

"Dymphna!"

Her sister's face was a hirsute mask of misery. "It was the baldness remedy," she whimpered.

Zipporah's voice sliced through the haze like a scythe. "Silly hen got too close to the cauldron."

"You asked me to stir it!" Dymphna wailed.

Zipporah turned, hands on broad hips, eyes like currents in a plump Easter bun. "At least we know it works!" She threw back her head and roared with laughter, sending the chickens scurrying from under the table and into the yard.

Merab fished a small knife from her pocket. "Here. Let me cut it off."

"No!" Dymphna raised both hands. "I tried. It just comes back all the thicker."

Merab thought back to the big leather book the leech kept chained to his wall. She'd read something about this. "Southernwood boiled in barleymeal?"

"That's for pimples," Zipporah snorted. She shuffled across the room and loomed over the dejected Dymphna. "So much ado! It'll probably be gone by morning. In the meantime . . ." She pointed toward a small table set in a corner near the cottage's only window. "There's the book and there's the quill. Write down the recipe before you forget."

Holding her skirt out before her, Dymphna struggled to her feet. She dumped the peas, bouncing and pattering, into a wooden bowl, then, dragging her stool along with her, crossed to the table and sat down. She turned the book to a fresh page and smoothed it out carefully with the flat of her hand. After a thoughtful moment, she dipped the quill into a flask of ink and wrote "Receipt for Baldness" in a precise, round hand.

Truth to tell, there weren't many recipes in the book. In the year since Squire and Mistress Weird had perished in a tragic encounter with a wild boar, leaving their three daughters with nothing save two gold coins and this rude cottage, the women had struggled to support themselves with spell craft, conjuring, dowsing, and the occasional exorcism. Hecate dropped in from time to time to offer advice, but Zipporah had little patience for the hag's old-fashioned ways.

"Surely, to be profitable, magic must be put to more practical use," Zipporah was fond of saying. "Moon drops!" she had sniffed after Hecate's last visit. "If I listened to her, we'd soon be dancing around our cauldrons like fairies in a ring!"

Under their older sister's guidance, then, they'd turned their eyes toward practicalities. Six months ago Merab had witched a well for Lord Lennox, and the news of her success had quickly spread. They'd had a recent commission from Lady Macbeth, and the baldness potion had been for King Duncan himself. "A royal charter!" Zipporah had enthused, rubbing her work-roughened hands together. Thinking about Dymphna, Merab hoped King Duncan wouldn't mind looking like a monkey.

Her musing was interrupted by the hollow pounding of hooves and the barking of dogs. The cat napping on the sill near Dymphna's scribbling hand arched its brindled back and hissed at something outside the glass. Zipporah was halfway to the door when the knocking began.

"Mistress! Open up!"

Merab's fingers curled tightly around the knife she still held while Zipporah reached for the broom, then cautiously lifted the latch. She eased the door open and, with one piercing black eye, peered through the crack. "Oh! It's you." Her shoulders relaxed and she threw the door wide to a young man Merab recognized by the badge on his tunic as a messenger from Inverness. "Come in." Zipporah held up a hand. "But wipe your feet first. I've just laid clean straw."

The messenger balanced unsteadily on their threshold, first on one foot and then the other, using the edge of his dagger to scrape layers of mud from his boots. "The Lady Macbeth sends her compliments," he wheezed. "She is riding this way and begs that you speak with her."

"We await her pleasure," said Zipporah.

Merab and Dymphna exchanged worried glances. Perhaps the potion hadn't worked. Soon they might be practicing their art from the bottom of the loch.

At Merab's invitation, the messenger dipped his drinking horn into a cask of barley water and drank deeply. Meanwhile, Dymphna threw another log on the fire and busied herself with the bellows.

But even before the messenger could drain his horn, Lady Macbeth stood tall in the doorway before them. She wore a blue robe, trimmed with pearls, and an overskirt embroidered with fine silver thread. A silver fillet held a square of pale gauze in place over her hair, which Merab could see was the color of burnished gold. "Greetings, Weird Sisters." The hand Lady Macbeth raised in salute was milky white, the fingers almost too narrow and delicate for the heavy rings they wore. "I've ridden all the way from Inverness to thank you."

Zipporah whisked a stool from under the table and bid their visitor sit. Lady Macbeth complied, settling her skirts prettily around her. Then she leaned forward, her voice low. "On Candlemas Eve, while my husband's servants were occupied preparing their master for bed, I slipped the potion you concocted into my husband's wine. Later when I crept into his chamber . . ." Astonishment sparkled in her violet eyes. "Never was there such a marvel! A veritable tent pole beneath the sheets!"

Lady Macbeth snapped her fingers and the messenger, who had been lounging negligently against the door frame, sprang to attention. "See to the dogs," she ordered. The youth scurried away. After he had gone, the lady continued. "As my lord is so fond of saying, 'Drink provokes the desire but takes away the performance.' But not that night. Saints, no! I think he was nearly as astonished as I."

Her eyes alight with joy, Lady Macbeth laid a hand on Zipporah's arm. "And now, I am with child, Mistress Weird!" She stroked her belly. "And I desire that this child shall be King of Scotland!"

"But, Lady!" Merab exclaimed. "Your husband is Thane of Glamis. The Thane of Cawdor stands between him and the kingdom, and both the Thane of Cawdor and King Duncan still live!"

Lady Macbeth's lips drew back in a smile, her teeth flashing white in the gathering dusk. "Exactly."

Merab's hand flew to her mouth, stifling a gasp.

Lady Macbeth drew her cloak more closely around her. "There must be some incantation, some potion to aid in our noble purpose."

Zipporah aimed a silencing glance at Merab, then bowed to the Lady. "Your wish is our command, dear Madam."

Lady Macbeth's gaze fell on each of the sisters in turn, then she winked. "My husband will be abroad tomorrow, hunting with his nobles on the heath." She rose from her stool and glided to the door as if she wore wheels rather than boots. Zipporah followed, bobbing up and down like a cork.

At the door, Lady Macbeth turned. From beneath her cloak she withdrew a small leather purse, shook it so the gold coins it contained clinked dully together, then placed the purse on Zipporah's upturned palm. "See to it, then." She smiled. "I can be very, very grateful." Waving a beringed hand, she caroled, "Farewell, my lovelies!" and in a miasma of sweet Arabian perfume, she was gone.

Zipporah latched the door and fell back upon it, both hands, still holding the purse, pressed over her heart. "What a triumph!" Suddenly her eyes narrowed. "Dymphna! Where are you?"

Dymphna emerged from the shadow of the wardrobe. Zipporah skewered the hapless girl with her eyes. "You did write it down, didn't you? The impotence cure? Tell me you wrote it down."

Dymphna's shaggy chin dipped to her chest. "The quill needed sharpening."

"You didn't write it down?" Zipporah's face grew dangerously red.

Dymphna shook her head. "But I'm sure I can remember!" she added brightly. "I have an excellent memory." She closed her eyes for a moment, then began speaking, as if reading the formula off the inside of her eyelids. "Mandrake root ground with seed of lemon, a pinch of St. John's wort, blue salts from the pools in the Sildenafil Hills . . ."

Zipporah's eyes grew hard. "How much salt?"

"I don't remember."

"A handful," Merab offered.

"And honey," Dymphna concluded. "That's all."

Zipporah sighed. "I pray you are right, sister. If not, it could take another one thousand years to recreate that formula!"

The next morning, two hours after the sun had gently nudged aside the moon, the Weird Sisters sat around their table amid a jumble of parchment scrolls and leather-bound volumes. Dymphna glanced up from the *Herbarium of Apuleius* she was perusing. "No poisons, Zipporah."

Merab nodded, her ebony curls bobbing vigorously. "I agree. No killing. I draw the line at killing."

Zipporah rested her chin on one hand. With the other she tapped her long fingernails on the tabletop.

"Maybe we can drive King Duncan away," Merab suggested. "Far, far away."

"But where?" Zipporah's nails clicked annoyingly against the wood.

"To England. I hear his son, Malcolm, is already there, petitioning King Edward for support."

"So?" Dymphna wanted to know.

"Macbeth is King Duncan's half-brother," Merab explained. "With both Duncan and Malcolm out of the country, Macbeth might well be declared King."

Dymphna stared at her sister, her eyes wide. "But Lady Macbeth expects us to meet her husband on the heath. Today!"

"We can still meet him . . ." Zipporah said.

"With no ready spell? No incantation? No potion?"

Zipporah smiled. "Remember when you fell into the loch and I gave you that bolus for leg cramps?"

Dymphna nodded.

"Sugar."

Dymphna's eyebrows disappeared under an untidy fringe of hair. "Sugar, you say? But it worked! It cured my cramps!"

"The sugar cured nothing more than your mind, dear sister. So, until we can brew the proper potion, let us play with his mind."

"But will he believe whatever nonsense we tell him?" Merab watched as her older sister crossed to the cupboard, opened a carved wooden casket, and withdrew a leather pouch and a looking glass that had once belonged to their mother.

Zipporah propped the mirror against a candlestick, spread the contents of the pouch on the table in front of her, then began fastening rounded pellets of sap to her forehead and chin, smoothing out the edges and blending them seamlessly into her skin. She reserved a particularly large and misshapen pellet for the tip of her nose. "He will, dear sisters, if we dress the part."

Zipporah turned and Merab fell over backwards, laughing, at her sister's transformation into a crone.

Zipporah's eyes darted appraisingly from Dymphna to Merab and back again. "Dymphna, you'll do as is."

Dymphna, whose beard had grown another two inches overnight, burst into tears.

"As for you, sweet Merab, you're far too comely for a midnight hag." Zipporah stuck her head into the wardrobe, rummaged about, and emerged in triumph a few moments later holding a tattered cloth of graying gauze. Holding it by the corners, she tossed it over Merab's head and watched as it settled lightly around her shoulders and hips, until its ragged edges just dusted the floor.

"You look like a plinth," Dymphna snuffled, dragging a frayed sleeve across her nose. "A cobweb-covered plinth."

Zipporah studied Merab's costume critically, the corners of her mouth turned down. "Don't just stand there, Merab. Wave your arms!"

Merab flapped her arms like a wounded stork.

"Now, moan."

The wounded stork keened and howled, as if near death.

Zipporah chortled. "That will have to do."

Merab dropped her weary arms and staggered about the room in a tight circle. "I can't see very well."

With a guiding hand on her back, Zipporah pushed Merab towards the door. "Never mind. You won't have to. Just follow my lead." She glanced over her shoulder at Dymphna, still sulking by the hearth. "Snap out of it, Dymphna! Come, now! It's show time!"

"Show?" Dymphna squeaked.

"Show!" cried her older sister.

"Show! Show! Show!" flapped the stork.

As the women had planned, Macbeth and his party stumbled upon the Weird Sisters on the banks of a rocky, babbling stream. Dymphna had coaxed some kindling and a pile of short logs into a hot fire and had set a small, three-legged cauldron, filled with water, over it to boil. When the steam began to rise, Zipporah tossed in a handful of greenish-yellow pellets. Singing "The Poor Soul Sat Sighing by a Sycamore Tree" in her reedy soprano, she circled the cauldron, round and round, until smoke boiled from it, spilled over the sides, and billowed across the brown furze thick as a winter's fog, licking hungrily at their ankles. The hunting party, with trumpets blaring and dogs braying, thundered to a halt a few hundred yards away, their banners fluttering in the mild breeze. While their steeds snorted and stamped, rattling their bridles, two men dismounted and approached warily.

"Banquo and Macbeth," Zipporah whispered. "I recognize them from the organized horse-battles last spring."

Dymphna pouted. "You'd think they'd be polite enough to remove their hats!" she complained.

Zipporah touched her sister's cheek. "Sweet Dymphna. Have you taken a good look at yourself?"

Dymphna's lower lip began to quiver dangerously under its new growth of beard. Zipporah held up a finger to silence her. "Shhhhhh. Here comes Banquo."

A tall man, wearing a rust-colored tunic with ties up the front and a cloak thrown over his broad shoulders, stopped twenty paces away, his left hand toying nervously with the hilt of his sword. "Who are you?" he demanded. His eyes narrowed. "At first I thought you were women, but then . . ." He squinted at Dymphna. "You are bearded!"

Dymphna stuck her chin out defiantly, but Merab could see that her sister's fingernails were digging deeply into her palms.

Merab felt Zipporah's elbow sharp against her ribs. "Whooo, whooo, whooo," she moaned.

Banquo staggered backward. "Are you not of this world?"

His companion raised a cautionary hand, then advanced with long, confident strides. Slightly shorter than his friend, Macbeth wore a Saxon tunic with a wide, embroidered hem and loose oversleeves. A belt, inlaid with precious stones, was buckled at his waist; he wore fine leather boots. "Speak!" Macbeth commanded.

Zipporah spread her arms wide. "All hail, Macbeth. Hail to you, Thane of Glamis!"

"All hail, Macbeth. Hail to you, Thane of Cawdor!" cried Dymphna, quickly catching on.

"All hail, Macbeth, who will be King hereafter!" finished Zipporah with another flourish of her arms.

Macbeth's eyes widened with astonishment. "But how can this be? The Thane of Cawdor still lives!"

"Eeyow, eeyow, eeyow!" Merab shrieked, completely ignoring the question.

"Wait a minute!" Banquo interjected, his face alight. "You've given my noble friend here a happy fortune. If you can really see into the future, what do you see in it for me?"

"Hail!" cried Merab.

"Hail!" croaked Dymphna.

"Hail!" shouted Zipporah. She leaned in Banquo's direction and whispered, "More is less and less is more."

Banquo's brow knit in puzzlement. "What is that supposed to mean?"

"Thou shall get kings though thou be none," chanted Zipporah.

Merab felt the sting of Zipporah's elbow again. She spun in a tight circle, arms pinwheeling. "Banquo and Macbeth, all hail!" she chanted. "Banquo and Macbeth, all hail!" until Zipporah touched her arm, signaling it was time for them to depart. The women turned their backs to the men and their faces toward the river.

"Wait a minute! Tell me more!" demanded Macbeth.

But Zipporah said nothing. With a theatrical gesture, she tossed another handful of pellets into the steaming cauldron. A choking mist arose, enveloping them all. "Come, sisters," she hissed into the fog. "Let us fly!"

Leaving the two men to stumble blindly back to their horses, the Weird Sisters scurried away, following the bank of the stream until they found themselves once again in the safety of the wood.

"Why did we run?" panted Dymphna, doubled over with her hands resting on her knees.

Merab had stripped off her shroud and was leaning against a tree. "Yes, why?"

"Always," Zipporah grinned toothily, "leave them wanting more." She peeled a wart off her cheek and laughed.

Two days later, the rising sun found the sisters gathered once more around their table. "It's a message from Lady Macbeth," Zipporah said as she spread the parchment out on the table in front of her. "Do you want the good news first, sisters, or the bad news?"

Merab circled the table, ladling pease porridge into their trenchers. "What does the message say?"

"The Thane of Cawdor has been executed for treason."

The ladle clattered against the pot. "That means . . ."

"Exactly," said Zipporah. "And King Duncan is coming to Castle Inverness *tonight.*"

"But we haven't had time to prepare the potion with the power of persuasion," worried Dymphna, her face once again clear and pink owing to the belated application of a paste made of lentils, blue-green algae, and flaxseed.

Zipporah shoved her porridge to one side. "I know. And the lady requires more of the sleeping potion, as well." She rose from her chair and crossed to the shelf, where she rummaged through the clutter of flasks, vials, and bottles assembled there. One by one, she lifted the stoppers and sniffed. "Ah, here it is." She set the flask aside. "Now," she said, "we've no time to lose! Quickly, Dymphna! Where did you put the recipe?"

In less time than it took to churn butter, the Weird sisters stood, once again, around a bubbling cauldron. "Double Bubble, spoil the hubble . . ." Zipporah read from the parchment Dymphna had produced.

Merab peered cautiously into the cauldron. "It's pink," she said in a worried voice. She dipped in an experimental finger. "And sticky."

Zipporah shook her head. "That's not right. It should be brown." She squinted suspiciously at the parchment, its edges brown and curling, the writing dense and crabbed. She held the parchment close to her nose, then at arm's length before sending an accusing glance in Dymphna's direction. "Are you sure this is the potion with the power of persuasion, sister?"

Dymphna nodded. "Would you like *me* to read it?"

Zipporah blinked twice, shrugged, then thrust the parchment toward Dymphna, "Very well. You read. I'll stir." She grasped the wooden paddle with both hands and began stirring, her whole body swaying rhythmically with each turn of the paddle.

> *Double, double, toil and trouble,*
> *Fire burn and cauldron bubble,*

read Dymphna.

> *Fillet of a fenny snake,*
> *In the cauldron boil and bake.*

Dymphna nodded at Merab, who selected a serpentine object from the ingredients laid out on the table in front of her and tossed it into the pot.

As the snake sank, Merab studied the pink mixture with rising panic. Surely it wouldn't make any difference? What could it matter that she'd collected that snake from the woods and not from the fen?

"Merab!" She was suddenly aware that Zipporah was shouting at her.

Merab returned her attention to her task. As Zipporah stirred and Dymphna chanted, Merab tossed the ingredients, as Dymphna called for them, one by one into the pot.

> *Eye of newt . . .*

Merab's heart began to hammer against her ribs.

> *And toe of frog.*
> *Wool of bat,*
> *And tongue of dog.*

Merab was breathing so rapidly she felt light-headed. Tongue of dog! O gods and goddesses! She hadn't been able to bring herself to do it. The mongrel had been brown and white, its tail wagging joyously, its nose wet and black against her cheek. Merab reached for a shriveled strip of dried venison and tossed it into the pot instead.

Zipporah stirred more vigorously, her heels rising in and out of her shoes. "Now!" she cried.

> *Double double, toil and trouble,*
> *Fire burn and cauldron bubble,*

the three sisters chanted in unison.

> *Scale of dragon, tooth of wolf,*

Dymphna continued.

> *Witches mummy, maw and gulf*
> *Of the ravin'd salt-sea shark,*
> *Root of hemlock digg'd i' the dark . . .*

Swift as raindrops flying before the wind, the magic words tumbled from Dymphna's mouth, and just as quickly, Merab tossed the ingredients, one after the other, into the pot. The mixture boiled thick and slimy—bubbles formed, swelled, and erupted on the surface of the sludge like breakfast porridge. As Merab watched, the porridge in her own stomach churning, the mixture gradually changed from pink to lavender, from lavender to gray, from gray to a dull brown. The storm raging in her stomach began to subside.

Zipporah blessed the mixture with a final counterclockwise stir. A pale finger of bluish smoke drifted toward the ceiling and swirled around the tied bundles of herbs drying in the rafters. "There! That should do it."

Merab stepped back from the cauldron with relief. "I'm curious about something, Zipporah. Back there on the heath. Why did you talk in riddles? Why didn't you tell Macbeth straight out that he'd be King?"

Using a wooden spoon, Zipporah ladled the potion into an earthenware jar that the Queen's messenger would soon take to the castle kitchens. "Men like conundrums," she explained. "It gives them something to puzzle over. If Lord Macbeth didn't have to figure some of it out for himself, no one could convince him we'd given him his money's worth."

It was quiet in the woodland cottage for the next several weeks. While Zipporah tended the garden—plucking weeds, loosening the dirt around the roots of the parsnips and carrots, picking bugs off the leaves of the lettuce plants—Merab brewed up a batch of comfrey for the butcher's bronchitis and a love potion for the tavern-keeper, whose wife had run away with the handsome, young ironmonger. Dymphna studiously copied recipes into her book.

On the second day of the third week, the sisters had just settled down for a dinner of roast capon and peas, when a sudden commotion on the roof of the cottage made them lay down their knives and look up at each other in alarm. A clatter like hail erupted from the hearth and smoke blew backwards down the chimney, scattering ashes in every direction.

Suddenly Hecate stood solid as a tree before them. From neck to ankles, the Mistress of the Moon was swathed in diaphanous silver robes; a cape spun of cobwebs shimmered from her shoulders. In contrast, her face was flushed with rage and her mouth worked up and down soundlessly.

Merab sprang to her feet, gingerly brushing a glowing cinder from her skirt. "Hecate! Why do you look so angry?"

Hecate shrugged out of her cape, letting it drift to the floor, where it settled in a glistening pool at her feet. "Haven't I good reason, you brazen hussies?" she hissed.

Zipporah rose from her chair, elbowed Merab out of her way, and stood before the enraged goddess. "I'm sure we don't have the slightest idea what you're talking about, Madam."

Hecate leaned forward, sputtering hellfire. "How *dare* you work spells on behalf of that man without consulting me?" Her eyes, cold as winter ice, locked with Zipporah's. "Amateurs! Bumbling amateurs! Do you know what you've done?"

Merab shook her head, eyes downcast, as Hecate's icy gaze settled on her.

"Do you?" Hecate shouted at Dymphna.

Dymphna recoiled.

Hecate jabbed a long, crooked finger in the direction of Dymphna's up-turned nose. "What on earth did you tell the man? What did you tell Macbeth?"

"Please, Madam. Sit." With the toe of her shoe, Zipporah pushed a stool cautiously in Hecate's direction. Hecate considered it for a moment, then reining in her temper like a team of wild horses, she swallowed her anger and sat down with a flump.

"We told him he'd be King," Zipporah confessed. "We thought we'd give him something to think about until we had time to prepare the potion that would actually make it happen."

Hecate's voice dripped with sarcasm. "Apparently the man and his lady wife were unwilling to wait."

"What?" Merab's hands flew to her cheeks, her mouth yawning wide.

Hecate nodded gravely. "Macbeth murdered King Duncan that very night."

Dymphna collapsed heavily on the hearth, her hands pressed between her knees. "Surely you're mistaken! Lord Macbeth a murderer? But he seemed so good-natured!"

"No mistake," said Hecate. "And they wasted little time moving their household from Inverness to the royal castle at Dunsinane."

"But what about King Duncan's bodyguards?" Merab wondered.

"Suspicion fell on them at first, of course," Hecate explained, "especially when they were found smeared with blood, sleeping with a bloody dagger between them."

"Sleeping?" Merab cried. "That makes no sense at all. Why wouldn't they have flown after committing so vile a deed?"

"They were locked—all unknowing—in Morpheus's arms." Hecate reached inside her purse and withdrew a familiar, pear-shaped object. "I discovered this flask near their cots."

Merab plucked the familiar flask from Hecate's hands, removed the cork, stared at the milky residue coating the bottom, and sniffed. She turned toward Zipporah, one eyebrow raised in surprise. "This is the sleeping draught we prepared for Lady Macbeth!"

Hecate leaned forward. "I rather thought so."

"So the Lady drugged the guards and murdered the King while they slept?"

"Not the Lady. Lord Macbeth himself."

Dymphna sprang to her feet. She had found her tongue at last. "But what of the other portion we prepared for the Lady?"

Hecate's eyebrows knit in puzzlement. "What other potion?"

"Our plan was bloodless, Madam, and twofold. Lady Macbeth was to introduce the potion into the mussel broth to be served at the banquet. It would bewitch King Duncan with an overwhelming desire to join his son in England. Then the nobles, equally enchanted and twice as fickle, would declare Macbeth King."

Zipporah groaned. "We sent complete instructions! Oh, why didn't Lady Macbeth use the potion? Why didn't she give it a chance to work?"

Hecate's words were blunt. "Maybe she did. Perhaps the fault lay in the potion."

Thinking about her secret economies, Merab felt herself shrinking inside her skin. Soon she would be as tiny as the field mouse that sometimes winked at her from the darkened corner near the hearth. If only she hadn't been so selfish! If she had it to do all over again, she'd pay whatever it cost for the newt eyes, she'd even sail to Constantinople and slice the nose off Sultan Ala-ud-din-Kaikobad himself.

"But we followed the formula," Dymphna protested. "Exactly."

Hecate's voice softened. "Yet something went quite wrong at the banquet, I fear. Lord Macbeth had a fever on the brain. He had visions of bloody heads. He saw Banquo's ghost. On and on he raved, until Lady Macbeth sent the guests home and hustled her husband, raving still, to his bedchamber."

"Perhaps he was drunk," Merab suggested.

"Besides," Zipporah added, "Banquo's not dead. We saw him ourselves not long ago. With Lord Macbeth. On the heath."

"Oh, Banquo's quite, quite dead." Hecate cast her eyes heavenward. "I passed his blameless soul as it soared over the moon, heading towards the stars."

"Who . . . ?" Dymphna's eyes grew wide.

"Three thugs, his spirit told me. Hired by Macbeth."

Zipporah bowed her head. "Macbeth is obsessed, 'tis certain, twisted by ambition. Even now, with the kingship firmly in his grasp, he rages on." She looked up. "Oh, Hecate! Does his lust know no bounds?"

"I must lay that responsibility at your feet, Zipporah. What did you put into that potion? Insane root?"

Merab stepped between Hecate and her older sister. "No potion's to blame, Madam. We told Banquo he would beget kings."

"And for that, he died," Dymphna whimpered.

Zipporah straightened. "Where's Macbeth now?"

"Pursuing Macduff," Hecate informed them.

"But surely I heard that Macduff is safely away with Malcolm in England?"

Hecate looked grave. "No one, I fear, is safe from Macbeth's evil designs and enterprises. But rest easy," she continued. "I believe I've found the solution. Remember the old sow's blood charm?" She grinned. "I used it to conjure up some apparitions for our impatient King. First a talking head. Then a bloody child. 'None of woman born shall harm Macbeth,' I bid the child say." She cackled, her mouth wide, revealing black and pointed teeth. "I'm particularly proud of that riddle."

"*All* men are born of woman," Dymphna insisted.

Hecate looked amused. "So it would seem."

Dymphna stared at the rafters for a moment, then shrugged and pointed at her sister. "Zipporah's good at riddles."

Hecate considered this information with a satisfied expression on her face. "Try this one, then: 'Macbeth shall never vanquished be until Great Birnam wood to high Dunsinane hill shall come against him.' "

The furrows deepened in Dymphna's brow. "How could a wood remove to the top of a hill?"

Zipporah spoke at last. "It can't, of course. That's what makes it so brilliant. With Macbeth secure in his kingship, the carnage should cease."

Dymphna clapped her hands. "Moon and stars be praised! What you said about Macduff troubled me greatly for it's not only he who's endangered, but his wife and precious children, too."

Hecate smiled modestly, then waved an impatient hand. "Speaking of danger, why didn't you answer my question? What *did* you put into that potion?"

Dymphna plucked the parchment from an earthenware pot where she had stored it, unrolled the document, and recited the ingredients, one by one, as her finger traced a path down the page. "Adder's fork, blind-worm's sting, lizard's let, howlet's wing, goat gall, yew . . ." When she had finished, she turned to Hecate. "Well?"

"It sounds right." Hecate sat in silence for a moment, thinking. "But in truth, I'm puzzled, because the insanity didn't stop with the King. Now it's Lady Macbeth who's gone stark-staring mad. Everybody's talking about it. The torches are always lit in the castle. She walks in her sleep. And lately I've heard reports of compulsive hand-washing." Hecate slid off the stool and hovered before them, her feet floating a hand's breadth above the floor. "I don't know what went wrong, but it's up to me, as usual, to set things right." Her eyes blazed. "Do you have any of that potion left?"

Zipporah nodded. "In the cupboard. In the large crock."

Hecate picked up the crock with both hands, crossed to the hearth, and emptied its contents into the cauldron. She glared at Merab. "Now, mistress, the rest of your stores!"

"Oh, no!" Merab wailed.

Hecate was firm. "It's the only way." While she stood to one side, heckling and prodding, the sisters reluctantly emptied all their potions, tonics, elixirs, tinctures, and physics, each bolus and pill, every ointment, syrup, and lotion, into the iron cauldron. Once, Hecate caught Dymphna's hand just as it disappeared into her pocket with a vial of syrup extracted from eastern poppies. "I said *everything*!" and Dymphna watched, long-faced, as the pain remedy joined its brethren in the pot, soon swirling with a malignant, purplish-green sludge.

Zipporah's eyes lingered on her jars, flasks, flagons, bottles, boxes, and bowls, all empty, lined up on the tabletop. "I think your measures excessive, Madam."

Hecate gathered up her gossamer cloak and, with a flourish, settled the shimmering fabric over her shoulders. She floated toward the door. "Next time perhaps you'll consult me before going off with your bows half-strung. Now," she commanded, pointing to the cauldron, "dump it—*all* of it—into the loch."

"Loch Ashie?" The mixture stared up at Merab like a malevolent blob and she vowed she'd never bathe in the clear, cool waters of Loch Ashie again.

"No, fool. Loch Ness." And with a final stab of her finger, Hecate vanished.

"Come!" Zipporah ordered. "Let's get this over with before that wretched hag returns. Dymphna, you fetch the wheelbarrow."

Merab already had her arms around the belly of the cauldron at its widest part. "Umph!" she grunted. "I can't do this by myself."

Zipporah helped Merab inch the cauldron across the floor of beaten earth toward the waiting wheelbarrow. "When I count to three, lift," Zipporah instructed. She adjusted her grip, took a deep breath—*one, two, three!*

"Oh!" shouted Merab, staggering under the sudden weight. She watched helplessly as the liquid swirled dangerously, reared over the lip of the cauldron with tentacle-like fingers, and sloshed, wet and slightly warm, all over her clothing. "Oh, dear," she exclaimed, but she was too busy to do anything but ignore it. Swearing and grunting, the women muscled the cauldron into the wheelbarrow, then stepped back, arms tingling with fatigue, to catch their breath.

Zipporah suddenly gasped. "Look, Merab! Look at your gown!"

Merab stared. Where once she had worn plain, gray homespun, scorched with pinholes and decorated with flecks of soil and food, her gown was now fine and white, spotless as a field of high mountain snow. "My spots!" she whooped. "They're gone!"

Dymphna smiled at Zipporah slyly. "I suppose you'll be wanting me to write this formula down, won't you, sister?" With her thumb and index finger, she penned an imaginary note against the cloudless blue sky. "Receipt for Spot Remover."

"What I want," Zipporah grumbled, "is to consign every drop of this loathsome liquid to the bottom of Loch Ness. Then, I plan to take up something safe, like midwifery, and forget we ever heard of the King and Queen of Dunsinane."

Merab's brow knit in puzzlement. "But I don't understand. If Macbeth . . ."

Zipporah pressed a finger, hard, against her sister's lips. "It's bad luck to say his name! I forbid it. From henceforth whenever we refer to that man, if we refer to him at all, it will be as 'that Scottish King.' "

She bent her knees, lifted the handles of the wheelbarrow, and with Dymphna straggling behind, rolled it down the path, through the garden, past the hives and into the wood. With the cat weaving about her ankles, Merab watched until Zipporah's silver head and Dymphna's copper one were lost among the shimmer of the early summer leaves. Merab gazed down in wonder at the pristine landscape of her gown. "Too bad it isn't blue," she said to the cat. And she went inside to consult the *Herbarium* to see what she could do about that.

Squinting at Death

BY EDWARD MARSTON

Edward Marston is the prolific author of plays, short stories, and novels, with his historical mystery *The Roaring Boy* being nominated for the Edgar Award for best novel in 1995. He is currently writing two series, one featuring Nicholas Bracewell, a stage manager for an acting company in Elizabethan England, the other with Ralph Delchard and Gervase Bret, two men who travel England investigating land claims in the eleventh century. His latest novel is *The Repentant Rake,* another mystery, set in Restoration England. A former chairman of the Crime Writer's Association in the United Kingdom, he lives in rural Kent, England.

Where is the number of our English dead?
(Herald shows him another paper)
Edward the Duke of York, the Earl of Suffolk,
Sir Richard Ketly, Davy Gam esquire:
None else of name; and of all other men
But five and twenty.
—THE LIFE OF KING HENRY THE FIFTH, ACT IV, SCENE 8

The battle was mercifully short but its actual progress was mercilessly brutal. Arrows, swords, daggers, lances, stakes, and clubs killed or maimed indiscriminately. Dead and dying men littered the muddy field of Agincourt, their blood intermingling with that of the countless horses that had been wounded or slaughtered. It was a scene of utter carnage, and it was difficult to see how such an accurate list of the deceased could be made so soon after the conflict. One thing was certain. It was a signal victory for King Henry and his army. France had suffered a defeat even more crushing than those of Crecy and Poitiers.

Fluellen listened to the record of enemy casualties with pride and exultation. The Welsh captain had been at the heart of the fighting, wielding his sword in the service of an English king and sending several Frenchmen to their Maker before their time. Fluellen was astonished at what he heard. Could they really have accounted for ten thousand of the enemy? That was the number announced by King Henry and it was buttressed by the news that the fifteen hundred prisoners included Charles, Duke of Orleans, nephew to the French King, Jean, Duke of Bourbon, and the redoubtable Jean Boucicaut, Marshall of France. Hopelessly outnumbered, the English army had somehow achieved a miracle. Like everyone else who had fought with King Henry, the Welsh captain was entitled to feel elated. The day was theirs.

But Fluellen's joy was tempered with concern. A Welsh name had jumped out at him from the abbreviated list of English dead. Davy Gam. Davy the Squint. Or to give him his full name, Dafydd ap Llywelyn ap Hywel from Breconshire, a veteran soldier and a close friend to Fluellen. The two men had grown up together. Other friends had fallen in the heat of battle but it was the death of Davy Gam that really saddened him. War was cruel. It gave him no time to bid farewell to a loved companion. When occasion served, Fluellen seized the opportunity to take King Henry aside.

"I crave a word with Your Majesty."

"As many as you wish, Captain Fluellen," said the King. "Your deeds at Agincourt have earned my deepest thanks and admiration."

Fluellen gave a shrug. "God chose to spare me. Others were not so fortunate."

"I grieve for all our casualties."

"So do I, Your Majesty, but I mourn for one man in particular."

"I think I can guess his name—Davy Gam."

"Is he really dead?"

"I fear so," confirmed the King, "but he died with honor. He was struck down near to the place where I was striving with the enemy myself. As he lay bleeding, I was able to reward him for his valor by touching him on both shoulders with my sword and creating him a knight. He may have followed me as Davy Gam Esquire but he quit this world as Sir Dafydd ap Llywelyn ap Hywel."

"His family will be consoled by that news."

"Bear it to them, Captain Fluellen."

"I will, Your Majesty," said the other. "But you say that you were nearby when he was mortally wounded. Did you see whose weapon inflicted death on him?"

The King shook his head. "I was too busy trying to protect my brother and myself. Thus it stood. The Duke of Alençon led a charge with fresh men against a part of the field where my brother, Humphrey, Duke of Gloucester, was embroiled with the men of Marle and Fauquemberghes. A knife thrust pierced Humphrey's belly beneath his cuirass and he fell to the ground. As soon as report of this was brought to me, I hastened to my brother's side with a bodyguard of archers and yeoman, men like Davy Gam and his son-in-law, Richard Vaughan of Bredwardine. Nobody fights as fiercely as the Welsh when they are in a tight situation."

"I can bear witness to that."

"My bodyguard shot and clubbed a pathway for me until I reached my brother. The fighting continued unabated all around me. It was only when we had subdued the French that I was able to take stock of our losses." The King heaved a sigh. "That was when I saw the gallant Davy Gam, lying in the arms of his page."

It was all the detail that Fluellen got. King Henry went off with his escort to walk the rain-soaked battlefield and see for himself the true extent of God's benevolence towards his army. His men did not rest. They spent the remainder of the day stripping clothes and armor from the corpses, searching for articles of value and confiscating discarded weaponry. Rings, brooches, coins, gold ornaments, and jeweled daggers were snatched uncaringly from the dead by looters. Any Frenchmen found alive in ditches or other hiding places were summarily killed and robbed. Loose horses were rounded up. Plunder was rampant.

Fluellen took no part in it. While most soldiers grabbed all that they could carry, he searched among the piles of bodies for a friend. Davy Gam was not easy to find. At the point where he fell, fighting had been particularly fierce and dozens of corpses lay haphazardly on the ground. All had met violent ends. Many were hideously mutilated, some had lost limbs in combat. When he eventually picked out his friend, Fluellen breathed a sigh of relief. Not only had Davy Gam been spared the butchery handed out to others, his body had not yet been reached by looters. He lay on his back with a serene expression on his face. The familiar black patch covered one eye. He no longer squinted at the world through the other. Fluellen knelt respectfully beside him and offered up a silent prayer for the salvation of his soul.

He examined the body more carefully, noting the wounds in the neck and the legs. They had bled profusely but had hardly been enough in themselves to kill so powerful a warrior as Davy Gam. There had to be a more serious injury somewhere. Fluellen was gentle but firm, putting hands under his friend so that he could roll him slowly over. Davy Gam was not heavily armored. His torso was protected by a nailed jerkin of filled leather over a mailed shirt and a bascinet warded off any glancing blows to the head. Sword and dagger were his preferred form of defense. He had none of the expensive plate armor worn by the King, lords, and knights. While they had been encased in heavy, cumbersome metal suits, he had valued freedom of movement. It had been his undoing. Fluellen was shocked by what he saw. Davy Gam had been stabbed in the back. A dagger had been worked in under his jerkin and sunk to the hilt with vicious force. It took an effort on Fluellen's part to extract the weapon. An even greater shock awaited him. It was no French dagger, thrust hard into the Welshman's back while he grappled with an enemy. The weapon was of English design. Davy Gam had not, it seemed, been killed in combat with a Frenchman.

He had been murdered by one of his fellows.

While plunder and celebration continued throughout that October evening, Fluellen was engaged in a hunt for the man who had killed his friend. The dagger was a vital clue. It was a long-bladed weapon with an elaborate handle into which the letter "P" had been carved. Since the hapless Davy Gam had died in the arms of his page, Fluellen first sought out Madog, the loyal young man who had fought beside his master. When he found the page shivering beside a campfire, he did not at first recognize him. Madog had been bruised and bloodied, the once-handsome face now scarred for life. One arm was in a sling. A wound in the thigh was heavily strapped. He looked close to exhaustion.

Fluellen bent over to peer more closely at him. He spoke in Welsh.

"Is that you, Madog?" he asked.

"What's left of me," replied the page. "I'll have painful souvenirs of Agincourt."

"None more painful than the memory of Davy Gam's death, look you."

"No, Captain Fluellen. That was a tragedy. To fight so bravely and then to be denied the privilege of sharing in the victory. It was heartbreaking."

Fluellen sat beside him. "Who actually killed Davy?"

"Some nameless Frenchman."

"Did you *see* the fatal blow delivered?"

Madog shook his head. "I was too busy fighting for my own life, Captain Fluellen. Then I heard this terrible cry from my master. By the time I struggled across to him, he had collapsed to his knees in a pool of blood. King Henry was close by."

"So I hear. He knighted Dafydd on the spot."

"Yes," said Madog sadly. "No sooner had he done that than my master died. I had no chance to carry him from the field. I had to defend myself, and as you see, I came off worst. When I'm recovered, I'll go in search of the body."

"There's no need," said Fluellen, "I've already found it." He produced the dagger for inspection. "Have you ever seen this before?"

"No, I haven't. Where did you get it?"

"I pulled it out of Davy Gam's back."

Madog shuddered. "Is this what killed him? No wonder he cried out."

"It was a cry of horror, not of pain. He was betrayed, Madog. Look at the dagger. No Frenchman would carry an English weapon like that. Davy Gam was murdered by someone in our army."

"Never!"

"It's not only a dreadful crime," said Fluellen, puce with anger, " 'tis expressly against the disciplines of war."

"Who could have done such a thing?" wondered Madog, dazed by the news.

"That's what you must tell me."

"How, Fluellen?"

"You may not have seen the murder but you were not far away when it happened. Who else was nearby? What other members of the King's bodyguard were close to Dafydd when you went across to him?"

"I didn't take much notice."

"You must have seen *someone*, Madog."

"Well, yes, I suppose I did. Let me think," said the page, face puckered with concentration as he teased out the names. "Iestyn Morgan must have been there. And I think I caught sight of Rhys Pugh. The only other person I can think of is Owain ap Meredyth ap Tydier."

"Nobody else?"

"I'm afraid not, Fluellen."

"But this is an *English* dagger," emphasized Fluellen, holding up the weapon. "That means an English hand was, in all probability, holding it. A Welsh hero was felled by English treachery. Was there no English soldier next to Dafydd?"

"Only one that I recall."

"Who was he?"

"That bragging knave who struts like a turkey-cock."

"Pistol?"

"That's the man, Captain Fluellen."

"Indeed, it is," said the other, vengefully. "I know the rogue well. Look at this letter carved in the dagger's handle. "P" is for Pistol just as clearly as "M" is for murderer. I'll match these initials to that scurvy, lousy, beggarly heap of ordure and call him to account. Davy Gam's death must be paid for in full."

Pistol was in his element. Having survived the battle, he had been among the first to search for plunder and was weighed down with booty stolen from French corpses. Pistol had hidden his cowardice behind a loud voice and a threatening manner. Reasoning that the largest bodyguard would belong to the King, he had stayed, for the sake of safety, close to Henry in the field and traded only a few blows with the enemy. Laden down with money, weapons, and assorted pieces of armor, he walked along with a jaunty stride and sang aloud. When he was suddenly confronted by a Welsh captain, he showed no fear.

"Out of my way, base Trojan!" he demanded.

"God pless you, Ancient Pistol," said Fluellen with mock deference.

"Ha! Art thou bedlam?"

"I desire a word with you, sir."

"Not for Cadwallader and all his goats."

"Do you remember my kinsman, Davy Gam?"

"What?" said Pistol contemptuously. "That one-eyed madman who spoke with a squint? Yes, I recall the knave. I'd know that ugly Welsh face of his anywhere."

"Then why did you stab him in the back?" yelled Fluellen, grabbing him by the throat and holding up the dagger. "If you meant to kill him, why not have the courage to look him in his one remaining eye while you were doing it?"

"Kill him?" gasped Pistol. "I killed nobody, you leek-eating loon!"

"This dagger has your initial on it."

Pistol could hardly breathe. "That doesn't mean that it's mine," he croaked. "I've never possessed a dagger as fine as that. I swear it!"

"No," said Fluellen, pushing him to the ground and forcing him to drop his stolen weapons. "What are these, you lying knave? There are three French daggers here worth twice as much as the one I hold."

"Presents for some friends."

"Whose backs are you going to sink these into?"

"Nobody's," said Pistol, cowering before him. "Spare me, Captain Fluellen. I'm no wild Frenchman. I fought on your side in the battle."

"Close to Davy Gam."

"He sought protection alongside a veteran soldier like me."

"A veteran liar, you mean!" exploded Fluellen, kicking him hard. "A veteran cheat, coward, braggart, traitor, and murderer. You stabbed Davy Gam in the back."

"As God's my witness, I didn't."

"Tell the truth for once in your life."

"That's what I am doing."

"Is it?" said Fluellen, drawing his sword to hold the point at Pistol's throat. "Confess, you railing villain, or I'll slice you up and feed your entrails to the birds."

"No, no!" begged Pistol, squirming on the ground. "Take my money, good Captain Fluellen. Take my loot. Take my clothes. Take my hair, if you wish, but leave me my entrails. We've been close friends these many years, and truly, sir, I'd not be parted from them."

"Speak honestly or prepare to die!"

"All hell will stir for this."

"I'll send you off to Satan with your tongue cut out."

"Take pity on me!" implored Pistol as the sword pricked his throat. "I've lost every friend I have and would not lose the one I love most, namely, my poor innocent self. Jack Falstaff died before we left England. Bardolph was hanged for some trifling offense, and our boy was killed when the French attacked our baggage train."

"Kill the poys and the luggage!" yelled Fluellen. "That was shameful. It was directly against the laws of arms."

"That was why I fought so hard against the villains. Why should I murder a fellow-soldier when there were so many French vipers to excommunicate from the battlefield? Spare me, good sir," he pleaded. "I may have mocked Davy Gam for his squint but I praise him for his bravery. When last I saw him, he was cutting a path through the enemy like a mower with a scythe."

Fluellen drew back his sword. "That sounds like Dafydd."

"I never got within five yards of him. Truly, I didn't. And even if I had," said Pistol, sitting up and spreading his arms, "I could not have stabbed him with that dagger. My only weapon was a bent sword I found at Harfleur."

"Then why does the dagger have your initial on it?"

"Ask Peter. Ask Paul. Ask Philip. Ask every Percy in our arm how his initial came to be inscribed on the weapon. You'll have hundreds to choose from. Why pick on me when there are so many others whose name begins with the fateful letter?"

"Because you're a cowardly, counterfeit cutpurse who hates the Welsh."

"Why, no, Captain Fluellen," said Pistol, beaming. "I revel in your company."

"You do nothing but pour scorn on us," retorted the other, angrily. "Only yesterday, you sneered at our leeks and called me a mountain-squire to my face."

" 'Twas all done in good humor."

"Is that how you killed Davy Gam? In good humor?"

"No, no!" bleated Pistol as the sword jabbed at him again. "I never touched him. It's you who have the squint now, my friend. You're looking at the wrong man."

"Am I?"

"On my word of honor."

"That's worthless."

"I swear that I did not murder your valiant countryman. And what is more, I'll prove it in the best way possible."

"How's that?"

Still sitting on the ground, Pistol did his best to strike a pose.

"By helping you to find the *real* killer," he declared.

Madog had mentioned three other people he had seen in the vicinity of Davy Gam during the battle. Fluellen decided to speak to each one of them. Having hidden his stolen armor in some bushes, Pistol trailed in his wake. Of the three men named by Davy Gam's page, one ruled himself out immediately. Iestyn Morgan had perished from wounds received in the first French charge. That left Rhys Pugh and Owain ap Meredyth ap Tydir. When Fluellen tracked down the first of them, he spoke to him in Welsh.

"A word in your ear, Rhys," he said.

"Where else are you going to speak it, Fluellen?" replied the other with a chuckle. "In my mouth? Up my arse?"

"This is no time for vulgarity. I want to talk to you about Davy Gam."

Pugh's face darkened. "Aye, poor man. Death finally closed his other eye."

"This is the weapon that killed him."

Fluellen handed him the dagger and watched him carefully as he examined it. Rhys Pugh was a big, powerful man with a black beard that was spattered with blood.

"An English dagger," he observed gruffly.

"Does it belong to you?"

"No, Fluellen. This 'P' on the handle doesn't stand for Pugh, I can assure you of that. Besides, why would I want to stab Davy Gam? We were fellows."

"That wasn't always the case."

Pugh nodded soulfully. "I confess it freely. We fought against each other in the past but we were indentured to fight beside each other this time. I was proud to call Davy Gam my fellow. He was a true soldier."

"You were close to him when he fell."

"That may be, Fluellen, but I was even closer to the two Frenchmen who were trying to kill me. I heard Davy cry out and wish I could have gone to his aid. Those two Frenchmen had other ideas. It took me an age to beat them off."

Fluellen could see that he was telling the truth. Rhys Pugh was not the assassin. He would be more likely to hack a man to death than to dispatch him with a sly dagger. Taking the weapon from him, Fluellen slipped it into his belt.

"Did you see anyone close to Davy?" he asked.

"Dozens of people, pressed all around him."

"Can you give me some names?"

"No," said Pugh, rubbing his beard. "In the middle of a battle, you don't stop to take a roll call of everyone nearby. I caught sight of Madog, his page, that I do remember. And I think that Iestyn Morgan was there somewhere. The only other person I remember was that other page."

"Who was he?"

"Owain ap Meredyth ap Tydir."

When his companion strode quickly away, Pistol had a job to keep up with him.

"What did he say, Captain Fluellen?" he asked.

"It wasn't him."

"I didn't understand a word of your heathen language."

"Welsh is an older and finer tongue than the one you speak."

"I could smell the leeks on his breath."

"Don't ridicule my nation," warned Fluellen, turning to him, "or I'll send you off to have a private conversation with Davy Gam."

Pistol quivered. "I'd prefer to stay alive, if it's all the same to you."

"Then hold your peace, you whoreson rogue!"

"I'll be as silent as the grave."

Owain ap Meredyth ap Tydir was a page in the King's household. Having acquitted himself well on the battlefield, he was resting with some friends in the shadow of a tree. Fluellen detached him so that he could speak to him in private. Pistol stayed within earshot but was bewildered when they lapsed into their native language. Owain was a personable young man, dark, well built, and well featured. He was momentarily saddened by the mention of Davy Gam's death but expressed no personal grief.

Fluellen was roused. "Aren't you sorry that he was killed?"

"I'm sorry that anyone from our army fell in battle," said Owain easily.

"But Davy Gam was your countryman!"

"Others who died also came from Wales."

"I expected more anguish from you."

"That will come at a later date, Captain Fluellen. I am still exulting in our victory now, as you should be. I have a personal triumph to celebrate as well," he boasted. "In recognition of my deeds at Agincourt, I've been promoted to the ranks of the Squires of the Body to the King. What do you think of that?"

"Don't look to me for congratulation," said Fluellen with vehemence. "While you glory in your own achievement, Davy Gam lies on the battlefield, squinting up to heaven. And it was no enemy weapon that killed him," he added, brandishing the dagger. "It was this, Owain. Someone thrust it into Davy's back. Was it you?"

"No!" denied the other.

"Are you sure?"

"Absolutely sure. I was on the same side as Davy Gam."

"So was his killer. This dagger was the work of an English craftsman."

"Then look for an English assassin," said Owain with indignation. "I'd not use a dagger like that. All my weaponry was made in my native Anglesey. Don't accuse me of this murder, if that's what it was."

"What else could it be?"

"Who knows? It's not my concern."

"Don't you *care* about Davy Gam?"

"Of course. But he was only one of thousands who fell today."

Fluellen was so enraged by his indifference that he wanted to strike the man. Owain turned away from him to walk back to his friends. He then paused and swung round again, fingers stroking his chin in meditation.

"I was not the only person close to Davy Gam," he said.

"I know. I've spoken to the others."

"To his page, Madog?"

"Yes."

"What about Iestyn Morgan?"

"He's dead," said Fluellen tartly. "Not that you'd be upset to hear that."

"That leaves Rhys Pugh."

"I've just questioned him."

"Only one more remains, then."

Fluellen's ears pricked up. "One more?"

"Yes," said Owain, thoughtfully. "I only had the merest glimpse of him, mark you, so I can't be certain of what I saw. But I had the impression that the person who got near enough to Davy Gam to see his squint was Rhodri ap Iorwerth."

Pistol had seen enough. When the bustling Fluellen tried to set off again, Pistol blocked his path and held up an appeasing hand.

"One moment, Captain Fluellen."

"Stand aside, you cur!"

"But I'm here to help you," said Pistol, "and I can't do that if you insist on talking in that foul language of yours. I take it that this young friend of yours was not the killer."

"He was not."

"But he gave you the name of another suspect."

"I'm on my way to question him right now."

"Let me hold the interrogation for you," volunteered Pistol.

"You?"

"Yes, Captain Fluellen. You are too direct in your examination. When you show them the dagger that killed Davy Gam, you give them time to invent their excuses. Where Welsh bluntness fails, English cunning may succeed."

Fluellen inflated his chest. "Nobody is more guileful than a Celt."

"We'll see about that."

"Begone, you pedlar's excrement!"

"Step on me and I'll stick to your shoe forever."

"I need to speak to Rhodri ap Iorwerth."

"Is that his name?" said Pistol. "Then hear my device. Give me the dagger and let me try my wiles on him. Stand off and watch us in secret. If he be innocent, you'll know it soon enough. If he be guilty, good Captain, I'll wager every penny I own that I'll tease out the proof of his guilt. Will this content you?"

"No, you dolt."

"Even a dolt can do a good deed sometimes."

Fluellen pondered. His own investigation had so far borne little fruit. The longer it was taking, the more frustrated he became. Pistol had a point. He had been too hasty to confront the others with the evidence of the dagger. Whoever killed Davy Gam would have an alibi and it would be readily produced when he saw the Welsh captain bearing down on him. If a different method of questioning could be employed, the only thing that could be lost was a little time.

"Very well," he said at length.

"First, we must trade."

"Find me the killer and I'll spare your stinking hide."

"I want more than that, Captain Fluellen," said Pistol. "Give me your word that you'll not beat me about my pate with a leek on Saint Davy's Day."

"I'm more likely to stuff it down your lying throat."

"I need your promise."

"Then you have it," said Fluellen testily. "Saint Davy's Day lies a long way off. The only Davy I'm interested in now is Davy Gam. The patron saint of revenge."

Rhodri ap Iorwerth was a short, stocky, vigorous man in his thirties with bow legs. He was sitting on a tree stump and chatting happily with two friends about their respective deeds in the battle. Glad to be alive, they were still surprised at their victory against such overwhelming odds. Fluellen approached furtively with Pistol until they reached the cover of some bushes.

"Which one is Rhodri?" whispered Pistol.

"The one in the middle."

"A wild-eyed rogue, if ever I saw one."

"With a hot temper," cautioned Fluellen. "Take care what you say."

"Watch and listen, good Captain."

"What will you do?"

"Teach you how to catch a Welsh fish with the right bait."

Leaving him concealed in the bushes, Pistol sauntered across to the three men. Tucked in his belt with the English dagger were the three French ones he had stolen from their dead owners. Pistol gave an elaborate bow.

"Good even, good sirs," he said. "Is there anyone here who speaks English? From the sound of your crucified consonants, you must be talking in Welsh."

"Mind your manners, you English pig," sneered Rhodri, "or we'll crucify your own consonants and disembowel your vowels."

"But I come as a friend."

"Then depart just as swiftly."

"Are you not interested in what I have to sell?" asked Pistol, plucking one of the French daggers from his belt. "Look here. This once belonged to a man of high degree, as you may see from the jeweled handle and fine workmanship. It's too precious an object for me but veterans like yourselves might prize such an object."

"What are you asking for it?" said one of the men.

"Make me an offer."

"Let me inspect it more closely first."

"Here," said Pistol, handing it over and taking a second weapon from his belt. "And here's its brother, made by the same craftsman, I daresay. Put them side by side and you can hardly tell them apart."

The man took the second dagger as well. "Where did you get them?"

"He filched them from corpses," said Rhodri.

"I found them lying on the ground, sir, and that's not theft. It's good fortune." He bared his teeth in a lopsided grin. "I've always been lucky."

"What's your name?"

"Pistol."

Rhodri laughed. "Do you hear that? This long streak of English piss is called Pistol. I doubt if he can fire a good fart, let alone a lead ball." The others joined in the mockery. "Pistol, is it? Beware his cock, boyos!"

Wanting to answer the taunts, Pistol schooled himself to be patient. He bestowed an understanding smile on Rhodri then whisked a third French dagger from his belt.

"This is the best of them all," he explained. "It came from the hand of a Duke."

"He gave it to you as a present, did he?" said Rhodri.

"No, my friend. He tried to stab me with it but I twisted it from his grasp. We are fellow-soldiers, you and I. Laugh at my name, if you wish, but recognize me as your comrade in arms."

"All I recognize is a scavenger. One that hides behind others when there's fighting to be done then sneaks across the field when the battle is over to plunder the dead and dying. Comrade in arms? You're nothing but a vulture."

Pistol smirked. "What will you give a vulture for this dagger?"

"A kick up the arse."

"Then I'll not trade with you," said Pistol, turning to the others. "Your friends know how to barter properly. They like what they see. Here, sir," he added, passing the third dagger to one of the men. "Feast your eyes on perfection."

"What's that last dagger in your belt?" asked one of the men.

"It's not for sale."

"Why not?"

"It belonged to a man who once did me a good turn. A Welshman, as it happens. And though he looked askance at me, I want his dagger as a keepsake. It will help me to remember the name of Davy Gam."

"Davy Gam?" said the man. "That was *his* dagger?"

"I found it lying beside his dead body."

"Give it here!" demanded Rhodri, coming forward.

"I'd not part with it for a king's ransom."

The Welshman raised a fist. "Hand it over while you still have strength to do so or I'll beat you all the way from here to London."

Pistol tried to back away but Rhodri reached out to grab him by the arm. With a swift movement of his hand, he snatched the English dagger from Pistol's belt. He held the weapon covetously.

"I'll keep this," he announced.

"But it's mine," argued Pistol.

"Not anymore."

"Davy Gam would've wanted me to have it."

"You will have it, if you're not careful—straight through the heart."

"Why are you so keen to have it, Rhodri?" asked one of his friends, going over to him. "These French daggers are far more costly. What's so special about that one?" His eye saw the letter carved into the handle. "It's your dagger," he said, pointing at it. "I swear it is, Rhodri. 'P' stands for Pomeroy. Isn't that the selfsame dagger you took from Sir Richard Pomeroy when you cut his throat at that skirmish in Harlech?"

"It is," admitted Rhodri.

"How did it come to be in Davy Gam's possession?"

"I'll tell you that!" roared Fluellen, bursting out of his hiding place to threaten Rhodri with a sword. "I pulled that dagger out of Davy's back and now I know who put it there. Rhodri ap Iorwerth," he said, "I arrest you on a charge of willful murder."

Pistol chuckled. "I told you I'd expose his villainy."

Rhodri blustered but there was no escape. His guilt was plain for them to see. Unable to lie his way out of the situation, he fell back on frantic self-justification.

"I did it for us, Fluellen," he gabbled. "I struck in the name of Wales."

"Welshmen don't stab their fellows in the back," retorted Fluellen.

"That's what Davy Gam did to us. Is your memory so short, mun? Owain Glyndwr may be hiding in a cave now but he was once a Prince of Wales that we were proud to follow. From Caerleon to Caernavon, we fought at his heels. But did Davy Gam join us in that war of liberation? No!" he said scornfully. "He stayed loyal to the King. He was ever a great stickler for the Duke of Lancaster. He betrayed us."

"That was one war," decided Fluellen. "This is another. A general amnesty was declared for all Welsh rebels who pledged themselves to fight for King Henry. You gave that pledge, Rhodri, and you broke it."

"Only in order to punish a traitor."

"Davy Gam fought honestly against the French."

"And dishonestly against the Welsh. Come, Fluellen," said Rhodri with an ingratiating smile. "What's one more death among so many? Davy Gam had too strong a squint to be allowed to live. Instead of looking to his own country, his eye fell instead on England. I did our nation a service by killing him."

"That's enough!" yelled Fluellen, using his sword to slash at his wrist so that the dagger was knocked to the ground. "Murder has no excuse to hide behind. Davy Gam, like his father before him, may have stayed loyal to the English but he paid a heavy price in loss of land and ransoms. He surrendered that eye of his in battle, remember, and it was a mere three years ago that he was kid-napped. A fearsome ransom had to be found."

"We should have killed him while we held him prisoner."

"That defies every article of war, Rhodri."

"Who cares about that?"

"Captain Fluellen does," said Pistol cheerily before turning to the other men. "Now, my friends, what are you going to offer me for those daggers?"

Fluellen took hold of his prisoner and marched him away. The sound of Pistol, haggling merrily, began to fade away in the background. Fluellen was content. He had no respect for Pistol but he had to admit one thing. A petty criminal had been responsible for solving a far more serious crime.

King Henry believed in summary justice. When the evidence was presented to him by Fluellen, he did not hesitate. Rhodri ap Iorwerth was convicted of murder and hanged on the spot. Distressed that a fellow Welshman had been the killer, Fluellen nevertheless took comfort from the fact that he had been brought to justice. He was ready to admit that Pistol's help had been of crucial importance.

"I might never have caught him without you, Pistol," he confessed.

"It takes an English hero to outwit a Welsh villain."

"Don't lay claim to heroism. That's too big a lie, even for you. You tricked the truth out of him. I'm grateful to you for that. Davy Gam can lie easy in his grave."

"Nobody can tease him about his squint now."

"He was loyal to his commander. That's vital in a soldier. Rhodri ap Iorwerth was treacherous. He fought under the King's banner but held firm to old loyalties. When he saw the chance to kill Davy Gam, he took it. Thanks to you, Pistol, disgusting maltworm, that you are, Rhodri is now dancing on air."

"Yes," said Pistol. "I'm glad of that. Like most of his nation, he was an ugly brute. Why does Wales breed such hideous ghouls? The only pretty Welshman I've ever seen was that one you talked to earlier."

"Who was that?"

"Owain something."

"Owain ap Meredyth ap Tydir."

"That's him. Except in a mirror, I've never seen such a handsome man."

"His handsome face will be his downfall," predicted Fluellen.

"Why?"

"Because it comes with a wandering hand and a seductive tongue. Brave soldier he may be but his finest conquests are in the bedchamber. The goatish instinct of Owain ap Meredyth ap Tydir will be the death of him in the end."

"Can you give his name a more English sound?"

"Owen Tudor," said Fluellen, waving a dismissive hand, "but it's not a name you need to remember. I don't think you'll ever hear of the Tudors again."

HISTORICAL NOTE: A certain amount of fact underlies this fictional tale. Fluellen and Pistol were, of course, created by Shakespeare but Davy Gam was a real person. He was a member of the premier family in Breconshire. His father, Llywelyn ap Hywel, stood firm in his support of the English crown. Davy Gam was equally loyal and was rewarded by Henry IV with the gift of confiscated lands. Until the revolt led by Owain Glyndwr finally petered out, Davy Gam was involved in regular skirmishes with his kinsman. He died at Agincourt in the way described by King Henry in this story, and was knighted before he passed away. He was killed by the enemy and not by an assassin.

Owain ap Meredyth ap Tydir is best known as Owen Tudor, grandfather of Henry VII. At the death of Henry V, he stayed on at Court and was appointed by the young Queen-Dowager, Catherine de Valois, to a prestigious position as Clerk of her Wardrobe. Their love affair led to a secret marriage and the birth of five children. Owen was eventually beheaded after the battle of Mortimer's Cross in 1461 on the orders of Edward IV. His son, Edmund Tudor, had already been created Earl of Richmond. Edmund's only son, Henry, was the victor at Bosworth in 1485 and set the Tudor dynasty in motion.

Exit, Pursued

BY SIMON BRETT

 Simon Brett's most recent novels are in his new Fethering series, *The Body on the Beach* and *Death on the Downs*. Adept at both the traditional mystery as well as the historical, his recent novels include *Mrs. Pargeter's Plot* and *Sicken and So Die.* He also created Charles Parys, an actor as well as amateur detective who stumbles into the middle of crimes usually set against the backdrop of the London theater scene. His other series concerns the mysterious Mrs. Pargeter, a detective who skirts the edge of the law in her unusual investigations. He's also quite accomplished in the short form as well, with stories appearing in the *Malice Domestic* series, as well as the anthologies *Once Upon a Crime* and *Funny Bones.* A winner of the Writer's Guild of Great Britain Award for his radio plays, he has also written nonfiction books and edited several books in the Faber series, including *The Faber Book of Useful Verse* and *The Faber Book of Parodies.* He lives in Burpham, England.

"Set on there. Never was a war did cease,
E'er bloody hands were wash'd, with such a peace."

Cymbeline's final couplet echoed around the Globe Theatre. From the tower above the stage, a trumpet sounded, to spell out to the stupidest of the ground-lings that the play was over. Applause came from the audience, but the sound was ragged, interspersed with catcalls, not the full-throated thunder that be-spoke success.

Charles Parys was behind the curtain of the tiring-house, waiting to see whether the cast would be called on to take a bow. In his fifties, cynical, he had witnessed too many first performances to take rejection by the audience personally. And yet, in the heart of all actors there always glows a little flicker of hope. *Cymbeline* still might work. The alchemy that made a play a success or failure was an arcane and inexplicable art.

He caught the sceptical eye of the actor playing Posthumus Leonatus, who had just come off the stage. "Don't think Master Shakespeare's got a winner this time," said Robert Hillard, brushing at the fine black velvet of his doublet where it had scuffed against the powdery paint of the curtain.

"They liked some of it," said Charles Parys, unwilling to condemn the play out of hand. "The fights . . . and the songs . . . and the Ghosts."

"Oh yes, and you coming down from the heavens on an eagle—that gave them a good laugh. But they really lost interest in the last bit, with all those explanations, tying up the loose ends of the plot. Most of this lot'd rather be at the bear-baiting than seeing a proper play. No taste, theatre audiences these days."

"Are we going out for a bow or not?" shouted the boy Ned Brackett, the fine vowels he'd used as Imogen giving way to his natural Cockney in a voice that would soon be too deep to play more heroines. Robert Hillard tried to catch the boy's eye, but his glance was deliberately evaded.

All the actors deferred to the book-holder, a harassed, balding man in a rough woollen jerkin. "Oh yes," he said. "Give them one bow. See how they take it."

The applause when the cast trooped sheepishly back on stage was at best lukewarm, and there were some boos. Most of the audience were already scram-bling for the exit, the groundlings held back by stage-keepers, as the gentry passed fastidiously over the debris of nutshells, orange peels, and rushes to the safety of their waiting carriages.

In spite of the feeble reception, Robert Hillard strutted and preened for the remainder of the audience. He cut a fine figure in black velvet doublet cut on silver tinsel and trimmed with silver lace. There was a regular crowd of merchants' wives who liked to stay at the end of the plays and ogle the actors. One in particular, a well-rounded, black-eyed mischief-maker, seemed to be staring with unambiguous interest towards Robert Hillard. With an angry swirl of ratty fur cloak, a long-nosed elderly man, who could only be her husband, put an arm around his chattel's shoulder and whisked her away from such riffraff. As he vanished into the crowd, he turned back and focused a look of sheer venom on his potential rival.

"Do you know that sour-faced pantaloon, Master Parys?" asked Hillard. "He seemed to be staring at you."

"I don't think it was at *me*. He did not like the interest his wife was taking in *you*, Master Hillard."

"Oh yes." Robert Hillard preened a little more. "That does happen quite often. It's something I've learned to live with."

Charles Parys reflected on the strangeness of the situation. The actor standing next to him had all the qualifications to be a ladies' man, except for even the mildest of interest in the ladies. Boys were Robert Hillard's dish of choice.

"But do you know him, Master Parys?"

"I believe he's an ironmonger and locksmith called Ezekiel Goodbody. Said to have made a lot of money and to have invested much of it in the business of entertainment."

"Ah. So maybe he will be our paymaster soon?"

"I don't think plays are the sort of entertainment he favors."

Back in the cramped tiring-house was a maelstrom of ribaldry and errant limbs, as too many actors vied to get out of their costumes and be first to the tavern. Above the chaos shrilled the voice of Rokesby Lander, the Master of Properties and Apparel. He was a huge man, swollen like an overfilled wineskin, and in spite of the cool May weather, sweating like a cheese in direct sunlight. The story went that he had been a boy actor and that an unscrupulous theatre manager had castrated him in an unsuccessful attempt to extend his days of playing female parts.

Lander's words were the same after every performance, and after every performance the actors ignored them. "Now don't just leave your costumes lying on the rushes! Fold them up and shake them out! Some got wet with the rain, and must be dried before they're used again! Come on, gentlemen, please!"

Nobody was sure when, if ever, *Cymbeline* would be performed again, but the costumes, particularly the fine ones, would be worn in other plays. They were among the chief assets of the King's Men, and Rokesby Lander had to account to the shareholders for every last lost button. Given the habitual untidiness of actors, his was not an enviable task.

He came across to Charles, who was struggling to free himself from the gold-painted pasteboard wings he'd worn as Jupiter. "Can I help you there?" the unsexed voice trilled.

Rokesby Lander was always offering to help, and during the quick change Charles had to make out of his Cloten costume into his Jupiter one, that help had been very much needed. There was always an ulterior motive to Lander's offers; his liking for Charles was more than just professional. Still, Charles himself had never had a moment's doubt since birth where his own interests lay, and the Apparel Master's fondness for him had sometimes proved useful in obtaining the odd favor.

Lander lowered his voice—in volume if not in pitch. "Will you be going to the tavern for a drink, Charles?"

"When did I not? Thirsty work, a new play."

"Yes." Rokesby Lander gestured hopelessly round the clutter of spangled costumes, left exactly where the actors had stepped out of them. "When I've finished this lot, I'll be going down to the Bull. Maybe see you there . . . ?"

Not if I see you first, thought Charles Parys.

The Bull was no worse than any other tavern South of the Thames, which is to say it was smoky, dingily lit by rush lights, damp from condensation and the sweat of bodies crammed inside. The smells of urine and sour ale fought for dominance, and it was a frequent complaint among the customers that the tavern-keeper served the one for the other. Since the Bull's regulars comprised a mix of stinking laborers, conmen, cutpurses, and whores, the actors fitted in very well. They frequented the tavern for the simple reason that it was in a crooked alley behind the Globe, but off the main thoroughfares which led the quality back to their relative elegance north of the river.

At five-thirty, particularly after the first performance of a play, most of the King's Men would gather in the Bull to commiserate about what had gone wrong, and gloomily assess the new work's prospects. They would drink for an hour or two. Only the rash or intrepid would stay longer. In May it was twilight by seven, and the Bankside was a rough area in which to loiter after dark.

"Come to the bear-baiting!" shouted a harsh voice as the actors approached the tavern door. "Tomorrow afternoon at three! See the dogs tear the living flesh from the bears! See the bears crush the dogs like piecrust! Don't bother with these long-winded plays! Come to the Bear Garden in Shoreside Lane! See some proper entertainment!"

The fellow trying to do them out of business was a ferret-faced man in a stained leather tabard on which had been painted a crude black outline of a bear harried by dogs. As the actors muscled forward to chase him from his pitch, he gave a sharp look towards Robert Hillard, before scampering off into the darkness of the surrounding alleys.

Inside the tavern door Charles Parys exchanged banter with the other *Cymbeline* actors while they waited to be served. There seemed to be only two potboys on duty to deal with the heaving mass, a skeletally thin old man and a lad scarcely into his teens who hobbled dangerously on legs warped by rickets. Between fusillades of insults at each other, the actors hurled oaths and exhortations to the potboys.

Charles was the butt of most of the company gibes. The parts he'd taken in the play ensured that. For the first four Acts he'd played Cloten, the brutish son of *Cymbeline*'s Queen, but after that character's decapitation, a headless dummy had been thrust into Cloten's costume, and Charles had had to don the awkward wings, scratchy beard, and shining robes of Jupiter. He'd then had to rush up the rickety stairs from the tiring-house to the hut above the stage, whence he'd been launched by uncaring stage-keepers on the back of an eagle. This was a rickety structure of cloth-covered basket-work, which wobbled dangerously on ropes as it was lowered to the stage. The descent of the mighty Jove had thus prompted more laughter than awe. The "thunder and lightning" specified in the book-holder's copy of the text had been forgotten by the stage-keepers, and the firework which should have gone off when Jupiter hurled his thunderbolt had failed to ignite, with the result that the bolt thudded feebly down on to the stage to a cry from some witty groundling of "Beware chicken droppings!" It hadn't been Charles Parys's finest hour.

Finally the limping boy brought their order and the actors' robust badinage gave way to a greater priority. Charles took a thankful sip from his cup of ale and, given the speed of the service, wished he'd ordered two. The ale was sour but welcome against his palate.

"Beware chicken droppings!" said a breaking voice at his side. Ned Brackett was dressed once more as a boy, but still retained some of Imogen's mincing elegance. Around his neck sparkled a gold chain with a pendant of inlaid pearls. The boy's voluptuous lips caressed a stick of brown sugar.

"Very amusing," said Charles. "So what's the painted bauble you have there?"

"Not painted, Master Parys. It's true gold. Given me by a gentleman of the Court."

"In return for what favors?"

The boy smiled coquettishly, and gave a suggestive lick to his sugar stick.

"It's no gentleman of the Court!" Robert Hillard staggered angrily across to join them. "Some jumped-up rascal in a borrowed doublet with a fancy for a young boy's arsehole."

Ned Brackett fluttered his eyelashes. "It takes one to know one, Master Hillard."

"Why, you . . . !" The actor who had played Posthumus drew his hand back as if to strike the boy, but seemed to think better of it. Hillard hadn't been in the tavern long enough to get as drunk as he appeared, and Charles realized the man was in the grip of violent emotion. He also realized the aptness of

Ned Brackett's words. Against the express orders of Rokesby Lander, Robert Hillard was still dressed in his black and silver doublet. His stage sword hung in its scabbard at his side.

The boy smiled smugly, knowing his power to hurt. "Now forgive me, Masters. I must go to join more select company."

And he teetered, emphasizing his Imogen walk, across to a tall figure in a purple doublet trimmed with gold. The man was as sallow as a Spaniard; a single pearl depended from one earlobe. On a ribbon round his neck was a pomander of cloves, but rather than foppish, he looked menacing. He laid a proprietorial hand on the boy's backside and smiled triumphantly across to Robert Hillard.

Charles Parys could feel the seething beside him; his fellow-actor's body was tensed to spring into violence. Charles laid a hand on the velvet of his arm. "Don't do anything. He's not worth it, Master Hillard."

" 'The boy disdains me.' " A void of misery lay beneath the actor's words. Charles continued the quotation from the play they had just completed.

> " 'He leaves me, scorns me; briefly die their joys
> That place them on the truth of girls and boys.' "

Hillard remained transfixed by the sardonic, challenging look of the man in purple. The anger still coursed his veins like molten metal, and his hand dropped instinctively to the pommel of his sword. "A man of the Court!" he shouted. "Put a monkey in a purple coat, and he'll pass for a man of the Court!"

His antagonist held silence, fondling Ned's bottom with one hand, and with the other fingering the boy's pearl pendant, goading Hillard on to further fury.

"So maybe he is a man of the Court! When the King himself is a lad-lover, what else would you expect? That this fellow is sent out by the King to bring back pretty bum-boys for the royal pleasure!"

The talk in the tavern dropped to silence. With a last, piercing look at Robert Hillard, the man in purple put an insolent hand on Ned Brackett's shoulder and led the boy out into the street.

"You fool, keep quiet!" hissed Charles, as conversations around them slowly came back to life. "To say that about the King is to risk your life."

"I say no more than the truth that everyone knows."

"Master Hillard, it doesn't matter whether it's true or not! There are spies everywhere, and saying stuff like that is foolhardy. It's not just us you put at risk. The King has revoked the license of other actors' companies for less."

The younger actor turned away in despair. "I don't care. I love Ned. I need him. If I can't have him, then nothing else matters."

"Master Hillard! Master Hillard," squeaked an approaching voice, shrill with affront. "You are a wicked man, and deserve a good beating!"

It was Rokesby Lander, sweating more than ever, forcing his bulbous body through the disrespectful crowd that milled around the tavern door.

Hillard turned to look at this new annoyance. "What is it, you vat of lard?"

"Your costume, Master Hillard. Players are expressly forbidden to leave the theatre wearing apparel owned by the King's Men! It is against the rules!"

"Rule me no rules, Master Tunbelly! Rules are for lesser men. You are now addressing the best actor in London!"

This defiant shout again brought the tavern to stillness. There were plenty of factions supporting other actors who would have challenged Robert Hillard's boast. Careless in his anguish for the loss of the boy Ned, he seemed set on a course of self-destruction.

"I must insist," Rokesby Lander said primly, "that you come back with me to the Globe this instant to return your apparel."

Robert Hillard's hand was again on his sword, and the fat man quailed before the balefulness focused on him. "A fig for your insisting, Master Doughbucket! I say to you—as Master Shakespeare has written in one of his more successful plays—'Sneck up!' "

And with that, the actor stormed out of the Bull Tavern. The hand tight on his sword handle ensured that the crowd shrank back to let him pass.

Conversation quickly reasserted itself. The Bull Tavern had witnessed too much drama to take much notice of one more flouncing exit.

"Could I buy you a drink, Master Parys?" wheedled Rokesby Lander.

The temptation was strong. The contents of his first cup had scarcely touched the sides of Charles's throat. But to accept the drink would oblige him to at least a polite minimum of Lander's conversation, and Charles didn't think he could face it. "No, no, I must be on my way shortly." There were other taverns to stop at between the Globe and his lodgings in Shoreditch. "But don't let me stop you . . ."

"I'm in no hurry," said the eunuch. "I'll have a drink after we've had a little chat."

"Oh." Charles Parys was uncomfortably suspended between tedium and downright rudeness. He made conversation. "What did you think of the play, Master Lander?"

The fat cheeks puffed out in disparagement. "Won't see many more performances of that one, I can tell you. As ever with Master Shakespeare—too many words and not enough action. Nor enough special effects to please the groundlings."

"There was me coming down on the eagle . . ."

Rokesby Lander giggled girlishly. "Yes, very funny too. But the public wants more than that these days. More spectacle. Like the masques that Master Jonson and Master Inigo Jones have devised for the Court. Prodigiously fancy costumes they have there, and fine music. What's more, being indoors, they can make magical effects with the lights. I tell you, Master Parys, the theatre of Shakespeare and his like is old-fashioned. The future lies with the masques . . . oh, and of course with the bear-baiting. The rich men of the future will not be the actors' companies but the owners of Bear Gardens like Master Ezekiel Goodbody."

Charles couldn't let that go by unchallenged. Not only did such a view offend his opinions, it also threatened his livelihood. "No, Master Lander, there will always be a place for the kind of theatre that challenges the mind to—"

But his case for the defense got no further. There was a shriek from the tavern doorway, and a seventeen-year-old whore, bare feet muddy beneath her ragged finery, burst in. "Sirs, come quickly! There has been murder in the streets!"

Charles Parys and Rokesby Lander were among the first to arrive at the scene of the crime. A frightened link-boy held a trembling torch over the body. Screams sounded from surprised whores and their clients in nearby alleys. Men shouted for the Watch to come.

Robert Hillard lay in the trickle of sewage that guttered down the middle of a narrow alley. Flames from the torch flickered on the mud, on the running water, on the blade half-drawn from the actor's scabbard, but also on the dark blood that had almost ceased to pump from the wound in his chest. Of the other sword—or whatever weapon had made the fatal thrust—there was no sign.

Charles Parys crouched down at his colleague's side, knowing he was too late. Hillard's eyes were dull in the torchlight, their fire extinguished.

Above him, Charles heard a piping wail from Rokesby Lander. "Oh, no! Look at the mess it's made of that doublet!"

Master William Shakespeare looked weary and melancholy. The dome of his head was furrowed, and more of the hair fringing it was white than when Charles Parys had last seen him. "So?" asked Charles.

"So we will do another performance of *Cymbeline*."

"That's good news."

The playwright shrugged. "I have just come from a meeting with my fellow shareholders. They took a lot of persuading. And do you know what finally convinced them we should give the play another try?" Charles shook his head. "Your bloody eagle, Master Parys. They said the King's Men had spent so much making the device that it must be used more than once. And doing another performance of *Cymbeline* would be cheaper—though only just—than commissioning a new play by a younger author, also containing the miraculous descent of someone on an eagle."

There seemed nothing to say that could ease the despair evident in his friend's words. So Charles suggested having a drink.

The meager May sunlight was sufficient that morning to justify standing out-side the Bull. The stenches were no less than inside, but at least more varied. Shakespeare drank sack, with the air of a man who intended to keep drinking sack all day. Charles Parys stuck to the ale. At three o'clock he had a perfor-mance to give in *Philaster* by Beaumont and Fletcher. The play's lines main-tained their customary tenuous hold on the sides of his brain.

"You have no thoughts, do you, Master Shakespeare, as to who might have killed Master Hillard?"

The playwright shook his head. He was too deep into his own failure to think about anything else. "Some jealous man . . . ?"

"Not a husband. Or if it was, he must realize he's got the wrong victim. By now all London knows Robert Hillard's tastes."

"I did not say a husband. Maybe some other worshipper of Sodom, whose bum-boy Hillard had seduced away . . . ?"

"It had happened the other way round. Ned Brackett . . . you know, Imogen . . . had just rejected Master Hillard."

"Then I don't know. But I'd still put it down to the workings of love . . . or love gone sour. Jealousy is the most powerful of the human emotions."

" 'The green-ey'd monster.' "

"Yes, Master Parys. A good line . . . that I wrote in the days when I still wrote good lines."

"Oh, come on. For heaven's sake. *Cymbeline* is full of good lines."

"Not enough of them. Whatever skill I once had, I have lost it. Or the public doesn't want it. They want younger writers. They want Beaumont and Fletcher."

"Or bear-baiting."

"They will always want bear-baiting," said Shakespeare despondently.

"Cheer up. It's not as if you haven't made a good living from the theatre."

The dark eyes fixed Charles's in a beam of unnerving intensity.

"You think the money matters when I cannot write?"

"It must cushion things a bit."

"No. It provides no comfort at all when the mind is dead."

"So . . ." Charles searched around for something to say, and felt embarrassed by the crassness of what he came up with. "Are you writing anything at the moment, Master Shakespeare?"

"There is something, but it's not working."

"What?"

"Master Greene wrote a tale called *Pandosto* . . ." Charles shook his head; the title meant nothing to him. "Well, it concerns the unreasoning jealousy of a king who believes his wife to be unfaithful, and he thinks he has had her killed for her imagined betrayal, but she's been hidden away and . . . oh, the usual stuff. Purification . . . regeneration . . . the road to self-knowledge . . . But I think I'm going to have to abandon it. The structure's not working."

"Why not?"

"Because the play's in two parts and there are sixteen years between them and . . . oh, don't let me bother you with my technical problems."

"So time comes into it again?"

"Yes, I'm even thinking of having Time as a character—a Chorus to bridge the sixteen years, but . . ." He seemed to lose himself in a far country. "I'm becoming obsessed by time."

To avoid metaphysical entanglements, Charles Parys resorted to a simpler question. "Do you have a title for the play?"

"I don't know. *Leontes and Hermione* . . . ? *A Tale for a Winter's Night*, perhaps? As I say, I probably won't finish it, so it won't need a title."

"Any good parts?" Charles asked diffidently.

"Good parts for a Clown?" For the first time that morning there was a light of wry humor in Shakespeare's eye. "There is one very good comic part—a peddler, a rogue, a coney-catcher. I've got a name from Ovid and Plutarch that I think will suit him. Autolycus." He saw the hope he had aroused and immediately extinguished it. "There is also the part of a lesser Clown. A shepherd, a gull. You could play *him*, Master Parys."

"Thank you," came the humbled reply.

"Good day, Master Shakespeare."

They looked up to see a young woman approaching them. Her face, soon to be ragged from the hardness of life, still wore the glow of youth. The dress looked even more tawdry in the daylight, gold paint cracked and flaking on its seams. She was still barefoot. It was the whore who had sounded the alarm in the Bull a few nights before.

"You are out early, Mistress Dorcas."

"And you could be *in* early, Master Shakespeare . . ." she replied unambiguously, ". . . if you so wish."

"I'll think about it."

"And while you think about it, I'm sure you'll buy a poor girl a drink."

He nodded. "Tell the potboy to put it on my reckoning."

Dorcas made a mock curtsey, and disappeared into the gloom of the tavern. For a moment Shakespeare avoided Charles's eye, then looked up defiantly. "So, if a man leaves a sour-faced wife minding his affairs in Stratford, may he not take a little pleasure when he is in London?"

"I never said you couldn't. If there's any guilt about, it's your own."

"It has not always been whores," said Shakespeare defensively. "There have been ladies of quality, the occasional pert merchant's wife. A man has needs."

"You don't need to tell me." Charles pondered the wobbly state of his own marriage.

The playwright continued his self-justification. "And Dorcas is a good girl, in spite of her calling."

"I never said she wasn't."

"No. And she has made me happy. Though for how much longer . . ." He looked pessimistically at the dwindling contents in his tankard of sack.

"It's the drink. 'Lechery, sir, it provokes, and unprovokes; it provokes the desire, but it takes away the performance.' "

Shakespeare smiled glumly. "Another line from the days when I could write. *Macbeth* was good."

"Yes . . ." Charles sighed wistfully, remembering past glories, ". . . and gave me my best part ever."

"A Drunken Porter. The part for which you had been rehearsing all your life, Master Parys."

"Well, I wouldn't say—"

"Then all was well with me. I could do no wrong. I'd written a play celebrating the King's Scottish lineage, so I found favor with him, and all the Court were—"

Charles interrupted once again to halt the slide into depression. "When we next do *Cymbeline*," he asked brusquely, "who will play Posthumus Leonatus?"

Shakespeare gave a hopeless shrug. "It will have to be me. I more or less know the lines. I'm too old for the part, but then you are too old for Cloten, Master Parys."

"Though not too old for Jupiter."

"I think it would be a hard task to be too old for Jupiter." A grin transformed his features. "Beware chicken droppings!"

Oh dear. Charles Parys knew he was never going to live that one down.

Shakespeare's grin transformed itself into a beam as Dorcas reemerged from the tavern, bearing a steaming cup of mulled wine. After a night spent on a draughty street corner, she needed something to warm her up.

"So what have you been up to, my little sugarplum?" asked Shakespeare.

"I've been talking to the Watch," she said proudly.

"What offense have you committed this time? Have you been insulting the gentry again?"

"No, no. The Watch wished to speak to me as a witness."

Shakespeare looked blank, so Charles Parys explained. "The young lady saw Robert Hillard stabbed."

"Well, not so much *saw*, but I was the first person to arrive after he had been stabbed."

"You didn't see the murderer then?"

"Maybe a flash of someone in a dark coat rushing away, but that was all . . ."

"Are you sure it was all?" Charles persisted. "You didn't hear any words . . . any other sound . . . anything else that was strange . . . ?"

"Well . . ." The girl hesitated, afraid that her words might sound foolish. "There was a smell . . ."

"A smell?" Shakespeare laughed. "So do we now identify a murderer by his smell? What was it—brimstone from the gates of hell?"

"No," said Dorcas sullenly.

"Why not by smell?" asked Charles. "It might be as good a means of identification as any other. So what was the smell, child?"

Dorcas blushed as she replied. "It smelt like a bear."

"A bear?" This struck Shakespeare as even funnier. "Are you saying that Robert Hillard was murdered by a bear? Not only that, but a bear that could wield a sword?"

Dorcas looked more uncomfortable. "As I say, it was just a smell."

"Plenty of bears pass those alleys when they're led from their kennels to the Bear Garden."

"I know that, Master Shakespeare," said the girl firmly, "but not after dark. And I did get a distinct fresh smell of bear." She punctuated her insistence by downing the rest of her drink. "I must get to work."

"You will find men about so early?"

"It's past noon, Master Shakespeare. Even the laziest cock will be ready to crow by now."

He smiled. She lingered. "So . . . will I see you?"

"I'll find you around three. When everyone I might drink with has gone to the theatre . . . to see the latest great success of Sir Francis Beaumont and Master Fletcher." He could not keep the bitterness out of his voice.

Dorcas left to trawl the alleyways for business. There was a clatter of the tavern door opening, and a tall, dark figure stalked out. By his clothes Charles recognized the man who had apparently seduced Ned Brackett away from Robert Hillard. In the daylight his purple doublet looked scuffed and worn; he was no genuine member of the Court.

He looked angry. Hard on his heels came Ned. The boy laid his hand on the purple sleeve and was shaken irritably off. The man strode away in a northerly direction. Ned Brackett stood still for an anguished moment, tears welling at his eyes. Then, seeing he was observed by Charles and Shakespeare, he rubbed a hand across his face and hurried off in the opposite direction from his former lover.

"Oh, the potency of dumb-show!" the playwright murmured. "A whole story told without words. I am sorry that the dumb-show is now thought old-fashioned. Mind you, most of what I do is now thought old-fashioned." The earlier anxieties continued to gnaw away at him. "I really thought I was on to something with *Cymbeline*. What really worries me is the fact that the groundlings didn't get behind it. They didn't seem interested even in the battles."

"It's the problem of nationality," Charles reassured him. "Always difficult when you're dealing with the Welsh. Scots, fine. You did that in *Macbeth*. Good play, great murder mystery. But Belarius and that lot in *Cymbeline* . . . you've hit a real difficulty there. Fine with one Welsh comic character like Fluellen. But when you've got lots of them . . . and they're meant to be heroic . . . I'm afraid it's virtually impossible to make the Welsh interesting to the rest of the people in this country."

"Hm," said Shakespeare.

"And Milford Haven's never going to sound great in blank verse."

"No," Shakespeare agreed. "Doesn't even scan."

"Come to the bear-baiting!" The ferret-faced man had resumed his pitch outside the Bull and went into his routine. "This afternoon at three! See the dogs tear the living flesh from the bears! See the bears crush the dogs . . ."

"Should we frighten him off?" asked Charles.

"Why bother?" Shakespeare replied. "We'd only be holding off the evil moment. The bear-baiting will win in the end."

Before Charles could remonstrate, an unmistakable voice squeaked "Master Shakespeare!" and the bulbous shape of Rokesby Lander wobbled towards them. Over his arm was draped a familiar black and silver doublet. "See, the laundresses and the seamstresses have done their best. Your doublet is as good as it was when you first had it made."

"Your doublet?" echoed Charles.

"Yes," said Shakespeare. "The doublet is mine."

Suddenly the man from the Bear Garden stopped in the middle of his sales pitch. He gave a piercing look towards Shakespeare and Charles, as if memorizing their faces. Then he turned sharply on his heel, and scuttled swiftly away.

"What was that about?" asked Shakespeare.

"Couldn't stand the competition? Knew what's happening at the Globe this afternoon will be better than any bear-baiting could be?"

"I doubt it, Master Parys. Perhaps, though. Not one of my doomed plays on today, one by the bright young Beaumont and Fletcher, so maybe it will be better than the bear-baiting."

There seemed nothing Charles could say that didn't dig Shakespeare deeper into his pit of gloom. He tried a change of subject. "What's all this about the doublet being yours?"

"It's true," said Rokesby Lander.

"Certainly is, Master Parys. When I bought New Place in Stratford, I imagined briefly that I was joining the local gentry and had clothes made accordingly. But I found the local gentry neither interested in me nor interesting in themselves, so I rarely wore my finery. Whatever you dress him in, an actor will always be a vagabond at heart."

"And a man is known by the clothes he wears."

"Exactly, Master Parys. I am glad you've been paying attention to the lines I've written for you in *Cymbeline*."

> " 'Thou villain base,
> Know'st me not by my clothes?' "

Softly, Shakespeare took up the cue from Cloten's speech, and gave the reply of Guiderius:

> " 'No, nor thy tailor, rascal,
> Who is thy grandfather: he made those clothes,
> Which, as it seems, make thee.' "

"It is good stuff," said Charles.

"Huh," came the cynical response. "Anyway, so I was in Stratford with these useless clothes and I thought, waste not, want not, and put this doublet—and the hose that went with it—back into the business."

"Another costume the King's Men did not have to buy."

"Precisely, Master Lander." Shakespeare took the garment and looked closely at the almost invisible black stitching of the repair. "To think this is the mouth through which a man's whole life spilled out . . ."

Fortunately, the Apparel Master had no time for an "Alas! poor Yorick" moment. "That's as maybe." Gathering up the doublet, Rokesby Lander waddled away. "I must get this to the tiring-house. See you later, Master Parys. Don't be late for *Philaster*. Or for me," he added coyly. "And not too much of the ale. Remember, you have a performance to give this afternoon."

The advice was good, but Charles still had a temptation to go on drinking. It was a temptation that seemed to arise with ever greater frequency as he grew older. He looked across to his companion, and saw that Shakespeare had once again slumped into gloom.

"I'd like to do something that lasts." The playwright was almost speaking to himself.

"I'm sure some of the plays will."

The lack of conviction in Charles's tone must have communicated itself. "I doubt it, Master Parys."

"Who knows what posterity will think? If it's not through your work, then maybe your name will live on through your children . . ."

The melancholy brown eyes fixed on his. "Do you have children, Charles?"

"A son. Also Charles. An idle boy. Has no talent for anything useful . . . so maybe he too will become a playactor. Maybe I will be father to a whole dynasty of playactors."

The dome of Shakespeare's brow wrinkled. "I'll have no dynasty. Not with the name of Shakespeare. My son Hamnet died fourteen years ago. He was only eleven."

"I'm sorry."

"Oh, it's just a life. These things happen. So far as the gods are concerned, we're just as flies to wanton boys."

" 'They kill us for their sport.' "

The playwright smiled wearily. "Yes. Dear oh dear. Repeating myself now."

"That was good, though," said Charles encouragingly. "*King Lear.* The groundlings loved it when Gloucester's eyes came out. That'll live on."

"I doubt it." Shakespeare was still locked in melancholy. "And no son to carry on my name. Two daughters. Susanna made me a grandfather a couple of years back. But another girl. Elizabeth Hall. Not Shakespeare. The line will die with me. And in my current mood, the sooner that death comes, the better."

"You are not ready for death."

"Oh, I am." Wryly, he quoted a line spoken by Posthumus Leonatus in his latest play. " 'Overroasted rather; ready long ago.' A failed husband, a failed father, a failed playwright . . . In fifty years the name of Shakespeare will be forgotten."

Charles Parys knew that this was all too probably true, but it didn't do to say so. Instead, he resorted to the cure-all of actors since time began. Forget that afternoon's performance in *Philaster.* "Potboy!" he called. "More drinks over here!"

And more drinks inevitably led to more drinks. Charles knew he had a duty to his profession, but he had a greater duty to keep Shakespeare from slumping further into gloom. As a result, by three o'clock he was in no state to give the best account of himself in Beaumont and Fletcher's *Philaster, or Love Lies A-Bleeding.*

The play was the usual tragicomedy of thwarted lovers and mistaken identities. In previous performances Ned Brackett had been highly praised for his acting as Euphrasia, who spends most of the play disguised as the page Bellario; and Robert Hillard had cut a striking figure in the title role. But the actor who'd been drafted in at short notice to take the lead lacked the dead man's charisma and had a very shaky hold on the lines. Also it rained heavily all afternoon, water dripping from the thatched eaves on to the disgruntled groundlings. Even the plays's cast were not immune. The "heavens," the roofing that should have protected the stage, had sprung many leaks, and new moves were added to those rehearsed as the actors dodged the drips.

The addition of a drunken Charles Parys to this mix did not improve the afternoon's theatrical experience. He was playing three parts—1st Woodman, A Country Fellow, and An Old Captain, but none of them came on till Act IV. As a result, during the first half Charles fell asleep in the tiring-house and, when woken for his cue by a very tetchy book-holder, had bleared vision and a sore head.

He stumbled onstage as 1st Woodman, realizing he'd forgotten his bow and arrows. The lines came back to him in a slightly jumbled form, which would not have pleased either Sir Francis Beaumont or Master John Fletcher. Still, he managed to get his laughs on the dirty bits, notably the description of one female character: "That's a firker, i'faith, boy; there's a wench will ride her haunches as hard after a kennel of hounds as a hunting saddle, and when she comes home, get 'em clapt, and all is well." The groundlings always liked jokes about venereal disease.

Things got worse, however, when Charles Parys reappeared—with minimal costume change—as the Country Fellow. He got laughs there too, but not for the right reasons. His swordfight with the ill-prepared substitute Philaster had the pair of them skidding over the wet rushes on the stage till both ended up flat on their arses. Though the groundlings loved it, Charles got a severe ticking-off from the book-holder.

And it was a very slurred Old Captain—again in minimally different costume—who marched on with "Citizens and Pharamond prisoner." He even failed to get the surefire laugh on his response to the 1st Citizen's suggestion of castrating their prisoner: "No, you shall spare his dowcets, my dear donsels."

The performance got worse. Charles seemed to have lost his concentration completely, and the other actors had to keep feeding the Old Captain his cues.

But in fact it wasn't the drink that distracted Charles Parys. It was something he had seen happening in the audience, something that made him feel suddenly stone cold sober.

The long-nosed merchant Ezekiel Goodbody was sitting with his black-eyed wife in one of the galleries, safe from the rain. Charles was aware of a movement behind them, and saw a thin figure in painted leather approach. It was the man from the Bear Garden, the one who had vanished so abruptly from outside the tavern that morning. He leant forward to whisper something in Ezekiel Good-body's ear. Whatever he said brought fury to the merchant's weasel face, a fury that gave way to an expression of pure evil.

Suddenly, everything fell into place for Charles Parys. He knew exactly what had happened to Robert Hillard. And he knew the same fate awaited someone else.

Sweat prickled on his temples as he gabbled through his last speech, which ended, rather appositely:

> " 'then to the tavern,
> And bring your wives in muffs. We will have music;
> And the red grape shall make us dance and rise, boys.' "

Never before had *Philaster* witnessed such a quick exit. As Charles hurled himself through the tiring-house, the book-holder's hissed words faded away behind him. "You'll be up before the shareholders for this, Master Parys! I've never witnessed such an unprofessional performance in the whole of my . . ."

William Shakespeare was sitting alone at a table in the Bull. On an opened leather carrying-roll was a sheet of paper; an unstoppered ink-bottle stood beside a cup of sack. The quill pen in his hand covered the page at speed, and there was a new luminosity in the dark eyes.

"Master Shakespeare!" cried a panting Charles Parys. "You are in danger!"

"Ssh! I can be in no danger. I am writing again. *A Winter's Tale*, it's called, and it's working! Bless Dorcas! 'I have,' " he went on, gleefully quoting *Cymbeline*, " 'enjoyed the dearest bodily part of my mistress.' Dorcas, for the moment, is sufficient muddy muse for me!"

"Master Shakespeare," Charles insisted. "Your life is in serious danger!"

"But my play is in no danger!" As he spoke, feverish with excitement, his hand continued, almost unconsciously, to spill words out on to the page. "I've nearly finished the Third Act. The scene is: 'Bohemia. A desert Country near the Sea.' Antigonus has saved the baby Perdita and is about to abandon her there. I just need a good exit for him and the scene will be nearly done."

"Listen!" Charles slammed his hand down on Shakespeare's. The quill dug into the paper in a splutter of ink.

"Why have you done that?" A dangerous fury came into the brown eyes. "I cannot be stopped when the ideas are flowing!"

"If you do not listen to me, you will be stopped for ever!"

This did finally engage Shakespeare's attention. "What do you mean?"

"I know who killed Robert Hillard, and now he is planning to kill you."

"How do you know this?"

"Have you heard of a locksmith called Ezekiel Goodbody?"

"The one who has put money into the Bear Garden?"

"The very same. He married a pretty young wife a year or so back, and it's the old May and December problem."

"She has a roving eye?"

"Yes, and she has needs that her husband cannot satisfy. He is mad with jealousy, to the point of killing anyone whom he suspects of making doe-eyes at his wife."

"So is that why he killed Robert Hillard? If so, he was certainly badly informed. Master Hillard was as much attracted to a pretty young wife as I am to a week-old herring."

"I know. But it was what Master Hillard looked like that caused his death. Ezekiel Goodbody has a spy, the scoundrel in painted leather we saw outside the tavern this morning."

"And?"

"And he must have seen someone leaving Mistress Goodbody's chamber wearing the doublet that poor Master Hillard wore as Posthumus Leonatus."

"So that is why he was killed?"

"Yes. But by now all London knows that Robert Hillard had no lust for woman's flesh. So the murderer knows he had the wrong victim. But then this morning Master Goodbody's spy was on hand to hear you say that *you* owned the doublet."

"Oh, my God!" The full gravity of the situation hit Shakespeare. "So he thinks I am the one who has been colting his wife?" Charles Parys nodded. "And will try to murder me too?"

"I fear so."

"Master Parys, how do you know all this?"

"I've been thinking about it a lot. The solution came to me during the performance of *Philaster*. I saw the spy whispering to Master Goodbody."

Shakespeare looked at him with new admiration. "I had not thought of you as a follower of clues, a diviner of mysteries."

Diffidently, Charles Parys spread his hands. "A small talent I have."

"If you have the skill to unmask murderers, I would not call that a small talent. I do not understand how you have enough information to reach these conclusions."

"Just a matter of logic and deduction," said Charles, with partial truth.

"I still find it strange . . . But to more immediate concerns. How am I to escape the avenging hand of Ezekiel Goodbody?"

"I have a plan, Master Shakespeare, that will not only save your life, but also see that the villain gets the punishment he deserves."

"We meet again," said the Constable.

A potboy instantly brought a cup of ale as the Constable lowered his considerable bulk on to a tiny stool. No payment would ever be requested for the drink. The tavern-keeper knew the wisdom of keeping on the right side of the law.

"Good to see you, Master Dewberry," said Shakespeare. "I hope you didn't take to heart any of those silly rumors that—"

"No, no, no, Master Shakespeare. I know people said there was a dissimilarity between me and the Constable in your play, but so far as I am conserved, it was, as the title goes . . ." He paused and chuckled heavily ". . . *much ado about nothing*. And the people who make such allocations that I am a fellow who gets words wrong, do nothing but show up their own ignominy. They do not seem to compromise that your character is *Dog*berry and mine is *Dew*berry, so there cannot be any caparison between the two, by any stretch of the invigilation."

"You're absolutely right," said Shakespeare, earnestly avoiding Charles's eye. "Now do you understand Master Parys's plan?"

"I do. And I think it a work of great genitalia. The Watch and I will do what is necessitous, and discharge ourselves like true offenders of the Crown."

"Good," said Charles Parys, earnestly avoiding Shakespeare's eye. "I knew I could rely on you."

Charles lifted the foul leather drape that hung over the Bull's window to see his plan unfold. William Shakespeare, full of hot sack for courage, had stepped boldly out of the tavern's door and set off on exactly the fatal route that Robert

Hillard had followed. The playwright paused at the corner, where the flickering torchlight melted to darkness, and sure enough, in that moment a dark figure in a fur cloak leapt towards him. Thin steel gleamed in the dwindling light.

Instantly Dewberry's men leapt from their hiding places, and the Constable himself bellowed out, "Stop, in the name of the Watch!"

The fur-cloaked figure, still only a dark outline against the greater darkness, turned on his heel and fled, with the ragged, shouting Watch in full pursuit.

William Shakespeare was unhurt, but shaken. Somewhat unsteadily, he made his way back to the safety of the Bull.

Charles Parys had changed from ale to sack, its tartness softened by sugar, warmed by the thrust of a red-hot poker. Shakespeare ordered the same and they settled down to put away a good few of them.

A little later, Ned Brackett came into the tavern and looked around disconsolately.

"Are you looking for your gentleman of the Court?" asked Charles.

"He's no more a gentleman of the Court than you are," said the boy venomously. "The chain he gave me is of painted tin, and all I am left with is a nasty discharge in my pizzle that will send me to the apothecary."

"Who will prescribe you a course of sweating to cure your clap," said Shakespeare.

"That's something to look forward to." The boy turned sullenly towards the tavern door. "Never again will I be taken in by rich apparel. In future I will find out the character of the man inside the clothes."

"You know," said Shakespeare as Ned Brackett trailed out, "maybe *Cymbeline*'s not such a bad play, after all. There's some good stuff in there about appearance and reality."

"Of course there is," Charles Parys agreed enthusiastically.

And then Dewberry appeared to report on the success of his mission. Once again, as the Constable sat down, a complimentary cup of ale appeared as if by magic in front of him.

A smile sat smugly on his broad features. "We have him, sirs, condemned by his own emission. I had hardly to mention the thumbscrews or the bastinado before he freely confused to the murder of Master Hillard. And omitted to the attempted murder of Master Shakespeare. He's now locked in chains of his own manufacture—a fitting fate for such an evil melon."

Charles Parys raised his eyebrows and mouthed, "Melon?"

"Felon," Shakespeare mouthed back.

Charles nodded, suppressing a giggle. "And was he easily caught, Master Dewberry?"

"By no means. He was fast for a man of his age, and ran back to the Bear Garden in Shoreside Lane, which he owns. There he thought to fructate the watch in the perusal of their duties by releasing one of the bears on us. But the beast, remembering the many cruelties of Master Goodbody, turned instead on his master. How it mauled and mammocked him! The beast chased him straight out of the bear-pit and into the expectorant arms of my faithful Watch."

A blissful, beatific expression had settled on Shakespeare's face. He dipped his quill in the ink bottle, and Charles Parys watched as he wrote: "EXIT, PURSUED BY A BEAR."

Charles was the last of the three to leave. Dewberry had bustled off after a few cups of ale, professing that he must find his wife to "raise up an object of great impotence." Dorcas had appeared, and Shakespeare had gone off to spend the night in the arms of his muddy muse, leaving enough money on the table to pay the evening's reckoning twice over.

As Charles Parys sipped at the warm sweetness of a new sugared sack, he wondered how long he'd leave it before persuading Rokesby Lander to lend him the black doublet once again, so that he could pay another—now risk-free—visit to the voluptuous and avid wife of Ezekiel Goodbody.

Richard's Children

BY BRENDAN DuBois

Brendan DuBois is the award-winning author of both short stories and novels. His short fiction has appeared in *Playboy, Ellery Queen's Mystery Magazine, Alfred Hitchcock's Mystery Magazine, Mary Higgins Clark Mystery Magazine,* and numerous anthologies. He has twice received the Shamus Award from the Private Eye Writers of America for his short stories.

He's also the author of the Lewis Cole mystery series—*Dead Sand, Black Tide, Shattered Shell,* and *Killer Waves.* His most recent novel, *Resurrection Day,* is a suspense thriller that looks at what might have happened had the Cuban Missile Crisis of 1962 erupted into a nuclear war between the United States and the Soviet Union. This book received the Sidewise Award for best alternative history novel of 1999. He lives in New Hampshire with his wife, Mona. Please visit his website at www.BrendanDuBois.com.

For mid-October, the weather in London was quite warm and the sun was out, another rare occurrence in this cloudy town. Kevin Tanner, assistant professor of English at Lovecraft University in Massachusetts, sat on a park bench in the middle of a small courtyard at the Tower of London. He still felt a bit jet-lagged, like everything he saw was too bright and loud, and the scents and sounds were too strong and forceful. He was near one of the largest stone buildings in the Tower of London complex, the White Tower, and there he waited. He had been here once before, as a grad student, more than sixteen years ago, and it seemed like not much had changed over the years. There were manicured lawns, sidewalks, and walls and battlements and towers, all representing nearly a thousand years of English history. And beyond the Tower complex, the soaring span of the Tower Bridge—looking ancient of course, but less than a hundred years old—and the wide and magnificent Thames.

At his feet was a small red knapsack, and just a half-hour ago—after spending nearly twenty minutes in line for the privilege of spending eleven pounds to gain entry—a well-dressed and polite security officer had examined his bag and its contents. Inside the bag was a water bottle, two candy bars, a thick guidebook to London, and secured in a zippered pouch within the knapsack, his passport and round-trip airline ticket. He supposed that if the security guard had been more on the job, he would have looked at the airline ticket and inquired as to how an assistant professor at a small college with a savings account of just over two thousand dollars could have afforded a round-trip, first-class airline ticket. Now that would have been something worth investigating.

Despite the oddity of this whole trip and the arrangements, he had enjoyed the flight over. He had never traveled business class in his life, never mind first class, and he felt slightly guilty at having all the attention and comforts of being up in the forward cabin. But after ten or so minutes, he quickly realized why it was so special. How could anybody not want to fly first class if they could afford it? The wide, plush seats, with plenty of elbow and legroom, and the flight attendants who were at his beck and call. That's when he felt that familiar flush of anger and embarrassment. Anger at being someone supposedly admired in society, a teacher of children, a molder of future generations, and the only way he could come to England and in first class was through the generosity of strangers. And embarrassment, for he was a grown man, had made grown-up choices, and he shouldn't be angry at that.

Still, he thought, looking down at his bag, it was going to be pleasant flying back.

He looked around him, seeing the crowds of tourists. There were two types: those moving about the grounds of the Tower by themselves, with brochures and maps, and those in large groups following one of the numerous Yeoman Warders, dressed in their dark blue and red Beefeater uniforms. Each uniform had ER written on the chest in fine script. *Elizabeth Regina.* Kevin crossed his legs, waited, checked his watch. It was 11 A.M., and a man came over to him, wearing a red rose in the lapel of his suitcoat. He was tall, gaunt, with thick gray hair combed back in a lion-like mane. The suit and shoes were black, as were the tie, and the shirt was white. The man came to him and nodded.

"Professor Tanner," he said in a cultured English accent that said it all: Cambridge or Oxford, followed by a civil service position at White Hall, relaxing in all the right clubs, following the cricket matches on the BBC.

"The same," Kevin said. "And Mister Lancaster?"

"As well," he said. "May I join you?"

He shifted on the park bench, turned so he could watch the man sit down, and see how he carefully adjusted the pleat of his pants. "I trust your flight was uneventful?"

"It was," he said.

"And your room is satisfactory?"

Kevin smiled. "The Savoy is just as it's advertised. I think even a broom closet would be satisfactory in that palace."

If he was hoping for a response from Mister Lancaster, it didn't happen. The older man nodded and said, "I see. I appreciate you coming here on such short notice. Will your university miss you?"

"No," he said, a note of regret in his voice, he realized. "I'm on sabbatical. Supposedly working on a book. Which is why I was able to drop everything to come here and see you."

"Really, then."

Kevin paused. "All right, I have to admit, you folks raised my curiosity. A round-trip first-class ticket, first-class accommodations, plus a stipend in pounds equal to about a thousand dollars. All to meet with you at the Tower of London. And to discuss what?"

"Quite," Lancaster said, folding his long hands over his knees. "History, if you don't mind. Some history old and history new, all starting here in England."

"Are you sure you want me?" he asked. "I'm an assistant professor of English. Not history."

The older man shrugged. "Yes, I know you're not a professor of history. And yet I know everything there is to know about you, Professor Tanner. Your residence in Newburyport, Massachusetts. Your single life. The courses you teach, your love of Shakespeare and Elizabethan England. Your solitary book, a study of gravestone epitaphs in northern New England, which sold exactly six hundred and four copies two years ago. And the fact that you are currently struggling on another book, one that will guarantee you receive tenure. But that book is nowhere near being completed, am I correct?"

Kevin knew he should be insulted by the fact that this pompous Englishman knew so much about his life, but he was almost feeling honored, that someone should care so much. "All right, you've done some research. To what purpose?"

"To help you with this book you're working on," Lancaster said.

"Excuse me?"

Lancaster turned away and said, "Look about you, Professor Tanner. Hundreds of years of history, turned into a bloody tourist attraction. The other day I was on a tour here, with a visitor from Germany. One of the Beefeaters told the tourists that the ER on his chest stood for 'Extremely Romantic.' Imagine that, making sport of our monarch, in this property that belongs to her. And think about all of the people who have been imprisoned here, from Lady Jane Grey to Sir Walter Raleigh to Rudolf Hess. And in this White Tower behind us, do you know what famous black deed happened there?"

He turned in his bench, looked at the tall building, the line of tourists snaking their way in. "The two princes."

"Yes, the two princes. Young Edward the Fourth and his younger brother Richard, the Duke of York. Imprisoned here by Richard the Third. You do know Richard the Third, do you not?"

"If you know my background, you already know the answer to that."

"Ah, yes, Richard the Third. One of the most controversial monarchs this poor green, sceptered isle has ever seen. Made even more famous by our bard,

Mister Shakespeare. 'Now is the winter of our discontent.' Either a great man or an evil man, depending on your point of view. And what happened to the young princes, again, depending on your point of view. What do you think happened, Professor?"

Kevin said carefully, "There's evidence supporting each view, that Richard the Third either had the princes killed, to remove possible claimants to the throne, or that he was ignorant of the whole thing. But the bones of two young boys were found there, buried under a staircase, some years later."

"Very good, you've given me a professor's answer, but not a scholar's answer. So tell me again, Professor, what do you think happened?"

Kevin felt pressure, like he was going up before the damn tenure board itself. "I think he had them murdered. That's what I think."

"And what's your evidence?"

"The evidence is, who profits? After Richard the Third seized the throne, he had to eliminate any possible rivals. Those two boys were his rivals. He did what he had to do. It was purely political, nothing else."

"Hmmm. And your book, the one you're working on, compares and contrasts our Richard, our Duke of Gloucester, with another Richard from your country, am I correct?"

"Jesus," Kevin exclaimed. "Who the hell are you people?"

"Never mind that right now," Lancaster said, leaning in closer to him. "Correct, am I not? Our Richard and your Richard, the Duke of San Clemente. Mister Nixon. Quite the comparison, eh? Richard the Third and Richard Nixon. The use of power, the authority, all that wonderful stuff. But tell me, the book is not going well, is it?"

Kevin thought about lying and then said, "Yeah, you're right. The book isn't going well."

"And why's that?"

"Because it's all surface crap, that's all," he said heatedly. "Sure, it sounds good on paper and in talking at the faculty lounge, but c'mon, Richard the Third and Nixon? Nixon certainly was something else, but he didn't have blood on his hands, like your Duke of Gloucester. And don't start yapping at me about Vietnam. He didn't start that war. Kennedy and Johnson did. And for all his faults, he ended it the best way he could. Messily, but the best way he could. And I think, and so do other historians, that his opening to China balanced that out. And that's why the book isn't going well. Because it's all on the surface, like it came from some overheated grad student's imagination."

Lancaster nodded again, plucked a piece of invisible lint off his suitcoat. "Perhaps you're ignoring the rather blatant comparisons."

"What do you mean?"

The older man gestured to the White Tower. "What crime was committed here. The murder of two young princes. And what kind of crime was committed in your own country. In 1963 and 1968. Two young princes, loved and admired, who promised great things to their people. Cut down at a young age."

Kevin was aghast. "The Kennedys?"

"Of course."

"You brought me all the way over here to spout conspiracy theories? Gibberish? Who the hell are you?"

"I told you, in a matter of—"

Kevin grabbed his knapsack. "And I'll tell you, unless you come straight with me, right now, I'm leaving. I'm not here to listen to half-ass Kennedy assassination theories. And you can cancel my room and airfare home, and I don't care. I'll pay my own way."

"And not finish your book?"

"That's the price I'll pay," Kevin said.

Lancaster smiled thinly. "How noble. Very well. Here we go. Leave now and your book will never be completed, you know that, don't you. Leave now and you won't get tenure. In fact, your life will start getting unwound. You will be forced out of your college, perhaps be tossed back into the great unwashed. Teaching English at high schools or what you folks call vocational technical schools. Or perhaps conjugating verbs to prisoners. Is that a better life than teaching at a comfortable university?"

Kevin felt his breathing quicken. "Go on."

"Stay with me and learn what I have to offer, and you'll not only write your book, you'll write a book that will become an instant best-seller. You will be known across your country and ours as well. If you want to stay at your university, that will be fine, but I can tell you, once this book comes out, Harvard and Yale and Stanford and Columbia will come begging at your door. That's your choice now, isn't it. To stay or go."

"Yeah, that's a hell of a choice," Kevin said.

Lancaster smiled. "But a choice nonetheless. It's a pleasant day, Professor Tanner. We're both alive and breathing and enjoying this lovely autumn day in the best city on this planet. Let me continue with what I have to say, and what I have to offer. And then you can leave and decide what to do next. All right? Don't you at least owe me some time, considering the expense that was incurred to bring you over to our fair country?"

Kevin lowered his knapsack to the ground. "All right, I guess I do owe you that. But make it quick and to the point. And I'm not going to do a damn thing until you tell me who you are, and why you spent all this money to have me fly over."

Lancaster nodded, folded his long hands. "Very well. That seems quite fair. Well, let's begin, shall we? Another history lesson, if you prefer. Let's set the stage, that place, as Shakespeare said, where we are all just actors. But this stage has a bloody history. Tell me, who runs the world?"

Kevin hesitated, thinking that he had fallen into the clutches of that odd group of loons and eccentrics who sometimes haunt college campuses. At one faculty luncheon some months ago, he remembered some physics professor bemoaning the fact that a junkyard dealer in New Hampshire had finally come across a Unified Field Theory, and wanted the professor's assistance in getting his theory published. So now it was Kevin's turn, and again, that temptation came up, to walk away from this odd man.

But . . . like the man said, it was a pleasant day, he had money and a nice room and a ticket back home, and if nothing else, at least he'd have a good story to tell at the next English faculty function.

So he nodded, gestured towards Lancaster. "All right, a fair question. Who does run the world? I'm not sure the world is actually run. If anything, I think it's hard to even come to an agreement as to who actually runs the country. As a conservative, I could say legally elected governments, in most cases, run most countries in the world. As a liberal, I suppose I could make a case that in some nations, corporations or the military have their hands in running things."

"Ah, not a bad answer," Lancaster said. "But let's try another theory, shall we? What would you say if I told you that royal families across this great globe actually . . . as you say it, run things?"

Oh, this was going to be a great story when he got back to Massachusetts, he thought. Kevin said, "All right, that's a theory. An odd one, but still a theory. But I'm not sure I understand you. Royal families, like the House of Windsor, actually run things?" Kevin found himself laughing. "Then you'd think they could do a better job in running their own personal lives, don't you?"

Lancaster didn't return the laughter. "How droll, I'm sure, Professor Tanner. But when I say royal families, I don't restrict myself to Europe. To make you feel more comfortable, let's discuss your own country, shall we?"

"The States?" He tried to restrain a laugh. "What royalty we have resides in Hollywood. Or Palm Springs. Or Wall Street. They're involved in entertainment or business, and they get their photos in *People* magazine when they become famous, and in the *National Enquirer* when they get arrested or sent into drug rehab. That's our royalty, Mister Lancaster. Your royalty's been written up by Mister Shakespeare himself. Our royalty, if that's what you call it, is a pretty ratty lot, if you ask me."

Lancaster's face seemed more drawn. "This isn't a joke."

"I'm sorry, I wasn't being amusing."

"You certainly weren't. And you're not taking this seriously. Not at all. And I suggest you do."

"Or what? Will you have me arrested?"

Lancaster's look was not reassuring. "That would be easier to accomplish than you think, Professor Tanner. So let's proceed, shall we? I was asking you about royalty in America. I don't care about your tycoons or your entertainers. What I do care about is the royalty involved in politics, the kind that actually, again as you say, 'run things.' "

Kevin didn't like the threat he had just heard, but he pressed on. "I'm sorry, I don't understand. We don't have any kind of royalty in the United States."

Lancaster's look was imperious. "Really? Look at your own history. What names in the last half of the twentieth century have either been in your Oval Office or nearby in your Congress? Let's try, shall we? Roosevelt, Kennedy, Rockefeller, DuPont, Bush, Gore, Byrd, Russell . . . wealthy families of influence who reside in and maintain the circles of power in your country. Tell me, Professor Tanner, are you really that naive?"

"No, I'm not that naive, and I'm also not that stupid," Kevin said, thinking again of what a great tale this would make once he got back home. "But you're reaching, Mister Lancaster, you're reaching quite a lot. Those families are political families, that's all, just like other families that have their backgrounds in oil, retail, or other kinds of business. Some families pick cattle, others pick politics. That's it."

"Really?" the man asked, his voice filled with skepticism.

"Really," Kevin said.

"These . . . families, as you call them, have been running your government and your lives for many decades, Professor Tanner. Just like the royal families in Shakespeare's time. In public they may show their good works and charities, as they run for office and for influence, but in private, it's quite different. They lie, they cheat, and they steal, and oftentimes, they kill. Look at your own news reports over the years, when famed members of these families would often die."

"What do you mean? They kill each other?"

Lancaster made a dismissive motion with a long hand. "Of course. Again, look at the news reports. Many times, members of your royal family—a Kennedy, a DuPont, a Rockefeller—perishes. Sometimes it's called a drug overdose. Other times, an accidental shooting. And in one memorable case a few years ago, a plane crash. Those are the cover stories. The real stories are darker, more malignant, as they kill each other, always vying for power, for influence, for money."

Kevin sighed. The shadows were getting longer, it was getting cooler, and he recalled the size of the bed waiting for him back at the Savoy. He said, "No offense, Mister Lancaster, but I think you're nuts. Again, no offense. The story of royal families in the United States, acting like characters from Shakespeare . . . well, it's too fantastic."

"Is it, now?" he asked. "Think of young John F. Kennedy, Jr., the one who died in that plane crash. He was a charming young man, of middling intelligence and skills. But what did he have going for him? Any extraordinary talents, any extraordinary gifts? Not really, am I right? He was just a pleasant young man. Yet tell me, Professor Tanner, if he had decided to enter politics, perhaps as a congressman, how long before he would be a leading candidate for president on the Democratic ticket? Two years? Four? Do you doubt that?"

And the truth is, Kevin couldn't doubt what the old man was saying about that particular subject, because it made sense. In his own home state of Massachusetts, old Teddy Kennedy was the proverbial 800-pound gorilla of politics, swatting down ineffectual opponents every six years, like King Kong on top of the Empire State Building, swatting down aircraft. Not to mention the Kennedy offspring that had been spun off from Massachusetts, setting up their own political dynasties in Rhode Island, New York, and Maryland . . .

"So you're telling me that John-John was murdered, is that it?" Kevin asked.

Lancaster slowly shrugged. "A possibility, that's all I can say. Just a possibility. But there's a reality we need for you to look at. A very real event that happened almost forty years ago. A lifetime, for sure, but the death of your two young princes is still a topic that bestirs the imagination, does it not?"

With this odd talk and the cooling weather and the harsh cries of the ravens—legend had it that if they were ever to leave the Tower, England would fall, which is why they had their wings clipped—Kevin was starting to get seriously spooked. The Tower of London no longer seemed to be the cheery tourist attraction that it had been earlier. His imagination could bring forth all of the bloody and horrible deeds that had taken place among these buildings, among these battlements. He suddenly wished that this gaunt man had never contacted him, had never pulled him away from his comfortable little life at Lovecraft University. He wished now he had tossed away that thick airmail envelope with ROYAL MAIL emblazoned in the upper right corner.

"Yes, the two princes—the two Kennedys—still bestir the imagination," Kevin said. "But I have to ask you again, who are you people? And why me?"

Lancaster shifted his weight. "Very well. A fair question. For the past few hundred years, ever since Shakespeare's time, this poor little globe has been under the influence of these families, who front companies, governments, and armies. As time passes, they have formed two alliances. Not a firm alliance—they are shifts here and there—but groupings of interest."

The old man made a noise like a sigh, as if he had worked hard every day, carrying a heavy burden on those thin shoulders. "Our group believes in the freedom of the individual, in concentrating power in the smallest possible arena. Where you have an open press, a Freedom of Information Act, legitimate elections, you can trust that our group or its allies have been behind it."

"So that's your group," Kevin said. "And the other one?"

"The second group has as its goal power: power of a government over people, a corporation over people, of one group of people over another. When you read about a newspaper in Russia being closed, when you read about Internet software that can track you on-line, when you read about Balkan tribes slaughtering each other, you can be sure this group is behind it. By their actions, by their deeds, they are the offspring of Richard the Third. For lack of a better phrase, we call them Richard's Children."

"You do, do you," Kevin said, now convinced that he was spending the afternoon with a madman. "And what do you call yourselves?"

A thin smile. "You're a bright young man. I'm sure you can figure it out."

Then it struck him. The red rose in the lapel. The last name. "The War of the Roses . . . the House of York fighting against the House of Lancaster. White rose versus red rose. Is that it?"

A crisp nod. "Very good. You're correct. It's been a long struggle, over generations and generations, but now we feel it's time to strike a blow. Despite the fall of the Berlin Wall and Communism, Richard's Children and their allies are gathering strength. It's time to bring things out in the open."

"Which is where I come in?"

"Exactly," Lancaster said. "Meaning no offense, but an anonymous professor from an obscure college comes across documentation and facts about the murder of America's two young princes. His book becomes a worldwide bestseller. The evidence he presents is irrefutable. The major news organizations, upset that such a scoop and story have escaped them over the years, perform their own research, based on the leads that this young professor had uncovered. And when these leads are followed, they will end up in some very interesting areas of inquiry. Richard's Children will have to retreat, maybe for decades, maybe long enough so that a true human civilization can emerge, a civilization based on the sanctity of the individual."

Lancaster reached into his coat pocket, withdrew a thick brown envelope. "In here you will find some evidence. But not the whole story, and nothing so directly offered, of course."

Kevin refused to take the offered envelope. "What do you mean, nothing so directly offered?"

"What I mean is that you will be offered leads, avenues to explore," Lancaster said. "It makes sense that way, does it not? For if everything is offered to you on a silver platter, then it will be shown that you performed little or no original research on your part. Your work, your published book, will be roundly criticized and ignored. But if you follow these leads"—he wiggled the envelope back and forth—"all will become clear. Everything. And your life will change in ways you can't imagine."

Kevin waited, watched the man who was offering so much. But what was behind that offer? Lancaster said, "Enclosed in the envelope, of course, is another stipend. About five thousand dollars."

Again, Kevin waited. He finally said, "There's no guarantee, you know. Publishers aren't exactly lining up outside my office, to sign me up for a new book. I could write this and nothing would happen."

"I doubt that," Lancaster said. "And speaking of doubts, don't believe that we won't be watching you. Do the research, do the work that goes into this book. Don't entertain any thoughts of going back home to your little place and pretend this meeting didn't happen, that you don't have an obligation. Have I made myself clear?"

His hand seemed to move of its own volition, as it grasped the heavy envelope. "Yes. Quite clear."

"Good. We'll be in touch."

Kevin bent over to place the envelope in his knapsack, and when he raised his head, Lancaster was gone. He looked around at the paths, now almost entirely deserted of tourists, and he got up himself and shouldered his bag.

Within a few minutes he was on a crowded sidewalk, heading for the Tower Hill tube station, and the knapsack—with the envelope safely inside—felt like he was carrying a boulder.

Two days later, in his room at the Savoy—which had cost as much as two months' rent in his apartment back home—Kevin looked at his meager collection of luggage. His head was still spinning, for in the two days he had by himself in London, he tried to put Mister Lancaster and that envelope out of his mind. He had caught an afternoon matinee performance at the London Lyceum of *The Lion King*, had spent an entire day touring the British Museum, and in one surprising sunny morning, he had actually caught the changing of the guard at Buckingham Palace. He found himself enjoying London and its people and the black taxi cabs and the tube system, even though at night, back in his room, he kept on being drawn to that envelope. He knew he should open it up and examine the evidence and the stipend, but no, he didn't want to spoil what little time he had in London. So the envelope had remained closed, like a tiny cage holding a dangerous reptile, one that he wanted to be very careful while opening up.

" 'Lord, what fools these mortals be!' " he quoted. "Yeah, Puck, you had that one right."

And he picked up his bags and left.

On the British Airways flight going home, again, he was luxuriating in the comfort and pleasure of flying first class, and he drank a little bit too much champagne. His head and tongue were thick, and he wished he could convince the pilot and crew to keep on flying around the world, stopping only to pick up food and fuel. He was sure that if that would happen, he would gladly spend the rest of his days in this metal cocoon, reading newspapers and magazines, sleeping in luxury, eating the finest food—compared to what he could whip at home in his own kitchen—served by conscientious helpers and watching the latest movies.

It would be an odd life, a strange life, but one worth it, so long as he could avoid thinking about his knapsack and that envelope, up there in the overhead bin.

He had one more glass of champagne, and then slept the rest of the way home.

His apartment was in an old house, built near the Merrimack River in Newburyport, Massachusetts. He knew he paid an extra hundred dollars a month for the privilege of a river view, and most days, he thought it was worth it. He sat in his office, brooding, staring at the piles of papers, books, and file folders that represented a book in progress, a book that was months, if not years, away from being finished. Kevin powered up his computer, looked at the little folder icon that represented his months of work. *Two Richards* was going to be the name of it, contrasting Richard III with Richard Nixon. And damn that Lancaster character—he knew he was nowhere near completing it on time, and in the way he wanted it done. At the beginning, he had wanted a dark, brooding book, full of facts and contrasts. A book that would safely secure his tenure, would at last make a mark in the world. And now?

Now, it was stuck in the mud, just like Lancaster had said.

Sitting in his dark office, he usually got a feeling of peace and tranquility, here among his books and papers. But not this evening, not after that strange meeting at the Tower. Those people—he doubted Lancaster could have pulled everything off on his own—had poked and pried into his life, knew almost everything about him. He picked up the envelope from his desk. Such a choice. Continue working on *Two Richards*, or dive into the ravings of a lunatic.

He looked up on the wall, where a tiny framed portrait of the Bard looked down at him. "Old Will," he said aloud, "did you ever have days like this? With odd people and noblemen coming to you, demanding you write about them or their families or adventures? Did you?"

The portrait remained silent. Of course. If Will had started talking to him, Kevin would have gotten up and driven to the hospital, demanding to be admitted.

Things were odd, things might be mad, but they weren't that bad.

Not yet.

He picked up the envelope, took a letter opener, and slit open the top.

Inside were three sheets of blank white paper, folded over. Inside was another cashier's check, drawn on the Midlands Bank, for three thousand pounds. About five thousand dollars, give or take. And beside the check and the paper, were two 8-by-10 glossy black-and-white prints, also folded over. He switched on the overhead lamp on his desk, flattened out both photos. The air in the office seemed to get suddenly cold and damp. Both photos he recognized, though he had never been at either location in his entire life. The first showed a black open-top Lincoln limousine, parked outside of a hospital. Police officers and reporters and other people were clustered around the luxury car, their mouths open in shock, some of the people holding up hands to their faces. It looked like a bright and sunny day, and near the car was an emergency room entrance to the hospital.

But of course. Parkland Memorial Hospital in Dallas. November 22, 1963.

The second photo was of a crowded hallway in a building of some sort, people clustered about, some reporters standing on chairs or tables, trying to get a better view, police officers trying to hold the crowd back. A man was on the ground, and only his feet were visible. As in the other photo, the people's faces were almost the same, mirroring shock, disbelief, anger.

And of course, the second photo was the Ambassador Hotel in Los Angeles. June 4, 1968.

America's two young princes. Murdered.

He stared at the photos for a long time, knowing of the official stories, the ones that said both men, both young princes, had been cut down by deranged men with dark passions and grudges. Kevin had never really paid that much attention to the various conspiracy theories and stories, but now, since his meeting with Lancaster . . . He looked again at the faces of the people in the crowds. Citizens of a nation, confident that their leaders and rulers were freely elected, every two, four, or six years. Not a nation like Shakespeare's time, ruled by royalty and extended families, with long knives and longer memories.

But what was the point of the two photos? What was their meaning? Back at the Tower, Lancaster said that only leads would be provided. Not information. Not direct clues. No, just leads, so that Kevin would have to work and work at it, to get the leads to uncovering the story of the century, and perhaps, the story of the millennium.

He sighed, went back to looking at each photo, sparing a glance up at the print of Shakespeare.

"What the hell are you looking at?" he grumbled as he picked up the first photo.

Kevin woke with a start, tangled up in his sheets and blankets. A dream had come to him, a dream of running along a muddy path, chased by wraiths armed with long knives and pikes, closing in on him. He rubbed at his eyes and mouth, feeling his legs tremble from the memory of the dream. He rarely ever had nightmares, but this one had been a doozy. He rolled over and sat up, looking out at the night. Like his office, his bedroom had a view of the Merrimack River, and he could make out the red and green navigation lights of a fishing craft, heading out to the cold Atlantic for a hard day of fishing.

He rubbed at the base of his neck, wondering what about the dream had disturbed him so. He had spent several hours holed up in his office before going to bed. He had looked at each photo until he was almost cross-eyed. He had gone on the Internet and had quickly been sucked into the strange world of conspiracies and plots. A few websites he had gone to had even hinted at the story Lancaster had been peddling, about powerful interests and families ruling the world, but those sites had gone off the edge with racist nonsense about religious cabals.

After a quick dinner of macaroni and cheese and an hour decompressing before the television, he had gone to bed and had instantly gone to sleep, until that dark dream had come upon him.

What in the hell was he doing, he thought. An obscure English teacher at an even more obscure college, supposedly holding the key to a worldwide conspiracy? Please. No doubt he had fallen in league with some elaborate prank by some eccentric Englishman, trying to gain some amusement by making Kevin run around like a fool, chasing down spirits and ghosts.

Spirits and ghosts, just like the wraiths chasing him in that dream, wraiths that were frightening and uniform in their appearance . . .

Uniform.

That thought stuck with him. Why?

Uniform. Uniform wraiths, armed and heading towards him . . .

He stumbled out of bed, almost fell as a sheet tripped him up, and he went back to his office, switching on the lights. The office looked strange, illuminated at such a time in the morning, but he didn't care. He grabbed both photos, took a magnifying glass, and started looking. His chest started thumping and the hand holding the magnifying glass began shaking. He took deep breaths, tried to calm down, and looked again.

Dallas, Texas. Outside of the hospital, holding back part of the crowd. A man dressed in a policeman's uniform, nose prominent, a nice profile shot.

Los Angeles, California. In the hallway of a hotel, holding back part of the crowd. A man dressed in a policeman's uniform, nose prominent, a nice profile shot.

In both pictures, there's an odd expression on the face, different from the crowd about him, those people shock and scared and horrified.

The expression . . . happiness? Sadness? Grief?

He blinked his eyes, looked again. It was the same man. Had to be. And what would be the chances that a police officer would be in Dallas the day JFK was killed, and would leave town and get a job in Los Angeles as a police officer, and then be present at the time RFK was killed?

What would be the chances?

He bounced back and forth again to the two photos, and then realized what the expression was on each face, frozen in time, almost six years apart.

It was satisfaction.

That's what.

Satisfaction for a job well-done.

He slowly got up and left the office, leaving the lights on, and then went back to bed and stayed awake until it was time for breakfast.

Three weeks after the night he had spent with the photos, Kevin was in a rental car, shivering, wondering if he would have the guts to take it this far. For nearly the past month, he had gone down a twisting and turning path, trying to identify the police officer who appeared in both photographs, separated by nearly five years and thousands of miles. Luckily for him, his university had a library that was one of the best in the region. Through its research assistants and some microfilm files and in searching old newspapers and magazines, he had found captions identifying the officer in the Dallas photo as Mike Mc-Kenna, and the officer in Los Angeles as Ron Carpenter. That had taken almost a week of back-breaking work, sitting in hard chairs, blinking as the black-and-white microfilm reels whirred by, almost like a time machine, taking him back to tumultuous times when it seemed like the two princes would make a difference in the American empire.

Once he had the names, what next?

Then came frustrating contacts with the police departments of Dallas and Los Angeles, trying to find out who Mike McKenna and Ron Carpenter were, and if they were still living. Another couple of days, blocked, for the departments weren't cooperative, not at all. Then, not really enjoying what he had to do next, he delved deeper into the outlands of the Internet, looking into the different conspiracy pages put up by people still investigating the deaths of JFK and RFK. Then, this was followed by flights to Dallas and Los Angeles—spending the latest money from Lancaster—to two separate offices, where obsessive men and women were keepers of what they felt was the real truth, he made some additional contacts. In turn, they led him to other people, who gave him two interesting facts: the names of Mike McKenna and Ron Carpenter still existed in the systems of the Dallas and Los Angeles police departments, and forwarding addresses for pension and disability information were exactly the same: 14 Old Mast Road, Nansen, Maine.

Unbelievable. So here he was, on a dirt road in a rural part of Maine, and after doing some additional work at the local town hall, looking at tax rolls, he found out who lived at 14 Old Mast Road: one Harold Brown, age seventy-nine. Retired. And that's it.

So here he was, at a place where the driveway intersected Old Mast Road, waiting in his rental car. The driveway—also dirt—went up to a Cape Cod house on top of a hill, painted gray. Smoke tendriled up from a brick chimney. Kevin rubbed at his chin, kept an eye on the house. Could this be it, right up here? All the years of controversy, investigations, claims, counterclaims, all brought to this one point, this little hill in a remote section of Maine? And all coming about because of him, Kevin Tanner, assistant professor of English?

Insane. It all sounded so insane.

And now what? That he had debated with himself for a couple of days, before he had worked up some courage, rented a car—his old Toyota would have never made it—and spent nearly four hours on the road. All along the way, he had practiced and repracticed his approach, what he would say, what he was going to try to come away with.

Now, it was time.

He opened the door, shivered from the early November cold. He walked up the muddy dirt driveway, looking at the old Cape Cod house, one of thousands sprinkled throughout the rural regions of Maine, Vermont, and New Hampshire. A very insignificant house, one easily ignored, except if the book was written and was published and became a best-seller, this sagging collection of wood and windows would become one of the most famous houses in the world.

The front lawn was brown, stunted grass, and Kevin went to the concrete stoop and knocked at the door. There was no doorbell, so he knocked again, harder. He could hear movement from inside. Kevin stood still, feeling his heart race away in his chest. Could this be it? Truly?

The door slowly opened, and an old man appeared, dressed in baggy jeans and a gray sweatshirt. His face was gaunt, his white hair was spread thinly across his freckled scalp, his eyes were watery and filmed, and his prominent nose was lined with red veins. Kevin felt his breath catch. This was him, the man in the photos.

"Yes?" he said, his voice almost a whisper.

Kevin cleared his throat. "Mister Brown? Harold Brown?"

"Yes," the man said. "Are you the tax assessor? Is that it?"

"No, no sir, I'm not," he said. "My name is Kevin Tanner. I'm a professor of English."

The old man blinked. "An English professor? Are you lost, is that it?"

"No, I'm not lost," Kevin said. "I was wondering if I could talk to you, just for a couple of minutes."

Brown looked suspicious. "You're not one of those door-to-door religious types, are you?"

"No, sir, I'm not. Just a professor of English. That's all."

Brown moved away from the door. "All right, come on in. I guess there won't be no harm in it."

Kevin walked into the house, breathing slowly, trying to calm down. The house had the scent of dust and old cooking odors, and he followed Brown as he moved into the living room. Kevin felt a faint flush of shame, watching the shuffling steps of Brown as he used a metal walker to move into the room. The black bedroom slippers he was wearing made a whispering noise against the carpeting.

Brown settled heavily into an old couch, and Kevin sat near him in an easy chair, balancing an envelope on his knees. The wallpaper was a light blue and there were framed photos of lighthouses and ships, but nothing that showed people. There were piles of newspapers around the floor of the small living room, and even piles on top of the television set. Brown coughed and said, "So. An English professor. Where do you teach?"

"Lovecraft University, in Massachusetts."

The old man shook his head. "Never heard of it. And why are you in this part of Maine?"

"To see you."

"Me?" Brown said, sounding shocked. "Whatever for?"

"Because I'm working on a book, and I think you have some information I could use," Kevin said.

"Me?" Brown said again. "I think you've come a long way for the wrong reason, young man."

Kevin remembered how he had thought how this would go, and decided it was time to just bring it out in the open, just barrel right ahead. He opened up the envelope and took out the two black-and-white photos that Lancaster had provided him, and passed them over. Brown looked at the photos and then fumbled in his shirt pocket, to pull out a pair of glasses. With the glasses on, Brown examined each photo, and then there was quick intake of breath. Kevin leaned forward, wondering if he would have to pull out the other bits of information he had, when Brown would deny that it was him in the photos. From the college newspaper research, he had additional photos, showing Brown in a variety of photos at each murder scene. From information supplied by the conspiracy buffs, Kevin had old police department records, placing him at each scene. Kevin waited for the answer, and when the answer came, he was shocked and surprised.

Brown looked up. "Are you here to kill me?"

Kevin said, "No, no, not at all. I really am a college professor, and I really am working on a book. About the deaths of both JFK and his brother. And my research led to these photographs, and then to you, Mister Brown. So that's really you, isn't it? You were present at both assassinations."

Brown's voice lowered to a whispered. "So long ago . . . so very long ago . . ."

Then, Kevin surprised even himself, as a burst of anger came up and he said, "Why? Why did you do it?"

Brown looked stunned at the questioning. "What do you mean, why? I did it because I was ordered to, that's why. I was younger back then, full of energy and purpose, and I did what I thought was right, and did what I was told. It was a different time, a turbulent time."

"And who ordered you to do it?"

Brown shook his head, lowered the photos down on the couch, kept his gaze on them both. "I'm not going to say a word. I'm an old man, living up here nice and quiet, and I'm not going to say another word."

"Was it Richard's Children? Was it?"

Brown's eyes snapped right back at him. "Who told you that?"

"That was part of my research. Richard's Children." Kevin took a breath, thinking, true, all true. That loon Lancaster was right. "I'm working on a book, Mister Brown, and I'm going to reveal your part in it, whether you help me or not."

Brown put his shaking hands in his lap. "It could be dangerous."

"Maybe so, but it'll be the truth."

Brown didn't say anything for what seemed to be a long time, and then he said, "I've been retired, for years . . . but I was a pack rat, you know. Against all orders. I kept documents and papers and photographs . . . lots of information . . ."

"You did?"

A slow nod from the old man. "I certainly did . . . a book. You said you're working on a book?"

"I am."

Brown said, "Would you like to see those materials?"

"God, yes."

Brown nodded, slowly got up off the couch, holding on to the walker with both gnarled hands. "You wait right here. I'll go get them."

Kevin clasped his hands together, his heart thumping yet again, thinking of how he would spend the day with the old man, debriefing him, figuring out all the angles of this story, the biggest story of the millennium, and all belonging to him. Kevin started smiling. Questions of tenure at old shabby Lovecraft U? Lancaster was right. When this book was done, he'd be considering offers from Yale and Harvard and—

Brown came back into the room. He moved quickly. He didn't have a walker with him, not at all, and he moved with the grace of an old man who had kept himself in shape. And there were no papers or books or photographs in his hand. Just a black, shiny, automatic pistol.

"You should have stuck with your Shakespeare," Brown said, his voice even and quite strong, and those words and the sharp report of the pistol were the last things that Kevin ever heard.

After receiving the news from a coded trans-Atlantic phone call, the man who sometimes called himself Lancaster and sometimes called himself York got up from his desk and walked across the room, to a thick oaken door. He rapped once on the door and entered at the soft voice that said, "Do come in."

The room was cozy, with long drapes and bookshelves lined with leather-bound volumes, some framed photos on the dull white plaster walls, and a wide window that looked down upon the windswept Thames. From his vantage point, looking over the desk and the comfortable chair that the old man sat in, Lancaster could make out the round shape of the rebuilt Globe Theatre.

The man wore a thick dressing gown, and his black hair was swept back, displaying a prominent nose. One arm was on the desk, and the other one, withered and almost useless, was propped up on the side of his chair. The old man was known as one of the richest and most philanthropic men in all the world, and on the wall were photos of him with the President of the United States, Prince Phillip of Great Britain, the Prime Minister, and several other notables. Including a small photograph of him with Richard Nixon, and Nixon was the one smiling the most, as if pleased at what had just been agreed to. He looked up and said, "You have news?"

"I do," Lancaster said. "The college professor has been removed. Mister Brown fulfilled our request admirably, and his compensation is en route."

"Good," the man said. "Any loose ends?"

Lancaster paused, and then proceeded, knowing that the man before him was always one for direct questions. "No, no loose ends. But I am just concerned about one thing, sir."

"Which is?"

Lancaster said, "I understand the whole point of this exercise. To locate those people with sufficient imagination and interest to look into our activities, and then see how far they can go before we eliminate them. And eliminate those they have contact with, who have supplied them with damaging information. But there's just one thing. Mister Brown, our man in Maine."

"Yes?" he asked.

"Don't you think he should be . . . taken care of, as well?"

The man at the desk turned and looked out at the mighty Thames and sat still. Lancaster knew better than to interrupt him when he was in such a reverie. Finally, he said, "No. I don't think so. And you want to know why?"

"Yes, I do."

"Loyalty," he said. "The man has done noble services for us, many times, over the years. He deserves our loyalty. So he shall remain alive. Understood?"

"Yes," Lancaster said.

"Good," said the man who called himself Richard. "As the Bard once said of my spiritual ancestor, 'I am determined to prove the villain, and hate the idle pleasures of these days.' Come, we have work to do."

"So we do, sir," he said. "So we do."

This World's Eternity
BY MARGARET FRAZER

Margaret Frazer's series of medieval mysteries featuring Dame Frevisse, a
Benedictine nun, now spans eleven novels, with *The Clerk's Tale* the most recent
and *The Bastard's Tale* forthcoming. She has won a Herodotus Award and twice
been nominated for Edgars, and her short stories appear in numerous anthologies, including *Murder Most Medieval* and *Murder Most Catholic*. She lives near
Minneapolis. The present story exactly follows the course of events in Shakespeare's play, with only the behind-the-scenes actions added.

*Death, at whose name I oft have been afeard,
Because I wish'd this world's eternity.*
—THE FIRST PART OF KING HENRY THE SIXTH, ACT II, SCENE 4

*There is advantage to be had, in great degree, in standing somewhat aside
from the general way of men. An advantage in having only one's mind, not
one's heart—let be the lower portions of one's anatomy—involved in the
matters that so consume most men.*

And women.

Oh, yes. Most definitely women.

An advantage to standing aside and letting them—men and women both—take their foolish courses, with need for me to do no more than slightly nudge them the way I'd have them go.

And so often hardly needing to do even that.

Whether the thought had been with him before, forming slowly and unnoticed, or came to him that day full grown, Gloucester never looked closely enough at himself to know. It was enough that when he clearly saw it, he chose to follow it.

The pity was that indeed he did love Eleanor. She was his very dear wife and had never failed him but in one way and even then through no willed fault of her own: their lack of a son was their mutual grief. But it remained that he was the Duke of Gloucester and son, brother, and uncle of kings, heir to generations of royal Plantagenet blood, and moreover, heir to the crown of England after his own nephew Henry VI, by God's grace presently King of England, France, and Ireland. He was all that and yet without heir of his own, and what was the worth of his love for Eleanor when set against that?

His chance and choice came out of the usual quarreling among the lords around the King. If only young Henry had been stronger, to take his lords in hand and keep them curbed, or else been stronger in his loins, to beget an heir to his throne on his Queen, things would have stood differently. But things were as they were, and that particular day, which had been intended for pleasant talk and pastimes among King Henry, Queen Margaret, and various lords and their ladies including Gloucester and Eleanor, was spoiled by a quarrel squalling up between the Duke of York and Duke of Somerset over which of them should be appointed Regent of England's lands in France, their claims and counterclaims fueled by that bastard Cardinal Beaufort and the Lords of Buckingham, Salisbury, Warwick, and damned Suffolk who, if he was not yet the Queen's paramour, would be before he was done, Gloucester would wager his dukedom on it.

The quarrel started up ugly and turned uglier, with King Henry as usual saying nothing and Queen Margaret too much, to the point of snapping at the

Earl of Salisbury when he demanded at Buckingham to show reason why Somerset should be preferred over York as Regent, "Because the King will have it so!"

Salisbury could hardly snap back at her; neither his rank nor blood allowed it. But Gloucester could and did, saying sharply at her, "The king is old enough himself to give his censure. These are no women's matters."

Margaret turned to sneer into his face, "If he be old enough, what needs your grace to be still Protector of the realm?"

He was still Protector, as he had been since Henry was a child newly come to the throne, because Henry, though now in his young manhood, had never seen fit to take the office from him and it was none of French-born Margaret's place to question that, but she had never liked him, had ever seen his nearness in blood to King Henry as a threat, and though never, never would Gloucester have harmed a hair on his nephew's head, there were jealous lords enough to follow her lead and on the instant the quarreling had turned from York and Somerset to him, with first Suffolk yapping to the attack and then damned Cardinal Beaufort, followed eagerly enough by Somerset and Buckingham, Queen Margaret goading them on and Henry saying nothing, until in a fury, wanting to throttle all of them to silence, Gloucester flung from the room, before he said things that he should not.

He thereby missed what followed but heard about it afterwards in fulsome detail from both Eleanor and half a dozen others. How Queen Margaret dropped her fan—"Deliberately, I swear!" Eleanor cried to him later—then ordered her to pick it up and, without giving time for Eleanor to obey even if she would—"And I would not have, I promise you!"—boxed her hard on the ear, there in front of everyone.

"And then cried me mercy!" Eleanor raged to him afterwards. "She said she'd not realized it was me. She said she thought I was a servant!"

There had been angry words then between them and something very like a threat from Eleanor before she stormed out, all of which Gloucester heard first from others who were there and then, on their way home, from Eleanor, still raging at the insult and humiliation of it all but containing herself better than he might have feared she would.

Nonetheless, well able to guess her control would not hold, once they were home he lingered in the great hall under pretext of talking to his chamberlain, to let her go on ahead of him to their bedchamber, that the worst be over before he joined her. When he did finally go to her, the worst of her fury was done, it seemed, though the thrown-about cushions and overturned chair showed something of how bad it had been, and as he came in, one of her harried ladies-in-waiting was ill-advisedly trying to soothe her with, "Maybe the queen is finally with child, my lady. That can unsort a woman's humors, you know."

To which, in answer, Eleanor snatched up a fallen pillow and threw it at the hapless woman, screaming, "You think *that* would be a good thing, you witless ninny? For her to have a son when I have none? Leave me! All of you!"

They none of them needed to be told a second time but snatched up their heavy skirts and crowded to be out the door, Gloucester himself closing it behind them before he crossed to Eleanor standing with her head clutched between her hands and sobbing. He judged her tears were still as much from rage as grief and kept a few steps back from her even as he asked with careful tenderness, "Do you still hurt, my heart?"

"No!" Eleanor cried fiercely, then piteously, "Yes," and on a final great heave of tears raised her head and held out her arms to him, letting him know she was ready to be comforted.

He went to her and put his arms around her and she leaned against him, her head on his shoulder as she added, sighing, "But only inwardly now. In my heart."

In her pride, she meant, and it was then, knowing both her pride and her heedlessness, that the thought came to him—full-grown as Minerva from the head of Jove and perhaps as long engendered without his knowing it—of how he might be rid of her without a breath of blame attached to him from her or anyone else. He had spies in his fellow-lords' households as surely as they had spies in his, all looking for any fault or flaw that could be used by one lord against another. Lady Eleanor was as watched as he was and now, when her rage against the Queen was all too likely to make her careless, now was when he should warn her not to be heedless, warn her to take extra care of what she said or did.

He didn't.

Instead, as if grieving with her, he said, "Dear heart, I'm sorry. If aught that I could do would curb her . . ."

Eleanor jerked up her head from his shoulder. "By holy God, you're the king's heir and there's naught can change that! It's what she can't abide about me. The knowing that if Henry dies . . ."

"Which God forbid," Gloucester put quickly in.

"God forbid," Eleanor said, with no fervor behind it. "That's what she can't abide. That I could be Queen in her place and have the crown off her proud, ugly head."

There was nothing ugly about Queen Margaret's head or form. The fault did not lie there but in the fact that she was young and still like to bear an heir and Eleanor was no longer either, and Gloucester knew he should say something to Eleanor's comfort, at least tell her that she was beautiful to him and nothing mattered so long as they had each other. It would have been near enough to truth and maybe enough to keep her from what came afterward. But again instead, on a grieving note he said, "Don't talk thus, Nell. Pray, rather, that King Henry lives long and his Queen bears him many sons. Don't, don't, I pray you, think of crowns and you and I." Knowing full well—who better after so many years of marriage?—her strong and contrary will.

Give them the toys to play with and leave them to find the sharp, hidden edges for themselves. Say only enough to urge them on against each other. Say to his face that young Warwick is ambitious and, let him deny it how he will, others, protective of their own ambitions, will turn on him. Or worry aloud over what the powerful Duke of York may be thinking to do with his power, and whether he is thinking to do anything or not, those already worrying about him will worry all the harder and soon begin to do more than worry. Give them such toys, then leave them to find and use the deadly edges by their own choice. Have I ever done more than that? Merely given them the chance, the choice, the sharp-edged toy, the weapon they do not have to use. Whatever comes after that is all of their doing.

Not mine.

Except in that I have hopes of how far they will go . . . of their own will
. . . toward their own destruction.

Things being as they were between Queen Margaret and Lady Eleanor, there
was no surprise a few days hence when Lady Eleanor did not ride north with
her husband and the great many lords and ladies going with King Henry and
his Queen to St. Alban's for the autumn hunting in green Hertfordshire. Instead
she stayed behind at Gloucester's Baynard's Castle in London, and there, in a
dark of the moon and the deep middle of a night, in the small garden below
the duchess's private rooms, the shadows between the high stone walls were
crowded in so thickly that the three black-robed figures were hardly to be seen
at all except they moved where otherwise nothing moved at all, and above
them at a window Lady Eleanor, likewise in black, likewise almost impossible
to see, leaned forward and at the whisper of the black-clad man beside her only
reluctantly straightened and stood back.

She had been told she would see little, hear almost nothing, until the Spirit
came, if it came at all, but she had paid well for these people's service and she
wanted more than vague movement and whisperings at the very edge of hearing. She wanted . . .

Below her, without warning, there was a sudden growl of thunder, like a
low-beaten drum, and then a sharp flare of green light, every shape in the
garden for an instant starkly lit before, as suddenly, the light and the thunder-
growl were both gone, the light's shape left in Eleanor's blinded eyes and the
silence frightening but not so frightening as the low, long, anger-edged groaning that replaced it, as from a tormented animal or a horribly twisted human
throat, and beside her Master Hume said in a raw, awed whisper, "They have
it."

And now she could see it, too. A darksome shape writhing inside the circle
she had been told her conjurers would make to contain and control whatever
spirit they summoned. For the first time she was glad of the darkness because
who would willingly look on a demon drawn from Hell? Even one she had
paid these people to find for her, to answer questions that now one of the men
below her was asking it in taut whispers that the demon growlingly answered.

First, what would become of King Henry . . . then of the Duke of Suffolk . . . then of the Duke of Somerset . . .

They had warned they could not hold the demon long, nor did they. The ill-green light flared and vanished again, leaving a thicker darkness after it than had been before, and Eleanor shuddered, glad to have it finished. But beside her Master Hume breathed a curse and at the same moment she saw below them in the garden too many shapes were in the darkness, far more than had been, and for one hideous moment Eleanor flared into horrible fear that instead of sending their one demon back to Hell the conjurors had somehow released a great many more. Then in the room behind her, yellow light burst bright and she shrieked and spun around, but it was only that the door to the next room had been thrown open, letting in sudden lamplight, and her heart nearly stopped with relief.

But her relief died a frightened death as men with the badge of the Duke of Buckingham on their doublets thronged into the room, and Master Hume's swearing with a steady anger as they seized him was nothing to her own despair that deepened the more as she swung around to the window again and saw the garden equally full of men, with torches now, and the Duke of York's badge on them and her demon-summoners held prisoner in their midst.

Leave them to their foolishness and wait. That's almost all I've ever needed to do. Oh, at the necessary moment say a word or perhaps a few to set them deeper into their foolishness but hardly ever more than that.

So little effort for such great pleasures.

The day's hawking had gone well enough that, riding between Henry and Suffolk up the easy slope from St. Alban's wide river meadows toward the abbey stretched along its hillcrest, Margaret was almost happy. Or as near to happy as she ever was in this god-benighted country with its too much rain and too many lords who did not want her here.

It had seemed so grand a thing to marry the King of England, to leave behind her father's impoverished French dukedom for a royal crown. She had not even begun to guess how ill it would turn, with a weakling husband, resentful lords, and worst of all thus far, no son yet to make her hold and claim on her crown secure. If once she had a son, then there would never be any chance for Henry to be forced into nay-saying their marriage. Without a son . . .

Beside her, Suffolk was being amusing over his tercel's failure to bring down a heron—"She was tipsy with the wind. Everyone knows falcons go as drunk on wind as we do on wine and today is fearsome windy."—but on Henry's other side, Gloucester and Cardinal Beaufort were sniping at each other yet again. This time at least, after a brief opening skirmish, their voices were low, no matter how certain their tone, and when the King asked what they were at, they both denied it was anything but talk of the hunt. She knew better and so should Henry. They were ever at it against each other, on and on like schoolboys with no better use for their wits and Henry doing naught to stop them except weakly protest that it was irksome to him. Not that they cared. They didn't because, like everyone else, they ignored him when they chose. Everyone ignored Henry when it suited them. Only she could not, ever, because everything she wanted for and in her life depended on him being King, on him staying King, on him being the man he did not want to be.

Margaret's throat tightened with familiar anger at both Henry and her own helplessness, and almost she was pleased to see the Duke of Buckingham riding down the hill toward them. Among the surfeit of lords around the King, Buckingham only quietly, rather than openly, resented that she was French, had brought no dowry with her, and had as yet produced no heir, and if nothing else, maybe his coming would divert Gloucester and Cardinal Beaufort from their bickering for this while. Surely he brought some sort of news; his face was grim enough as he drew rein, bowed to them all from the saddle, and King Henry asked, "What tidings with our cousin Buckingham?"

Gloved hand to his breast, Buckingham bowed again and answered, "Such as my heart trembles to unfold." But the tremble in his voice was of excited pleasure, Margaret now saw, and there was triumph in his glance aside at Gloucester as he went on to tell in detail of how Lady Eleanor, Duchess of Gloucester, had been caught in the company of conjurors, in the very act of raising a Spirit out of Hell, to demand of King Henry's life and death.

Exclaims of horror passed among the lords and ladies around the king and the word "treason," from more than one while Cardinal Beaufort leaned over to whisper, smiling, something into Gloucester's ear, to which Gloucester, pale as proverbial death and without taking his eyes from Buckingham, said something back that Margaret could not hear and King Henry raised his hands to heaven, praying fervently, "O God, what mischiefs work the wicked ones, heaping confusion on their own heads . . ."

Be damned to confusions, Margaret thought, triumph searing through her. Lady Eleanor had wrought better than confusions. She had destroyed herself and Gloucester with her, and Margaret cut across her husband's prayer to taunt at Gloucester, "See the tainture of your nest, my lord. Look you be unstained by it."

For once Gloucester, always so swift and glib of tongue, fumbled his answer, mixing protest of his innocence with a weak defense of Lady Eleanor that nonetheless ended with his complete rejection of both her and of her crime, all in one stumbling speech that was almost enough, for now, to satisfy Margaret but only because she knew there would be more sport to be had from him later.

And there was, because for once King Henry's piety was useful, keeping him from any inclination toward pity for people guilty of so foul a crime as trafficking with demons. Say what the conjurors did about all they had done being trickery—that they had summoned no actual demon, had merely made a deception with cloaks and darkness and clever acting, that all of it was pretense—they had nonetheless and undeniably questioned and spoken of the King's death and that was straightforwardly treason and death the penalty.

But not for Lady Eleanor. That her rank preserved her from accompanying them to their deaths was at first a disappointment to Margaret, until she understood how Lady Eleanor's torment was to be far longer than simple execution would have allowed. Rather, despoiled of her honor, doomed and humiliated, standing with bowed head before the King and lords and ladies where she had lately stood in pride, she was condemned to walk under guard, barefoot and wearing only her shift, through London, to be the gaze and mock of everyone, and then be taken to live out her life, a prisoner, on the Isle of Man.

Even for Margaret that would have been, for now, enough, but dear Suffolk, with Cardinal Beaufort's help, had been working to good purpose on King Henry's horror of Lady Eleanor's sin, so that when barely she had been led from the judgment chamber and Gloucester, humiliated with her, humbly asked for leave to go, too, and hide his misery, King Henry, with Suffolk and Cardinal Beaufort close behind him to keep him firm, asked Gloucester to resign as Lord Protector of the realm and, in token of that, give up his gold-banded staff, tall as himself, that was sign of that office.

To have Henry—her King, her lord, her husband—at last take to himself all of his rightful power was something Margaret had wanted for years, but Henry, as ever, spoiled it. Rather than with proud command, he asked almost humbly for Gloucester's resignation, murmuring more in apologetic explanation than assertion, "God shall be my hope now," and adding gently, "Go in peace, no less beloved than when you were Protector to your King."

That, surely, had *not* been among the things he was supposed to say, to judge by Suffolk's scowl of black anger and Cardinal Beaufort's face suffused with a scarlet rich as his cardinal's robes. It was Gloucester's disgrace they wanted, not King Henry's mild forgiveness of him, and out of patience with them all, Margaret stepped forward, her hand thrust out, and ordered with all the force Henry had refused, "Give up your staff, sir, and give to the King his realm."

Ignoring her, his gaze fixed on Henry, Gloucester said, "Willingly at your feet I leave it as others would . . ." He bent and lay the staff at Henry's feet, his glance flicking coldly toward her only as he straightened. ". . . ambitiously receive it." He stepped back and bowed deeply. "Farewell, good King. When I am dead and gone, may honorable peace attend your throne."

He took another backward step, made another bow, and turned and left, gone at last but his calm, like Henry's humbleness, more spoiling it than not for Margaret as she moved forward to snatch up the staff and thrust it into Henry's hand.

With need for nothing from me now except to stand aside this while and leave them to their triumph, having moved them, goaded them, to here. For

England's good, not for mine own. Therein lies the difference between their ambitions and mine. What I want, I want for England. Want that King Henry be brought to governing on his own, without Gloucester having claim to any power, so that the lords may then unite behind their King rather than be split into factions all around him and against each other.

Then whoever governs Henry governs all.

And I mean, as I've meant all along, for that whoever to be me.

Who better?

Unable to settle, driven by her discontent, Margaret had paced her chamber until she hated all its walls and now was pacing the covered walk around the palace garden, wrapped in her cloak against the day's damp and chill and aware her ladies were not happy, huddled by the door where she had ordered them to stay, not wanting the distraction of their murmured talk and company. Their unhappiness did not disturb her. Why should they be happy? She was not. Her head hurt with this constant trying to think of everything, the things that others never seemed to see or worry over, this constant striving to be sure she missed nothing vital in the twisty ways of everyone around her. It wasn't fair. She shouldn't need to do it. It was the husband's place to protect and have care and take forethought like this but Henry was useless and worse than useless at anything but praying. He was her danger where her safety should have been, her burden where he should have been her strength.

Forget Henry for now, she told herself sharply, turning the corner of the walk to bring her back toward her ladies. There was never trouble in out-thinking Henry. But Gloucester, who should have ceased to be a trouble now . . .

Not even the sight of Suffolk coming toward her along the walk gave her pleasure just now. He saw that immediately and made his bow lower than need be, asking as he straightened from it, "What is it? Is there aught that I may do?"

If Henry had been anything like to him . . . able to see her when he looked at her, wanting her happy, willing to do what he could to make her so . . .

"Walk with me," she ordered and said as he fell into step beside her, "It's Gloucester."

Because it had taken her these few days of brooding on it to put words at last to the root of her unease, she forgave Suffolk his pause before he echoed, openly puzzled, "Gloucester?"

"Gloucester," she repeated and turned around with a sharp swirl of her cloak to walk in the other direction, away from her waiting women, saying as Suffolk followed her, "The day he gave up his staff, he wasn't grieved enough."

"Grieved enough? Dishonored by his wife, disgraced before us all, I can't think how much more grieved we can hope for him to be," Suffolk protested. "The man I keep in his household sends word he's hardly spoken nor gone out at all except the once to see his bitch wife walk her last through London. When they met, she said much, he said little, they parted, and he's been mostly silent ever since."

"But what is he feeling? What is he thinking?"

"He's thinking all is lost to him," Suffolk said readily. "He's feeling shame. Humiliation. Grief. All that we could want for him. You saw him when he gave up his staff."

"It's what I didn't see then that troubles me."

"Troubles you? He's broken. There's nothing left for you to trouble over. He's finished."

Margaret refused that with a shake of her head. "I grant you he said what needed to be said, and he *showed* the feelings he should have shown. My doubt is that he *felt* them."

Suffolk started to protest that but she jerked an impatient hand at him and said, "I know. It's maybe foolishness even to doubt he's broken but something wasn't right." She pressed her hand to her breast, half jesting at herself but more serious than not. "A feeling. And I swear Cardinal Beaufort frowned as he listened to Gloucester with the rest of us. As if he felt something was not right. As if he had doubts, too." She frowned, remembering it. "I want to know more."

"About Cardinal Beaufort?" Suffolk asked, surprised.

"Of course not," Margaret snapped, then recollected herself—Suffolk was her ally, not her enemy—and said more gently, smiling at him, "About Gloucester. I'd have you find out for me what may have passed between him and his wife of late that he might not regret her loss as greatly as we thought he would. I'd know, too, besides this outward show of grieving, what else he's doing. I'd know anything that's aside from what should be." She laid a hand, the one not holding her cloak closed to her throat against the cold wind finding its way along the walk, upon his arm, and lowered and softened her voice, more as if promising him something than asking for his help. "You'll find out for me?"

The expected warmth kindled in Suffolk's eyes and his own voice was low and rich with promises besides the one he outward made in answering, "I'll find out."

And in surprisingly few days he did, though he was not comfortable with what he'd learned, Margaret readily saw as they walked along the garden walk again, a cold, fine rain falling this time and their cloaks bunched high around their ears, muffling their voices from anyone except each other, Suffolk saying as soon as they were well away from her women, "I've talked with my man in Gloucester's household about the night Buckingham and York broke in on Lady Eleanor at her foul play."

Though Suffolk himself had not been there, Margaret knew the hand he had had with Buckingham and York in setting up her rival's fall. "And?" she demanded.

"When asked directly, he admitted surprise at how easily all of it went."

"Easily? You and Buckingham and York all have your paid informers in the household. They let you know that she was at something vile and, when the time came, sent word to Buckingham and York and likewise had the necessary doors unlocked for them when they came. Why shouldn't it have been easy?"

Suffolk hesitated, unhappy over something, before he said, "The man who was bribed not to notice when my man took the keys to open the outer door and garden that night has just a few days ago been given a grant of a small property in Derbyshire. He's already left to claim it."

"From you?" Margaret asked, thinking that had been unnecessarily generous to a man who anyway would not dare to say what he had done. "Or was it Buckingham or York thought it needful?"

Suffolk shifted uncomfortably under his cloak. "It was Gloucester," he mumbled. "Gloucester gave it to him."

"Gloucester," Margaret hissed. "Gave him a reward? When? *Why?*"

"It seems he was given it the day after Gloucester lost his office of Protector. I don't know why. My man in Gloucester's household doesn't know."

Fierce with impatience—why was she the one who always had to think these things through?—Margaret said, "Gloucester should be purging his household, trying to find out who betrayed his wife. Isn't he?"

"No."

The terseness of Suffolk's answer showed he was uncomfortable with that and well he should be, Margaret thought, and lest her watching women wonder if there was trouble, did not alter her strolling pace; but her thoughts were racing and she said, "Instead he's given a grant of land to his own man who made her capture easy. That's not right."

"There's something else," Suffolk said, his discomfort greater. "He's approached the archbishop about divorce, his wife being so utterly disgraced before man and God."

Margaret waved an impatient hand. "Yes. I know that." Then she heard the tone of Suffolk's voice and, women or no women, stopped short and faced him. "You're going to tell me he's already started to look for another wife, aren't you?"

Suffolk nodded. "He has, my lady."

Margaret struck her fisted hands together, hard enough to hurt. "The fatnosed cur! He means to get himself a new wife and try to get a son and heir on her the way he couldn't on Lady Eleanor! That's why it went so easily against her. He wanted it. He knew what you were at. He *meant* for her to be disgraced so he could be rid of her."

"Surely not . . ."

"Surely yes. Look at it. She can't bear him any sons, that's plain, but he had no grounds for divorcing her. Now, by way of you, he can. Damn him!"

"Surely, old as he is . . ."

"He's not all that old and it's the wife's age that matters anyway." Too angry to stand still, Margaret began to walk again. "That's why he wasn't hurt enough by losing the Protectorship. He knew he couldn't keep it forever anyway. Sooner or later he'd have to give it up. Doing so now was merely by the way. The whole point of it all was to be rid of his wife to leave him free to find a new one. You have to stop him."

"Stop him?" Suffolk echoed. "How? The divorce will come easily enough, with the grounds he has, and if he wants to marry again, who's to gainsay him?"

Between her teeth she said, impatient at Suffolk for seeing so little, "I don't want to 'gainsay' him. I want him *stopped*. For now and ever afterward. Surely, my lord, you can think of the surest way to that?" Daring him to admit he could and seeing realization and agreement come into his face.

I'd had to be unsure if anyone besides myself would see the next necessary step and had wondered how much I must needs do to set them on to it but as it happened nothing was needed from me. They did it all themselves and brought the thing on swiftly, their flood of hatreds and ambitions at last bringing Gloucester down, with nothing needed from me except I mostly stand aside and let them do it.

Standing at bay in the council chamber he had all unwittingly entered, with the broad sunlight of a bright day still falling through the windows but darkness closing on him fast, Gloucester stared at the lords grouped before him, one charge of treason after another pouring from them, all at him and all too much and too fast for him to make any reasonable answer, not when faced with that much hatred—Cardinal Beaufort's eyes glittering with all the malice Gloucester had known was in him, Suffolk's face cloudy with a stormy hatred worse than Gloucester had ever guessed he had, Buckingham's mouth twisted with the sour, sweet taste of envy and triumph mixed bitterly together, York's carefully kept mask showing nothing of his deep, long-hidden ambitions except for one quirked corner of his mouth and a hard pleasure behind his eyes, while Henry, poor Henry, stood looking from one side to the other, from Gloucester to the baying pack of lords, offering no more than, feebly, his hands knotted into a

white-knuckled lump more overwrought than prayerful, "Uncle, my conscience tells me you're innocent," to no use at all.

Hot-hearted Margaret, jealous of anything she could not claim and control
for herself, quelled him with one sentence and urged the rest on with another,
and Gloucester with all of them against him and nothing left to him, not even
hope, cast up his head, drawing on all the pride of royal blood and high place
that had been his until now, and cried out—not so much to his King as to
Despair, "I know their plot is to have my life!" and after that—at overweening
Buckingham's order—let Cardinal Beaufort's guards take him away, because
what else was there for him to do . . .

. . . except to die, when the time very shortly came.

*Nor do I judge it sin to take pleasure in that thought, as assuredly I do,
though mayhap there's sin in my great satisfaction that I made sure of his
death by a slight murmur in the right ears of how unwise it would be for
Gloucester to come to any kind of trial or be given any chance of appeal to
Henry's all-too-ready mercy. But, well, I left it to them to choose what to
do with that small thought and so I'd say the greater blame was theirs, that
they proved sensible in the matter.*

*Though not so sensible as they might have been. Surely Suffolk could have
found a way to Gloucester's death that made it not so obvious how he died.
Not even Henry, looking on Gloucester stretched starkly out on his bed with
bulging eyes and swollen, blood-blackened face, dead hands still clutched
into the bedclothes, could deceive himself Gloucester had been anything but
brutally smothered. But even so, who could have foreseen how the Commons
in Parliament, that great sprawl of gentry, merchants, knights, and nobodies
who, for reasons passing understanding, have ever favored Gloucester against
anyone except King Henry himself, would rise up in so much protest against
his death and Suffolk who had caused it.*

"And you let them tell you what to do!" Margaret raged at Henry. "On their
word you've exiled him! Exiled Suffolk. Of all the men in your realm, the one
who's served you best!"

"And maybe the one most likely to bring me to mischance," Henry said back to her with all the set-mindedness of a weak man brought finally to some decision. Or else with the steady vengeance of a man who had understood more than Margaret had, until now, ever thought he did.

That thought, come out of nowhere, stopped her in mid-plea for Suffolk, turned her wary with wondering what else might be behind the flat brown stare Henry so often turned on her.

But the chill was momentary. Henry never stood long against anyone near enough to press their will on him, and now that Gloucester was gone, she meant for there to be no one so near to him as her ever again. If not today, then tomorrow or the day after or however long it took to work his will to hers, she would have Suffolk back.

She was thinking that, and of how she would accomplish it, when Cardinal Beaufort moved forward from where he had been waiting quietly aside, and with a bow said to Henry and hardly a look at her, "My lord, might we talk awhile together?"

Henry, ever ready to talk to churchmen before anyone else, turned immediately away from her, saying with the willingness he seemed to have for everyone but her, "Of course, my lord uncle."

His other uncle, Margaret suddenly thought, watching them walk away, heads close together. The King's only uncle now that Gloucester was dead. The King's uncle and a cardinal of the Church, without either wife or any claim to the throne, only immense ambition and no longer Gloucester to stand in his way.

Or Suffolk either. No one, Margaret saw him thinking, to come between him and his King now. Not even her because she was, after all, no more than a woman.

And something in her hardened and darkened with cold anger at being faced with a fight she had already fought and did not want to fight again. Not now, when she knew the ways there were around it.

A mistake on my part.
    Not to foresee . . . that once I'd shown her the way to what is possible . . .
she would go on to other . . . possibilities.

Difficult to believe . . . I was blind to that.
Difficult to believe . . . even now . . . so near to . . . dying.
To believe she'd . . . poison . . . me.
Damning us both.
Cardinal and Queen.
Together.

Cleo's Asp

BY EDWARD D. HOCH

Edward D. Hoch is past president of Mystery Writers of America, winner of its 2001 Grand Master Award and its Edgar Award for best short story of 1968. He has published nearly 850 stories as well as anthologies, collections, and novels. He has been Guest of Honor at the annual Bouchercon mystery convention and received its Anthony Award for best short story. In 2001 he received the convention's Lifetime Achievement Award. In 2000 he received The Eye, the life achievement award of the Private Eye Writers of America. He resides in Rochester, New York, with his wife, Patricia.

I am remembering back to a time, thirty years before the birth of Christ, when I was still a very young man. Egypt was my home in that final year of Cleopatra's reign, and I was but a nameless clown from the rural regions who brought figs and other fruits to the palace and often stayed to amuse the Queen with my jests. I called her Cleo when not in her presence, because I likened her so much to a young girl. It seemed impossible that she was nearing forty, old enough to be my mother, and had been the mistress of the legendary Julius Caesar and now the wife of Mark Antony. Her face still held an almost mystic appeal for me, and I never tired of gazing upon it as one might look upon the countenance of a goddess.

Though Cleo traveled much and had lived in Rome for many years, it was following her return to Egypt and her marriage to Mark Antony that I knew her best. Her palace at Alexandria was a thing of beauty, towering over the harbor. Alexander the Great had founded the city some three hundred years earlier, with an elaborate system of cisterns that served as enormous reservoirs belowground, ensuring a supply of fresh drinking water for all. Conduits drew the water from a canal leading to the Nile River. There was also a mole or breakwater nearly a mile in length stretching to the nearby island of Pharos. The mole enclosed a spacious harbor with the fabulous Pharos Lighthouse guiding the way to it. As a boy I would often play on the mole and near the castle, getting to know the servants and slaves who tended to it. Sometimes I went to the mausoleum of Alexander, where Cleo would retreat when she wished to be alone.

Cleo herself called me the Clown, and encouraged me in my antics. I amused her, and I was happy to become a fool if it meant spending time in her royal presence. With Antony, my relations were cooler. He regarded me as one of many country youths who frequented the castle. Perhaps he feared that I spied on his activities for Cleo, and in truth I was well aware of his friendship with her attendants, Charmian and Iras.

Charmian was the older of Cleo's two lady attendants. She must have been near to thirty, with a dusky skin and brown eyes that seemed always on me. Iras, younger and almost pale by comparison, seemed more like one of my sisters, always eager to partake in some game when Cleo was away or alone with Antony.

A year earlier, violence had erupted. Caesar's heir Octavian declared war on Cleopatra and Antony, no doubt goaded by the fact that Antony had been married to his sister before falling under Cleo's spell. Octavian defeated them in a naval engagement at Actium. They fled back to Alexandria, and Octavian awaited his opportunity to strike at our homeland.

At this time in late summer, so dreadful to remember, I had wandered in the early morning onto the mole to watch the activity in the harbor. For no reason that I could determine, the fishing boats with their distinctive swept-back sails were making for shore. Then a man emerged from the high light-house at the end of the breakwater, running to spread the word. "Octavian's fleet has been sighted, coming this way!"

I ran back along the mole to tell Cleo, but the news had already reached the palace. "My little clown," she told me, still lovely even in the tension of the moment, "Antony has already left to do battle with them. We expect the Romans will come ashore somewhere west of here, near the mausoleum of Alexander. It would be safest for you to return to your village."

"I wish to remain here," I insisted. "These are dark days for you, my Queen. If I can cheer you in any way—"

"No, no," she began, but then I observed a change in her expression. She seemed deep in thought for a moment, and then said, "There is a way in which you might help me, Clown. I suspect an enemy in my midst, perhaps one of my own attendants."

"Your guards?"

She shook her head. "It is known that Iras and Charmian are friendly toward Antony. I suspect one might be in the pay of Octavian, informing him of Antony's plans. How else can I explain our defeat at Actium last year?"

"It could not be Iras!" I insisted, quick to defend her as I would my sister.

"I hope I am wrong, but you can help."

"What can I do?"

"Find out if it is one of them! They trust you and you can move among the palace staff without creating suspicion." Speaking those words to me, intoxicating me with her fervor, I could almost understand how men of the greatness of Caesar and Antony could fall under her spell. Perhaps the wiles she had used so successfully on them were beginning to fade, but she was still a magnetic presence to a young man of my age.

"If you desire it, my Queen," I replied, putting aside my own qualms at her request. I did not really want to spy on these two comely handmaidens who had always shown friendship toward me.

I went to the palace kitchen, a great open room with storage bins for the baskets of fruit I often delivered, bartering with the cook for coils of silver or

copper weights that could later be swapped for something of equal value elsewhere. There were Egyptian coins in limited circulation, and one had been
minted in our city to honor its founder, Alexander, but many people still
preferred the old system of bartering.

After completing my business with the cook, I saw that Iras was there,
wearing a white linen sheath with short billowy sleeves and sandals made from
papyrus leaves. "Clown" she called me, because Cleo's naming of me had passed
on to the others, "will you be returning to your village tonight?"

"I expect to, miss," I answered. "My brothers are picking more fruit for me
to deliver on the morrow."

"What do you have besides figs?"

"There are dates, grapes, and pomegranates too. What is your wish?"

She handed me a tall loaf of fresh bread, newly delivered by the baker. "This
for your journey. Bring me some grapes tomorrow. Now tell me true, have
you seen Antony today?"

"He is not with the Queen," I said. "Octavian's ships have been sighted off
shore. He has gone to engage them in battle."

"I know of the ships. These are dark days." Her face was troubled. "If you
see Antony, tell him I must speak with him." It had been some months since
last we played our games and I wondered if those days were forever behind us.
She had changed recently, grown to an adult woman even as I watched.

"I will do that," I assured her.

But I had one more stop before heading across the sand to our village in the
delta oasis where the sycamore fig trees grew. My brothers had asked me to
obtain some bread and Iras's gift of a loaf had reminded me. The large bakery,
providing the city's most important food, was located near the harbor but some
distance from Cleo's palace. There women used rollers on stones to grind the
wheat or barley. Bakers kneaded together flour, yeast, and water, sometimes
adding fruit or spices. Then two-piece clay pots were filled with the dough and
set over hot coals. The molds ensured that all the loaves had roughly the same
appearance, nearly a foot high and roughly conical in shape.

The head baker, whose name was Wabet, knew me from many previous visits. "What have you to barter this day, Clown?" he asked with a smile.

I took out the coil of silver I'd received at the palace for the basket of figs. "How many loaves of bread for this?"

We dickered back and forth until I finally obtained a dozen loaves, enough to feed our family and leave some for bartering with neighbors. "You drive a hard bargain, Clown," Wabet told me as I departed. "Mark Antony himself could learn from you."

I paused and asked, "Have you seen Antony today?"

"He was here early, then rode off toward the sea." I was about to leave when he asked, "In your village do you have honey or fruit to flavor my breads?"

"We have honey only when we search it out among the hives, but this is a good time for fruit. I could bring you an assortment when I come in tomorrow."

My village was about four miles from the city and I set off with my loaves of bread. It was later than I'd thought and the family was already gathering for supper when I arrived. "You did well," my oldest brother told me with a smile. "Tomorrow we will send you for beer."

Although the brewery was located quite near the bakery, I knew our father would never allow us to bring beer to the house. Drinking it while in Alexandria was bad enough. But several days' supply of bread was welcomed by all. There were fish for supper because my brother had caught them with his nets. At night the nets would hang above our beds to ward off biting insects. There was a use for everything in our little house.

After supper I went out to the grove to gauge how many more figs remained on our trees. I could see that our neighbor's grapes were doing well too. "Be careful," my brother warned me. "The nest of asps is still near the water."

"I'm not afraid of them," I said. The art of handling poisonous serpents had come naturally to me at an early age.

Our trees had almost been picked clean, but my brother was not concerned. "Our neighbors have not yet begun to pick their groves, and we can barter with them for as many figs as we need." I knew he was right. That was the way it had worked in past seasons. It would always be the same, even if the Romans were to conquer the city. They would still need fresh fruit from the countryside, just as Wabet needed it for his bread.

The following morning I journeyed first to the bakery with the basket of fruit I'd promised Wabet. The other workers had not seen him since they arrived at dawn, but some thought he might be stoking the coal for the fires. I went back to the ovens and found him all too soon. He was crumpled against the wall, bleeding from a head wound. One of the pottery bread molds lay nearby, also covered with blood. Wabet had been struck with it, perhaps more than once.

I tried to prop him up, while shouting for help. "Warn the Queen," he told me, gasping for breath. "There is a traitor in her midst. One of her women attendants is in league with Octavian."

"Which—?" I started to ask, but he closed his eyes and said no more. I shouted again and the other bakers came running, but it was too late.

"Did you kill him?" one of them asked.

"No. You can see the blood on the floor is drying in some places. He was struck down earlier and only now succumbed to his wounds. Did anyone come here from the Queen's palace?"

An elderly man shook his head. "Only the bakers are here this early. No one comes from the palace, except Antony on occasion."

But I was remembering something from the previous day. "Fresh bread is delivered to the palace quite early. Who takes it?"

"That would be Peneb, one of our apprentices."

"Is he here?"

"He has already left for the palace."

Because Wabet had ordered the fruit from me, the other bakers took it, paying me in a few coins and silver coils. Then I was off in pursuit of Peneb. If Cleo's attendants had not visited the bakery, it meant that this man Peneb might be the only conduit for information. When I arrived at the palace kitchen, I found Charmian preparing a light meal for Cleo. I set down my basket of figs and she uncovered it, choosing a few of the best for the Queen.

The grapes I'd brought for Iras were left on the counter where she would see them. "Has the fresh bread been delivered yet?" I asked casually.

She nodded. "Within the hour. There may be an extra loaf for you if you can make me laugh on such a dour day as this."

"Where is Peneb, the baker's apprentice who delivered it?"

Charmian shook her head. "Somewhere in the castle. He said he had to speak with someone."

"And why are you so dour?" I wanted to know, trying to cheer her up. "Has Antony been here?"

She nodded sadly. "He and Cleopatra have clashed. Antony believes she has betrayed him to Octavian because the Roman has once again been victorious off our shores. Come with me now." She picked up the tray of food.

I followed Charmian into the Queen's presence and found her in a state of high agitation. Iras was there too, and Mardian, a dark and husky man who was one of Cleo's male attendants.

"Did you bring my grapes, Clown?" Iras asked, stroking the fuzz on my cheek in her old girlish manner.

"They are on the counter in the kitchen."

"Make mirth, Clown," Cleo commanded, her eyes dark and brooding.

I started some juggling and turned a few flips, but it was no help. "Even you cannot lift my spirits with your antics this day." Cleo turned to her ladies. "Help me, my women!" she pleaded.

It was Charmian who answered with a suggestion. "To the mausoleum! There lock yourself, and send Antony word that you are dead."

Cleo gave it a few moments' thought and then agreed. "To the mausoleum! Mardian, go tell him I have slain myself, say that the last I spoke was his name. Then bring me word of how he takes my death."

The husky man bowed and hurried away on his mission. But I was troubled by this deceit and wondered why she had done it. Soon after, when Iras and Charmian had gone about their chores, I told Cleo, "The baker Wabet has been slain. I was there when he died and he told me to warn you that one of your women attendants is a traitor in league with Octavian."

"Slain?" Her hand went to her throat. "When?"

"This morning, in the dawning hours."

Cleo shook her head. "Both Charmian and Iras were here all morning. Neither of them could have done it."

"An apprentice named Peneb may be the guilty one. He delivers bread here each morning and is known to your attendants. I believe him to be somewhere in the palace at this moment."

"Then it is wise that I retire to the mausoleum." She thought for a moment and grew sad, the lines of age beginning to crease her brow. Perhaps she was wondering if her appeal was waning. "You have mentioned the family of asps that inhabit your orchard. Are they still a problem?"

"Not if we are careful. I have no fear of them."

"Is it true that their poisoned bite is painless?"

"So it is said," I told her, growing uneasy.

"Could you bring me one of the best, hidden in a basket of figs?"

"Tomorrow?"

"Today, before nightfall."

"I could try," I answered reluctantly.

"You will be rewarded," Cleo promised, touching my cheek. "Go now, so you may return as quickly as possible. I will be in the mausoleum with my attendants."

I left her alone and hurried down the stone steps toward the kitchen area. The task she had assigned me was a grave one indeed, and I hoped I would be worthy of her trust. The kitchen was empty now except for Charmian, who saw me and asked, "Do you still seek the apprentice Peneb?"

"Is he here?"

"I saw him enter the storeroom with Iras."

Quickly I ran down a few more steps to the storage area used for grain. A single oil lamp lit the room, its linen wick burning with a dancing flame. "Do you seek me, Clown?" asked a voice from the shadows.

"I do, if your name is Peneb."

I saw before me a young man not much older than myself. He might have been twenty at most, and in each hand he held a dagger poised for thrusting. "What do you want?"

"You killed the baker Wabet. No one from the castle came there except Antony, yet Wabet knew Cleopatra was being betrayed by one of her attendants. You were the only link to them, bringing the fresh bread here each day. Wabet found out and you bashed his head in with a pottery bread mold. Tell me, Peneb, who has betrayed my Queen? Is it Charmian or Iras?"

By way of an answer the apprentice lashed out with the right-hand blade, just missing my stomach. I danced around him, seeking any weapon I could find, as his knives came closer with each swing. Finally I grabbed the lamp and swung it at him. The flame singed his right hand and one dagger clattered to the floor. Holding him at bay with the flame, I stooped to grab it. He came at me then, right on top of me, seeking a target for his blade. Somehow I flipped him over my back and brought my fist down on his jaw.

He was unconscious when I left him there, hurrying back up to the kitchen. Neither Charmian nor Iras was in sight, and the grapes were still on the counter. I left the palace by the rear entrance, intent on the mission assigned me by Cleopatra.

I made good time on my journey to the village, reaching the grove of fig trees when the sun was highest. Carefully I approached the area of the asps' nest, beneath some jutting stones near the water's edge. I hoped my father or my brothers would not see me. The asp is a form of Egyptian cobra, usually more active at night, and when I located one, it was curled and sleeping. I knew it could probably kill up to three men, since it was said less than half the venom was released with each bite. I used a forked stick to pin its head to the ground. Then, holding it tightly by the neck and tail, I managed to place the serpent in my basket, covering it with figs and closing the lid firmly.

I was nervous as I made my way back to the palace, all too aware of my angry cargo in the basket. I'd been gone nearly four hours in all, and as I approached the mausoleum, I saw Cleo's attendant Mardian, all distraught, and knew that something was amiss. "What has happened, Mardian?"

He wrung his hands in grief. "I delivered the message to Mark Antony, saying Queen Cleopatra was dead. He did not hurry back to the mausoleum as planned, but instead threw himself on his own sword in despair. When he learned she was still alive, he had himself carried here. I heard his words: *I am dying, Egypt, dying. Give me some wine, and let me speak a little.*"

"Where is he now?" I asked.

"She took him inside the mausoleum and he perished. Octavian has been here to demand her complete surrender."

"Who is with her now?"

"Only Iras and Charmian."

"I must go to her. I have brought the figs she requested."

The mausoleum, which lay to the west and adjoined the temple of Isis, was locked and guarded by a single soldier. He needed permission from Cleo for my entry, but this was quickly forthcoming. I followed the guard through this house of the dead, past burial niches dating from Alexander's time, and finally into Cleo's presence. It was a large room with windows overlooking the beach and the sea beyond. They bathed the room in a glow so bright that no lamps were needed. Cleo was stretched out on a sofa, one arm shielding her eyes from the glare.

"All is woe, Clown," she told me as the guard left us. "My husband Anthony has expired here, and I shall soon follow."

"Do not say that!" Charmian urged. "Octavian offers you life."

Cleo merely shook her head. "Julius Caesar took me to Rome as his lover. Octavious Caesar would take me there as his slave, in chains."

"You must live," Iras told her.

"Why? So one of you traitors can deliver me to him and claim your reward?"

"She is the traitor," Charmian accused, pointing her finger at Iras. "She gave information to the baker's apprentice who was in league with the Romans."

"It is you who cries treason but is guilty of it!" Iras countered. "You slept with the apprentice and told him Antony's every move."

I thought for a moment the two might come to blows, and I hastened to intervene. "We will ask the apprentice Peneb which is the guilty one," I told Cleo.

"But Peneb is dead," she told me. "Did you not kill him yourself in the storage room under the kitchen?"

"We fought there," I admitted, "but he was alive when I left him. Tell me how he died."

"Stabbed in the back with his own dagger," Charmian informed me. "I found him myself shortly after you departed."

"So he tells no tales," Cleo said. "Did you not kill him, Clown?"

"We fought and I felled him with my fist. I never took a knife to him."

She shifted her gaze to the two trusted attendants. "If what he says is true, then one of you killed this man after he departed."

"Why would we?" Iras asked, trembling with fright or guilt.

"To keep your treason a secret, of course." Her hand had moved to the lid of the fig basket I'd delivered.

"Iras went to the storage room with the apprentice," Charmian insisted. "I told the Clown they were down there together."

"It is a lie!" Iras insisted. "I was not even in the storage room today."

"Clearly one of you lies." Cleo agreed, shifting her gaze to me. "Can you tell me which one, Clown?"

"Charmian did tell me Iras was with Peneb," I confirmed. "But I saw no evidence of it."

The two women faced each other, and for a moment we were frozen in place. Then Cleo turned to Iras and said, "Give me my robe, put on my crown. I have immortal longings in me. Methinks I hear Antony call."

As Iras approached with the robe and crown, Cleopatra smiled and lifted the lid from the basket of figs. "Come then, dear Iras, and take the last warmth of my lips. Feed me a fig from the basket."

Iras, her face white with fright, bent as commanded and let out a gasp. She fell dying to the floor.

"What is this?" Charmian asked. "Some sort of witchcraft?" But then she saw the asp in Cleo's grasp, and moved back in terror.

"Peace, peace, Charmian. You have been the loyal one. Do you not see the baby at my breast that sucks the nurse asleep?"

And saying that, my Cleo died, her body giving a final convulsion as the serpent's poison did its work.

"A tragedy has been visited upon us," Charmian said, letting out a sob of grief.

I corrected her. "A tragedy has been visited upon me. I have condemned an innocent young woman to death."

"How is that?" she asked, her eyes still on Cleo's body and the serpent that entwined it.

"Iras was innocent. It is you who betrayed my Queen to Octavian's armies."

She turned on me. "Your tongue is as forked as this serpent's!"

"No, no. I believed Iras to be the guilty one because you told me she was in the storage room with Peneb the apprentice. But I saw her not, and the grapes she wanted were still where I'd left them in the kitchen. She did not pass that way or she would have taken them. It was you who conspired with Peneb, you who stabbed him when you found him unconscious, because you feared he would implicate you. The scheme to tell Antony of the Queen's death was yours, and it was you who urged her to surrender to Octavian."

"But now she is dead," Charmian told me with a smile. "And I am safe."

"Safe from Cleopatra, perhaps, but not from me!" I seized the asp from Cleo's breast and brought it to her.

I heard the soldiers of Octavius Caesar at the mausoleum entrance. Quickly I gathered the serpent from Charmian's body and escaped with it through the window to the beach. They would find nothing, unless they noticed the marks of the serpent's fangs on the bodies. It would not bring Cleo back, but in some small measure I had avenged her death along with Antony's.

Much Ado About Murder
by Kathy Lynn Emerson

Kathy Lynn Emerson has written mysteries and historical fiction for both children and adults, several books of nonfiction, and both category and single-title romance. Her twenty-seventh published book, the sixth in the Face Down mystery series featuring Susanna, Lady Appleton (sixteenth-century gentle-woman, herbalist, and sleuth), is *Face Down Across the Western Sea* (August 2001). Her short stories have appeared in *Alfred Hitchcock's Mystery Magazine* and in several anthologies. She lives in rural Maine.

"The vii day of March began the blazing [star] at night and it did shoot out fire."
—DIARY OF HENRY MACHYN, 1555/6

An ominous portent first appeared in the sky over England on the same evening Robert Appleton brought Lord Benedick and his wife to Leigh Abbey. It was a blazing star with a long tail. Half the size of the moon, it much resembled a gigantic torch burning fitfully in the wind.

"A sure sign of disaster," muttered a maidservant, casting her baleful glance at the comet high above. She sent an equally suspicious look toward the new arrivals dismounting by rushlight in the inner courtyard.

Ignoring her tiring maid's comment, Susanna Appleton wrapped a wool cloak more closely around herself and went forward to greet her husband and his guests. Jennet could find evil omens and harbingers of impending doom in the twisted branches of a bush or the discolored grass beneath a mushroom. She relished dire predictions, though she always professed herself well-pleased when they came to naught. No doubt she imagined her own warnings had somehow prevented catastrophe.

The visitors were a richly dressed young couple traveling with two elderly servants. As Susanna watched, the husband lifted his wife out of her saddle and set her gently on her feet on the icy cobbles. He lifted her gloved hand to his lips, then held it tight as he slipped the other arm around her waist to steady her. He was rewarded with a smile of such radiance that Susanna felt a twinge of envy. True devotion between spouses was rare and it was sadly lacking in her own marriage. Robert would always love wealth and position more than he cared for any woman.

"Lord Benedick comes to England from Padua," Robert said after he'd presented Susanna to that nobleman. "Padua is part of the powerful Venetian Republic, where he is held in great regard. And his wife here is niece to the governor of Messina."

Titles impressed Robert more than they did Susanna, but she was as well informed as he on the subject of various political alliances. He did not need to tell her that Messina was part of Sicily, or that Sicily was under Spanish rule. So, some would say, was their own land, ever since Queen Mary's marriage to King Philip.

Robert's reason for inviting Lord Benedick to visit his home was just as clear—he hoped a friendship with this well-connected young sprig of the nobility would ease him back into favor at court. He'd made the mistake of backing the Lady Jane Grey's attempt to take Mary Tudor's throne away from her and had spent several uncomfortable months in prison before being pardoned and released.

Susanna had also supported Queen Jane. Now her loyalty was to the Lady

Elizabeth, Queen Mary's half-sister, although it was not wise to say so. These visitors, she decided, must be looked upon as the enemy, a danger to certain clandestine activities practiced at Leigh Abbey during Robert's frequent absences.

Forcing a smile, Susanna gestured toward the passage that led to the great hall. "If you will come this way, Lady—"

Impulsively, Lord Benedick's wife took both Susanna's hands in hers. She spoke charmingly accented English. "Let us be comfortable together, Beatrice and Susanna. What need we with formality when we are destined to be great friends?"

"Destined?"

Beatrice laughed. " 'Tis written in the sky." She gestured toward the comet. "Under another such dancing star was I born. How can any doubt this new one is a sign of good things to come?"

With great ease, Susanna thought.

As she led the way into the house, she realized that Beatrice's "dancing star" must have been the one that streaked across English skies in 1533. Susanna had not been born until the following year, but she had heard the stories as a child. That particular portent, it was said, foretold the divorce of Henry VIII from Catherine of Aragon. To those of Susanna's religious upbringing, putting aside both Queen Catherine and the Church of Rome had been cause for rejoicing. Catholics viewed the matter in a different light.

The divorce of her parents had been one of the first things Queen Mary set aside when she came to the throne. Now it was her sister, Elizabeth, daughter of Anne Boleyn, who was accounted a bastard. And those who would not renounce the New Religion and return to the Roman Catholic fold faced arrest, even martyrdom, on charges of heresy. The plight of many of Susanna's late father's friends had driven her to devise a way to help them escape persecution.

When wine and cheese and dried fruit had been served, Robert spoke. "We have been granted permission to hunt in the royal deer park on the morrow," he announced. "We will retire early to be up betimes."

Seated before the fire in the great hall, Susanna shifted to allow the warmth to reach more of her. Because Robert wished to impress their guests, he kept them in the largest and draftiest of the rooms instead of retiring to one of the smaller, warmer chambers. While beads of perspiration formed on her forehead from the heat, her back felt cold as a dead man's hand.

"Do you go with them, Beatrice?" she asked.

"I take no pleasure in killing." Beatrice sipped from a glass goblet containing a Gascon wine.

"She prefers slow torture," Lord Benedick commented, *sotto voce.*

Ignoring him, Beatrice remarked upon the color of the claret. "Bright as a ruby, as it should be."

Susanna could not resist. "I am told that if a claret wine has lost its color, one may take a pennyworth of damsons, or else black bullaces, and stew them with some red wine of the deepest color and make thereof a pound or more or syrup, which when put it into a hogshead of claret wine, does restore it to its original shade."

One foot resting on the back of a firedog, Robert stirred the fire with a poker. "The study of herbs," he confided to Lord Benedick, his manner implying a shared masculine indulgence of female weakness, "is my wife's little hobby."

"A very proper occupation." Lord Benedick lounged on a bench with a low back, his legs stretched out in front of him with the ankles crossed. He lifted his goblet in a toast to both women. "Mine delights in devising new uses for holy thistle."

"A universal remedy," Beatrice said with a smug smile. The twinkle in her eyes and the quick exchange of glances with her husband alerted Susanna to the play on words.

"*Carduus benedictus,*" she murmured.

Belatedly catching on, Robert laughed.

Jennet hovered close by, ears stretched to catch every word, but she did not understand the pun. Beatrice's companion, an old woman named Ursula, also seemed oblivious, or else she'd heard the joke too many times before to find it amusing. She sat near the hearth, placid as a grazing cow, her gnarled hands busy with a piece of needlework.

"If you have an interest in herbs other than the one that shares its name with Lord Benedick," Robert said to Beatrice, "you must ask my wife to show you her new storeroom."

Concealed by her skirts, Susanna's hands clenched into fists. Trust Robert to focus attention on the one thing she wished to hide. "I fear it is most noisome," she protested. "I have been conducting experiments to determine which herbs are most effective for killing fleas and other vermin." She'd intended the pungent smell keep Robert at bay. Now she must hope the odor was also strong enough to deter curious visitors.

"Poison would never be my wife's weapon of choice," Benedick remarked. "No more than the bow. She prefers a blade."

"He means I speak poniards and every word stabs." Beatrice gave her husband a playful swat on the shoulder.

This couple bandied words like tennis balls, Susanna thought, and yet each one was served with affection. She glanced at Robert, then away.

Benedick grinned at his wife before returning his attention to his host. "I cherish the hope that this visit will allow me to gain some small understanding of English women, for I do find my wife a most puzzling creature."

"*Your* wife, sir?"

"Did you not know? Beatrice was born in England."

"My mother," she explained, "was Spanish. She came to these shores in the entourage of Queen Catherine of Aragon. But she married an Englishman."

"Have you family here, then?" Susanna asked.

"Alas, no. When both my parents died, Ursula there was obliged to take me back to Spain to be raised by my mother's sister."

Hearing her name, the old woman glanced their way. She sent a fond smile winging toward her former charge, then took up her embroidery once more.

The conversation turned to the delights of travel in Spain and Italy. To Susanna's relief, there was no further mention of the new storeroom she'd caused to be built in an isolated spot beyond her stillroom and herb garden.

Before dawn the next day, Susanna rose to watch the hunting party depart, then made her way to what she privately called "the mint room." It was well, she thought, that the three "heretics" she'd had hidden at Leigh Abbey a few days earlier had left before Robert and his guests arrived. And a great pity that another had turned up right on their heels.

She glanced over her shoulder as she turned the key in the lock. No one was in sight and the sun had yet to burn off a concealing early morning mist. With luck, she could spirit the fellow away before Beatrice or her servant rose from their beds.

About the members of her own household she had no concerns. None would betray her. They had been loyal to her father in his time and they were loyal now to her. Further, they regarded Robert as an interloper and doubtless always would. He'd gained legal control of Leigh Abbey only because he'd married her.

The near overwhelming scent of mint rolled out of the storehouse the moment Susanna opened the door. Inside the small, brick-lined, stone building were great bales of garden mint, watermint, and pennyroyal. Taking a deep breath of fresh air first, Susanna plunged inside, skirting the bales to reach another door, this one concealed by a panel in the back wall.

She did not see the body until she tripped over it.

Susanna knelt beside a man sprawled face up on the floor, an expression of agony on his face. She knew even before she touched him that she was far too late to render aid.

As her fingers found a lump on the back of his skull, her own head began to swim. Startled by her find, she'd forgotten to hold her breath.

Was this how he'd died? In fear of suffocation, his heart failing under the strain of trying to take in untainted air?

Eyes streaming, coughing fit to choke, she fled the storeroom. In the yard, doubled over, she inhaled in great gulps, all the while fighting for control of a roiling stomach. When someone took her hand to guide her to a nearby bench, she let herself be led. She assumed Jennet had come to her rescue, but it was Beatrice's voice that spoke, in calm, well-modulated tones.

"I have heard the odor of pennyroyal attracts fleas, then smothers them, but I'd not have thought it would work so well on a man. Was he your particular enemy?"

Susanna stared at the other woman in shock and horror. "I did not kill him!"

"He is dead." Beatrice looked distraught, as who would not, having come upon such a scene.

"A tragic accident."

"Yes," Beatrice murmured. But she did not sound convinced.

What else could it have been? Susanna buried her face in her hands, although she had no intention of giving way to tears. For just a moment, she needed to hide from Beatrice's too-perceptive gaze.

The odor in the mint room had been well nigh overpowering. If he'd dropped the key she'd given him, then panicked as he tried to find it and could not, confusion and the struggle to breathe could have caused him to stumble and fall, striking his head. On what? She had no notion, but she'd felt the lump. The blow alone might have killed him. Or, as she'd first thought, he could have had a weak heart and been snuffed out by sheer terror. She was certain of only one thing. The pennyroyal alone was not to blame. As Beatrice had implied, a man was a great deal bigger than a flea.

"Inconvenient, no matter how he died," Beatrice remarked. "If he is found here and can be identified as a heretic, his presence will endanger your efforts on behalf of the Marian exiles."

Startled, Susanna sat bolt upright. She felt a chill that had naught to do with the cold, damp morning. "What do you know of the work we do here?"

The calm, composed countenance above a sable-trimmed cloak of red velvet inspired confidence, as did Beatrice's words. "Benedick and I have many friends in the English community at Padua."

Susanna's head pounded, an aftereffect of her coughing fit. She found it difficult to order her thoughts. Did she mean Benedick had befriended men driven into exile by Queen Mary's religious policies? Or that he was acquainted with Englishmen already there before Mary took the throne? The University of Padua had long drawn students from England, in particular those with an interest in medicine, but not all of them were followers of the New Religion.

"I see I must be blunt with you." Beatrice glanced around to make sure they were unobserved. "Some of the most recent arrivals reached Padua only because of your efforts on their behalf." She named three men Susanna had hidden at Leigh Abbey on their way out of England. "What you do here is of vital importance, Susanna. Benedick and I may not share your faith, but we approve of saving lives."

"Robert would not, if he knew." The bitter words slipped out before she could censor them.

"I am glad to hear that you have kept your ambitious husband in the dark."

"He is a loyal subject!" She stood up too fast, making her head spin.

"Aye, so loyal and so bent on advancement under your present monarch that he might be tempted to betray his own wife. There would be a risk. He might be blamed for your folly. But if you alone were found guilty, he would benefit from your downfall."

That Beatrice spoke the truth did not make her observations any more palatable, but her words also reminded Susanna that she had a more pressing problem. "I dare not call in the coroner. He would ask too many questions."

"Then we must remove the body from the premises at once," Beatrice said, "before anyone else comes along and sees it. Have you a barrel or a buck tub to hide him in while we transport him?" She glanced toward the dark interior of the storeroom, as if considering the dead man's size. "Or mayhap an empty wine butt?"

Susanna rejected Beatrice's more colorful suggestions in favor of a plain blanket to wrap him in. "There is one in the stable," she said. After closing and locking the storeroom door, she led the way there. "He rode in on an old bay mare. We can use her to carry him away again."

"Is there a river or stream nearby?" Beatrice asked. "If we leave him in the water, it will appear that he was thrown when he attempted to ford it and drowned after hitting his head on a rock."

"And the rushing water will wash away the smell of the mint." Susanna had to admire Beatrice's quick thinking. In spite of a tendency toward the over-dramatic, she had a practical bent.

"But what was he doing in your storeroom? Why did he come out of hiding?"

Susanna covered her hesitation by fumbling with the stable door. Beatrice appeared to be an ally. She knew Susanna smuggled heretics out of England and that one of them was dead. But she might not realize that the storeroom had a secret inner chamber concealed behind its back wall. She had no need to know of its existence, Susanna decided.

"You must have told him to remain out of sight," Beatrice persisted.

"When do men ever do what they are told?" Susanna felt a wry smile twist her lips when she heard the asperity in her own voice. "Had it been Robert, he'd have risked venturing out at night to make sure his horse had been cared for." He doted on Vanguard. "That, I think, is the most logical reason for the stranger to have been wandering about in the dark."

"Why go into your storeroom?"

"Curiosity?"

"Do you know his name?" Beatrice fired questions in a barrage and Susanna volleyed answers back.

"I never ask for names."

"Then how—"

"A password."

The system had been devised with the help of Sir Anthony Cooke, a dear friend of her father's. He was himself in exile now, but one of his daughters had remained behind to maintain a station along an escape route for fellow "heretics" similar to the one at Leigh Abbey.

"Saddle the bay and two other horses," Susanna instructed Mark, one of the grooms. When he hurried off to do her bidding, she turned to her companion. "You must not involve yourself in this, Beatrice."

"You cannot manage the body alone."

"Mark will assist me. All else aside, you are scarce dressed for the task. And you can better serve me by staying here. It will help allay suspicion. You can pretend to be closeted with me in my study while I am gone."

Common sense warred with an overabundance of zeal, but in the end Beatrice agreed to Susanna's suggestion.

"Does he appear to have struck his head on a rock?" Susanna asked. Although the brook flowed fast and deep with spring runoff, a strong man in good condition, such as this one had been, might have been able to pull himself out if he had not been knocked unconscious.

Even with her stalwart young groom's assistance, it had been no simple undertaking to move the body. The deceased had been dead weight.

"He'll do, madam," Mark said, "and we must away before anyone comes upon us."

"Free his horse," she ordered. "Set her wandering in the woods." She was tempted to order Mark himself to "find" the bay and instigate a search for its rider, but she was loath to do anything to call attention to Leigh Abbey.

Had she thought of everything? she wondered as they rode home. Belatedly, she remembered that he'd had a pack with him when he arrived. That might contain some clue to his identity. All she knew at present, from his appearance, was that he had seen more than forty winters. The better to go unnoticed on his journey, he'd worn plain clothes that gave no hint of his occupation, but he'd had the speech of a gentleman.

The ride back took less than a quarter hour. She'd not dared transport the body any farther now that it was full daylight.

"Go you to the kitchen and dry off," she told Mark. He'd gotten soaked positioning the body.

Susanna went straight to the mint room, pausing only long enough to collect a lantern. When she'd locked herself in, she hurried to the inner door, her key at the ready. A moment later, she was safely inside the second room and had shut out the overpowering smell.

No one had disturbed the hiding place she'd had purpose-built to conceal refugees from Queen Mary's religious persecution. Long and narrow, it took up one end of the windowless storehouse and contained sleeping pallets, a chair and table, and a supply of food and drink stored in a tall, freestanding cupboard.

Suspicions had begun to nag at Susanna as soon as the initial shock of discovering a body had passed. In the aftermath, transporting it and throwing it into the brook, she'd had no time to ask herself questions, but now that she had leisure to consider them, she discovered a disconcerting dearth of answers.

Susanna contemplated her surroundings. The dead man had arrived with a pack. She remembered seeing it. Brown leather, of good quality. The type of bag that hung over a saddle. It must be somewhere.

So, too, should there be a key, a duplicate of the one she'd just used.

She began a methodical inspection of the chamber, end to end, floor to ceiling, but she reaped no more reward for her pains than a splinter in one thumb and sore knees.

No pack.

No key.

Covering her mouth and nose with a cloth, Susanna conducted a quick but thorough search of the storeroom before she emerged into the crisp afternoon air. There was nothing in the mint room but mint.

The hairs on the back of her neck prickled as she made her way to the stable. She glanced over her shoulder, certain someone was watching her, but there was no one in sight. Had he felt this way? she wondered. For all that Mark and the other grooms slept in the room above, the dead man could have gotten into the stables unseen and unheard. Then what? She studied the neat rows of stalls. Had he merely checked on his bay? Or had he come to hide something? More to the point, had he feared some enemy, someone who had, indeed, caught up with him?

As long as the duplicate key to the mint room remained missing, Susanna was forced to consider the possibility that the stranger had been murdered, that someone had trapped him in the storeroom, struck him on the head, and left him there to die . . . locking the door on the way out.

"Oh, there you are, madam!" Jennet exclaimed, rushing into the stable. "Mark said you were back."

Beatrice arrived a moment later, closely followed by Ursula.

"Can she be trusted?" Beatrice demanded, glaring at the tiring maid. "She got the whole story out of your groom before I could prevent it."

"I am obliged to trust you both," Susanna told her. "There is no time to waste. It will not do for Robert to return and find me here. I have never shown an interest in the horses before."

"Why *are* you in the stable?" Jennet asked.

"To search for the stranger's missing pack."

When she had described its appearance, they spread out. Beatrice spoke in rapid Spanish, giving Ursula instructions. The reminder that both women were foreigners, for all that Beatrice had been born in England, gave Susanna pause. It seemed odd to her that Beatrice was so determined to help.

For a short while, no one spoke. Susanna inspected the stall where the old bay mare had been kept, the one in the darkest corner, where its occupant had stood the best chance of escaping notice. Stabling the refugees' horses was the riskiest part of her enterprise. Robert paid little attention to people, but he was devoted to his cattle. There had always been a chance he'd notice unauthorized additions.

Mare's droppings aside, Susanna found nothing in the stall. She moved on to the next one.

Jennet's cry of triumph brought them back to the center aisle of the stable. She had found the missing pack in the tack room. She hurried toward Susanna, carrying it in one hand and waving a paper in the other.

"A letter!" Beatrice cried, intercepting Jennet and plucking it from her fingers. "This must be destroyed before it can be used against you."

"Wait!"

But Susanna was too late. Beatrice had opened the nearest lantern and thrust the parchment into the candle flame. By the time Susanna reached her, the paper had been reduced to ash.

"Now, then," said Beatrice, pulling at the pack, "we must do likewise with this."

Jennet tried to keep hold of her prize, but Beatrice was a strong woman. She tugged it free and, giving Susanna no chance to protest, swept out of the stable with it. Ursula trailed along in her wake.

"Is she mad?" Jennet asked.

"It is my hope that she is only overzealous. I intended to destroy the pack myself, but I had planned to examine the contents first."

"It is the fault of the star with the long tail," Jennet muttered darkly. "An evil omen. Did I not say so? Death and destruction. Terror and—"

"Enough! Nothing supernatural caused that man's death, or Beatrice's actions, either." She fixed Jennet with a commanding stare. "What did the letter say?"

"Oh, madam, how could you think that I—"

"What did it say, Jennet?" Susanna tapped her foot and waited. All Leigh Abbey servants were taught to read, and if Jennet had one besetting sin, it was an abundance of curiosity. She'd been caught more than once hiding behind an arras to listen to the private conversations of others. Susanna had no doubt that she'd skimmed the letter before announcing her discovery, or that she'd found it in the first place by searching the pack.

"It was a letter of introduction. I did not have time to read the whole of it." Jennet's affronted tone spoke volumes.

"Repeat the words you did see, exactly as you remember them."

"To Sir Anthony Cooke, Strasbourg. I recommend unto you Master William Wroth."

"Go on."

"That is all I saw, madam."

"What of a signature? Who sent it?"

"I could not make out the name, but the letter was written from Staines on the second day of March. Where is Staines, madam?"

Susanna frowned. "It is some fifteen miles west of London, along the way to Salisbury." Of more importance was the identity of the person in that place who'd sent William Wroth to Leigh Abbey.

"Fetch Mark," she instructed. "I've a message to dispatch. Then find quill and ink and paper and write down every item you noted in Master Wroth's pack."

"The dead man had no mark of violence upon him." Robert paused to refill his goblet with a sharp white wine from Angulle.

He and Lord Benedick and their servants had been stopped on the way home from the hunt by the coroner, who had been called in as soon as the body was discovered. Robert had been asked if he could identify the deceased. He claimed he'd never seen the fellow before.

"No mark at all?" Susanna asked as she and Beatrice exchanged a worried glance. Had no one noticed the lump on his head? This was a complication they had not foreseen.

"The fish had nibbled him," Robert said.

"He must have drowned, then," Beatrice murmured. "Will your coroner declare the death an accident?"

"He is reluctant to do so without knowing the identity of the victim. And he has some suspicion that the fellow may have taken his own life. He cannot be buried in hallowed ground if that is the case."

"What's to be done then?"

"The coroner has persuaded the justices to look more deeply into the matter."

Susanna's fingers clasped her wine cup so tightly that her knuckles showed white. They suspected murder. She was sure of it.

Beatrice did not seem to share her fears. "Officials are wont to fuss and fume and make themselves look important," she declared with a little laugh. "This will all turn out to be much ado about nothing."

The next morning, when Robert and Lord Benedick had left for a second day of hunting, Susanna, Beatrice, Jennet, and Ursula gathered in Susanna's study, a pleasant room full of books and maps, with windows that overlooked Leigh Abbey's fields and orchards to the east and the approach to the gatehouse on the north.

"The man's name was William Wroth," Susanna announced.

Ursula gasped, made the sign of the cross, and fumbled for her rosary.

"You know this man Wroth, good Ursula?" Susanna had not expected any reaction. She'd brought up Wroth's name as a preliminary to a discussion of how to convince the authorities his death was an accident.

The old woman's deeply lined face crumpled further and her eyes, filmed with age, sought her mistress, but she did not speak.

Beatrice laid a hand on her arm. Her voice was gentle. "You must tell us if you know who this man was, Ursula."

"He was evil, mistress," Ursula answered.

Or rather, that was what Beatrice told Susanna and Jennet she had said. She and Ursula spoke in Spanish, a language the others did not understand.

"Why does she think he was evil?" Susanna demanded.

Their incomprehensible conversation resumed. Beatrice asked questions and paused now and again to translate when Ursula answered, but it seemed to Susanna that the waiting gentlewoman took a great many words to convey very little. She began to wonder how much Beatrice was holding back.

"She knows nothing of help to us," Beatrice said at last. "Only that when she was in my mother's service here in England, there was a man by that name who was well known for his hatred of all things Spanish. This was many years ago, for I was still a small child when my parents died."

"Did she ever meet William Wroth?" He'd have been a young man in his twenties then.

"She knew him by reputation. She says he was wont to pick fights with the servants of Spanish merchant families in London. And their sons."

"And no one stopped him?"

"Why should they, once Queen Catherine had been set aside? I remember a little of that time myself, for all that I was so young. My mother would cry herself to sleep over what had happened to her mistress. Once King Henry divorced her, men who felt as Wroth did had few restraints on their behavior. It was a popular belief that the only good Spaniard was a dead Spaniard."

"That must have made things difficult for your parents."

A great sadness clouded Beatrice's countenance. "Since I have been back in England, I have felt their loss the more, but when they were alive, they knew great happiness. My father loved my mother as much as Benedick loves me and she returned his feelings tenfold."

Through the north-facing window, Susanna caught sight of an approaching rider. She knew him by his bright green cloak and dappled horse. By the time her neighbor, old Sir Eustace Thornley, who had served as a justice of the peace since Susanna was a girl, had been shown to the study, all four women were seated in a circle, applying their needles to a large piece of tapestry work.

"I am sorry to trouble you," he apologized after he'd been presented to Beatrice, "but I seek information about a man seen in the area of late." He gave particulars of William Wroth's appearance but did not say he was dead. Susanna suspected that Sir Eustace, who had never married, clung to the quaint notion that women should not trouble their pretty little heads about such matters as sudden death and coroners' inquests.

"That is a passing general description, sir," she said with flutter of eyelashes and a pout. "Has he no distinguishing characteristic?"

Flustered, Sir Eustace mumbled, "A faint smell of mint clung to his clothing and beard." He cleared his throat and pressed on. "It is not, I think, a common perfume."

"Mint has many uses." Susanna's voice was level but her heart raced triple time. She could scarce deny knowledge of the herb. Every woman received some training in the stillroom. "I steep the leaves of garden mint to make an infusion. Drinking one to two cups of this daily, but not for more than one week at a time, is an excellent remedy for sleeplessness and helpful to the digestion, as well. Mayhap the gentleman spilled his medicine."

"I prefer to distill mint," Beatrice said. "One must use freshly cut, partially dried plant tops, cut just before the plants come into flower. An overmature plant produces an oil with a sharp, bitter aroma, but if the process be done aright, it yields a hot, pungent aroma."

The justice's eyes began to glaze over.

Taking her cue from Beatrice, Susanna launched into a detailed description of the preparation of a stimulant using mint and other herbs. She gave up all pretense of stitching. She was not much of a needlewoman in the best of circumstances.

"Well done, Susanna," Beatrice said when Sir Eustace took his leave a few minutes later. "How quick men are to lose interest in domestic matters!"

"A pity. I so wanted to tell him that some mints are cultivated as an aid to love. Why pennyroyal, given to quarreling couples, is even supposed to induce them to make peace."

"It is also a protection against evil," Beatrice remarked.

"Well, then," Susanna said with a smile, "we have nothing to fear. With all the mint we have stored at Leigh Abbey, 'tis certain we are safe from further trouble from Sir Eustace."

The next day Susanna and Beatrice rode with their husbands to Canterbury to visit the cathedral. On the way back, Robert stopped at Sir Eustace's manor house, sending the others on ahead without him. Susanna had no opportunity for a private word with him until they retired to their bedchamber for the night.

"Do you hunt again tomorrow?" she asked.

"Aye." He sounded disconsolate. "Lord Benedick cares for naught but hunting, hawking, and dallying with his own wife. He has no intention of attaching himself to the court."

Concealing a smile, Susanna made a sympathetic sound and continued to take pins out of her hair.

"You are a clever woman, Susanna. Can you find a way to give Beatrice a dislike of you?"

She fought a sense of disappointment as she brushed her long, thick hair. Robert believed it was a waste of his time to entertain Lord Benedick any longer, but he did not want to be the one to offend him, just in case Benedick turned out to have some use, after all. Robert expected Susanna to do his dirty work for him.

"I see no reason to discourage her friendship. Beatrice is most pleasant company."

"What do you know of her family?"

The question surprised her. "Her mother was in the household of Queen Mary's mother. I'd think such a connection would be helpful to you."

"Any benefit is overshadowed by what happened afterward. Beatrice's mother killed her English husband, then took her own life."

Aghast, Susanna put down her hairbrush and demanded details.

"Their family seat was at Staines," Robert said. His voice was muffled as he settled himself for the night. "That is all Sir Eustace told me." Their neighbor was well known for his long memory and love of gossip. If he'd had more information, he'd have repeated it.

Susanna crossed to the bed and pulled aside the bright blue damask hangings to glower at her spouse. Staines. The location could not be a coincidence. "Did Wroth come here because of Lord Benedick and his wife?"

Just before his eyes shifted away from her unrelenting gaze, she read the truth in them. He recognized Wroth's name. Had he known all along who the dead man was?

The belligerent jut of Robert's jaw warned her he did not intend to answer questions, but two could play at that game. She did not intend to explain how she'd discovered Wroth's identity. She perched on the foot of the bed and deftly began to braid her hair.

"I am as anxious as you that you regain favor at court." How else could she hope to continue her rescue efforts? "But if I do not know as much as you do, Robert, then I may make some mistake or say the wrong thing. If this dead stranger, for example, is the same Wroth who had such a reputation for hating all things Spanish—"

"God save me from meddling females!"

"He sounds the worst sort of extremist." She could not regret that Wroth was dead, knowing the sort of man he had been, but neither could she continue to ignore the possibility that he had been murdered. "He brought no credit to the cause he claimed to espouse."

"Nor was he faithful to it."

"What do you mean?" Her hands stilled in her hair.

"When last I was in London, I heard a rumor that Wroth, who had been in prison under sentence of death, had agreed to do some service for Queen Mary in order to save his own skin."

The possibility that Wroth had come to Leigh Abbey as a spy made Susanna's blood run cold, but she did not dare ask Robert any more questions for fear of arousing *his* suspicions. Beatrice had been right. Susanna's husband would turn her in himself if he saw any profit in it.

Mark returned to Leigh Abbey the next day, bringing a reply to the message Susanna had sent to Sir Anthony Cooke's daughter. The verbal questions had been accompanied, as proof of the sender's identity, by a sprig of rosemary. Margaret Cooke's answers came back with a bit of rue. She sent word that no one in Staines should have known what went on at Leigh Abbey, but that

Wroth himself owned property there. He'd bought the estate of a man—Margaret could not remember his name—who had been murdered by his wife.

"Good news," Mark added, unaware that his mistress had been obliged to take a tight grip on the arms of her favorite carved oak chair to quell the sudden trembling in her hands. "When I passed through the village, I heard that Sir Eustace took another look at the body and this time noticed the lump on the dead man's head. The death will be ruled an accident. No more questions will be asked."

"Good news, indeed," Susanna murmured, giving Mark a reward for his services and sending him back to his usual duties.

Sunk deep in thought, it was some little time before Susanna realized that Jennet, who had come into the study with Mark, had remained when he was dismissed. She had a talent for disappearing into the woodwork when she did not want to be noticed.

"What did Beatrice do with the dead man's pack?" Susanna asked.

"Cut it into small bits and burnt them."

Trust Jennet to know. The list she'd made had been helpful, too. Wroth's pack had contained only clothing. No papers. No key.

"Why do you think she did that, Jennet?"

"To protect you, madam?"

"I wonder."

"Madam?"

"Yes, Jennet?"

"It is possible I missed seeing a key in Master Wroth's pack." At Susanna's start of surprise, she rushed on. "I do not know how else she could have got hold of it."

"Beatrice?"

Jennet nodded. "She must have been the one who sent old Ursula to get rid of it, since metal will not burn. I saw it clear when I followed Ursula to the fishponds. The key caught the sun as she threw it in."

Susanna found Beatrice and Ursula in the small parlor. Beatrice had pulled the Glastonbury chair close to the window in order to read by the light streaming in through the panes. Ursula sat close to the fire, mending a stocking.

"Did you arrange to meet Master Wroth here?" Susanna asked. If Robert wanted her to give the other woman a dislike of them, an accusation of murder should suffice.

Beatrice's demeanor remained calm. She marked her place in *Liber de Arte Distillandi* and met Susanna's eyes before she answered. "No."

"But you recognized him when you saw him?"

"No," she said again.

Susanna believed her, but she felt certain Beatrice was hiding something. "If you sought to trap Wroth in the mint room, intending to hold him there until Lord Benedick could deal with him—"

"Why all these questions?" Beatrice asked. "I thought you deemed Wroth's death an accident, even if Sir Eustace does not."

It was on the tip of her tongue to correct Beatrice, but at the last moment, she decided to keep the justice's most recent conclusion to herself. "Someone must have struck Wroth down, then locked him in the storeroom afterward," she said instead. "If he simply fell, I'd have found the key. Tell me, Beatrice, what is the connection between William Wroth and the death of your parents?"

With an abrupt movement, Beatrice rose from the chair and went to stand by the window and stare out at the bleak landscape. Her view encompassed the ornamental gardens, but at this time of year they showed no sign of life.

"You recognized Wroth," Susanna said in a voice she hoped conveyed her sympathy. "You locked him in, doubtless meaning to fetch Lord Benedick to deal with him, but by the time you returned, Wroth was dead."

"Benedick knows nothing of this!" As soon as the words were out, she looked stricken, but it was too late to call them back.

If Benedick had seen the body, Susanna realized, it would have been long gone by morning. But if Wroth had not been locked in to await interrogation by Benedick, then Beatrice must have meant to kill him. Unless . . .

"Ursula," Susanna whispered. "Ursula was the one who recognized Wroth. She locked him in."

With obvious reluctance, Beatrice nodded. She returned to the chair. "I see I must tell you everything. Yes, she locked him in. Then she came to me. It took some time to sort matters out. It was the middle of the night. She had to extract me from my bed without waking Benedick, then explain who Wroth was and what she'd done and why. I had been told my parents were carried off by a fever. It was a great shock to learn that my mother had been accused of killing my father and of taking her own life. Ursula insisted that Wroth was to blame for both deaths."

"Has she any proof?"

"No. My mother took her aside one night at Staines, gave her money, and told her she must take me back to Spain without delay. Then she led Ursula to a window and pointed to a man—Wroth—and said we must avoid being seen by him when we left, that he was dangerous. Within the hour, Ursula and I were on our way to Calais. It was there that word reached us that my parents were dead."

"And Ursula did nothing?"

"What could she do? She knew Wroth's reputation. She was sure he had killed them, but she feared for her own life and mine if she remained on English soil long enough to accuse him. But now—now she is old. She no longer fears death." She smiled faintly. "And because she is old, her bones ache, preventing sleep. She was up in the middle of the night and chanced to look out a window. She recognized Wroth at once, for the situation was much as it had been when she'd seen him all those years ago. She went out for a closer look, followed him into the storeroom, caught him by surprise, hit him on the head, and took the key to lock him in. She reasoned that, together, she and I might be able to persuade him to confess to his crimes, but by the time I heard her explanation and dressed and went with her to the storeroom we were, as you have guessed, too late. He was dead."

"But why just leave him there? You must have known he'd be found."

"It was too close to sunrise to do anything else. As it was, I scarce had time to lock the door again and return to my bed before Benedick woke. I meant to go back and dispose of him as soon as Benedick left on the hunt, but you were there ahead of me."

Susanna wanted to believe her. If Wroth's death had been an accident, the matter was closed. And she'd had a narrow escape, for had he lived to be accused, the existence of the inner room and its purpose would have been exposed. She'd have ended up in gaol alongside Will Wroth. And although he might well have been acquitted, she'd have been certain to be executed for treason. She swallowed hard.

"We will say no more of the matter."

Beatrice frowned. "Benedick and I plan to return to Padua soon, where we will be safe from English law, but the smell of mint made Sir Eustace suspicious of you, Susanna. What if he continues to investigate? What if he discovers that Wroth died in your storeroom?"

"I am confident he will not." Had the return of the hunting party not interrupted her at that moment, Susanna would have gone on to share the verdict on Wroth's death with Beatrice.

"I thought they meant to leave this morning," Robert complained the next day. "What is Beatrice doing in your storeroom?"

"Stillroom, Robert. She's preparing her secret recipe for *aqua vitae* as a parting gift, using pennyroyal to add protective properties to the distillation."

"Do we need protection?" He sounded suspicious.

Susanna smiled. "No, my dear, but Beatrice took note of the way Jennet carries on, fearful of evil in the wake of the star with the long—"

She broke off, beset by a vague sense of alarm as she remembered that, as far as Beatrice knew, Susanna also had need of protection—from Sir Eustace. First they'd been distracted by the arrival of their husbands and then the bustle of preparations for Beatrice and Benedick's departure had occupied the rest of the afternoon and evening. Susanna's intention to tell Beatrice there was no longer any need to worry had completely slipped her mind.

Robert failed to notice Susanna's distraction. "She will not be at it much longer," he said after a few moments of consideration. "Not with the goodly fire she had Benedick build for her in your storeroom."

"Stillroom," Susanna corrected. "And a stilling pot must be heated over a soft fire. Be patient, Robert. The day is young."

"Storeroom," Robert insisted, "and this was no temperate blaze."

Susanna felt her face drain of color. *Aqua vitae* had another name. It was called "burning water" because it so easily turned into flame.

"Storeroom?" she whispered.

No one heard her. The explosion drowned out all other sounds. It blew the storeroom walls outward as the fire, in one bright flash, consumed the incriminating bales of mint. It did not spread, nor was Beatrice harmed. She'd taken care to avoid both consequences when she planned this parting gift for her hostess.

"The fire was too rash." Benedick's cheerful wink told Susanna that he was now in his wife's confidence. His generous offer to pay for the damage mollified Robert and prevented him from asking awkward questions.

Beatrice, Susanna thought, had also been too rash, but only because she'd believed she owed it to Susanna to protect her from Sir Eustace's suspicions.

"Will you rebuild your storeroom?" Robert asked as they watched their guests ride away a few hours later. Jennet had come out too. And Mark.

"There is no need." From now on, she'd hide escaping heretics in the stable with their horses.

"But where will you store pennyroyal?" Jennet asked. "Won't you need a great deal more of it to keep Leigh Abbey safe from the star with the long tail?"

"No, indeed," Susanna assured her, "for Beatrice had the right of it all along. Your ominous portent, Jennet, is in truth a dancing star, and a sure sign of all the good things to come."

The Serpent's Tooth

BY P. C. DOHERTY

Paul Doherty is the author of many historical novels and mysteries, all of which have been widely praised in both the United Kingdom and America. His books have been published by Robert Hale, Headline, and Constable Robinson in the British Commonwealth, and by St. Martin's Press in America. He studied history at Liverpool and Oxford Universities and gained a doctorate at Oxford for his thesis on Edward II and Isabella. He is headmaster of a school in London, and lives with his wife and family near Epping Forest.

The riders emerged from the mist two days before midsummer. The hot sun had not yet burnt off the misty wisps swirling across the water meadows, in amongst the elms, willows, and alders that fringed the banks of the Avon. Despite the rutted, cobbled track, they came quietly, the leading rider dressed like Death Himself. Despite the threatening heat, he was garbed in black like some raven come to feast, his cloak hung easily on a silver chain round his neck. He did not drape this over his shoulders but wore it loosely so it fell in folds over the back of his saddle. His black leather jerkin was unbuttoned down to the midriff, his crisp white shirt, loose at the neck, displayed a leather cord from which some half-concealed medallion hung. He wore black hose pushed into stout riding boots of the same color, silver gilt spurs that clinked and jingled. He rode effortlessly, reins loosely in one hand, the other resting on his thigh as if ready to draw the great pistol fastened in its holster or stretch across for the basket-hilted rapier strapped to his left side, its ermine-covered scabbard edged with bronze. "A dangerous-looking man" is how one farmer, going down towards the meadows, described this strange visitor to Stratford. "A Raven in human form!"

"Mind you," another declared, "his companion looked as fearsome. He was dressed in brown and green, head and face hidden by a cowl like some outlaw riding out of the forest."

Nevertheless, it was "Raven" who caught people's attention. He rode with an easy arrogance, "As sure as a cock on a dung hill," the farmer described him.

At first the "Raven" seemed to be journeying nowhere but rode around Stratford as if on pilgrimage and wished to memorize certain sights. He rode along the three great streets that ran parallel with the River Avon. He paused before the archery butts near old Clopton's bridge, where a boy heard him mutter a line from one of the great playwright's works about, "Sad eyed justice" and another verse no one could later place, "Thou shalt have justice more than thou desirest." He then rode on, lips moving soundlessly as if quoting the poetry of the man whose town he had come to visit.

No one really knew what happened that day yet they would always remember the man, dressed like a raven, riding the boundaries of their town. He went across Clopton's bridge, along Bridge Street up to where High Street and Henley Street debouched into the marketplace. He visited the Bear tavern and rode along Henley Street to the house where Master Shakespeare had been born. He asked a few questions of early risers and stared intently at the black timbers and white plaster, the glass-filled casement windows. He even dismounted and strode along the narrow alleyway as if to savor the roses growing in the gardens behind. He returned and stood on the cobbles before the front door staring up at the eaves, as if trying to catch something ephemeral, the very substance of the place. He laughed softly, shrugged, and remounted his horse. He then paused at Rogers, the old apothecary shop, where confections of roses, liquorice, and the imports from the New World were being laid out on the stalls, protected against the sun by a leather awning. He asked a few questions of the apprentices and continued to "The King's House," where the scullions and maidservants were still heavy-eyed with sleep. The "Raven's" companion held the horses while his master took a tankard of ale in the great panelled room, slouched in a chair staring at the wall paintings from the Book of Tobit, all decorated with embroidered letters, friezes, and suitable texts from the Bible. Once he had finished his tankard, the "Raven" ordered another and took it out to his companion: he drank quickly before handing it back to the tap boy. The bill was settled, the "Raven" remounted his horse and continued his journey, down to New Place, a five-gabled house built slightly off the street, protected by a small courtyard with barns, gardens, and small orchards at the back. Again the "Raven" and his companion sat on their horses, staring up at the upper-storey windows under the red-tiled roof. Afterwards they turned their horses past the Guildhall, along the road into Old Stratford. They dismounted at the lych-gate of Holy Trinity Church. The "Raven" told his companion to look after the horses before walking up the long, haunting path, lined by lime trees, in through the main door of the church.

The sexton, preparing to ring the bell, espied the stranger, and went hurrying over all a-blabber. The "Raven" waved him away and walked up the wide vaulting nave into the chancel, where the tombs of the Cloptons and other town notables were buried. He paused and stared down at Master Shakespeare's tombstone. The sexton, who had followed him from afar, later reported how the "Raven" loudly whispered the words of the great playwright's epitath:

> "GOOD FREND FOR JESUS SAKE FORBEARE,
> TO DIGG THE DUST ENCLOASED HEARE:
> BLESTE BE YE MAN TY SPARES THES STONES,
> AND CURST BE HE TY MOVES MY BONES."

The "Raven" stood, head bowed, hand on the basket hilt of his sword as if saluting an old friend. The sexton, embarrassed, was about to turn away when he heard the "Raven" add a line certainly not inscribed on the stone:

"Truth will come to light, Murder cannot be hid long!"

The "Raven" walked abruptly away, the sexton hid in the shadows, quivering like a mouse: he did not stir until the clatter of boots and the clink of spurs faded like evensong on a soft summer's evening. The grave-digger busy in the churchyard, moving bones to the old charnel house, saw the "Raven" leave: he grasped his reins, mounted, and determinedly cantered away from the church, back up the street towards New Place.

On this occasion they didn't tarry but hammered on the gates of the court-yard. A servant came hurrying out to be brusquely ordered, "To open in the King's name!" The "Raven" and his companion entered. The gates slammed behind them and that's all the good people of Stratford ever knew about the "Raven's" arrival in Stratford. They never really learned why he had come or why he was closeted with Physician John Hall and his wife, Susanna. They did not know what passed between them. Oh, of course, rumours abounded.

"Something to do with Shakespeare's will," one gap-toothed gossip at the Swan declared.

"Oh no," another riposted. "More to do with his death and burial."

For surely Master Shakespeare, with his powerful friends in the city and court, deserved a better resting place than the musty old chancel of Holy Trinity Church?

Of course the servants at New Place were questioned time and again, when-ever any of them put a foot across a tavern doorway or went into the market to shop among the stalls. Someone would always pluck at their sleeves but the servants were no help. All they could say was that the "Raven" was a King's man, also a physician, a certain Doctor Paul Siggins of Cambridge. One cham-ber maid added a more relishing piece of tittle-tattle. "How Siggins was not only a King's man, but," she added in a more sinister whisper, "A busy scurrier who worked for the Office of the Night."

Those who knew more than they should always turned away as if the con-versation was finished. They did not wish to be caught up in such business. The Office of the Night was often whispered about by sheriffs' men and those who worked for the local Justices. How the Office of the Night took its name from the dark, cavernous rooms at the Tower of London where the King's spies pored over manuscripts by lighted candles or sat round tables and whispered, in those dark, velvet-draped chambers, how they would counter the plots and mischief of the King's enemies both at home and abroad. Yet those in the know would later reflect what could the sinister Office of the Night possibly want with the Shakespeare family? The gentle-eyed, sad-faced John Hall and his feisty wife Susanna? Many would have loved to have known but it was too dangerous to question further. After a few months discretion, rather than curiosity, ruled the day and the visit by the "Raven" from the Office of the Night was never mentioned.

At New Place the two arrivals soon made their authority felt. Siggins and his friend, whom he introduced simply as "Adam, a son of Eve," were led into the oak-panelled hall where Physician John Hall sat at his great table on the dais pretending to fill in his notebook. In truth, he had done little writing but hid his anxiety beneath the pretense of business. Hall's wife, Susanna, came in and out like a bird from its nest, supervising the maids, dusting the massive oaken furniture or rearranging the four great quilted chairs before the man-telled hearth. Physician John Hall almost leapt to his feet, knocking over an ink horn as Siggins and his companion slunk like hunting cats into the chamber. Hall stood for a while peering through the poor light. The main hall was still rather dark despite extra windows being built at either end or the best beeswax candles blazing in their bronze and iron holders.

"Dr. John Hall?" Siggins's voice was soft but carrying. "Physician John Hall of New Place Stratford? My name is Siggins, from the Office of the Night."

Hall decided that standing so poised had little effect upon his visitors: still holding his quill, he walked round the table, off the dais, and down the hall to where the two strangers stood in the open doorway. Behind them Susanna, her auburn hair pulled tight and coifed behind her head, stood anxious-eyed. She did not seem so resolute or stubborn now: her face was rather pale, full lower lip jutting out more than it usually did. She had decided not to wear her best dress to grace her visitors but a dark blue kirtle, slightly pinched at the waist, with a silver-grey girdle to match and fine white ruffs around neck and cuffs. She had also cast her best buckled shoes to one side in favor of soft buskins, as if she realized this was not a day for chatter and laughter but sharp questioning and keen wits. Hall glared at her, gesturing with his head that the door be closed. Susanna could only stare back. Siggins hadn't moved but stood, blocking the way, as if uncertain whether to stay or leave. Hall felt nervous: sweat pricked his neck and back. He didn't think the walk would take so long. All he was aware of were those two faces staring at him.

"You are a physician, Master Siggins?" He stretched out his hand, eager to break the silence.

Siggins took a step forward, clasped it, and stood away. Hall could now make out his visitor, his agitation only deepened. Siggins was soft-faced, with large dark eyes and a pleasant smiling mouth, yet he exuded a menace, a threatening authority. Hall cursed his own imagination. He just wished Siggins wouldn't stand there, lips slightly parted, studying him from head to toe. His companion, Adam, was just as broody, with his dark face under a black thatch of hair, sharper-featured with keen watchful eyes. Like his master, Adam was clean-shaven: a man composed, at peace with himself but deeply interested in what was happening around him.

You are like actors, Hall thought. You've made this entrance many a time. You are trying to make us nervous.

"Are you nervous, Dr. Hall?"

Siggins was smiling, his hand beating a tattoo on the side of his black leather jacket.

"You are a physician," Hall replied. "You are like me." He coughed nervously. "You search a man for symptoms."

"I was a physician."

Siggins was now staring around the hall. He studied the plate above the wooden panelling, the soft turkey carpets on the floor, the gilt-edged paintings; the best mugs, platters, and cups arranged on the top of a large oaken dresser.

"I was a physician," Siggins repeated. "And so was my friend Adam. Now we work for the Crown to cure the body politic of all manner of malignant diseases."

"Surely the Crown does not believe a malignant disease flourishes here in Stratford?" Susanna asked sharply.

"I beg your pardon?"

Siggins looked at Susanna for the first time. He sketched the courtliest bow, sharp, slightly mocking; he grasped her fingers and kissed them lightly.

"You must be Susanna? Master Shakespeare's daughter?"

"I am," she stammered. "But, sir, must you stand in the doorway like actors on the stage? We are busy people, we do not know your business here."

"You can read?" Adam spoke up. He slouched forward, opened the wallet on his belt, and plucked out a scroll of parchment.

Susanna almost snatched it from his hand and went to stand by her husband, who unrolled the parchment. Siggins watched Hall, his sad, furrowed face fringed by greying hair. The physician was still clearly nervous; he glanced up quickly.

"It does not say much."

"What does it say?" Siggins insisted.

"What the bearer of this document has done, he has done for the good of the King, the Crown, and the security of this realm. All loyal officers of the King and all faithful subjects are bound, on their loyalty, to cooperate fully and provide all assistance and sustenance needed."

"And who signed it?" Siggins demanded.

"The King himself," Hall whispered. "Jacobus Rex." He tapped the parchment. "That's his secret seal."

"Good! Good!" Siggins plucked the parchment from Hall and tossed it at his companion.

"Now, Master Hall, I have travelled far. I have not broken my fast. . . ."

Hall, glancing quickly at his wife, waved the two visitors to the chairs beside the fireplace.

"Do you wish some food?"

"No, just some wine. No, on second thoughts." Siggins held a hand up. "No wine before midday, yes, as Hippocrates says? Perhaps a jug of ale, the same for my companion? Then we'll begin."

Mistress Susanna made to protest but her husband warned her with his eyes.

"No servants," Siggins called out, taking off his sword belt and cloak. "Mistress Susanna, you may serve us."

They took their seats. Siggins and Adam on one side, Hall on the other. The physician shuffled his feet. He tried to make conversation but Siggins glanced owl-eyed back, not harshly or unkindly, just a long, searching stare. Susanna returned with a tray bearing two jugs of ale and goblets of watered wine for herself and her husband. She served them and sat down.

"You had a good journey, Master Siggins?"

"Master Shakespeare died," Siggins declared abruptly. "Let me see now, on Tuesday twenty-third April, St. George's Day. He was buried two days later on Thursday the twenty-fifth. He was hurried quickly to his grave?"

"What do you mean?" Susanna could no longer control her temper. She placed the goblet on the floor beside her and leaned forward. "What do you mean, sir, by such a remark? Why are you here?"

"I arrived in Warwick yesterday," Siggins replied slowly as if addressing a child. "I sent a servant with a letter which, I understand, you received at midday. I explained my status and my office. I said I would be with you long before noon today and that I would question you about your father's death, which took place two months ago. I am not here, Mistress Hall, for gentle chatter, empty gossip, or for the hot words of a scold's sarcasm. I want certain questions answered without any obfuscation or obstruction, without hindrance or let." Siggins allowed his threat to hang heavy.

"My wife is upset," John Hall intervened. "She is still in mourning. My father-in-law's death was, is, a great blow to us."

"But not to him," Siggins replied. "Didn't he write that he welcomed death as a lover? To go gently into the night, I forget the specific lines. . . ."

"You are a follower of his?" Hall sipped at his goblet.

"A follower, sir?" Siggins cradled his own tankard. "A follower? Why, Physician Hall, can't you recognise the symptoms? I was Master Shakespeare's most ardent admirer. As a boy my father took me to the 'Globe,' to its every masque, its every play." Siggins seemed lost in his own reverie. "I have been taken to ancient Athens, Caesar's Rome. I have stood amongst the archers at Agincourt and gasped in terror at Macbeth's foul deeds. I was even in the 'Globe' on that fateful day, twenty-ninth June 1613 . . . !"

"You mean the fire?" Hall intervened.

Siggins held a hand up for silence. "Yes, the fire. Your father-in-law's company had put on a new play, *Henry VIII*: in that play there's a masque of Cardinal Wolsey's house, a marvellous scene! Cannons were shot off and" he waved his hand—"the rest you know. The 'Globe' caught fire." Siggins sipped from his tankard. "No one was hurt but the playhouse was destroyed. Shortly afterwards your father came home to die. Was he a sickly man? He seemed hale and hearty enough when he left London."

"My father had a susceptibility to fever."

"And you called a physician?"

"I am a physician," Hall retorted. "You know that. I treated my father-in-law myself. He had a weakness of the chest, a tendency of the lungs to cough sour phlegm. The spring this year was cold and, as you know, contagion was rife."

"Your father was fifty-two years of age when he died."

Siggins pulled out a leather pouch from his jerkin: he opened this and drew out a piece of parchment folded neatly in a square, which he undid and laid across his lap.

"What is that?" Susanna demanded.

"Just a few jottings." Siggins smiled. "At the end of March this year the lawyer Francis Collins?"

"And a leading member of this town's council," Hall intervened.

"Francis Collins," Siggins continued, ignoring the interruption. "Attended your father on the twenty-fifth March to carry out a second draft of the first page of his will. I have read that will."

"I have not yet had it passed through probate," Hall declared. "I intend to do so, travel to London tomorrow."

"Never mind, never mind." Siggins gestured. "In that draft of twenty-fifth March, Master Shakespeare described himself as 'in perfect health and memory, God be praised.' Was he in perfect health?"

"Well," Hall stammered. "That was just a formula, lawyer's words."

"So, he wasn't in perfect health and memory?" Siggins countered.

"He was well enough to redraft his will," Susanna intervened. "He was sound of mind and body, but despite my husband's best ministrations, he suddenly sickened and died. The corpse was viewed by all his friends and family. My own mother, Anne . . ."

"She resides here?" Siggins intervened.

"She has her own quarters," Susanna retorted. "She waits for you in her chamber."

"I do not wish to see her," Siggins snapped. "Nor your sister Judith."

The King's man leaned back in the chair studying the carving above the mantel hearth, cherubs crowning a maiden.

"Was your father a papist? Rumors abound," Siggins continued. "That Master Shakespeare had papist sympathies?"

"He was a loyal subject," Hall retorted. "A member of the established Church. True, his family, his father . . ."

Something about Siggins made him falter. Hall busied himself with his own goblet, aware of how closely his visitors were studying him. For the first time in months John Hall experienced true panic, a bubbling terror. He glanced sideways at his wife. Susanna, usually so forthright, was sitting pale-faced, eyes constantly blinking, now and again gnawing on thin, bloodless lips. She no longer appeared so resolute, devoid of that fiery temper Hall feared so much: her face was softer, her determined jaw relaxed, as if she had drunk too much or experienced a shock. She kept running her finger round and round the rim of her goblet, lost in her own thoughts.

From across the hearth Siggins studied both of them. Susanna, he could understand: her appearance confirmed all he had learned about her: a determined woman, those grey-green eyes, like pieces of glass, revealed a resolute character and a strong will. Siggins tried to see her father in her features but was unable to: perhaps the line of the cheek, the deep-set eyes, the broad brow? He quietly admired her calm, the way she was able to curb the anger seething within her. Hall was a different character: slightly shorter, sturdy with a slightly bulging midriff. He had what Siggins would describe as a kindly face framed by lank iron-grey hair, the moustache and beard well-trimmed.

"What's your favourite play?" Siggins asked. "Your father's work you most admire?"

"The play about ancient Rome," Hall answered.

"Which one, *Coriolanus* or *Julius Caesar*?"

"*Julius Caesar*," Hall replied quickly.

"And you, mistress?"

"Why, *Othello, The Moor's Tale*."

"Ah, in which the hero strangles his wife?"

Hall laughed abruptly. Susanna's face coloured; she lowered her head.

"And yours, Master Siggins?"

"*Macbeth*." Siggins smiled. "Adam and I would pay gold to see that play again. I even bought a copy of the folio at St. Paul's. I've studied the text most closely. What fascinates me is, was Macbeth a murderer from the start? Or did his ambitious wife change him? Strange, isn't it?" Siggins stretched out his leg to ease the cramp. "At the end of the play Macbeth is the stronger whilst his wife grows witless. Ah yes, murder is a terrible crime. Anyway, we were talking about your father's will." He pushed himself up in the chair. "On the twenty-fifth March he was hale and hearty but, a month later, he was dead. You say of the rheums, a sickness of the lungs?"

Hall stared back.

"Now, let's look at this Will." Siggins snapped his fingers, and his companion handed across a small scroll. "Let me see." Siggins unrolled the parchment. "Your father left your sister Judith one hundred pounds as a marriage portion, which would rise to one hundred and fifty pounds if she gave up any claim to the cottage in Chapel Lane. Another one hundred and fifty pounds was settled on her conditionally if she was still alive in three years' time. However, that was under the condition her husband settled a similar sum on her and any children. Now." Siggins glanced up from under his eyebrows. "Master Shakespeare did not seem to have any great confidence in either Judith or his new son-in-law, who is it? Ah yes, Master Thomas Quinney . . ."

"If you have studied us," Susanna spoke up. "You know the reason."

"No, you tell me," Siggins murmured.

Susanna moved uneasily in her chair. Siggins became aware of how dark the hall was growing as if the shutters had been pulled across the windows. He glanced quickly at one of these. Was the day proving to be cloudy, was it his imagination, or something else? The chamber he sat in was sumptuous, elegant: its wainscoting skillfully carved, the furniture of the very best, chairs, couches, and footrests all beautifully quilted and covered. The fragrance of the beeswax candles wafted through the air like perfume, the ale he drank was good, yet there was evil here.

"Well, Mistress Susanna?" Siggins glanced across.

"My sister Judith married late," she began haltingly. "She was thirty-one when she married in February this year."

"And her husband?"

"Thomas Quinney, a vintner."

"I believe he was excommunicated? Summoned to the consistory court at Worcester? Why was that?"

"They were married outside the proper liturgical season, against the law of the Church."

"Why?" Siggins insisted.

"Because my sister is pregnant," Susanna retorted. "The baby is due in November."

"Ah yes. Ah yes." Siggins nodded as if hearing the news for the first time. "Marry in haste, eh, and repent at leisure." He smiled. "Your father wasn't pleased with the match?"

"He considered Master Vintner a rogue, a scoundrel. Someone looking for a rich heiress."

"Well, he was disappointed, wasn't he?" Siggins lifted up the will and peered at it as if his eyesight was poor. "The real beneficiary of this will, apart from a few gifts to this friend or that, are yourself, Doctor Hall and your good wife, Susanna. Let us see. The bulk of his estate . . ." He rattled the piece of parchment. "This mansion, New Place: the houses in Henley Street: the lands in Old Stratford, Bishopton, and Welcomb, not to forget the house in Blackfriars London and all his moveables, chattles, leases, plates, jewellery, clothing . . ." Siggins glanced up quickly. "I understand these leases include your father's very profitable shares in the 'Globe' and Blackfriars theatres." Siggins smiled across at this precious pair. "I also understand you are both executors of the will whilst those who witnessed it are either friends of yours or servants in this house. . . ."

"What are you implying?"

Susanna sat rigid, body quivering with anger: the skin on her face was tight: her eyes had lost that dull look and were gleaming malevolently at Siggins. When she spoke, her lips hardly moved, the words being spat out.

"I am implying nothing." Siggins sniffed. "Nothing at all, not for the moment. But let's go back to your father. He lies buried in the chancel of Trinity Church, yes? True?"

"You know he is," Hall replied softly.

"And the cause of his death?" Siggins ran a finger round his lips. "Do you remember the play *Troilus and Cressida*? Master Shakespeare talks of 'The rotten diseases of the south: guts griping, ruptures, catarrhs, gravel in the back, lethargies, raw eyes, rotten livers, wheezing lungs, incurable bone ache'?" Siggins closed his eyes. "I can't remember the rest." He opened his eyes. "Which of these did your father die of?"

"We told you, of a fever!"

"Not the plague?"

"Why do you mention that, sir?"

Hall would have sprung to his feet but Siggins gestured at him to stay still.

"I've made careful research." Siggins puckered his lips. "You buried your father so hastily, seventeen feet down beneath the chancel stones of Trinity Church."

"That will become a family grave," Susanna added quickly.

"In which case." Siggins snapped his fingers: Adam handed across another scrap of parchment. "This epitaph:

GOOD FREND FOR JESUS SAKE FORBEARE,
TO DIGG THE DUST ENCLOASED HEARE:
BLESTE BE YE MAN TY SPARES THES STONES,
AND CURST BE HE TY MOVES MY BONES.

Who composed that?"

"My father," Susanna replied. "While he was lying sick."

"Why should he write such a verse?" Siggins demanded. "I mean, who would dig up a man's corpse seventeen feet below sacred ground?"

"Sometimes," Hall intervened brusquely, "tombs can be opened by the sexton, the bones removed to the charnel house."

"Nonsense!" Siggins leaned forward. "Arrant nonsense, sir, and you know it! Who would dare to dig up the corpse of this kingdom's greatest poet and toss his bones as if they were the remains of a dog into some charnel house? Who would dare disturb the resting house of such a notable? The richest burgess in Stratford? Nonsense! Flibberty-gibbet nonsense and you know it!"

"I agree, sir." Susanna tried to appear submissive, lifting one hand elegantly, finger extended. "But my father was also concerned, he had powerful friends at court. . . ."

"Ah, I see," Siggins interrupted. "The great Shakespeare's coffin could be exhumed and moved to some more worthy resting place like St. Paul's or the Abbey." The smile faded from his face. "Madam, do you take me for a fool?"

"I take you for my enemy!" she hissed back. "I demand to know why you are here."

"Truth will come to light and murder cannot be hid long. Do you know the line?" Siggins demanded. "From the second scene of the second act of *The Merchant of Venice*?"

"Are you saying my father was murdered?"

"No, but someone else does."

"Who, my sister?" Susanna no longer tried to control her temper. "She's bound up with envy, hate."

"No, not her!"

"Then that damnable Quinney, who desires our wealth!"

"No, not him."

Hall sprang to his feet. "Sir, you are no longer welcome here."

"I know I am not: that's why I am here on the King's authority. I shall not

leave sir until I have had my say, and when I've had my say, you may summon
me to any court in the kingdom. I'll be there with you cheek to cheek, jowl to
jowl. But sit down, Master Hall, and control your feelings: the play is not done
and I have not had my say. As for you, Mistress, remember a line from your
father's play: 'The lady doth protest too much methinks.' Now, I told a lie,"
Siggins continued. "My favorite play is not *Macbeth* but *King Lear*: there's a
line there, fourth scene first act. What is it now? 'Ingratitude thou marble-
hearted fiend. / More hideous when thou showest thee in a child than a sea
monster.' The sentiment is only surpassed by another in the same speech. . . ."

" 'How sharper than a serpent's tooth it is, to have a thankless child.' "

Siggins glanced surprised at this interruption from his companion Adam.

"You know the play well, Mistress?"

Adam had hardly moved from his chair: for most of the conversation he'd
kept his eyes down, lips moving soundlessly.

"Do you know the play, Mistress?" Adam repeated. "It's about an old king
with ungrateful children."

"Are you saying my father was murdered?" Susanna rasped. "You come into
this house and claim my father was murdered, as if this was a play written by
himself."

"I believe your father was murdered," Siggins agreed. "By slow and subtle
poisoning. Doctor Hall, I understand you keep a journal of the patients you
treat? Do you have the notes you made when tending Master Shakespeare?"

Hall gestured over at the fireplace. "They were personal, private: I had them
burnt."

"Did you now? Did you now?" Siggins breathed the words out. "I think you
poisoned him."

"No!" Hall roared, jumping to his feet: he seized the iron poker resting in
the corner of the hearth.

Siggins's hand went beneath his black leather jacket while Adam plucked
the dagger from the top of his boot.

"Sit down, Master Physician," Siggins warned. "Do not strut like a peacock or even think of raising that poker against the King's emissary. My friend here will split you in two, then then I shall arrest you!"

Hall, his face puce red, stood leaning on the poker breathing noisily through his nose.

"Now you shall listen to me." Siggins's voice remained calm. "And I shall finish this tale. Let us go back to your father. Many people believe he left London in 1613 because of the fire at the 'Globe,' yet fires in theatres are common. Did he leave London for that reason, Mistress Susanna? Or because you, his beloved daughter, had been accused of adultery?"

Susanna sat, hands in her lap, face turned slightly away. She gazed at Siggins from the corner of her eye: a blood-chilling, hard look.

"That was all a nonsense," Hall growled.

"Was it?" Siggins asked. "I understand Master John Lane, a young gentleman of good family, claimed Mistress Susanna had been naughty with one Ralph Smith at John Palmer's house."

"Slander!" Susanna turned to face him squarely. Her face was pale except for the red spots of anger high in her cheeks. "Master Lane slandered me and was summoned before the consistory court at Worcester: he was excommunicated and that was the end of the matter."

"Perhaps it was!" Siggins tapped his boots against the stone-paved floor. "But it was enough to bring your father home, and when he arrived, perhaps he didn't like what he saw? His young Susanna married to Physician John Hall, his natural heir, his beloved, being naughty like some strumpet on Bankside? Did he begin to think again about his will and who should be his heir? And then Judith, your sister, the old maid of the family, suddenly marries a vintner, carrying his child. Did you pour poison in your father's ear? How Judith's husband was really after his wealth? Did you fear that the child, due to be born later this year, would be a boy, a male heir?"

"You have no proof of this!" Susanna hissed.

"Did your father begin to reflect? We know he had already redrafted the will to give Judith more. Only the good Lord knows what would have happened if your sister gave birth to a beautiful boy? Would Master Shakespeare think it fairer and more equitable to divide everything evenly between his daughters? I warrant he did. Then he falls ill and is helped into the dark by your husband." Siggins pointed to the physician. "He may be a poor Macbeth but you'll fill the role of that villain's wife most aptly. What poison did you use, Master Hall? Some plant, some herb, a fusion? Italianate, French, or English? And of course, being a physician you were most wary, that's why Shakespeare's body was buried within forty-eight hours." Siggins paused. Of course you had to face the problem of the corpse of such a venerable and venerated man being possibly moved, so you arranged for the coffin to be buried seventeen feet deep. As the playwright died"—Siggins smiled at the pun—"you played upon his mind. Was it you, Doctor Hall, or your good wife, Susanna? What did you whisper in his ear? How he might not be allowed to lie in peace? Would it be best to write an epitaph which would lay a curse upon anyone who even considered it?" He glanced at Susanna. "Your father wrote that epitaph, did he not?"

"He did."

"At your behest?"

Susanna remained silent.

"Your father knew he was dying. He also realized he was being poisoned, but being imprisoned here, kept close by you, he could do nothing about it, so he obeyed your wishes."

Siggins picked up the piece of parchment from his lap and handed it across to a pallid-faced Hall, who sat all a-tremble, his face an ashen grey.

"Did your father think of the lines he wrote for Macbeth? *'I have lived long enough. My way of life is falling into the* sewer.' Look at the epitaph, Master Hall. Read it out to me again."

Hall sat, hands shaking.

"Read it out!" Siggins's voice rose to a shout.

Hall coughed and cleared his throat; his mouth, throat, and lips were so dry he found it difficult to speak.

"Then I shall read it for you." Siggins plucked the parchment back and read the epitaph.

"Did you know?" Siggins glanced up. "That if you used the letters from that epitaph and rearrange them, all but a few, the epitaph contains another message:

"SUSANNA AND JOHN HALL MURDERED ME,
GOOD SHAKESPEARE.
CURST BE YE TO REST MY BONES,
FOR BEST BE YE TO DIGG THE STONES."

"Nonsense!" Susanna leaned forward, her face a mask of hateful malice, lips curled back like a dog.

"Your father told me you murdered him," Siggins evenly declared. "As he has told the world."

Susanna pulled herself back in the chair, grasping the arms and sitting like some malevolent queen on her throne.

"Have you studied the classics?" Siggins turned to Hall. "Cicero's speech, 'Pro Milone'? Cicero asks one question about a murder, 'Cui Bono?' Who profits from it?" Siggins used his fingers to emphasize the points. "Your father came back to Stratford in 1613: the very year, the very month Susanna was accused of adultery. Judith, his rather neglected daughter, was married last February and is now heavy with child. Master Shakespeare was definitely considering changing his will and the small alteration he ordered was in her favor. Your father was hale and hearty in March when he made that change." Siggins paused. "A month later he is dead. You pair are the principal beneficiaries of that will. You tended your father during his sickness, whatever that was. You were executors of his will and those who witnessed it were either your friends or servants. I believe"—Siggins sifted among the manuscripts on his lap—"Ah yes, there it is! One of the witnesses was a certain Robert Whatcott, who reported to you, Mistress Susanna, Master Lane's jibe about being naughty with another man. You buried your father seventeen feet deep in the chancel of that church. You made him compose an epitaph so no one would ever disturb that tomb and examine his corpse. Your only mistake was not to scrutinize that epitaph more carefully."

Susanna moved her hand and grasped that of her husband. The color had now returned to her face.

"You are not here on the royal commission. You are here because you were a friend of my father."

"You flatter yourself and you flatter me," Siggins murmured. "I wish I was your father's friend. I was, and am, his most fervent admirer. I met him just before he left London, and when I heard of his death, I mourned. I cried myself to sleep. I wanted to learn the details and they came like drops of water pouring through a hole. So I asked my royal master if I could come here to make my own devotions, to breathe my requiem by his tomb, to visit his assassins!"

"If you believe what you say, then arrest us!"

Susanna brushed a hair from her face.

"I do believe what I say," Siggins replied. "I believe your father wrote the truth!"

"In an epitaph?" Susanna scoffed. "A few words etched into stone!"

"Where better?" Siggins half-smiled. "To etch the truth? Parchment crumbles, a great deal of what we write disappears, never to be seen again. But stone, particularly the tombstone of a famous poet? To misquote the gospels: 'You and I will pass away. Time will pass away but your father's words will stand.' "

"I don't believe it!" Susanna flung her hand out. "I don't believe you can interpret his epitaph and glean such a message."

"I thought you'd say that." Siggins gestured at Adam. "My companion is a skilled scribe. He has written out the epitaph yet again, your father's hidden message beneath." Siggins took a thin scroll of fresh parchment from Adam. "Read it, Mistress Susanna! I have numbered every letter in the epitaph. You can see how the same letters were used in your father's secret message: its evidence enough. There!" He tossed the parchment at her, and she caught it deftly.

"Unroll it!" he snapped. "Face the truth."

Susanna, hands shaking, did so: she stared down at the lines carefully inscribed, each letter carefully numbered:

1 2 3 4 5 6 7 8 9 10 11 12 13 14 15 16 17 18 19 20 21 22 23 24 25 26 27 28 29

"GOOD FREND FOR JESUS SAKE FORBEARE,

30 31 32 33 34 35 36 37 38 39 40 41 42 43 44 45 46 47 48 49 50 51 52 53 54 55 56

TO DIGG THE DUST ENCLOASED HEARE:

57 58 59 60 61 62 63 64 65 66 67 68 69 70 71 72 73 74 75 76 77 78 79 80 81 82 83 84 85 86 87

BLESTE BE YE MAN TY SPARES THES STONES,

88 89 90 91 92 93 94 95 96 97 98 99 100 101 102 103 104 105 106 107 108 109 110 111 112 113

AND CURST BE HE TY MOVES MY BONES."

---

15 16 17 19 8 44 27 48 69 9 15 11 52 85 79 54 46 58 67 40 6 32 7 55 21 39 102 26

"SUSANNA AND JOHN HALL MURDERED ME,

1 2 3 4 18 98 68 20 29 41 73 50 74 24 38

GOOD SHAKESPEARE.

91 92 93 94 95 96 97 65 66 30 31 12 43 49 36 107 108 109 110 111 112 113

CURST BE YE TO REST MY BONES,

5 47 75 25 14 60 61 63 64 21 53 42 84 51 33 34 35 70 37 56 82 83 103 87 62 72

FOR BEST BE YE TO DIGG THE STONES."

"Now you understand, Mistress Susanna? As for your arrest . . ." Siggins picked up the other parchments, handed them to his companion, and got to his feet.

"I shall not arrest you, not for your sakes but for your father's. He probably accepted that very few would realize what he had truly written on his gravestone; perhaps he didn't care. Every time you go to that church, Mistress Susanna"—Siggins stepped forward and leaned over her—"you'll hear your father's voice mouth those words. His accusation will ring along that hollow nave. Others will not hear it but you will. The angels will, as will the demons in Hell. In one of his plays your father wrote: *'The evil that men do lives after them.'* Think upon that, Mistress Susanna, in the late hours of the night, when the shadows gather about you." Siggins glanced towards the physician. "As for you, Doctor, I shall give you a reading list. Go through Master Shakespeare's plays and see what happens to evil men, as well as those who allow evil to make its presence felt."

Siggins picked up his cloak and sword belt thrown over the back of the chair, he walked towards the door, and his companion followed softly. Siggins turned and glanced at the murderous pair still sitting in their chairs, hands clasped, locked together in their own guilt.

"Nothing comes of nothing!" Siggins called out. "Think about Macbeth, Lear, and Othello. You may prosper for a while, but when the play is finished, only then will you know the truth."

And beckoning to his companion, Siggins opened the door and walked out into the courtyard.

AUTHOR'S NOTE: Everything written in this short story is based on fact, although my conclusion is original! Shakespeare's will, the redraft of March, the hasty burial, the place of burial, and the epitaph: the same applies to the terms of the will and the beneficiaries. Dr. Hall's second notebook was never found. Finally, by 1693, Shakespeare's direct line—male/female—was extinct. For the historical details, see Schoenbaum's "William Shakespeare: A Compact Documentary Life" (Oxford University Press, 1977; New American Library, 1986).

The Duke's Wife

BY PETER ROBINSON

 Peter Robinson is the author of the Inspector Banks series, which includes the Edgar-nominated *Wednesday's Child* and *In a Dry Season*. *In a Dry Season* won the Anthony and Barry Awards for best novel of 1999 and was also nominated for the Arthur Ellis, Hammett, and Macavity Awards. Robinson's award-winning short stories have been collected in *Not Safe After Dark and Other Stories*, published by Crippen & Landru in 1998.

I was absolutely speechless. After everything that had happened, there he stood, bold as brass, telling all the world we were going to be married. *Married*! You would have been speechless, too.

Let me give you a little background. My name is Isabella, and until that moment I was all set to enter a convent. I fear I have a wayward and impulsive nature that needs to be kept in check, and the convent I had in mind, the votarists of Saint Clare, was one of strict restraint. Imagine my feelings when, head swimming from the twists and turns of recent events, I heard I was to be married to the Duke!

But there's more, much more.

A short while ago, the Duke realized that he had become lax in his duties, being of too mild and gentle a nature to enforce the laws of the land to their fullest. Of special concern to him, because it ate away at the very institution of marriage itself, was the law that forbade, on pain of death, a man to live with a woman to whom he was not married.

Fearing that the people would revolt if he were suddenly to change course and start enforcing the law rigorously himself, the Duke thought it better to slip away for a while and leave his deputy, Angelo, in charge. Thus, Angelo was invested with all the Duke's powers and charged with cleaning up Vienna.

Mistake. Big mistake.

Where do I come into all this, you might be wondering? Well, it so happens that my brother Claudio had plighted his troth to his fiancée Juliet, and they were sleeping together. The problem was that they had kept their marriage contract a secret in the hope that Juliet's family would in time come to favor their union and provide a dowry, and this brought them within the scope of the law against fornication.

Now, Angelo *could* have exercised mercy, realizing that this was a very minor infringement indeed, and that the two were, in all but the outward ceremony itself, legally married, but Angelo is a cold fish and a sadistic, ruthless dictator. He likes to hurt people and make them squirm; it gives him pleasure. Believe me, I *know*.

Finding himself so suddenly and inexplicably condemned to death, Claudio asked me to intercede with Angelo on his behalf and see if I could secure a pardon. This I did, with disastrous results: Angelo told me he was in love with *me*, and he would let Claudio go only if I slept with *him*.

Now, while I do realize that in many people's eyes to give up one's virginity for one's brother's life might not seem too much to ask, you must bear in mind that I was to join the votarists of Saint Clare. I was to be married to God. This was my life, my destiny, and all of that—my very *soul* itself—would be sacrificed if I gave in to Angelo's base demands.

And don't think I didn't care about Claudio. Don't think for a moment that the thought of complying didn't cross my mind, but I wasn't going to give in to that kind of blackmail. I didn't trust Angelo, anyway. For all I knew, he might take my virginity *and* have Claudio executed as well—which, as it turned out, was exactly what he had in mind!

The whole process was degrading, me pleading passionately for my brother's life, going down on my knees on the cold stone to beg, Angelo making it clear that only by yielding up my body to his will could I save Claudio. Humiliating.

When I told him my decision, Claudio wasn't at all understanding. Of everyone, he should have been the one to see how important my virginity was, but no. He even had the effrontery to suggest that I should reconsider and commit this vile sin to save his life. Claudio was afraid of death, and all he could talk about was his fear of dying when *I* was facing a much greater enemy than death.

I told him he would find his comfort in the bosom of the Lord. He didn't seem to agree.

Where was the wily Duke during all this? You may well ask. As it turns out he was secretly directing events, disguised as a friar, and he was the one who came up with a cunning plan. He might be of a tender and mild disposition, but he has a devious mind, and he likes to play games. Nor does he always stop to think who might get hurt by them.

Angelo had once been betrothed to a woman called Mariana, but her dowry went down on the same ship as her brother Frederick, and Angelo left her in tears, pretending he had discovered some stain on her honor when it was, in fact, the loss of the dowry that turned him against her. If you needed any more evidence of his worthlessness, that's the kind of person he is.

Now, if I were to go back to Angelo and pretend to agree to his demands, the friar suggested, we could arrange things so that Mariana went to his chamber in my stead, breaking no laws and saving both my virginity and Claudio's life.

It seemed a very good plan, and it worked, though the friar did have to do a little juggling with severed heads later on to convince Angelo that Claudio had indeed been beheaded. Then, for reasons of his own, the friar let me go on believing that Claudio had been executed—I did say he liked to play games, didn't I?—until the final scenes had been played out.

He had Mariana beg for Angelo's life, and the poor woman importuned *me* to beg with her! Thus, I found myself on my knees for a second time, this time pleading for the life of a man I hated, the man who, I thought, had killed my brother even though, he thought, he had enjoyed the treasures of my body.

So is it any wonder I was speechless when in walked Claudio, as alive as you or I, and the Duke announced that I was to be his Duchess?

I could have said no, I suppose, but at the time I was too stunned to say anything, and the next thing I knew, we were married.

Though it took me many months, I got over the shock of it all and adapted myself as best I could to my new life. I hadn't actually taken my vows, so there was no legal problem with the marriage. The Duke took over Vienna again and enforced the law himself, tempered with mercy and charity, and things went back to an even keel. I'm not saying that fornication ceased. That could never happen here. We Viennese are an odd lot, our lives full of secret vices and lies, and anyone with an interest in the human mind and perverse behavior would have a field day studying us.

Being the Duke's wife had many advantages, I soon found, though I did have some trouble adjusting to his husbandly demands. He wasn't a young man, but he was certainly vigorous, though he needed certain props to help him perform those functions he liked so much. In particular, he liked to dress as a friar and intone Latin vespers when he took me from behind, as was his wont. That, I could deal with, but I drew the line when he asked *me* to dress as a nun. That would have been far too much of a travesty for me to take, given everything that had happened.

So time passed, and on the whole I was quite enjoying the life of idleness and luxury. I loved my horses, enjoyed the theatre and the frequent grand balls, and I came to rely on the kind attentions of my maids and the delicious concoctions of my cooks. As I say, the sacrifices were bearable. Once in a while, I had a wistful thought for the life I might have led, but I must confess that when I hosted a magnificent banquet or walked the grounds and gardens of our wonderful palace, the thought of a bare, cold, tiny cloister lost much of its appeal. Mind you, I still attended church regularly and prayed every night, and we gave generously to the votarists of Saint Clare.

You might be interested in knowing what happened to the others. Claudio and Juliet were married, after which they moved to the country. By all accounts, they are happy enough, though we don't see them very often. Angelo and Mariana were also married—it was *her* wish, the Duke's dictate, and in accord with the law—but their story didn't end happily at all. Well, how could it with an evil, sadistic pervert like Angelo for a husband? Mariana is very sweet, but she is *such* a naïf when it comes to men. Even back when I was headed for the convent, I had more idea than she did.

So I wasn't at all surprised when she came to me in tears about six months after her marriage.

"Dry your eyes, dear," I said to her, "and let's walk in the garden." It was a beautiful spring day, with a warm gentle breeze wafting the scents of flowers through the mild air.

"I can't go on," she said.

"What's wrong?"

"It's Angelo."

"What about him?"

"He doesn't love me anymore."

He never did love her, I could have said, but I held my tongue. I doubted that was what she wanted to hear at the moment. "What makes you think that?" I asked.

She looked around, then leaned in towards me and lowered her voice. "He has other women."

I could have laughed out loud. Just about every husband in Vienna has other women. I suspect even my own Duke has one from time to time, but if it spares me the friar's costume and the Latin vespers for a night, who am I to complain? But Mariana, I could see, was really upset. "It's just men, Mariana," I told her. "They're like that. They can't help themselves. It's their nature. Every time they see an attractive woman, they just have to conquer her."

"But am *I* not attractive?"

"That's neither here nor there. You're his *wife*. That's all that counts."

"Yes, I am his wife, so why does he have to sleep with other women? I'll sleep with him anytime he wants. I'll do *anything* he wants me to, even if it hurts me, even that disgusting thing with the—"

"Mariana! I told you, it's just their nature. You'll have to learn to live with it or your life will be a very unhappy one."

"But I already *am* unhappy. I can't live with it. I want to die."

I took her arm. "Don't be so histrionic, Mariana," I said. "You'll get used to it."

She broke away. "I won't! Never! I want to die. I'm going to kill myself."

I sighed. "Over a man? There must be better reasons. Look, who is this woman he's been seeing?"

Mariana looked at me. Her eyes were so full of pain that my heart cried for her, even though I thought she was being foolish. "It's not just *one* woman."

"How many?"

"I don't know."

"Two, three?"

"I told you. I don't know."

"You must have some idea. Is it three, four, or five?"

"About three. I think that's about right."

"So he's sleeping with three other women?"

"Three a week. Yes."

"*What?*"

"He has them sent to him. There's a man called Pandarus, a Greek I think, a despicable human being, and Angelo pays him to procure young women. Usually young virgins from the provinces who are new in town and haven't settled into employment. They're so young. They don't . . . I mean they don't all know what to expect."

"He forces them?"

Mariana nodded. "I've heard cries. Screams, sometimes, and he swears they will die terribly if they ever speak of what happened."

Mariana's story was starting to interest me. I had heard of this Pandarus, though I had never met him, and I knew that he affected a respectable enough surface and was able to move among varying levels of society. Procuring wasn't new to Vienna, even at the higher echelons—nothing to do with sex is new to Vienna—but this Pandarus intrigued me all the same. "How do you know all this?" I asked.

"A dear friend told me. She had a conversation with one . . . with one of the girls."

"And you're certain it's true?"

Mariana nodded. "One night I lay in wait, hiding in the bushes, and watched. We have always had separate quarters, and Angelo maintains the same chamber he used . . . do you remember that night when I went to him in your stead?"

I nodded. It wasn't a memory I cared to dwell on. Not one of my finest moments.

"They come in the darkest of night, and he burns no candles. Everything is just as it was that night."

"I see," I said. I had hated Angelo long and deeply enough for what he had inflicted on me that even as we spoke, the beginnings of a plan began to form itself effortlessly in my mind.

"What can I do, dear Isabel? Pray, tell me, what can I do?"

I took her hand. "Do nothing," I said. "At least not for the moment. I know it pains you, but bear with it. I'm certain there's a solution and I promise that your suffering will come an end ere long."

Her eyes widened and lit up at that little sliver of hope. "Really? You promise? Oh, Isabel, is it possible I can be happy again?"

"We'll see," I said, busy thinking. "We'll see."

I was finally satisfied enough with my changed appearance and the peasant clothes I had painstakingly made to venture out into the city streets in the guise of a country girl seeking employment. Through further, cautious questioning of Mariana, I had already determined that Pandarus tended to prey on his victims in the busy public square near the coach station, often approaching them the very moment they arrived in the city. He had, I imagined, a skilled eye and knew exactly who was vulnerable to his approach and who best to leave alone. I affected to look lost and weak, and on my second visit, a man came up to me. His clothes and his bearing signified a certain level of wealth and influence in society, and his general manner was that of a gentleman.

"Are you new here?" he asked.

"Me?" I responded shyly, keeping my head down. "Yes, sir."

"Where are you from?"

I named a distant village I had once heard one of my husband's ministers mention.

"And what, may I ask, brings you to Vienna?"

"I seek employment, sir."

"You do, do you? And what skills do you possess?"

"I can cook, sir, and wash, and mend clothes."

"Valuable skills, indeed. Come, walk with me."

I couldn't just go with him, not that easily. I had to play the shy country girl. "I cannot, sir."

"Cannot? Why not?"

"I don't know, sir. It just seems so . . . forward. I don't know you."

"Forward? Walking alongside a perfect gentlemen in a public place?" He smiled. He really did have a warm smile, the kind that leads you to trust a person. "Come, come, don't be silly."

So I walked beside him. He offered his arm, but I didn't take it. That didn't seem to upset him too much. "You know, I think I might be able to help you," he said, stroking his moustache.

"Help me, sir? You mean *you* require my services?"

He laughed. "Me? Oh, no. Not me. A friend of mine. And I will speak for you."

"But you don't know me, sir. How can you speak for me? You don't even know my name."

He stopped walking and put his fingers under my chin, lifting my face. He was taller than I, so I had to look up, though I tried to keep my eyes down under my fluttering lashes. I felt myself blush. "I am an excellent judge of character," he said. "I believe you to be an honest country maiden, and I believe you are exactly what he has in mind." He let me go and carried on walking. This time I picked up my pace to keep up with him, showing interest. "He does, however, have one peculiarity I must mention," he went on.

"What might that be, sir?"

"He prefers to conduct his business at night."

"That is strange, indeed, sir."

He shrugged. "It is a mere trifle."

"If you say so, sir." As a county girl, I could, of course, have no idea of the ways of city folk.

"So, should you be interested—and he is a most kind, considerate, and bountiful master—you must go to him through his garden at night and he will acquaint you with his needs. You need have no fears. He is an honorable man, and I shall be close by."

Again, I had to remind myself that I was playing the role of a simple country girl. "If you think so, sir."

"Tonight, then?"

I hesitated for just as long as necessary. "Tonight," I whispered finally.

"Meet me here," he said, then he melted into the crowds.

My plan was simple enough. I intended to gain entry to Angelo's chamber under cover of darkness and. . . . Well, I hadn't really thought much past there, except that I planned to confront him and expose him for what he was. If necessary, I would claim that I went to visit my friend Mariana and that he attempted to ravage me, but I doubted it would come to that. One of the many advantages of being the Duke's wife is that subjects tend to fear my husband's power, and I had no doubt that Angelo would give up his nightly escapades if faced with their possible political consequences. A wife's railing is easy enough to ignore, but the power of the Duke is another matter entirely.

I could not help but feel restless all evening as I waited for the appointed hour. After the usual antics with cassock and vespers, I slipped a sleeping draught into the Duke's nightcap, and he went out like a snuffed candle. When the servants were all in bed, I donned my disguise and slipped out of the house.

The dark streets frightened me, as I had not gone out alone at night before, and I feared lest some drunken peasant or soldier should molest me. In case of just such an incident, I carried a dagger concealed about my person, a present to the Duke from a visiting diplomat. But either the denizens of the night are better behaved than I had imagined, or I was blessed by fortune, for I made my way to the square without any hindrance whatsoever. When I got there, I was surprised at how many people were still out and about at such a late hour, lounging by the fountain, talking and laughing in the light of braziers and flaming torches. I had no idea that such a world of shadows existed, and I found that the discovery oddly excited me.

Pandarus appeared at my side as if by magic, wrapped in dark robes, his head hooded, as was mine.

"Are you ready?" he asked.

I nodded.

"Then come with me."

I followed him through the narrow alleys and across the broad cobbled courtyards to Angelo's quarters, where we paused at a gate in the high wall surrounding the garden.

"This gate is unlocked," said Pandarus. "Cross the garden directly to the chamber before you, where you will find the door also unlocked. Enter, and all will be explained."

I managed to summon up one last show of nerves. "I'm not certain, sir. I mean . . . I do not . . ."

"There's nothing to fear," he said softly.

"Will you accompany me, sir?"

"I cannot. My friend prefers to conduct his business in private."

He stood there while I gathered together all my strength, took a deep breath, and opened the gate. There were no lights showing beyond the garden, so I had to walk carefully to make sure I didn't trip and fall. Finally, I reached the door of Angelo's chamber, and it opened when I pushed it gently, hinges creaking a little. By this time, I could make out the varying degrees of shadows, so I was aware of the large canopied bed and of the silhouette standing before me: Angelo.

"Come in, my little pretty one," he said. "Make yourself comfortable. Has my friend Pandarus told you what you must do?"

I curtsied. "Yes, sir. He told me you might have a position for me, but that you only conduct interviews at night."

Angelo laughed. "He's a fine dissembler, my Pandarus. But in that, he is not all wrong. I do, indeed, have a *position* for you."

With this he moved towards me, and I felt his lizard-like hand caress my cheek. I should have drawn back, I know, and at that moment told him who I was and why I was there, but something in me, some innate curiosity, compelled me to continue my deception.

Angelo led me slowly to the bed and bade me sit, then he sat beside me and began his caresses again, this time venturing into more private territory than before. I took hold of his hand and moved it away, but he was persistent, growing rougher. Before I knew it, he had me on my back on the bed and his hand was groping under my skirts, rough fingers probing me. I struggled and tried to tell him who I was, but he put his other hand over my mouth to silence me.

All the time he manhandled me thus, he was calling out my name. "Isabella . . . Oh, my beautiful Isabella! Do it for me, Isabella. Please do it for me!" At first, this confused me, for I was certain he hadn't recognized me. Then I realized with a shock that he *didn't* know who I was, but that this must be what he said to all his nighttime visitors. He called them *all* Isabella.

And then I understood.

The whole thing, the recreation of the exact same conditions as the night I was to visit him in exchange for Claudio's life—the hour, the insistence on absolute darkness. Though Mariana had gone to him in my stead, Angelo either refused to believe this, or thought that by duplicating the trappings he could enjoy the treasures of my body time after time in the darkness of his vile imagination.

As we struggled there on the bed, disgust and outrage overcame any simple desire I harbored for justice, and I knew then what I had been planning to do all along. Angelo's behavior just made it all that much easier.

I slipped out my dagger and plunged it into his back with as much force as I could muster. He stiffened, as if stung by a wasp, and reared back, hand behind him trying to stanch the flow of blood.

Then I plunged the dagger into his chest and said, "This for Mariana!"

He croaked my name: "Isabella . . . My Isabella . . ."

"Yes, it's me," I said. "But I'm *not* yours." And I plunged the dagger in again. "This is for me!" I said, and he rolled to the floor, pleading for his life. I knelt over him and plunged the dagger in one more time, into his black heart. "And this is for not being able to tell us apart in the dark!"

After that, he lay still. I didn't move for several minutes, but knelt there over Angelo's body catching my breath until I was sure that no one had heard. The house remained silent.

Knowing that Pandarus was probably still lurking by the garden gate, I left by the front door and hurried home through the dark streets. Nobody accosted me; I saw not a soul. When I got home, in the light of a candle in my chamber, I saw that my clothing was bloodstained. No matter. I would burn it. As soon as that was done and I was washed clean of Angelo's blood, all would be well. Mariana might shed a tear or two for her miserable, faithless husband, but she would get over him in time and he would never hurt her or anyone else again.

And as for me, as I believe I have already told you, there are many advantages to be gained from being the Duke's wife, not the least of which is the unlikelihood of being suspected of murder.

"Let the Game Begin!"

A Master Hardy Drew Mystery

BY PETER TREMAYNE

Peter Tremayne is the pseudonym of Peter Berresford Ellis, a Celtic scholar who lives in London, England. He conceived the idea for Sister Fidelma, a seventh-century Celtic lawyer, to demonstrate that women could be legal advocates under the Irish system of law. Sister Fidelma has since appeared in nine novels in the U.S., the most recent being *Our Lady of Darkness,* and many short stories, which have been collected in the anthology *Hemlock at Vespers and other Sister Fidelma Mysteries.* His other series character is Master Hardy Drew, a constable in Elizabethan England. He has also written, under his own name, more than twenty-five books on history, biography, and Irish and Celtic mythology, including *Celtic Women: Women in Celtic Society and Literature* and *Celt and Greek: Celts in the Hellenic World.*

"Let the Game begin!"
—*THE LIFE OF KING HENRY THE FIFTH*

When the shrill voice of a boy, accompanied by an incessant thudding against his door, awoke Master Hardy Drew that morning, the Constable of the Bankside Watch was not in the best of moods.

He had retired to his room, which he rented above The Pilgrim's Wink Tavern, in Pepper Street, in the early hours that morning. Most of the night he had been engaged in dispersing the rioters outside the Cathedral of Southwark. It had been a well-organized protest at the publication of the Great Bible, which had been authorized by King James. The Great Bible had been the production of fifty scholars from the leading universities resulting in a work that the King had ordained to be the standard Bible used throughout his realms.

While it had been obvious to Master Drew that the Catholics would seize the opportunity to express their outrage at its publication, he had not expected the riots organized by the Puritan Party.

Not only were there rumors and reports of Popish plots and conspiracies this year but the activities from the extreme Protestant sects were far more violent. King James's moderate Episcopalian governance angered the Puritans also. Only last month the Scottish Presbyterian reformer, Andrew Melville, had been released from the Tower of London in an attempt to appease the growing anger. The King had admitted that his attempt to break the power of the Presbyterian General Assembly in Scotland had not met with success. Rather than placate the Presbyterians, Melville's release had increased the riots and he had fled into exile in France where, rumour had it, he was plotting his revenge. James had fared little better with imposing his will on the English Puritans.

The kingdoms of England and Scotland echoed and reechoed with treasonable conspiracies. Indeed, a few months previously, another attempt to install James's cousin, Arabella Stuart, on the throne had resulted in the unfortunate lady being confined to the Tower. Times were dangerous, Master Hardy Drew had been reflecting on this while quelling the outburst of anger of Puritan divines. Even his position of Constable was fraught with political danger. There were many who might falsely inform on him for his religious affiliations or, indeed, for his lack of them, in order to secure the position of Constable for themselves together with the small patronage that went with it.

The knocking increased in volume and Master Drew rolled out of his bed with a groan.

"Ods bodikins!" he swore. "Must you torture a poor soul so? Enter and have a good reason for this clamor!"

The door opened a fraction and a dirty young face peered round.

Master Drew glared menacingly at the child.

"You had better have a good reason for disturbing my sleep, little britches," he growled.

"God save you, good master," cried the young boy, not entering the room. "I've been sent to tell you that a gen'lemen be lying near done to death."

Master Drew blinked and shook his head in a vain attempt to clear it.

"A gentleman is . . . ? Who sent you, child?" he groaned.

"The master what owns the inn in Clink Street. The Red Boar. Master . . . Master Pen . . . Pen . . . some foreign name. I can't remember."

"And precisely what did this "Master Pen" ask you to tell me?" Master Drew inquired patiently.

"To come quick as the gen'lemen be stabbed and near death."

Master Drew sighed and waved the child away.

"Tell him that I'll be there shortly," he said.

Had the news been other than that of a gentleman stabbed in an inn, he would have immediately returned to his interrupted slumber. London was full of people being stabbed in taverns, alleys, or along its grubby waterfront. They were usually members of the lower orders of society whom few people of quality would miss much less shed a tear over. But a gentleman . . . now that was a matter serious enough to bring a Constable of the Watch from his warm bed.

Master Drew splashed his face with cold water from a china basin and hurriedly drew on his clothes. Below, in the tavern, he spent a half-pence on a pot of beer to cut the slack from his dry throat and, outside, chose an apple from a passing seller to munch for the balance of his breakfast.

Clink Street was not far away, a small road down by the banks of the Thames, along the very Bankside which was Master's Drew's main area of responsibility. He knew of the Red Boar Inn but had little occasion to frequent it. Perhaps "inn" was too grand a title, for it was hardly more than a waterfront tavern full of the usual riffraff of the Thames waterfront.

There was a small crowd loitering outside when he reached there. A small boy was holding forth to the group, waving his arms and pointing up to a window. Doubtless, this was the same urchin who had brought the message to him. The boy pointed to the Constable as he approached and cried: "This is 'im naw!" The small crowd moved back respectfully as Master Drew halted before the dark door of the inn and pushed it open.

Although the morning was bright outside, inside candles were alight, but even so, the tap room was still gloomy, filled with a mixture of candle and pipe smoke, mingling with odors of stale alcohol and body sweat.

A thin, middle-aged man came hurrying forward, wiping his hands on a leather apron. He had raven black hair but his features were pale, which caused his shaven cheeks to have a bluish hue to them.

"We do be closed, good sir," he began but Master Drew stopped him with a cutting motion of his hand.

"I am Constable of the Bankside Watch. Are you the host of this tavern?"

The man nodded rapidly.

"That I do be, master."

"And your name?"

"Pentecost Penhallow."

Master Drew sniffed in disapproval.

"A Cornishman by your name and accent?"

"A Cornishman I do be, if please you, good sir."

Master Drew groaned inwardly. This day was not starting well. He did not like the Cornish. His grandfather had been killed in the last Cornish uprising against England. Not that he was even born then, but there were many Cornish who had come to London during the reign of the Tudors and stayed. He regarded them as a people not to be trusted.

The last uprising had been caused by the introduction of the English language into church services in Cornwall. The Cornish rebels had marched into Devon, even captured the suburbs of Exeter after a siege before defeating the Earl of Bedford's army at nearby Honiton. That was where Master Drew's grandfather had been killed. The eventual defeat of the Cornish rebels by Lord Grey, and the systematic suppression of the people by fire and sword, the execution of their leaders, had not brought peace to Cornwall. If anything, the people had become more restless.

Master Drew knew that the English Court feared a Catholic-inspired insurrection in Cornwall, as well as other of the subject nations on the isles. Cornwall was continuing to send her priests to Spain to be trained at St. Alban's College of Valladolid.

Master Drew took an interest in such things and had read John Norden's recent work surveying Cornwall in which it was reported that, in the western part of the country, the Cornish tongue was most in use among its inhabitants. Master Drew felt it best to keep himself informed about potential enemies of the kingdom for these days they all seemed to congregate in the human cesspool which London had become.

He realized that the innkeeper was waiting impatiently.

"Well, Master Pentecost Penhallow," he asked gruffly, "why am I summoned hither?"

"If you would be so good as to go above the stair, good master, you may find the cause. One of my guests who do rent the room above do be mortally afflicted."

Master Drew raised an inquisitive eyebrow.

"Mortally afflicted? The boy said he was stabbed? What was the cause? A fight?"

"No, no, good Master Constable. He be a gentleman and quite respectable. A temperate, indeed he be. This morning, as is my usual practice, I took him a noggin of mead. He do never be bestirring of a morn without his noggin. That 'twas when I discovered he be still abed with blood all over the sheets. Stabbed he be."

"He was still alive?" demanded Master Drew, surprised.

"And still be but barely, sir. Oh, barely!"

"Godamercy!" exclaimed Master Drew in annoyance. "Still alive and yet you sent for me and not a physician?"

Pentecost Penhallow shook his head rapidly.

"Oh, sir, sir, a physician was sent for, truly so. He do be above the stair now. It be he who do be sending for thee, Master Constable."

The Constable exhaled angrily.

"What name does your gentleman guest go by and which is his room?"

The innkeeper pointed to the head of the stair.

"Master Keeling, do be his name. Master Will Keeling. The second door on the right above the stair."

Master Drew went hurrying up the stairs. On the landing he almost collided with a young girl carrying a pile of linen. He caught himself but the collision knocked some sheets from her hand on to the floor. The Constable swiftly bent down and retrieved them. The young girl was an exceptionally pretty dark-haired lass of perhaps no more than seventeen years. She bobbed a curtsy.

"*Murasta, mester,*" she muttered and then added in a gently accented English: "Thank'ee, master."

The Constable gave a quick nod of acknowledgment and entered the door that the tavern owner had indicated.

A thin-faced man, with a shock of white hair, clad in a suit of black broadcloth, making him appear like some Puritan divine, was sitting on the edge of a bed. On it a pale-faced young man lay against the pillows. Blood stained the sheets and pillows. Some bloodstained clothes were pressed against the man's chest. The thin-faced man glanced up.

"Ah, at last. You have not come a moment too soon to this place, Master Constable. He has barely a moment more of life."

"God send you a good morrow, Doctor Tate," replied Constable Drew in black humor. He knew the elderly physician and acknowledged the man before he moved to the bedside.

The young man was, indeed, barely conscious and obviously feverish. There was a bluish pallor that lay over his kin, which showed the swift approach of death.

"Master Keeling," he said loudly, bending to the dying man's face. "Who did this thing? Who stabbed you?"

The young man's eyes were open but they were wandering about the room. He seemed to be muttering something. The Constable leaned closer. He could just hear the words, and their diction indicated a person of some education.

"What's that you say, good fellow? Speak clearly if you can."

The lips trembled.

"Oh for . . . for a Muse of fire . . . that would ascend the . . . the brightest heaven of invention . . ."

Master Drew frowned.

"Come, good fellow, try to understand me. Answer you my simple question . . . what manner of knave has done this to you?"

The young man's eyes brightened and Master Drew suddenly found a hand gripping his coat with a power that one would have not thought possible in a dying man. The lips moved, the voice was stronger.

"Once more unto . . . unto . . ." He began to cough blood. Then suddenly he cried loudly, "Let the game begin!"

The voice choked in the man's throat. The pale blue eyes wavered, trying to focus on the Constable's face, and then the pupils dilated as, for a split second, the young man realized the horror of the imminent fact of death.

The Constable gave a sigh and removed the still-clutching hand from his jacket and laid it by the side of the body. He whispered softly: "Now entertain conjecture of a time, when creeping murmur and the pouring dark fills the wide vessel of the universe . . ."

"What's that?" demanded the physician grumpily.

"No matter," Master Drew replied as he moved aside and gestured to the body. "I think he has run his course."

It did not need the physician's quick examination to pronounce that the man was dead.

"What was the cause of death?" asked Master Drew.

"A thin blade knife, Master Constable. You will see it on the table where I placed it. It was left in the wound. One swift incision was made in the chest, which I deduced caused a slow internal bleeding, thus allowing him to linger between life and death for the last several hours."

"Presumably not self-inflicted?"

"Most certainly not. And you will notice that the window is opened and a nimble soul might encounter little difficulty in climbing up with the intention of larceny."

"You have an observant eye, Master Physician," smiled the Constable thinly. "Can it be that you are interested in taking on the burdens of Constable?"

"Not I!" laughed the physician. "I need the prospect of a good livelihood."

Master Drew was turning the knife over in his hands. It told him nothing.

"Cheap," he remarked. "The sort that any young cockscomb along the waterfront might carry at his waist. It tells me little."

Doctor Tate was covering the body with the bloodstained sheet.

"Poor fellow. I didn't understand what he was saying at the end. Ranting in his fever, no doubt?"

"Perhaps," replied the Constable. "But articulate ranting nonetheless."

Doctor Tate frowned.

"I don't understand."

"Perhaps you don't frequent the Globe?" smiled the Constable. "He was reciting some lines out of Master Shakespeare's play *The Life of King Henry the Fifth*."

"I didn't take you for one who frequents the playhouses."

"A privilege of my position," Master Drew affirmed solemnly. "I am allowed free access as Constable. I find it a stimulation to the mind."

"There is too much reality to contend with than living life in make believe," dismissed Doctor Tate.

"Tell me, good Doctor, did the young man say ought else before I came?"

"He said nothing but raved about battles and the like. Something about St. Crispin's Day but that is not until next October, so I do not know what he meant by it."

The physician had turned from the body and was packing his small black bag.

"I can do no more here. The matter rests with you. But I would extract my fee before I depart."

"Take your fee and welcome," sighed the Constable, glancing round the room. It was untidy. It appeared as if someone had been searching it and he asked the physician if the room had been disturbed since he had arrived. The physician was indignant.

"Think you that I would search for a fee first before I treated a gentleman?" he demanded.

"Well, someone has been searching for something."

"And not carefully. Look! Some jewels have been left on the table there. I'll take one of those pearls in lieu of a coin of this realm."

Master Drew pulled a cynical face.

"A good profit in that, Doctor Tate. However, I'll not gainsay your right."

The physician swooped up the pearl and held it up to the light. The smile on his face suddenly deepened into a frown and he placed the pearl between his teeth and bit sharply. There was a crack and the physician let out a howl of rage.

"Paste, by my troth!"

Master Drew walked over and examined the other pieces of jewelry scattered nearby. There were some crushed paste jewels on the floor. A small leather purse also lay there with a few coins in it. He took out the coins.

"Well, paste jewels or no, he was not entirely destitute. There is over a shilling here, which will pay for a funeral if we cannot find his relatives. And here, good physician, three new pennies for your fee."

He grinned sourly. "I wager that the three pennies are closer to the value of your service than ever that pearl, had it been real, would have been."

"Ah, how is a poor physician to make a decent living among the impoverished derelicts along this riverbank, Master Constable? Answer me that, damme! Answer me that!"

The physician, clutching his coins, left the room.

Master Drew gazed down at the shrouded body of the young man and shook his head sadly.

An educated young man who could recite lines from popular theatrical entertainment but who used cheap paste jewelry. Surely this was a curious matter? He turned and began to search the room methodically. The clothes were many and varied and, while giving an appearance of rich apparel, on closer inspection were actually quite cheap in quality and often hastily sewn.

He noticed that there were some papers strewn around the room, and bending to pick them up, he saw a larger pile on the floor under the bed. He drew these out and examined them. It was a text of the play, *The Life of Henry V* by Will Shakespeare. The lines of Henry V had been underlined here and there.

"Well, well, Master Keeling," the Constable murmured thoughtfully. "This sheds a little light in the darkness, does it not?"

He gathered up the script and turned out of the room, closing the door. There was nothing more he could do there.

The innkeeper was awaiting him at the bottom of the stair. He appeared anxious.

"The physician says the gentleman do be dead now, Master Constable. Did he identify his assailant?"

"Indeed he is, Master Penhallow. Some words with you about your gentleman guest." Master Drew frowned suddenly and an idle thought occurred to him. "Pentecost, is that your first name you say?"

"That it be," agreed the man, somewhat defensively.

"Your parents being no doubt pious souls?"

"Not more so than anyone else." He was defiant but then he realized what was in the Constable's mind. "Pentecost be a good Cornish name; the name of my mother's family. *Pen ty cos* means dwellers in the chief house in the wood."

Master Drew found the explanation amusing.

"Well now, Master Pentecost Penhallow, how long has Master Keeling been residing here?"

"One, nay two months."

"Do you know what profession he followed?"

"Profession? He be a gentleman. What else should he do? You've seen his clothes and jewels?"

"Is that what he told you? That he was a gentleman?"

The innkeeper's eyes narrowed suspiciously.

Suddenly a dark-haired woman appeared from a shadowy corner of the tavern. Twenty years ago she must have looked much like the young girl whom he had encountered on the landing, thought Master Drew. She began to speak rapidly to him in a language that Master Drew did not understand. It sounded a little like Welsh but he guessed that it was Cornish.

"Wait a moment, good woman," protested Master Drew. "What is it you say?"

"*Meea navidna cowza Sawsneck,*" replied the woman in resignation.

"*Taw sy!*" snapped her husband, turning with an apologetic smile to the

Constable. "Forgive my wife, sir. She be from Kerrier, and while she has some understanding at her of English, she does not be speaking it."

"So, what does Mistress Penhallow say?"

"She complains about the late hours Master Keeling did keep, that's all."

"Was he late abroad last night?"

"He was."

"When did you last see him alive?"

"At midday but my wife saw him when he came in last night." He turned and shot a rapid series of questions at his wife in Cornish.

"She says that he came in with his friend, another gentleman, about midnight. They were a little the worst for drink."

The woman interrupted and repeated a word that sounded like *tervans.*

"What is she saying?" demanded Master Drew.

"That they were arguing, strongly."

"Who was this man, this friend?"

There was another exchange in Cornish and then Master Penhallow said: "My wife says that he was a young man that often used to drink with Master Keeling. Another gentleman by name of Cavendish."

A satisfied smile spread over Master Drew's face.

"Master Hal Cavendish? Was that his name?"

"That do be the name, Master Constable. A fine gentleman, I am sure. Have you heard tell of him?"

"That I have. You say that the two came here last night, drunk and arguing? Is it known when Master Cavendish left Master Keeling's room?"

"It was not by the time that my wife and I retired."

"Where were you when Master Keeling came in that you did not see him?"

"I was out . . . on business."

"On business?"

The man hesitated, with a swift glance at his wife, as if to ensure that she didn't understand, then he drew the Constable to one side.

"You know how it be, good master." He lowered his voice ingratiatingly. "A few shillings can be made from cock fights. . . ."

"*Kessynsy!*" sneered his wife.

"You were gambling, is that it?" Master Drew guessed the meaning of her accusation.

"I was, master. I confess I was."

"So you did not return until late? Was all quiet then . . . I mean, you heard nothing of this argument overheard by your goodwife?"

"All was quiet. The place was in darkness."

"And when was this?"

"About the middle watch. I heard the night cryer up on the bridge."

London Bridge stood but a few yards away. Master Drew computed that was between three and four o'clock. He rubbed his chin thoughtfully.

"And did your daughter notice anything before she went to bed?"

Master Penhallow's brows drew together.

"My daughter?"

"The girl that I met on the landing; I presume that she is your daughter? After all, she addressed me in your Cornish jargon."

A look of irritation crossed the man's face.

"I do be apologizing for that, master. I know 'tis thought offensive to address one such as yourself in our poor gibberish. I will speak harshly to Tamsyn."

Master Drew stared disapprovingly at Pentecost Penhallow for he heard no genuine regret in his voice.

What was it Norden had written? "And as they are among themselves litigious so seem they yet to retain a kind of concealed envy against the English who they affect with a desire of revenge for their fathers' sakes by whom their fathers received their repulse." He would have to beware of Penhallow's feigned obsequiousness. The man resented him for all his deferential speech, and Master Drew put it down to this national antipathy.

"Is that her name? Tamsyn?" he asked.

"Tamsyn Penhallow, if it please you, good master."

"Did she notice anything unusual last night."

"Nay, that she did not."

"How do you know?"

"Why, wouldn't she be telling me so?"

"Perhaps we should ask her?"

"Truly, good Master Constable, we cannot oblige you in this for she had only just left to go to the market by the cathedral."

Master Drew sighed.

"I will be back soon. In the meantime, no one must enter into the room of Master Keeling. Understand?"

Pentecost Penhallow nodded glumly.

"But when may we clear the room, master? It is not pleasing to have a corpse lying abed there for when the vapors do be emanating . . ."

"I will be back before midday," the Constable cut him short and left the Red Boar Inn, still clutching the script he had gathered from the floor of Keeling's room.

Although it was still early in the day, he made his way directly to the circular Globe playhouse, which was only a ten-minute walk away. He was greeted by the elderly gatekeeper, Master Jasper.

"A good day, Master Constable. You are abroad early." The old man touched his cap in respectful greeting.

"Indeed, I am, and surprised to see you here at this hour."

"Ah, they are rehearsing inside this morning." The old man jerked his thumb over his shoulder.

"I had hoped as much. I'll lay a wager with you, good Jasper," smiled the Constable in good humor. "I'll wager you what new play is in rehearsal."

The old doorkeeper laughed.

"I know well enough not to lay wagers with the Constable of the Watch. But for curiosity's sake, do make your guess."

"*The Life of King Henry the Fifth.*"

"The very same," chuckled Master Jasper in appreciation.

"Is Master Hal Cavendish playing in it?"

"You have a good memory for the names of our players," observed the old man. "But young Hal Cavendish be an unhappy man because Hal cannot play Hal in this production."

"Explain?" asked Master Drew, allowing the old gatekeeper a few moments to chuckle at his own obscure joke.

"Young Hal Cavendish fancied himself as playing the leading part of King

Hal but now must make do with the part of the Dauphin. He is bitter. He is understudying the part of King Hal, but if he could arrange an accident to he who plays the noble Harry Fifth, young Cavendish would lief as not be more than content."

Master Drew stroked the side of his nose with a lean forefinger.

"Is that the truth of it?"

"Aye, truth and more. Hal Cavendish is a vain young man when it comes to an assessment of his talents and that is no lie. Mind you, good Constable, all those who tread the boards beyond are of a muchness in that vanity."

"Do you also have a player called Will Keeling in the band of Kings Players?"

To his surprise Master Jasper shook his head.

"Then tell me, out of interest, who plays the part of Henry the Fifth, whose role Hal Cavendish so desires?"

"Ah, a young Hibernian. Whelton Keehan. He has newly joined the company."

Master Drew raised a cynical eyebrow.

"Whelton Keehan, eh. What manner of young man is he? Can you describe him?"

Master Jasper was good at descriptions, and at the end of his speech, the Constable pursued his lips thoughtfully.

"I would have a word with Master Cavendish, good Jasper," he said.

The old man saw the grim look in his eyes.

"Is something amiss, Constable?"

"Something is amiss."

Master Jasper conducted the Constable through the door and led the way into the circular auditorium of the theater.

An elderly, lean-faced man was standing on stage with a sheaf of papers in his hand. There were a few other people about but the central figure was a young man who stood striking a pose. One hand held a realistic-looking sword while the other hand was on his waist and he was staring up into one of the galleries.

"Crispian Crispian shall never . . ." he intoned and was interrupted by an angry stamp of the foot of the lean man, who shook his wad of paper at him.

"God's wounds! But you try my patience, Master Cavendish! *Crispin* Crispian shall ne'er go by . . . ! Do you aspire to rewrite the words of Master Shakespeare or can it be that you have grown indolent as the result of your previous success as Macduff? Let me tell you, good Master Cavendish, an actor is only as good as his last performance. Our production of *Macbeth* ended last night. You are now engaged to play the Dauphin in this play of Henry the Fifth, so why I am wasting time in coaching you to understudy the part of King Hal is beyond me."

The young, fair-haired man waited until the torrent had ended and then he began again.

"Crispin Crispian shall ne'er go by
From this day to the ending of the world
But we in it shall be remembered.
We few, we happy few, we band. . . ."

His voice trailed off as he suddenly noticed Master Hardy Drew standing nearby with folded arms.

The lean-faced man swung round.

"And who might you be who puts my players out of rhythm with their parts? Can you not see that we are in rehearsal?"

Master Drew smiled easily.

"I would have a word with Master Cavendish."

"Zoots!" bellowed the man and seemed about to launch into a tirade when Master Jasper drew him to one side and whispered something.

"Very well, then," sighed the man in irritation.

"Ten minutes is all we can spare. Have your word, Master, and then depart in peace! We have a play to put on this night."

The young man was frowning in annoyance as Master Drew approached him.

"Do I know you, fellow?" he demanded haughtily.

"You will, fellow," the Constable replied in a jaunty tone. "I am Constable of the Bankside Watch."

The announcement registered little change of expression on the player's features.

"What do you want of me?"

"I gather that you are a friend of Master Whelton Keehan."

Hal Cavendish's features formed a grimace of displeasure.

"A friend? Not I! An unwilling colleague on these boards, this will I admit to. But he is no more than an acquaintance. If he is in trouble and needs money to bail him, then pray go to Master Cuthbert Burbage, who manages our company. Perhaps he will feel charitable. You will not extract a penny from me to help him."

"I am afraid that he is beyond financial assistance," Master Drew smiled grimly. Then without explaining further, he continued: "I understand that you accompanied him back to his lodgings last night?"

Hal Cavendish sniffed dismissively.

"If you know that, then why ask?"

"Let me make it plain why I ask," Master Drew's voice rose in sudden anger at the young man's conceit. "You stand in danger unless you answer me truthfully. Why was he known at his lodgings as Will Keeling?"

"It's no crime," Cavendish replied indifferently. "He was but a few months arrived in this city from Dublin and thought to better his prospects by passing himself off as an English gentleman at his lodgings. Poor fool—he had not two farthings to jingle in his pocket. I'll grant you, he was a good actor, though. He borrowed props from here, costumes and paste jewelry to maintain his image at his lodgings and thus extend his credit with that sly old innkeeper. Ah . . . tell me, has his ruse been discovered? Are you carting him off to debtors' prison?"

Hal Cavendish began to laugh in good humor.

Master Drew waited patiently for him to pause in his mirth.

"Why should that give you cause for merriment, Master Cavendish?"

"Because I now can play the part of King Hal in this production. Keehan was never right for the part. In truth, he was not. A Hibernian playing King Hal! Heaven forfend! That is why we argued last night."

"Tell me, Master Cavendish, how did you leave Master Keehan? What was his condition?"

"Truth to tell, I left him this morning," the young man admitted. "He was not in the best of tempers. We had been drinking after the last performance of Macbeth and visited one or two houses of . . . well, let us say, of ill repute. Then we fell to discussing tonight's play."

"You were arguing with him."

"I do not deny it."

"About this play?"

"About his inability to lay his role. He had the wrong approach to the part which rightfully should be mine. He had the audacity to criticize my part as the Dauphin and thus we fell to argument. A pox on the man! May he linger a long time in the debtors' jail. He deserves it for leading the innkeeper's daughter on a merry dance with his assumed airs and graces. She, being a simple, country girl, was beguiled by him. There is no fun in debauching the innocent."

Master Drew raised an eyebrow.

"Debauching? In what way did he lead Master Penhallow's daughter on?"

"Why, in his pretence to be an English gentleman with money and fortune. He gave the poor Penhallow girl some of his worthless jewels and spoke of marriage to her. The man is but a jack-in-the-pulpit, a pretender."

The Constable considered this thoughtfully.

"You say that Keehan promised to marry the Penhallow girl?"

"Aye, and make her a rich and great lady," agreed Cavendish.

"He gave her paste jewels?"

"Poor girl, she would not know the like from real. I think she had set her heart on being the mistress of some great estate which only existed in Keehan's imagination. He gambles the pittance that Master Burbage pays us and visits so many whorehouses that I doubt if he has not picked up the pox which will cook his goose the sooner. I have never known a man who had such an excess of love for his own self. I rebuked him for it. By the rood! He had the audacity to recourse to a line from this very play of ours, *Henry V* . . ."

The young man struck a pose.

" 'Self love, my liege, is not so vile a sin as self-neglecting.' One thing may be said of Master Keehan, he never neglected himself."

"This Master Whelton Keehan does not sound the most attractive of company," agreed the Constable.

"I doubt not that this view is shared by the father of the Penhallow girl. I never saw a man so lost for words when he espied Master Keehan treading the boards last night and realised that Keehan was none other than his gentleman lodger."

"What?" Master Drew could not stay his surprise. "Do you mean to tell me that Master Pentecost Penhallow knew that his lodger was a player and residing at the Red Boar under a false name?"

"He knew that from last night. He was there in the ring having paid his penny entrance to stand in the crowd before the stage. Keehan did not see him but I did. In fact, as I was coming off stage, Master Penhallow accosted me to confirm whether his eyes had played him false or not. I had to confess that they had been true. He went away in high dudgeon. He was in no better spirits when I saw him later at the Red Boar."

"You saw Master Penhallow at the Red Boar? At what time was this?"

Master Cavendish considered for a moment.

"I confess to having indulged in an excess of cheap wine. I scarcely recall. It was late, or rather, it was early this morning. He was coming in as I was going out."

The elderly white-haired man came forward clicking his tongue in agitation.

"Sirrah! Can you desist with your questioning? We have a play to rehearse and . . ."

Master Drew held up his hand to silence him.

"Cease your concern, good master. I shall leave you to your best efforts. One thing I have to tell you. You must find a new player for the part of King Hal this evening. Master Keehan is permanently indisposed."

"Confound him!" cried the elderly man. "What stupidity has he indulged in now?"

Master Drew smiled grimly.

"The final stupidity. He has gotten himself murdered, sir."

Arriving back at the Red Boar Inn, he found Master Pentecost Penhallow moodily cleaning pewter pots. He started as he saw the dour look on the Constable's face.

"You lied to me, Master Penhallow," Master Drew began without preamble. "You knew well that Will Keeling was no gentleman, nor had private mean. You knew that he was a penniless player named Keehan."

Pentecost Penhallow froze for a moment and then his shoulders slumped in resignation.

"I knew," he admitted. "But I only knew from last night."

"Are you a frequent playgoer then, Master Penhallow?"

The innkeeper shook his head.

"I never go to playhouses."

"Yet you paid a penny and went to the Globe last night. Pray, what took you there?"

"To see if I could identify this man Keeling . . . or whatever his name was."

"Who told you that he was a player there?"

"Two days ago, one of my customers espied him entering the inn and said, 'That's one of the King's Players at the Globe.' When I said, nay, he be a gentleman, the man laid a wager of two pence with me. So I went and there I saw Master Keeling in cavorting pretense upon the stage. God rot his soul!"

"So you realized that he was in debt to you and little wherewithal to honor that debt?"

"Indeed, I did."

"So when you returned home in the early hours of this morning, you went to his room and had it out with him?"

When Penhallow hesitated, Master Drew went remorsefully on.

"You took a knife and stabbed him in rage at how he had led you and your family on. I gather he gave faked jewels to your daughter and promised marriage. Your rage did wipe all sense from your mind. It was you who killed the man you knew as Will Keeling."

"I did . . ." began Master Penhallow.

"*Na! Na, tasyk!*" cried a female voice. It was the young woman the Constable had seen on the landing that morning. Penhallow's daughter, Tamsyn.

"*Cosel, cosel, caradow,*" Penhallow murmured. He turned to Master Drew with a sigh. "This Keeling was an evil man, Constable. You must appreciate that. He used people as if they meant nothing to him. Yet every cock is proud on his own dung heap. He crowed at his vice when I challenged him. He boasted of it. His debt to me is but nothing to the debt that he owed my daughter, seducing her with his glib tongue and winning ways. All was but his fantasy and he ruined her. No man's death was so richly deserved."

The young girl came forward and took her father's arm.

"*Gafeugh dhym, tasyk,*" she whispered.

Penhallow patted her hand as if pacifying her.

"*Taw dhym, taw dhym, caradow,*" he murmured.

Master Drew shook his head sadly as he gazed from father to daughter and back to father. Then he said:

"You are a good man, Master Penhallow. I doubted it for a while, being imbued with my prejudice against your race."

Penhallow eyed him nervously.

"Good Master Constable, I understand not . . ."

"Alas, the hand that plunged the dagger into Master Keehan was not your own. Speak English a little to me, Tamsyn, and tell me when you learnt the truth about your false lover?"

The dark-haired girl raised her eyes defiantly to him.

"*Gorteugh un pols!*" cried Penhallow to his daughter but she shook her head. She spoke slowly and with her soft accent.

"I overheard what was said to my father the other night; that Will . . . that Will was but a penniless player. I took the jewels which he had given to me and went to the Dutchman by the Black Friars House."

Master Drew knew of the Dutchman. He was a jeweler who often bought and sold stolen goods but had, so far, avoided conviction for his offenses.

"He laughed when I asked their worth," went on the girl, "and said they were even bad as faked jewels and not worth a brass farthing."

"You waited until Will Keehan came in this morning. But he came in with Hal Cavendish."

"He was in an excess of alcohol. He was arguing with his friend. Then Master Cavendish departed and I went in to his room and told him what I knew."

Her voice was quiet, unemotional. Her face was pale and it was clear to Master Drew that she had difficulty controlling her emotions. "He laughed—laughed! Called me a Cornish peasant who had been fortunate to be debauched by him. There were no jewels, no estate and no prospect of marriage. He was laughing at me when. . . ."

"Constable, good Constable, she does not know what she is saying," interrupted Pentecost Penhallow despairingly.

"That was when you came in," interrupted Master Drew. "One thing confused me. Why was it left until morning to raise an alarm? I supposed it was in the hope that Keehan would die before dawn. When he did not, good conscience caused you to send for a physician but hoping that he would depart without naming his assailant. That was why you asked me if he had done so. That was your main concern."

"I have admitted responsibility, Master Constable," Penhallow said. "I will admit it in whatever form of tale would best please you."

"You are not a good teller of tales, Master Penhallow. You should bear in mind the line from this new play in which Keehan was to act which says, as I recall it to mind, 'men of few words are the best men.' Too many words allow one to find an avenue through them. Instead of saying nothing, your pretense allowed me to discover your untruths."

"I admit responsibility, good Constable. She is only seventeen and a life ahead of her, please . . . I did this . . ."

"Enough words, man! Unless you wish to incriminate yourself and your family," snapped the Constable, "I have had done with this investigation." He put his hand in his pocket and drew out a purse. "I found this in Master Keehan's room. The physician took his fee out of it. There is enough to give Master Keehan a funeral. Perhaps there might be a few pence over, though there is not enough to clear his debt. But I think that debt has now been expunged in a final way."

Pentecost Penhallow and his daughter were staring at him in bewilderment.

Master Drew hesitated. Words were often snares for folk but he felt an explanation was needed.

"Law and justice sometimes disagree. You have probably never heard of

Aristotle but he once wrote: 'Whereas the law is passionless, passion must ever sway the heart of man.' Rigorous adherence to the letter of the law is often rigorous injustice."

"But what of . . . ?"

"What happened here is that a penniless player met his death by the hand of a person or persons unknown. They might have climbed the wall and entered by the open window to rob him. It often happens in this cruel city. Hundreds die by violence and hundreds more by disease among its teeming populace. The courts give protection to the rich, to the well-connected, to gentlemen. But it seems that Master Keehan was not one of these; otherwise I might have had recourse to pursue this investigation with more rigor."

He turned for the door, paused, and turned back for a moment.

"Master Penhallow, I know not what conditions now prevail in your country of Cornwall. Do you take advice, and if it be possible, return your family to its protective embrace and leave this warren of inequity and pestilence that we have created by the banks of this foul-smelling stretch of river. I doubt if health and prosperity will ever be your fortune here."

The young girl, eyes shining with tears, moved forward and grasped his arm.

"*Dursona dhys!*" she cried, leaning forward and kissing the Constable on the cheek. "*Durdala-dywy!* . . . Bless you, Master Constable. Thank you."

Smiling to himself, Master Drew paused outside the Red Boar Inn before wandering the short distance to the banks of the Thames. The smells were overpowering. Gutted fish and offal. The stench of sewerage. Those odious smells, to which he thought that a near lifetime of living in London, had inured him, suddenly seemed an affront to his nostrils. Yet thousands of people were arriving in London year after year, and the city was extending rapidly in all directions. A harsh, unkind city which attracted the weak and the wicked, the hopeful and the cynics, the trusting and the swindler, the credulous and the cheat. Never was there such an assemblage of evil. The Puritan divines did not have to look far if they wished to frighten people with an image of what hell was akin to.

He sighed deeply as he glanced up and down the riverbanks.

A boy came along the embankment path bearing a placard and ringing a handbell. Master Drew peered at the placard.

It was an announcement that the King's Players would be performing Master Will Shakespeare's *The Life of King Henry the Fifth* at the Globe Theatre that evening.

Master Whelton Keehan would not be playing the role of King Hal.

Master Hardy Drew suddenly found some lines from another of Will Shakespeare's plays coming into his mind. Where did they come from? *The Tragedy of Macbeth*! The last performance Whelton Keehan had given.

"Tomorrow, and tomorrow, and tomorrow,
Creeps in this petty pace from day to day
To the last syllable of recorded time;
And all our yesterdays have lighted fools
The way to dusty death. Out, out brief candle!
Life's but a walking shadow, a poor player
That struts and frets his hour upon the stage
And then is heard no more."

Ere I Killed Thee

BY ANNE PERRY

 Anne Perry writes, "I was born in Blackheath, London, in 1938. From an early age, I enjoyed reading and two of my favorite authors were Lewis Carroll and Charles Kingsley. It was always my desire to write, but it took twenty years before I produced a book which was accepted for publication. That was *The Cater Street Hangman*, which came out in 1979. I chose the Victorian era by accident, but I am happy to stay with it, because it was a remarkable time in British history, full of extremes, of poverty and wealth, social change, expansion of empire, and challenging ideas. In all levels of society there were the good and the bad, the happy and the miserable."

The audience rose to its feet and thundered applause. Oscar Wilde might be the sensation of the day, but there was nothing to excel the music of Shakespeare and the passion and tragedy of Othello. And of all the brilliant actors who had taken that role, there was no one who had invested it with more immediacy than Owain Glenconnor. There was no Iago more serpentine than Idris Evans.

Usually Owain's wife, Dierdre Ashbourne, had received standing ovations as well. Her Lady Macbeth was classic, but as Desdemona she was no more than good. Something of the fire and the luminosity was absent. As Owain stood on the stage next to her, taking the very last bow, he saw the shadow in her face and knew the bitter disappointment she felt. It happened to all actors sometime or another, but it had been many years since she had played second to anyone at all, certainly not to stand by graciously while a relatively minor actress like Idris's wife, Amelia Ryecroft, was thrown roses.

As soon as the curtain finally fell, they swapped brief words of enthusiasm, and then each returned to their dressing rooms. Dierdre had only to take off her gown and a little of the paint before being ready to go on to the party. She did not want or need a wig. Her own glorious tawny hair was perfect for the role and the public expected to see it. It was part of who she was. It only needed an expert twist and a few pins and it was ready for her appearance to celebrate.

Amelia was much the same. Idris had only to change his clothes and get rid of the jewelry of Iago and he was ready. Perhaps he should wash off a little of the extra color, but that was quickly done.

Owain had to get rid of every scrap of the black paint necessary for his part alone, not only from his face and neck, but from his hands as well. It was a long job, and as usual by the time he joined the rest of the cast, they were already sipping champagne and entertaining guests with stories of past performances, anecdotes about other plays, and hilarious stories of triumph and disaster on tour.

He stared across the room with its heavy pre-Raphaelite wallpaper, gas lamps he knew would be gently hissing, but at the moment were drowned by the sound of voices and laughter and the clink of crystal. As usual, Dierdre was the center of a group of admirers. She stood on the lowest step of the stairs, her pale apricot skirts unshadowed by anyone else, catching the light like the center of a Rembrandt painting, making everyone else seem dull by comparison. By heaven, the woman knew how to draw the eye!

Owain walked in casually, a little swagger in his step. He was wearing his favorite loose white silk shirt with full sleeves, hardly conventional eveningwear, but very flattering, very dramatic. He saw Idris grin at him and raise his glass. He read the scene exactly.

There was a drop in the buzz of conversation and half a dozen heads turned. Someone called out "Congratulations!," and others joined in. Immediately he was passed champagne and took it, relishing the sweet-sharp flavor. Someone had treated them to a very good vintage. He raised the glass high. "Thank you, whoever gave us this!" he said clearly. His voice was magnificent, dark and full of emotion. If he had not been a great actor, he might have sung at least well. But being one in a male voice choir, however good, had not the drama or the glory of a sublime solo performance.

Dierdre turned and looked at him, smiling with devastating charm. Most of the men in the room were watching her. That was not unusual, but tonight perhaps they were waiting to see how she would take having been upstaged by her husband and Iago, even Iago's young wife. If any imagined she would sulk, they did not know her. She was standing beside Idris now. She linked her arm in his and he responded gallantly. They had known each other for years, and ridden the crest of the waves and the troughs together.

Owain walked over to her and put his arm around her on the other side. "Who treated us to the champagne?" he asked casually. Better not to make any reference to the performance.

She glanced at Idris and away again quickly, and loosed herself from his arm, her face bleak for a moment before turning to Owain. "Kennedy," she answered, referring to Kennedy Williams, the theatre manager. "And Idris." She looked awkward; as if it were a confession and something he might mind. Perhaps he did. He would like to have been included, and apparently they had not thought of him.

"I see," he said coolly. "Well, it's excellent." He upended the glass and drank all the rest of it, then signalled to the footman, who offered him another, which he took then straight away set it down on one of the small tables and ignored. He turned to Kennedy Williams and one of the supporting cast and began conversation with them.

Idris shrugged and looked back to Dierdre again, but instead of resuming their previous discussion, she moved away from him and stood beside Owain, smiling at him a little nervously.

"It really wasn't anything," she began, looking at him, then at Kennedy.

He did not answer.

"Owain, believe me!" she pleaded.

This was not the place to mention such a tiny, ridiculous matter. The only way to deal with it was to forget it. Talking about it in front of others, especially Kennedy, was embarrassing. He affected not to know what she was referring to. He stared at her blankly, but he knew his annoyance showed. "If whatever it was—wasn't anything, then we should dismiss it," he said coolly.

She handed him another glass, holding it out in a graceful gesture. She had beautiful hands and she used them marvellously, like a dancer. "The drink, darling . . ."

This was absurd. She was creating out of nothing a drama to be the center of. It was his own stupidity to have set the scene for her. The applause for Amelia must have hurt her more than he had appreciated. It was miserable to have an audience you thought was yours pass you by, even for one performance, for someone else younger, if not prettier. And Amelia was charming, but she would never have Dierdre's fire, or her grandeur. She could have been allowed this one triumph. A little generosity wouldn't hurt.

He took the champagne. "Of course." He sipped it, holding her gaze steadily. They had been married for over ten years. They could read each other so well. He could put warmth into his face, and it would deceive everyone else, but not her. "Thank you," he added, smiling back at her.

"And Idris?" she asked so softly only Kennedy would have heard her.

He held the glass up. "To his health!" It still sounded a little sharp.

She relaxed and turned to the others, ready for the next tale, the next remembrance and joke.

Owain forgot the matter altogether in a week of superb performances. The critics were enthusiastic, especially about his own final scene, and about the individual quality and power of Idris in the role of Iago. But of course no matter how good they were, there were always rehearsals, just to keep up the fluidity and polish. It was at one of these that he found himself unintentionally quarrelling with Idris. He did not really know how it came about. One minute they were all standing together in the wings while Kennedy spoke to the man who was in charge of the limelights, a highly technical job, and one on whose skill their safety depended, the next minute Deirdre was walking across the boards in the light and putting her arm through Idris's.

Owain saw Amelia turn and the quick flash of displeasure in her face. She was young and still very much in love with Idris. She was in awe of Dierdre's glamour, and Owain had noticed the vulnerability in her, the fear of being less interesting, less beautiful. She always played the second lead, not the first, except privately with Kennedy Williams. For him she was the first and the best, although she seemed quite unaware of it.

Owain stepped forward, intentionally interrupting them. "Dierdre, try that entrance again now that they have the lights correct," he ordered. It was rude and interfering, out of character for him, but it had the desired effect of breaking the scene. She looked at him with wide eyes, almost as if she were frightened. She glanced over at Kennedy Williams. Idris frowned.

"Yes, of course, Owain," Dierdre said meekly, and with downcast eyes she moved away.

"What the devil's the matter with you?" Idris demanded, his voice low, but the anger in his face unmistakable. "You've been playing Othello too long! Your imagination's overtaken you."

Owain was stunned. "Othello! Don't be ridiculous. It was nothing to do with me! Didn't you see Amelia's face?"

"What's Amelia got to do with it?" Idris was startled. "Dierdre's hurt, she needs a little compassion, a word of gentleness, and you don't seem to want to give it." There was criticism in his face and his dark eyes were cold.

"Compassion!" Owain said incredulously. "Don't be idiotic! There's nothing wrong with her that wouldn't be cured by a good notice or a little more applause."

Idris regarded him with total disgust. "I didn't think I'd hear you say anything so cold-blooded, Owain. I thought you had more humanity, and less selfish pride."

Owain was lost for words. His confusion must have shown in his face even before he spoke. "You're falling over yourself to give compassion to my wife, and leaving your own wife to wonder what's going on, and you despise me for it?"

The color washed up Idris's face, and embarrassment made him angrier. "Amelia knows perfectly well I have only friendship and admiration for Dierdre . . . as have all the rest of us."

"And compassion!" Owain said sarcastically. "Don't forget that! Your heart no doubt bleeds for her because your wife got the longer applause from the audience. I daresay Amelia wonders why you aren't proud of her. It's not as if she'd upstaged you."

"I'm not talking about applause, you fool!" Idris snarled, keeping his voice down only with difficulty.

Kennedy Williams was staring at them now, undecided whether to come over or not. He glanced at Amelia and his feelings were naked for an instant in his eyes.

"I'm talking about her sister!" Idris replied to Owain.

Owain was completely at a loss. "Sister?"

Idris's eyebrows shot up. "Her sister died last week, man! Don't stand there as if you don't know what I'm talking about. She must have been your sister-in-law. I think Dierdre has the superb courage and selflessness to go on stage every night, and all you can do is accuse her of being jealous because Amelia is getting recognition at last. I thought better of you." He turned away and took a step as if to leave.

Owain caught him by the shoulder and half spun him around.

Idris's whole body clenched as if he intended to strike back, and he restrained himself only when his fist was half raised.

"She hasn't got a sister!" Owain said between his teeth, still quietly enough for Kennedy Williams not to hear. "I don't know what the devil she's told you, but she's an only child!"

Idris stood motionless, his eyes wide. "What?"

"She's an only child!" Owain repeated.

Idris drew in his breath sharply as if to respond. Neither man was sure whether to believe the other or not.

The moment was broken by Dierdre returning, her face anxious. She glanced at Kennedy Williams, then smiled a little tentatively at Idris before turning to Owain.

"The lights are right. Please let's get on with the scene. Then we can go and"—she lifted her shoulder elegantly—"and have a pleasant afternoon doing whatever we wish. I need a little rest before tonight, don't you?"

He saw a moment of something like fear at the back of her eyes, but she was right, they all needed to leave the theatre and have a break from work and a good meal before giving all the passion and concentration, even the physical effort, of a good performance this evening. He did more than anyone. Othello was an immense role.

"Yes, of course," he agreed, and without referring to anyone except Williams, he moved straight into the scene.

But a couple of days later the quarrel erupted again. Dierdre was playing the grand romantic lead, as she always had done. It was a dinner party with friends on a Sunday evening. There were perhaps a dozen people present. The chandeliers blazed on creamy shoulders, exquisite hair, and an array of jewels fit to grace the necks of duchesses. The table was set with crystal and porcelain. Roses spilled over the silver bowl in the center and sprays of honeysuckle twined around the silver cruet sets. Footmen waited discreetly by the side tables and maids in black dresses and white lace caps and aprons served each dish in its turn. Dierdre was flirting outrageously, particularly with Idris. Owain could see Amelia's face becoming more and more strained.

Four times he cut across the conversation, trying to draw Dierdre to speak to him, flirt with him, anything to break the sparkling bond between her and Idris, which must be becoming plainer all the time, not only to Amelia but to everyone else as well. He tried current events, other people's plays, Oscar Wilde was taking London by storm and his wit was becoming more and more outrageous. Owain even tried theatre gossip, and comments on the music hall, but nothing worked until finally it became ridiculous and everyone was looking at him.

Afterwards when the ladies retired to the withdrawing room, he caught Idris alone in the hall, returning from the cloakroom.

"For God's sake, pull yourself together and stop behaving like a fool!" he said angrily. "You've got a wife who adores you, and you spend the entire dinner ignoring her! She may not be as much fun to show off with as Dierdre, but she's worth treating with a little dignity in public, whatever you do alone."

Idris coloured scarlet, and Owain thought at first it was fury, then as he looked more closely he realized with a wave of relief that it was shame.

"I'm sorry," Idris said quietly. "Dierdre is so . . . so full of wit I forgot myself. I wish Amelia had more . . ."

"Confidence?" Owain said with an edge to his voice. "You don't give her much help, do you!" That was a criticism, not a question.

"You don't need to add to it," Idris replied. "It won't happen again."

At that moment Kennedy Williams came out of the dining room and Idris turned and walked away quickly, his face still scarlet.

Owain dismissed the matter from his thoughts until nearly a week later when he saw Amelia coming down the stairs of the hotel. It was late breakfast time, a meal not all of them took. She looked pale and unhappy. Dierdre came hurrying after her. She was wearing a loose robe over her nightgown and her hair was around her shoulders in a dark bronze wave. She was flustered and her cheeks were bright pink. She caught up with Amelia on the bottom step.

"It isn't what you think!" she said urgently. Her voice was something of a stage whisper, giving the impression of a desire for privacy, but actually carrying so far that even Kennedy Williams in the dining room entrance must have heard it.

"Isn't it?" Amelia said sarcastically, swivelling on the step and facing Dierdre. "If there is some alternative reason for you coming out of my husband's bedroom in your night-clothes, I should be interested to hear what it is? You are certainly giving a grandstand performance of being a whore!"

Owain took a step forward. This was going too far.

"Amelia, I swear . . ." Dierdre began, putting her hand on Amelia's arm.

But Amelia snatched herself away. "Don't insult us all!" she hissed. "You're a trollop. Owain may be prepared to put up with it. Maybe he's still enough in love with you he can't break free of you. But I certainly can, and I will!"

"Wait!" Dierdre cried out, her voice now carrying a note of real desperation. "Idris wasn't in there, and I knew he wasn't! I was looking for you! I know how . . . how close you are! Idris adores you! I expected when you weren't in your own room that I'd find you there . . . where else would you be?"

Amelia stopped and turned back. She was struggling to believe. Owain could see it in her eyes, the trembling of her lips. Perhaps it was true . . . just conceivably? He believed it himself. What she wanted was drama, not passion. She had no use for Idris, except as a prop for her glamour.

"And what did you want me for?" Amelia asked huskily.

"A tisane," Dierdre said with an anxious smile. "I have a terrible headache, and my maid has forgotten to get any more."

"I see."

Owain could not tell whether Amelia believed her or not. Perhaps she wanted to so badly she would not even ask Idris or attempt to find out. Or she might have cared too much not to put it to the test, and not allow herself the agony of ever afterwards being tormented with doubt.

Now it was a matter of stopping the embarrassment.

"Dierdre!" he said firmly, taking her by the elbow. "For heaven's sake, get the hotel management to fetch you a tisane, and stop giving rise to the most awful speculation by half the dining room!"

As it happened, there was no chance for him to learn more of it. That evening just before the fourth act, he was alone in his dressing room, still looking for his favorite shirt, which either he or his dresser must have misplaced, and more importantly for his Moorish dagger, which he hung on the wall in every theatre, whether he was playing Othello or not, when he heard a shrill and terrible scream. He knew immediately that it was not temper or someone caught by surprise, it was sheer and absolute horror.

He dropped the jacket in his hands and ran through the door and along the passage towards the sound. Cassio and Bianca were standing at Idris's door and it was she who was screaming, but even as Owain arrived, Cassio put both arms around her and pulled her back.

Owain pushed past him and saw Idris lying on the floor on his face, the Moorish dagger sunk into the middle of his back, where the scarlet blood spread wide and dark around its hilt. It was stupid to imagine he could still be alive with a wound like that, but it was a desperate instinct. Owain pushed past the other two and knelt down beside Idris, feeling for the pulse in his neck. He knew there would be nothing there, and yet he was suddenly sick with disappointment. He looked at Idris's face. His dark eyes were wide open and he seemed surprised, as if he had seen death coming.

Should Owain close his eyes in decency, or leave him exactly as he was for the police? There would have to be police. There was no possibility at all that this was anything but murder.

He stood up slowly, startled to find himself shaking. "You'd better tell Kennedy," he said awkwardly. "There'll be no conclusion to tonight's performance. He'll have to make an announcement." He pulled the door closed. "And get someone to guard this till the police come!"

It was less than thirty minutes before Inspector Morgan arrived, dark as Idris himself, a little overweight and with a voice like melted treacle.

"Well now," he said grimly. "Idris Evans, is it? What a tragedy! A fine actor, but it's Iago he plays, isn't it?"

"Yes," Owain agreed.

Morgan raised one eyebrow. "And no need to ask you who you are, sir. I've watched you many a time. One of the best Othellos of your generation, they say. I'd say the best, and no mistake. What happened here, do you know?"

"No, I don't."

"After Act Four, they tell me. So you weren't on stage before the interval, and neither was Mr. Evans, poor soul. Nor Desdemona . . . that'd be Miss Ashbourne."

"That's right," Owain agreed.

"Well, well," Morgan said thoughtfully. "You'd better tell me everything you did from the time you left the stage, until you heard Bianca scream, if you don't mind. And then I'll have everyone else do the same."

It was a long and tedious job establishing where everyone was, but in the end the conclusions were plainer than might have been supposed. No one had come in through the stage door from the start, so whoever had killed Idris had of necessity been one of the cast or dressers, or a stagehand, or Kennedy

Williams. Morgan was dogged and perceptive. He wrote everything down in tiny, scratchy writing with lots of little figures, and at shortly before one in the morning when they were gathered in the greenroom, except for Amelia, who was lying down. He announced that the only people who were not accounted for by someone else were Kennedy Williams, who said he had been alone in the manager's office, Amelia, who was upset and had closed her dressing room door and, since she shared a dresser with Bianca, was alone at that time, and Owain himself, also in his dressing room alone. The only other person seen by no one was the stage doorman, and Dierdre said that she had gone to collect a note from an ardent admirer, and she had seen him.

"He was there, on his stool," she said in a whisper. She looked ashen and her hands were locked together as if to keep them from shaking. She seemed to find difficulty in speaking and kept looking from Owain to Inspector Morgan as if she dreaded something even more tragic happening but was helpless to prevent it.

Kennedy Williams stood limply against the door, leaning on it to support himself. The lines of his thin face all dragged downward. He looked as if he had been up for days, not hours.

"You're sure of that, Miss Ashbourne," Morgan asked, but not as if he doubted her. It was just one more fact to be ticked off on his list.

"Yes, Inspector," she replied, then hesitated.

"Was there something else?" Morgan asked.

"No!" she answered a trifle too quickly.

Morgan waited.

Still she said nothing, but looked more and more wretched.

"I think perhaps I should speak to you alone again, Miss Ashbourne," he said.

"No, I . . . I really have nothing else I can tell you," she assured him. "I don't know who killed Idris. He was a brilliant actor and a dear friend—to my husband as well as myself." She said the last directly, almost aggressively, as if she had already been challenged on it.

Kennedy Williams stared at the floor.

Morgan glanced at him, then back at Dierdre with his eyebrows raised ages. "Some friends can quarrel, Miss Ashbourne."

"Oh, of course!" she acknowledged. "And I expect you've heard that Owain and Idris did, but it was all just over misunderstandings. Nothing that mattered, I assure you. Oh no! You can't . . ." Then she stopped and lowered her eyes. "If it's anybody's fault, it's mine. I was foolish, but no more than that, I swear. And Owain knows me better than to imagine otherwise."

"I've seen the play, Miss Ashbourne," Morgan told her. "I know Desdemona's innocent of everything."

She gave him a tearful smile.

"And it's Othello and Desdemona who end up dead!" Owain snapped. "Not Iago . . ."

"I always thought that was a pity, myself," Morgan looked at him coolly. "If anyone ever deserved a bad end, it was Iago. Terrible sin, jealousy, whatever it's of . . . power, money, honor, the love of a woman, anything at all. Can spoil more lives than almost anything else."

"I know," Dierdre whispered. She gulped and controlled herself with a visible effort.

Morgan looked across at Owain, and Owain saw the hostility in his eyes. For the first time Owain realized that he was in danger. It was preposterous, but Morgan really considered he might have killed Idris. His first instinct was to deny it, to point out that there was rivalry between himself and Idris, but it was constructive, each one helping the other's performance! Then he looked around the room and saw Kennedy's haggard face, full of guilt and apology. Dierdre beautiful and tragic, and Morgan who loved the theatre and had seen him play Othello, indeed thought him the best in the part he knew. It was nothing to do with acting . . . it was Dierdre! With a churning sickness, he remembered the quarrels he and Idris had had over the last few weeks, all of them seen by Kennedy. He knew what Morgan had drawn from him, and knew Kennedy would see it from Amelia's point of view. He was a fine manager, but he was no actor, his feelings for her were an open book for anyone to read.

"That's all for tonight," Morgan said at last. "But I'll see everyone tomorrow. Don't leave the hotel, if you please."

Owain went back to the dressing room to change into his own clothes. He still couldn't find his favorite shirt and was obliged to seek out another. He came out and was told that Dierdre had already left for the hotel. He walked the half mile or so alone in the dark, trying to think. He had no time to grieve for Idris. That would have to come later, and it would—they had been friends most of their professional lives. Owain had loved his humor, his strength, and above all his intelligence. They had brought out the best in each other, both as actors and as friends.

Now he had to wrestle with what had happened and find his way out of the net of suspicion that was already a circle around him. He found it almost impossible to believe that either Kennedy or Amelia could have killed Idris, and yet the facts seemed to leave no other answer. Why? Jealousy. Always it came back to jealousy. Either one of them might have believed for an insane hour or two that Idris and Dierdre were really having an affair. Amelia was young and in love, only married a couple of years. Until the last week or two she had been by Dierdre on stage, and now it looked as if Dierdre were taking her husband also. Perhaps there was more fire of passion in her than even Idris had known?

But why did she kill Idris and not Dierdre?

Who could know what quarrel had taken place between them?

Or Kennedy? Was he more in love with Amelia than any of them had guessed, and he had killed Idris for betraying her . . . and in turn to free her for himself?

Owain crossed the dark street under the gas lamps and walked towards the lights of the hotel. Either answer hurt him for people he cared about deeply, but he felt dangers closing in, and only the truth would save him.

He did not see Dierdre. She had apparently already retired. She preferred to sleep alone. She was a woman of personal mystery. Her vanity required she did not share the secrets of her toilette with anyone but her maid. He had understood, even approved. It allowed him a similar privacy, and since he often liked to learn his lines late at night, it suited him very well. They were together when they chose.

He slept badly and went out without breakfast to see if he could learn anything more at the theatre. Morgan was already there, but he managed to avoid him.

By eleven o'clock he had a thumping headache, but had succeeded in finding a stagehand who had seen him go into his dressing room and then spoken to Idris afterwards. He had then been in sight of the door and seen Owain leave to go in the opposite direction at about the time Idris must have been killed.

Brimming over with relief, he half dragged him to tell Morgan.

However, after a miserable luncheon the stagehand found Owain in the hotel lounge.

"I'm sorry, Mr. Glenconnor, sir," he said wretchedly, shifting from one foot to the other in his embarrassment. "But it wasn't last night that I saw you. It was the night before. I'd say that it was because I know you couldn't 'ave 'urt Mr. Evans for the world, but Miss Ashbourne saw me where I really were, an' she'd 'ave to tell the truth, like, 'cos she already 'as done. I'm terrible sorry, sir."

"Yes, of course you have to," Owain agreed, horrified to find himself shivering. He clenched his body and forced himself to look at the man. "Thank you for coming to me."

"I'm sorry, sir."

"It's all right." But it wasn't. It was made plain how very wrong it was when Dierdre herself came to him an hour or so later. She was dressed in very sober black, her bright hair contrasting with the pallor of her face.

"Owain, I'm so sorry," she said urgently. "I'd already told that miserable policeman that I'd seen the stagehand, whatever his name is. Otherwise I would never have mentioned it. I didn't realize how much it was going to mean to you. I'd have lied, if I'd known!"

"You don't have to lie for me!" he said sharply.

She winced, almost as if he'd struck her. "I know!" She looked down, avoiding his eyes. "I know you would never have killed Idris no matter what you thought about him and me."

"I didn't think anything," he said, hearing his own voice rise with a desperate note in it. "Except that you were behaving selfishly, and Idris was being a fool! Idris was my friend!"

She looked up now. "And I'm your wife! Lesser men than you have been jealous . . . and discovered too late that their wives were innocent of any wrong greater than a little harmless flirting, a little high spirits. I know perfectly well you are innocent . . . I just wish Inspector Morgan was as sure of it as I am." There was no conviction in her voice, only fear, and it settled like a coldness around Owain until he was almost paralyzed by it.

Then in the theatre that afternoon he found the shirt, his own beautiful white shirt with the gathered sleeves. It was stuffed behind a piece of scenery, with only a white tip sticking out above the painted flat. He pulled it and saw with horror tight in the pit of his stomach the bloodstained sleeve, dark red-brown, and caked together. The left sleeve, as it would have been if he had worn it when killing Idris. He was the only left-handed one in the cast.

Had anyone else seen him? He stared around him in the dimly lit backstage, peering into the shadows of the wings, and then up to the galleries where the drops were winched up. He saw no one. He could barely make out the shapes so far up, but why would anyone be up there in the dark when there was no performance this evening?

He pushed the shirt under his jacket and hurried into the corridor, his hands shaking. Morgan was somewhere about. He must destroy the shirt when he had a chance, but he could not risk being found with it now. Where could he put it? Anyone would know it was his as soon as they asked. And yet it was perfectly obvious that whoever murdered Idris had worn it. Why? There was only one answer . . . to blame him.

Where would he put the thing now? he thought with a black humor of Macbeth. Blood . . . the blood of his friends already on his clothes. And yet he was guilty of nothing. But how could Morgan, or anyone else, believe that? Except whoever had worn his shirt to murder Idris.

Where would nobody look for anything? He must be quick. Morgan was not far away. He suspected him already. Behind a flat no one ever moved? Well, they certainly were not performing Othello again for a while, and the Venetian scene belonged to this theatre. It did not travel with them. He stuffed it behind the painting of the palace backdrop against the canal and straightened up just as the constable came across the stage and spoke to him. He managed to answer almost normally, but his heart was pounding so violently he knew that were the footlights lit, the man would have seen him shake.

And of course, Morgan did have the theatre searched, even though he was uncertain what he was looking for, only that whoever had killed Idris must have had blood on them, on their clothes. Something was missing, some garment. Had Owain's shirt remained where it was? Morgan would have to have found it. At least it was not visible where he had put it now, and unless someone removed the heavy flats altogether, it would not be. Owain had a breathing space until he could get back there unobserved and destroy it.

But that was not what caused the dark, cold terror inside him, it was the knowledge that whoever had taken his Moorish knife off the wall and driven it into Idris's back, had also deliberately taken his shirt as well, and worn it to commit the murder. They could only have done it with the intention of blaming Owain. They had left the shirt where it would be seen. They wanted it found . . . and Owain hanged. He struggled and twisted his thoughts, tortured them into all kinds of unlikely paths, but every one of them led back to the same conclusion. Someone wanted him destroyed every bit as completely as Idris had been, in a way more so. Idris was a tragic victim. Owain would be remembered not as a great actor, the greatest Othello of his generation, but as the Othello who reversed the drama and murdered Iago . . . a miserable man who resented another man's talent and charm and in a fit of jealousy plunged a knife into his back.

Who?

Only Kennedy or Amelia. Amelia could have done it. It was physically possible. Did that quiet face and light, charming manner hide a woman of such deadly purpose?

They were all in the green room waiting when Morgan came back to tell them that the search was completed.

"Did you find anything, Inspector?" Dierdre asked quietly. She looked very tense this morning, and she kept glancing curiously at Owain. Sitting here now, waiting for Morgan to speak, he realized he had not seen her alone since the evening before, and that had been brief. She had left within minutes, claiming a headache, which was more than likely true, in the circumstances. He had thought little of it at the time.

Morgan was saying that he had found nothing that he knew to be of relevance to the murder, and they were free to move about the theatre as they wished.

Owain looked across at Dierdre and saw the flash of surprise on her face, masked almost instantly. Then he knew what Idris must have felt the moment the dagger pierced him from a hand he had thought to be that of a friend. Dierdre had expected Morgan to find the shirt, and she could not understand why he had not, because she had put it there!

Why? Had she and Idris really been lovers after all? A quarrel? Or had she pursued him and he had rebuffed her, and he had concealed it with lightness of touch, laughter, to spare Owain's feelings?

He was sitting perched on an old horsehair sofa in the familiar greenroom, like that in any of scores of theatres up and down the country, and he felt sick. Why would Dierdre, his own wife, beautiful, melodramatic Dierdre, try to have him hanged for a murder he had not committed?

Had she killed Idris herself? Or was it brilliant opportunism, a chance to blame him seen and taken on the spur of the moment?

And what could he do to save himself?

Someone came in with the newspapers. He forced his attention to them. It was Cassio, and his face was a mixture of horror and fascination as he read the accounts aloud. Some were simple reporting of the facts. Brilliant actor Idris Evans had been murdered in the theatre during a performance of Othello, in which he played the villain Iago. Police were investigating, but so far had no clear leads as to who was responsible.

But others rehearsed the plot of Othello, the passionate jealousy which had destroyed a great man and resulted in one of the most powerful tragedies ever portrayed on the stage. There were photographs of Dierdre in costume as Desdemona, looking beautiful and radiantly innocent, but with a shadow across her eyes as if she already knew she was the unwitting catalyst of death.

She rose now and took the newspaper from Cassio and Owain watched her face as she looked at the photograph of herself. He saw the flush on her cheeks, her body straighten a little and the soft satisfaction in her eyes the moment before she lowered them. She was the star again. Idris might be dead and Owain cast as the villain, a true Othello, a man whose love for his wife, and his jealousy over her, had caused him to commit murder. But Amelia was forgotten, and Dierdre was in the centre of the stage.

Now he knew why she had done it.

He looked away quickly. He must not meet her eyes. As long as she did not know he knew, he had one slender advantage. He must leave, before his face gave him away. He was one of the best actors alive, but even he could not control the ashen colour of his skin or force from his mind the horror and the fear which must be somewhere in the stiffness of his movement, the clumsiness he felt, as if his arms and legs scarcely belonged to him.

He stood up and walked out, passing Kennedy Williams, who looked like his own ghost. Now, when Morgan had already just looked, would be the time to get the shirt and destroy it. It would be impossible ever to remove the stain. He knew blood was one of the hardest things to wash out. Cold water before it was dried was about the only way. Now he would have to burn the whole thing.

He went almost blindly up the passage, tripping on the step, lucky not to fall. He had always known Dierdre was vain, ambitious, fed on admiration. But then had she not had an element of that in her character, she would never have been the actress she was. He understood it. Heavens, had he not enough of it in himself? He loved to stand in the lights with a thousand faces towards him and how every heart and mind was feeling the emotion that rang in his voice or cried out in the physical energy of his being. To make them part of his dream, to carry them into passion and thought they had never known before, was the fabric of his life.

But so was friendship. So was love. How could he have been so desperately wrong about Dierdre? Had everything between them been an act for her? Or was this madness grown only since she had lost the limelight to Idris and Owain? And she had lost it, a little. It was slipping out of her grasp. He could see that more clearly now, looking over the last few months.

He reached backstage and went to the heavy flats where he had stuffed the shirt. He pushed his hand into the crevice and fished for the touch of silk. There was nothing there. He reached in further. He had not thought he had put it so far! It was still not there.

He must stop shaking and keep control of himself. It had to be there. If Morgan had found it, he would have said so. Owain would already be under arrest. It was his shirt, everyone knew it, and if they didn't, Dierdre would have told them.

But where was the shirt? He had pushed his arm as far as he could into the crevice. He was right up to the shoulder, and there was nothing there! There was nowhere it could have dropped to. His fingers were right to the end of the space, and he could feel the floorboards at the bottom.

Ice filled the pit of his stomach and the sweat broke out on his face. Someone had removed it. Dierdre! God in heaven . . . what had she done with it? And he knew the answer before the question was fully formed in his mind. She had put it where Morgan would find it.

He stood up slowly, stiffly. Where? Where had she put it? Would she lead Morgan to it, or was it somewhere Morgan would find it himself? If the latter, then why had he not found it just now?

Was there still time for Owain to get it and destroy it? Would Morgan look in the places he had already looked before? Perhaps not. That would be the one area it would be safe. Where? One of the dressing rooms. His? She would never dare on her own! Or would she? Yes—of course. She had the nerve for anything.

He started to walk quickly, lightly, along the open spaces into the corridor, up the narrow stairs, and along the passage, past his own room and into Dierdre's. There was no one there. Heaven only knew when there would be another performance. He closed the door and started to go through the rack of gowns. Nothing. Of course not. Too obvious. What about the cupboard? He pulled open the door and went through the contents, blouses, underwear, stockings . . . no shirt. He turned and stared around the room. Where else? There were two wigs on stands, not for the part of Desdemona. Dierdre was too proud of her own hair to cover it unless she had to. The wigs were not hers. He pulled one off its stand. It must belong to some other actress. He looked at the second, then pulled it off as well. It came off the pole easily. It was stuffed with a white silk shirt, blood-stained sleeve stiff and dark.

The door opened and Morgan stood in the entrance. Dierdre and Kennedy Williams behind him.

"Well then, Glenconnor," Morgan said sadly. "Now I was really hoping it wasn't you, but that in your hand makes it impossible for me to go on holding on to that dream, doesn't it." He put his arm forward. "Give it to me."

There was no point whatever in arguing. Owain held it out and Morgan took the crumpled bundle.

"I hope you're not going to tell me it isn't yours, are you, sir?"

Owain had difficulty finding his voice. "No. But I didn't kill Idris, in spite of what it looks like." That was futile, but he said it from passion, not thought.

"Didn't you now. There's blood all over it, sir. Please don't tell me you cut yourself, and hid it here in Miss Ashbourne's room in case we thought you were guilty of Mr. Evans's murder. Because, you see, you must have hidden it before he was found, sir, which would be very difficult to explain, now, wouldn't it?"

"I didn't say the murderer wasn't wearing it," Owain answered him. "I said it wasn't me!"

"But Owain, the blood is on the left sleeve!" Dierdre said huskily. "And you're the only one who is left-handed! Oh God! I'm so sorry! I knew you were jealous, but I never dreamed it would come to this!" She covered her face with her beautiful hands and stood sobbing silently, a picture of womanly grief.

Morgan turned round very slowly to look at her. "Left sleeve, you say, Miss Ashbourne?"

She lifted her face, eyes wide. "That's right, Inspector. Owain is the only one of us who is left-handed. I'm . . . so . . . sorry!"

"I'm sure he is, ma'am," Morgan said very slowly, his face still sad, his brow furrowed. "But how did you know the shirt was stained on the left sleeve, seeing that we just found it?"

She looked bewildered, but Owain saw her stiffen. "What?" she breathed out. She was shaking now.

Morgan repeated the question. "How did you know it was the left sleeve that was stained, ma'am?"

"I . . ." she started to explain, then saw in Morgan's eyes that it was too late. She swung around to Kennedy Williams.

But understanding filled his face as well and he took a step backward away from her, shaking his head a little.

"Jealousy's a terrible thing," Morgan said softly. "Cruel as the grave. But I am not sure that the love of glory's any better. Anything that'd drive a person to kill one man and see another hanged for it has got to be a tragedy, any way you look at it."

Dierdre lifted her chin high and stared at him defiantly. She was magnificent. Owain felt a lurch of pity for her, for all that she had been in her best moments, the laughter and the hunger for life, and above all for what she could have been. But mostly he grieved for Idris, who had been just as alive, as gifted, as hungry to create the magic of theatre and hold an audience in his spell.

Dierdre stood very stiff. This would be her last act, and she would be more Lady Macbeth than Desdemona, but at least she would be center stage, sharing the limelight with no one. It seemed that was what mattered more than all else.

Owain found there were tears on his face as he watched her walk out next to Morgan and disappear down the corridor, the light still bright in her burnished hair.